JEEVES AND
RIGHT H
AND OTHE

P. G. Wodehouse was born in Guildford, Surrey, in 1881 and educated at Dulwich College. After working for the Hong Kong and Shanghai Bank for two years, he left to earn his living as a journalist and storywriter.

During his lifetime he wrote over ninety books, and his work has won worldwide acclaim. He was hailed by *The Times* as 'A comic genius recognized in his lifetime as a classic and an old master of farce.' P. G. Wodehouse said: 'I believe there are two ways of writing novels. One is mine, making a sort of musical comedy without music and ignoring real life altogether; the other is going right deep down into life and not caring a damn.'

In 1975 he was created a Knight of the British Empire and he died on St Valentine's Day in the same year at the age of ninety-three.

ALSO IN ARROW BY P. G. WODEHOUSE

Jeeves and Wooster: The Code of the Woosters and Other Stories

Jeeves and Wooster: The Mating Season and Other Stories

P. G. Wodehouse

JEEVES AND WOOSTER
RIGHT HO, JEEVES
AND OTHER STORIES

ARROW BOOKS

Arrow Books Limited
20 Vauxhall Bridge Road, London SW1V 2SA

An imprint of the Random Century Group

London Melbourne Sydney Auckland Johannesburg
and agencies throughout the world

This edition first published in 1992 by Arrow Books

1 3 5 7 9 10 8 6 4 2

Printed and bound in Great Britain by
Cox & Wyman Ltd, Reading, Berkshire

ISBN 0 09 914201 5

CONTENTS

To RAYMOND NEEDHAM, K.C.
With Affection and Admiration

P. G. Wodehouse

RIGHT HO, JEEVES

1

'Jeeves,' I said, 'may I speak frankly?'

'Certainly, sir.'

'What I have to say may wound you.'

'Not at all, sir.'

'Well, then – '

No – wait. Hold the line a minute. I've gone off the rails.

I don't know if you have had the same experience, but the snag I always come up against when I'm telling a story is this dashed difficult problem of where to begin it. It's a thing you don't want to go wrong over, because one false step and you're sunk. I mean, if you fool about too long at the start, trying to establish atmosphere, as they call it, and all that sort of rot, you fail to grip and the customers walk out on you.

Get off the mark, on the other hand, like a scalded cat, and your public is at a loss. It simply raises its eyebrows, and can't make out what you're talking about.

And in opening my report of the complex case of Gussie Fink-Nottle, Madeline Bassett, my Cousin Angela, my Aunt Dahlia, my Uncle Thomas, young Tuppy Glossop and the cook, Anatole, with the above spot of dialogue, I see that I have made the second of these two floaters.

I shall have to hark back a bit. And taking it for all in all and weighing this against that, I suppose the affair may be said to have had its inception, if inception is the word I want, with that visit of mine to Cannes. If I hadn't gone to Cannes, I shouldn't have met the Bassett or bought that white mess jacket, and Angela wouldn't have met her shark, and Aunt Dahlia wouldn't have played baccarat.

Yes, most decidedly, Cannes was the *point d'appui.*

Right ho, then. Let me marshal my facts.

I went to Cannes – leaving Jeeves behind, he having intimated that he did not wish to miss Ascot – round about the beginning of June. With me travelled my Aunt Dahlia and her daughter Angela. Tuppy Glossop, Angela's betrothed, was to have been of the party, but at the last moment couldn't get away. Uncle Tom, Aunt Dahlia's husband, remained at home, because he can't stick the South of France at any price.

So there you have the layout – Aunt Dahlia, Cousin Angela and self off to Cannes round about the beginning of June.

All pretty clear so far, what?

We stayed at Cannes about two months, and except for the fact that Aunt Dahlia lost her shirt at baccarat and Angela nearly got inhaled by a shark while aquaplaning, a pleasant time was had by all.

On July twenty-fifth, looking bronzed and fit, I accompanied aunt and child back to London. At seven p.m. on July twenty-sixth we alighted at Victoria. And at seven-twenty or thereabouts we parted with mutual expressions of esteem – they to shove off in Aunt Dahlia's car to Brinkley Court, her place in Worcestershire, where they were expecting to entertain Tuppy in a day or two; I to go to the flat, drop my luggage, clean up a bit, and put on the soup and fish preparatory to pushing round to the Drones for a bite of dinner.

And it was while I was in the flat, towelling the torso after a much-needed rinse, that Jeeves, as we chatted of this and that – picking up the threads, as it were – suddenly brought the name of Gussie Fink-Nottle into the conversation.

As I recall it, the dialogue ran something as follows:

SELF: Well, Jeeves, here we are, what?

JEEVES: Yes, sir.

SELF: I mean to say, home again.

JEEVES: Precisely, sir.

SELF: Seems ages since I went away.

JEEVES: Yes, sir.

SELF: Have a good time at Ascot?

JEEVES: Most agreeable, sir.

SELF: Win anything?

JEEVES: Quite a satisfactory sum, thank you, sir.

SELF: Good. Well, Jeeves, what news on the Rialto? Anybody been phoning or calling or anything during my abs.?

JEEVES: Mr Fink-Nottle, sir, has been a frequent caller.

I stared. Indeed, it would not be too much to say that I gaped.

'Mr Fink-Nottle?'

'Yes, sir.'

'You don't mean Mr Fink-Nottle?'

'Yes, sir.'

'But Mr Fink-Nottle's not in London?'

'Yes, sir.'

'Well, I'm blowed.'

And I'll tell you why I was blowed. I found it scarcely possible to give credence to his statement. This Fink-Nottle, you see, was one of those freaks you come across from time to time during life's journey who can't stand London. He lived year in and year out, covered with moss, in a remote village down in Lincolnshire, never coming up even for the Eton and Harrow match. And when I asked him once if he didn't find the time hung a bit heavy on his hands, he said, no, because he had a pond in his garden and studied the habits of newts.

I couldn't imagine what could have brought the chap up to the great city. I would have been prepared to bet that as long as the supply of newts didn't give out, nothing could have shifted him from that village of his.

'Are you sure?'

'Yes, sir.'

'You got the name correctly? Fink-Nottle?'

'Yes, sir.'

'Well, it's the most extraordinary thing. It must be five years since he was in London. He makes no secret of the fact that the place gives him the pip. Until now, he has always stayed glued to the country, completely surrounded by newts.'

'Sir?'

'Newts, Jeeves. Mr Fink-Nottle has a strong newt complex. You must have heard of newts. Those little sort of lizard things that charge about in ponds.'

'Oh, yes, sir. The aquatic members of the family *Salamandridae* which constitute the genus *Molge*.'

'That's right. Well, Gussie has always been a slave to them. He used to keep them at school.'

'I believe young gentlemen frequently do, sir.'

'He kept them in his study in a kind of glass-tank arrangement, and pretty niffy the whole thing was, I recall. I suppose one ought to have been able to see what the end would be even then, but you know what boys are. Careless, heedless, busy about their own affairs, we scarcely gave this kink in Gussie's character a thought. We may have exchanged an occasional remark about it taking all sorts to make a world, but nothing more. You can guess the sequel. The trouble spread.'

'Indeed, sir?'

'Absolutely, Jeeves. The craving grew upon him. The

newts got him. Arrived at man's estate, he retired to the depths of the country and gave his life up to these dumb chums. I suppose he used to tell himself that he could take them or leave them alone, and then found – too late – that he couldn't.'

'It is often the way, sir.'

'Too true, Jeeves. At any rate, for the last five years he has been living at this place of his down in Lincolnshire, as confirmed a species-shunning hermit as ever put fresh water in the tank every second day and refused to see a soul. That's why I was so amazed when you told me he had suddenly risen to the surface like this. I still can't believe it. I am inclined to think that there must be some mistake, and that this bird who has been calling here is some different variety of Fink-Nottle. The chap I know wears horn-rimmed spectacles and has a face like a fish. How does that check up with your data?'

'The gentleman who came to the flat wore horn-rimmed spectacles, sir.'

'And looked like something on a slab?'

'Possibly there was a certain suggestion of the piscine, sir.'

'Then it must be Gussie, I suppose. But what on earth can have brought him up to London?'

'I am in a position to explain that, sir. Mr Fink-Nottle confided to me his motive in visiting the metropolis. He came because the young lady is here.'

'Young lady?'

'Yes, sir.'

'You don't mean he's in love?'

'Yes, sir.'

'Well, I'm dashed. I'm really dashed. I positively am dashed, Jeeves.'

And I was too. I mean to say, a joke's a joke, but there are limits.

Then I found my mind turning to another aspect of this rummy affair. Conceding the fact that Gussie Fink-Nottle, against all the ruling of the form book, might have fallen in love, why should he have been haunting my flat like this? No doubt the occasion was one of those when a fellow needs a friend, but I couldn't see what had made him pick on me.

It wasn't as if he and I were in any way bosom. We had seen a lot of each other at one time, of course, but in the last two years I hadn't had so much as a postcard from him.

I put all this to Jeeves:

'Odd, his coming to me. Still, if he did, he did. No argument about that. It must have been a nasty jar for the poor perisher when he found I wasn't here.'

'No, sir. Mr Fink-Nottle did not call to see you, sir.'

'Pull yourself together, Jeeves. You've just told me that this is what he has been doing, and assiduously, at that.'

'It was I with whom he was desirous of establishing communication, sir.'

'You? But I didn't know you had ever met him.'

'I had not had that pleasure until he called here, sir. But it appears that Mr Sipperley, a fellow student of whom Mr Fink-Nottle had been at the university, recommended him to place his affairs in my hands.'

The mystery had conked. I saw all. As I dare say you know, Jeeves's reputation as a counsellor has long been established among the cognoscenti, and the first move of any of my little circle on discovering themselves in any form of soup is always to roll round and put the thing up to him. And when he's got A out of a bad spot, A puts B on to him. And then, when he has fixed up B, B sends C along. And so on, if you get my drift, and so forth.

That's how these big consulting practices like Jeeves's

grow. Old Sippy, I knew, had been deeply impressed by the man's efforts on his behalf at the time when he was trying to get engaged to Elizabeth Moon, so it was not to be wondered at that he should have advised Gussie to apply. Pure routine, you might say.

'Oh, you're acting for him, are you?'

'Yes, sir.'

'Now I follow. Now I understand. And what is Gussie's trouble?'

'Oddly enough, sir, precisely the same as that of Mr Sipperley when I was enabled to be of assistance to him. No doubt you recall Mr Sipperley's predicament, sir. Deeply attached to Miss Moon, he suffered from a rooted diffidence which made it impossible for him to speak.'

I nodded.

'I remember. Yes, I recall the Sipperley case. He couldn't bring himself to the scratch. A marked coldness of the feet, was there not? I recollect you saying he was letting – what was it? – letting something do something. Cats entered into it, if I am not mistaken.'

'Letting "I dare not" wait upon "I would", sir.'

'That's right. But how about the cats?'

'Like the poor cat i' the adage, sir.'

'Exactly. It beats me how you think up these things. And Gussie, you say, is in the same posish?'

'Yes, sir. Each time he endeavours to formulate a proposal of marriage, his courage fails him.'

'And yet, if he wants this female to be his wife, he's got to say so, what? I mean, only civil to mention it.'

'Precisely, sir.'

I mused.

'Well, I suppose this was inevitable, Jeeves. I wouldn't have thought that this Fink-Nottle would ever have fallen a victim to the divine p., but, if he has, no wonder he finds the going sticky.'

'Yes, sir.'

'Look at the life he's led.'

'Yes, sir.'

'I don't suppose he has spoken to a girl for years. What a lesson this is to us, Jeeves, not to shut ourselves up in country houses and stare into glass tanks. You can't be the dominant male if you do that sort of thing. In this life, you can choose between two courses. You can either shut yourself up in a country house and stare into tanks, or you can be a dasher with the sex. You can't do both.'

'No, sir.'

I mused once more. Gussie and I, as I say, had rather lost touch, but all the same I was exercised about the poor fish, as I am about all my pals, close or distant, who find themselves treading upon Life's banana skins. It seemed to me that he was up against it.

I threw my mind back to the last time I had seen him. About two years ago, it had been. I had looked in at his place while on a motor trip, and he had put me right off my feed by bringing a couple of green things with legs to the luncheon table, crooning over them like a young mother and eventually losing one of them in the salad. That picture, rising before my eyes, didn't give me much confidence in the unfortunate goof's ability to woo and win, I must say. Especially if the girl he had earmarked was one of these tough modern thugs, all lipstick and cool, hard, sardonic eyes, as she probably was.

'Tell me, Jeeves,' I said, wishing to know the worst, 'what sort of a girl is this girl of Gussie's?'

'I have not met the young lady, sir. Mr Fink-Nottle speaks highly of her attractions.'

'Seemed to like her, did he?'

'Yes, sir.'

'Did he mention her name? Perhaps I know her.'

'She is a Miss Bassett, sir. Miss Madeline Bassett.'

'What?'

'Yes, sir.'

I was deeply intrigued.

'Egad, Jeeves! Fancy that. It's a small world, isn't it, what?'

'The young lady is an acquaintance of yours, sir?'

'I know her well. Your news has relieved my mind, Jeeves. It makes the whole thing begin to seem far more likely a practical working proposition.'

'Indeed, sir?'

'Absolutely. I confess that until you supplied this information I was feeling profoundly dubious about poor old Gussie's chances of inducing any spinster of any parish to join him in the saunter down the aisle. You will agree with me that he is not everybody's money.'

'There may be something in what you say, sir.'

'Cleopatra wouldn't have liked him.'

'Possibly not, sir.'

'And I doubt if he would go any too well with Tallulah Bankhead.'

'No, sir.'

'But when you tell me that the object of his affections is Miss Bassett, why, then, Jeeves, hope begins to dawn a bit. He's just the sort of chap a girl like Madeline Bassett might scoop in with relish.'

This Bassett, I must explain, had been a fellow visitor of ours at Cannes; and as she and Angela had struck up one of those effervescent friendships which girls do strike up, I had seen quite a bit of her. Indeed, in my moodier moments it sometimes seemed to me that I could not move a step without stubbing my toe on the woman.

And what made it all so painful and distressing was

that the more we met, the less did I seem able to find to say to her.

You know how it is with some girls. They seem to take the stuffing right out of you. I mean to say, there is something about their personality that paralyses the vocal cords and reduces the contents of the brain to cauliflower. It was like that with this Bassett and me; so much so that I have known occasions when for minutes at a stretch Bertram Wooster might have been observed fumbling with the tie, shuffling the feet, and behaving in all other respects in her presence like the complete dumb brick. When, therefore, she took her departure some two weeks before we did, you may readily imagine that, in Bertram's opinion, it was not a day too soon.

It was not her beauty, mark you, that thus numbed me. She was a pretty enough girl in a droopy, blonde, saucer-eyed way, but not the sort of breath-taker that takes the breath.

No, what caused this disintegration in a usually fairly fluent prattler with the sex was her whole mental attitude. I don't want to wrong anybody, so I won't go so far as to say that she actually wrote poetry, but her conversation, to my mind, was of a nature calculated to excite the liveliest suspicions. Well, I mean to say, when a girl suddenly asks you out of a blue sky if you don't sometimes feel that the stars are God's daisy chain, you begin to think a bit.

As regards the fusing of her soul and mine, therefore, there was nothing doing. But with Gussie, the posish was entirely different. The thing that had stymied me – viz. that this girl was obviously all loaded down with ideals and sentiment and what not – was quite in order as far as he was concerned.

Gussie had always been one of those dreamy, soulful birds – you can't shut yourself up in the country and live only for newts, if you're not – and I could see no reason why, if he could somehow be induced to get the low, burning words off his chest, he and the Bassett shouldn't hit it off like ham and eggs.

'She's just the type for him,' I said.

'I am most gratified to hear it, sir.'

'And he's just the type for her. In fine, a good thing and only to be pushed along with the utmost energy. Strain every nerve, Jeeves.'

'Very good, sir,' replied the honest fellow. 'I will attend to the matter at once.'

Now up to this point, as you will doubtless agree, what you might call a perfect harmony had prevailed. Friendly gossip between employer and employed, and everything as sweet as a nut. But at this juncture, I regret to say, there was an unpleasant switch. The atmosphere suddenly changed, the storm clouds began to gather, and before we knew where we were, the jarring note had come bounding on the scene. I have known this to happen before in the Wooster home.

The first intimation I had that things were about to hot up was a pained and disapproving cough from the neighbourhood of the carpet. For, during the above exchanges, I should explain, while I, having dried the frame, had been dressing in a leisurely manner, donning here a sock, there a shoe, and gradually climbing into the vest, the shirt, the tie, and the knee-length, Jeeves had been down on the lower level, unpacking my effects.

He now rose, holding a white object. And at the sight of it, I realized that another of our domestic crises had arrived, another of those unfortunate clashes of will between two strong men, and that Bertram, unless he remembered his fighting ancestors and stood up for his rights, was about to be put upon.

I don't know if you were at Cannes this summer.

If you were, you will recall that anybody with any pretensions to being the life and soul of the party was accustomed to attend binges at the Casino in the ordinary evening-wear trouserings topped to the north by a white mess jacket with brass buttons. And ever since I had stepped aboard the Blue Train at Cannes station, I had been wondering on and off how mine would go with Jeeves.

In the matter of evening costume, you see, Jeeves is hidebound and reactionary. I had had trouble with him before about soft-bosomed shirts. And while these mess jackets had, as I say, been all the rage – *tout ce qu'il y a de chic* – on the Côte d'Azur, I had never concealed it from myself, even when treading the measure at the Palm Beach Casino in the one I had hastened to buy, that there might be something of an upheaval about it on my return.

I prepared to be firm.

'Yes, Jeeves?' I said. And though my voice was suave, a close observer in a position to watch my eyes would have noticed a steely glint. Nobody has a greater respect for Jeeves's intellect than I have, but this disposition of his to dictate to the hand that fed him had got, I felt, to be checked. This mess jacket was very near to my heart, and I jolly well intended to fight for it with all the vim of grand old Sieur de Wooster at the Battle of Agincourt.

'Yes, Jeeves?' I said. 'Something on your mind, Jeeves?'

'I fear that you inadvertently left Cannes in the possession of a coat belonging to some other gentleman, sir.'

I switched on the steely a bit more.

'No, Jeeves,' I said, in a level tone, 'the object under advisement is mine. I bought it out there.'

'You wore it, sir?'

'Every night.'

'But surely you are not proposing to wear it in England, sir?'

I saw we had arrived at the nub.

'Yes, Jeeves.'

'But, sir – '

'You were saying, Jeeves?'

'It is quite unsuitable, sir.'

'I do not agree with you, Jeeves. I anticipate a great popular success for this jacket. It is my intention to spring it on the public tomorrow at Pongo Twistleton's birthday party, where I confidently expect it to be one long scream from start to finish. No argument, Jeeves. No discussion. Whatever fantastic objection you may have taken to it, I wear this jacket.'

'Very good, sir.'

He went on with his unpacking. I said no more on the subject. I had won the victory, and we Woosters do not triumph over a beaten foe. Presently, having completed my toilet, I bade the man a cheery farewell and in generous mood suggested that, as I was dining out, why didn't he take the evening off and go to some improving picture or something. Sort of olive branch, if you see what I mean.

He didn't seem to think much of it.

'Thank you, sir, I will remain in.'

I surveyed him narrowly.

'Is this dudgeon, Jeeves?'

'No, sir, I am obliged to remain on the premises. Mr Fink-Nottle informed me he would be calling to see me this evening.'

'Oh, Gussie's coming, is he? Well, give him my love.'

'Very good, sir.'

'And a whisky and soda, and so forth.'

'Very good, sir.'

'Right ho, Jeeves.'

I then set off for the Drones.

At the Drones I ran into Pongo Twistleton, and he talked so much about this forthcoming merry-making of his, of which good reports had already reached me through my correspondents, that it was nearing eleven when I got home again.

And scarcely had I opened the door when I heard voices in the sitting room, and scarcely had I entered the sitting room when I found that these proceeded from Jeeves and what appeared at first sight to be the Devil.

A closer scrutiny informed me that it was Gussie Fink-Nottle, dressed as Mephistopheles.

2

'What ho, Gussie,' I said.

You couldn't have told it from my manner, but I was feeling more than a bit nonplussed. The spectacle before me was enough to nonplus anyone. I mean to say, this Fink-Nottle, as I remembered him, was the sort of shy, shrinking goop who might have been expected to shake like an aspen if invited to so much as a social Saturday afternoon at the vicarage. And yet here he was, if one could credit one's senses, about to take part in a fancy-dress ball, a form of entertainment notoriously a testing experience for the toughest.

And he was attending that fancy-dress ball, mark you – not, like every other well-bred Englishman, as a Pierrot, but as Mephistopheles – this involving, as I need scarcely stress, not only scarlet tights but a pretty frightful false beard.

Rummy, you'll admit. However, one masks one's feelings. I betrayed no vulgar astonishment, but, as I say, what-hoed with civil nonchalance.

He grinned through the fungus – rather sheepishly, I thought.

'Oh, hullo, Bertie.'

'Long time since I saw you. Have a spot?'

'No, thanks. I must be off in a minute. I just came round to ask Jeeves how he thought I looked. How do you think I look, Bertie?'

Well, the answer to that, of course, was 'perfectly foul'. But we Woosters are men of tact and have a nice sense of the obligations of a host. We do not tell old friends beneath our roof-tree that they are an offence to the eyesight. I evaded the question.

'I hear you're in London,' I said carelessly.

'Oh, yes.'

'Must be years since you came up.'

'Oh, yes.'

'And now you're off for an evening's pleasure.'

He shuddered a bit. He had, I noticed, a hunted air.

'Pleasure!'

'Aren't you looking forward to this rout or revel?'

'Oh, I suppose it'll be all right,' he said, in a toneless voice. 'Anyway, I ought to be off, I suppose. The thing starts round about eleven. I told my cab to wait . . . Will you see if it's there, Jeeves?'

'Very good, sir.'

There was something of a pause after the door had closed. A certain constraint. I mixed myself a beaker, while Gussie, a glutton for punishment, stared at himself in the mirror. Finally I decided that it would be best to let him know that I was abreast of his affairs. It might be that it would ease his mind to confide in a sympathetic man of experience. I have generally found, with those under the influence, that what they want more than anything is the listening ear.

'Well, Gussie, old leper,' I said, 'I've been hearing all about you.'

'Eh?'

'This little trouble of yours. Jeeves has told me everything.'

He didn't seem any too braced. It's always difficult to be sure, of course, when a chap has dug himself in behind a Mephistopheles beard, but I fancy he flushed a trifle.

'I wish Jeeves wouldn't go gassing all over the place. It was supposed to be confidential.'

I could not permit this tone.

'Dishing up the dirt to the young master can scarcely be described as gassing all over the place,' I said, with a touch of rebuke. 'Anyway, there it is. I know all. And I should like to begin,' I said, sinking my personal opinion that the female in question was a sloppy pest in my desire to buck and encourage, 'by saying that Madeline Bassett is a charming girl. A winner, and just the sort for you.'

'You don't know her?'

'Certainly I know her. What beats me is how you ever got in touch. Where did you meet?'

'She was staying at a place near mine in Lincolnshire the week before last.'

'Yes, but even so. I didn't know you called on the neighbours.'

'I don't. I met her out for a walk with her dog. The dog had got a thorn in its foot, and when she tried to take it out, it snapped at her. So, of course, I had to rally round.'

'You extracted the thorn?'

'Yes.'

'And fell in love at first sight?'

'Yes.'

'Well, dash it, with a thing like that to give you a send-off, why didn't you cash in immediately?'

'I hadn't the nerve.'

'What happened?'

'We talked for a bit?

'What about?'

'Oh, birds.'

'Birds? What birds.'

'The birds that happened to be hanging round. And the scenery, and all that sort of thing. And she said she was going to London, and asked me to look her up if I was ever there.'

'And even after that you didn't so much as press her hand?'

'Of course not.'

Well, I mean, it looked as though there was no more to be said. If a chap is such a rabbit that he can't get action when he's handed the thing on a plate, his case would appear to be pretty hopeless. Nevertheless, I reminded myself that this non-starter and I had been at school together. One must make an effort for an old school friend.

'Ah, well,' I said, 'we must see what can be done. Things may brighten. At any rate, you will be glad to learn that I am behind you in this enterprise. You have Bertram Wooster in your corner, Gussie.'

'Thanks, old man. And Jeeves, of course, which is the thing that really matters.'

I don't mind admitting that I winced. He meant no harm, I suppose, but I'm bound to say that his tactless speech nettled me not a little. People are always nettling me like that. Giving me to understand, I mean to say, that in their opinion Bertram Wooster is a mere cipher and that the only member of the household with brains and resources is Jeeves.

It jars on me.

And tonight it jarred on me more than usual, because I was feeling pretty dashed fed with Jeeves. Over that matter of the mess jacket, I mean. True, I had forced him to climb down, quelling him, as described, with the quiet strength of my personality, but I was still a trifle shirty at his having brought the thing up at all. It seemed to me that what Jeeves wanted was the iron hand.

'And what is he doing about it?' I inquired stiffly.

'He's been giving the position of affairs a lot of thought.'

'He has, has he?'

'It's on his advice that I'm going to this dance.'

'Why?'

'She is going to be there. In fact, it was she who sent me the ticket of invitation. And Jeeves considered – '

'And why not as a Pierrot?' I said, taking up the point which had struck me before. 'Why this break with a grand old tradition?'

'He particularly wanted me to go as Mephistopheles.'

I started.

'He did, did he? He specifically recommended that definite costume?'

'Yes.'

'Ha!'

'Eh?'

'Nothing. Just "Ha!" '

And I'll tell you why I said 'Ha!' Here was Jeeves making heavy weather about me wearing a perfectly ordinary white mess jacket, a garment not only *tout ce qu'il y a de chic*, but absolutely *de rigueur*, and in the same breath, as you might say, inciting Gussie Fink-Nottle to be blot on the London scene in scarlet tights. Ironical, what? One looks askance at this sort of in-and-out running.

'What has he got against Pierrots?'

'I don't think he objects to Pierrots as Pierrots. But in my case he thought a Pierrot wouldn't be adequate.'

'I don't follow that.'

'He said that the costume of Pierrot, while pleasing to the eye, lacked the authority of the Mephistopheles costume.'

'I still don't get it.'

'Well, it's a matter of psychology, he said.'

There was a time when a remark like that would have had me snookered. But long association with Jeeves has developed the Wooster vocabulary considerably. Jeeves has always been a whale for the psychology of the individual, and I now follow him like a bloodhound when he snaps it out of the bag.

'Oh, psychology?'

'Yes. Jeeves is a great believer in the moral effect of clothes. He thinks I might be emboldened in a striking costume like this. He said a Pirate Chief would be just as good. In fact, a Pirate Chief was his first suggestion, but I objected to the boots.'

I saw his point. There is enough sadness in life without having fellows like Gussie Fink-Nottle going about in sea boots.

'And are you emboldened?'

'Well, to be absolutely accurate, Bertie, old man, no.'

A gust of compassion shook me. After all, though we had lost touch a bit of recent years, this man and I had once thrown inked darts at each other.

'Gussie,' I said, 'take an old friend's advice, and don't go within a mile of this binge.'

'But it's my last chance of seeing her. She's off tomorrow to stay with some people in the country. Besides, you don't know.'

'Don't know what?'

'That this idea of Jeeves's won't work. I feel a most frightful chump now, yes, but who can say whether that will not pass off when I get into a mob of other people in fancy dress. I had the same experience as a child, one year during the Christmas festivities. They dressed me up as a rabbit, and the shame was indescribable. Yet when I got to the party and found myself surrounded by scores of other children, many in costumes even ghastlier than my own, I perked up amazingly, joined freely in the revels, and was able to eat so hearty a supper that I was sick twice in the cab coming home. What I mean is, you can't tell in cold blood.'

I weighed this. It was specious, of course.

'And you can't get away from it that, fundamentally,

Jeeves's idea is sound. In a striking costume like Mephistopheles, I might quite easily pull off something pretty impressive. Colour does make a difference. Look at newts. During the courting season the male newt is brilliantly coloured. It helps him a lot.'

'But you aren't a male newt.'

'I wish I were. Do you know how a male newt proposes, Bertie? He just stands in front of the female newt vibrating his tail and bending his body in a semicircle. I could do that on my head. No, you wouldn't find me grousing if I were a male newt.'

'But if you were a male newt, Madeline Bassett wouldn't look at you. Not with the eye of love, I mean.'

'She would, if she were a female newt.'

'But she isn't a female newt.'

'No, but suppose she was.'

'Well, if she was, you wouldn't be in love with her.'

'Yes, I would, if I were a male newt.'

A slight throbbing about the temples told me that this discussion had reached saturation point.

'Well, anyway,' I said, 'coming down to hard facts and cutting out all this visionary stuff about vibrating tails and what not, the salient point that emerges is that you are booked to appear at a fancy-dress ball. And I tell you out of my riper knowledge of fancy-dress balls, Gussie, that you won't enjoy yourself.'

'It isn't a question of enjoying yourself.'

'I wouldn't go.'

'I must go. I keep telling you she's off to the country tomorrow.'

I gave it up.

'So be it,' I said. 'Have it your own way . . . Yes, Jeeves?'

'Mr Fink-Nottle's cab, sir.'

'Ah? The cab, eh? . . . Your cab, Gussie.'

'Oh, the cab? Oh, right. Of course, yes, rather . . . Thanks, Jeeves . . . Well, so long, Bertie.'

And giving me the sort of weak smile Roman gladiators used to give the Emperor before entering the arena, Gussie trickled off. And I turned to Jeeves. The moment had arrived for putting him in his place, and I was all for it.

It was a little difficult to know how to begin, of course. I mean to say, while firmly resolved to tick him off, I didn't want to gash his feelings too deeply. Even when displaying the iron hand, we Woosters like to keep the thing fairly matey.

However, on consideration, I saw that there was nothing to be gained by trying to lead up to it gently. It was never any use beating about the b.

'Jeeves,' I said, 'may I speak frankly?'

'Certainly, sir.'

'What I have to say may wound you.'

'Not at all, sir.'

'Well, then, I have been having a chat with Mr Fink-Nottle, and he has been telling me about this Mephistopheles scheme of yours.'

'Yes, sir?'

'Now let me get it straight. If I follow your reasoning correctly, you think that, stimulated by being upholstered throughout in scarlet tights, Mr Fink-Nottle, on encountering the adored object, will vibrate his tail and generally let himself go with a whoop.'

'I am of the opinion that he will lose much of his normal diffidence, sir.'

'I don't agree with you, Jeeves.'

'No, sir?'

'No. In fact, not to put too fine a point upon it, I consider that of all the dashed silly, drivelling ideas I ever heard in my puff this is the most blithering and futile. It won't work. Not a chance. All you have done is to subject Mr Fink-Nottle to the nameless horrors of a fancy-dress ball for nothing. And this is not the first time this sort of thing has happened. To be quite candid, Jeeves, I have frequently noticed before now a tendency or disposition on your part to become – what's the word?'

'I could not say, sir.'

'Eloquent? No, it's not eloquent. Elusive? No, it's not elusive. It's on the tip of my tongue. Begins with an "e" and means being a jolly sight too clever.'

'Elaborate, sir?'

'That is the exact word I was after. Too elaborate, Jeeves – that is what you are frequently prone to become. Your methods are not simple, not straightforward. You cloud the issue with a lot of fancy stuff that is not of the essence. All that Gussie needs is the older-brotherly advice of a seasoned man of the world. So what I suggest is that from now onward you leave this case to me.'

'Very good, sir.'

'You lay off and devote yourself to your duties about the home.'

'I shall no doubt think of something quite simple and straightforward yet perfectly effective ere long. I will make a point of seeing Gussie tomorrow.'

'Very good, sir.'

'Right ho, Jeeves.'

But on the morrow all those telegrams started coming in, and I confess that for twenty-four hours I didn't give the poor chap a thought, having problems of my own to contend with.

3

The first of the telegrams arrived shortly after noon, and Jeeves brought it in with the before-luncheon snifter. It was from my Aunt Dahlia, operating from Market Snodsbury, a small town of sorts a mile or two along the main road as you leave her country seat.

It ran as follows:

Come at once. Travers.

And when I say it puzzled me like the dickens, I am understating it, if anything. As mysterious a communication, I considered, as was ever flashed over the wires. I studied it in a profound reverie for the best part of two dry Martinis and a dividend. I read it backwards. I read it forwards. As a matter of fact, I have a sort of recollection of even smelling it. But it still baffled me.

Consider the facts, I mean. It was only a few hours since this aunt and I had parted, after being in constant association for nearly two months. And yet here she was – with my farewell kiss still lingering on her cheek, so to speak – pleading for another reunion. Bertram Wooster was not accustomed to this gluttonous appetite for his society. Ask anyone who knows me, and they will tell you that after two months of my company, what the normal person feels is that that will about do for the present. Indeed, I have known people who couldn't stick it out for more than a few days.

Before sitting down to the well-cooked, therefore, I sent this reply:

Perplexed. Explain. Bertie.

To this I received an answer during the after-luncheon sleep:

What on earth is there to be perplexed about, ass? Come at once. Travers.

Three cigarettes and a couple of turns about the room, and I had my response ready:

How do you mean come at once? Regards. Bertie.

I append the comeback:

I mean come at once, you maddening halfwit. What did you think I meant? Come at once or expect an aunt's curse first post tomorrow. Love. Travers.

I then dispatched the following message, wishing to get everything quite clear:

When you say 'Come' do you mean 'Come to Brinkley Court'? And when you say 'At once' do you mean 'At once'? Fogged. At a loss. All the best. Bertie.

I sent this one off on my way to the Drones, where I spent a restful afternoon throwing cards into a top hat with some of the better element. Returning in the evening hush, I found the answer waiting for me:

Yes, yes, yes, yes, yes, yes, yes. It doesn't matter whether you understand or not. You just come at once, as I tell you, and for heaven's sake stop this back-chat. Do you think I am made of money that I can afford to send you telegrams every ten minutes. Stop being a fathead and come immediately. Love. Travers.

It was at this point that I felt the need of getting a second opinion. I pressed the bell.

'Jeeves,' I said, 'a V-shaped rumminess has manifested

itself from the direction of Worcestershire. Read these,' I said, handing him the papers in the case.

He scanned them.

'What do you make of it, Jeeves?'

'I think Mrs Travers wishes you to come at once, sir.'

'You gather that too, do you?'

'Yes, sir.'

'I put the same construction on the thing. But why, Jeeves? Dash it all, she's just had nearly two months of me.'

'Yes, sir.'

'And many people consider the medium dose for an adult two days.'

'Yes, sir. I appreciate the point you raise. Nevertheless, Mrs Travers appears very insistent. I think it would be well to acquiesce in her wishes.'

'Pop down, you mean?'

'Yes, sir.'

'Well, I certainly can't go at once. I've an important conference at the Drones tonight. Pongo Twistleton's birthday party, you remember?'

'Yes, sir.'

There was a slight pause. We were both recalling the little unpleasantness that had arisen. I felt obliged to allude to it.

'You're all wrong about that mess jacket, Jeeves.'

'These things are matters of opinion, sir.'

'When I wore it at the Casino in Cannes, beautiful women nudged one another and whispered: "Who is he?" '

'The code at Continental casinos is notoriously lax, sir.'

'And when I described it to Pongo last night, he was fascinated.'

'Indeed, sir?'

'So were all the rest of those present. One and all

admitted that I had got hold of a good thing. Not a dissentient voice.'

'Indeed, sir?'

'I am convinced that you will eventually learn to love this mess jacket, Jeeves.'

'I fear not, sir.'

I gave it up. It is never any use trying to reason with Jeeves on these occasions. 'Pig-headed' is the word that springs to the lips. One sighs and passes on.

'Well, anyway, returning to the agenda, I can't go down to Brinkley Court or anywhere else yet awhile. That's final. I'll tell you what, Jeeves. Give me form and pencil, and I'll wire her that I'll be with her some time next week or the week after. Dash it all, she ought to be able to hold out without me for a few days. It only requires will power.'

'Yes, sir.'

'Right ho, then. I'll wire "Expect me tomorrow fortnight" or words to some such effect. That ought to meet the case. Then if you will toddle round the corner and send it off, that will be that.'

'Very good, sir.'

And so the long day wore on till it was time for me to dress for Pongo's party.

Pongo had assured me, while chatting of the affair on the previous night, that this birthday binge of his was to be on a scale calculated to stagger humanity, and I must say I have participated in less fruity functions. It was well after four when I got home, and by that time I was about ready to turn in. I can just remember groping for the bed and crawling into it, and it seemed to me that the lemon had scarcely touched the pillow before I was aroused by the sound of the door opening.

I was barely ticking over, but I contrived to raise an eyelid.

'Is that my tea, Jeeves?'

'No, sir. It is Mrs Travers.'

And a moment later there was a sound like a mighty rushing wind, and the relative had crossed the threshold at fifty m.p.h. under her own steam.

4

It has been well said of Bertram Wooster that, while no one views his flesh and blood with a keener and more remorselessly critical eye, he is nevertheless a man who delights in giving credit where credit is due. And if you have followed these memoirs of mine with the proper care, you will be aware that I have frequently had occasion to emphasize the fact that Aunt Dahlia is all right.

She is the one, if you remember, who married old Tom Travers *en secondes noces*, as I believe the expression is, the year Bluebottle won the Cambridgeshire, and once induced me to write an article on What the Well-Dressed Man is Wearing for that paper she runs – *Milady's Boudoir*. She is a large, genial soul, with whom it is a pleasure to hob-nob. In her spiritual make-up there is none of that subtle gosh-awfulness which renders such an exhibit as, say, my Aunt Agatha the curse of the Home Counties and a menace to one and all. I have the highest esteem for Aunt Dahlia, and have never wavered in my cordial appreciation of her humanity, sporting qualities and general good-eggishness.

This being so, you may conceive of my astonishment at finding her at my bedside at such an hour. I mean to say, I've stayed at her place many a time and oft, and she knows my habits. She is well aware that until I have had my cup of tea in the morning, I do not receive. This crashing in at a moment when she knew that solitude and repose were of the essence was scarcely, I could not but feel, the good old form.

Besides, what business had she being in London at all? That was what I asked myself. When a conscientious housewife has returned to her home after an absence of seven weeks, one does not expect her to start racing off again the day after her arrival. One feels that she ought to be sticking round, ministering to her husband, conferring with the cook, feeding the cat, combing and brushing the Pomeranian – in a word, staying put. I was more than a little bleary-eyed, but I endeavoured, as far as the fact that my eyelids were more or less glued together would permit, to give her an austere and censorious look.

She didn't seem to get it.

'Wake up, Bertie, you old ass!' she cried, in a voice that hit me between the eyebrows and went out at the back of my head.

If Aunt Dahlia has a fault, it is that she is apt to address a *vis-à-vis* as if he were somebody half a mile away whom she had observed riding over hounds. A throwback, no doubt, to the time when she counted the day lost that was not spent chivying some unfortunate fox over the countryside.

I gave her another of the austere and censorious, and this time it registered. All the effect it had, however, was to cause her to descend to personalities.

'Don't blink at me in that obscene way,' she said. 'I wonder, Bertie,' she proceeded, gazing at me as I should imagine Gussie would have gazed at some newt that was not up to sample, 'if you have the faintest conception how perfectly loathsome you look? A cross between an orgy scene in the movies and some low form of pond life. I suppose you were out on the tiles last night?'

'I attended a social function, yes,' I said coldly.

'Pongo Twistleton's birthday party. I couldn't let Pongo down. *Noblesse oblige.*'

'Well, get up and dress.'

I felt I could not have heard her aright.

'Get up and dress?'

'Yes.'

I turned on the pillow with a little moan, and at this juncture Jeeves entered with the vital oolong. I clutched at it like a drowning man at a straw hat. A deep sip or two, and I felt – I won't say restored, because a birthday party like Pongo Twistleton's isn't a thing you get restored after with a mere mouthful of tea, but sufficiently the old Bertram to be able to bend the mind on this awful thing which had come upon me.

And the more I bent same, the less could I grasp the trend of the scenario.

'What is this, Aunt Dahlia?' I inquired.

'It looks to me like tea,' was her response. 'But you know best. You're drinking it.'

If I hadn't been afraid of spilling the healing brew, I have little doubt that I should have given an impatient gesture. I know I felt like it.

'Not the contents of this cup. All this. Your barging in and telling me to get up and dress, and all that rot.'

'I've barged in, as you call it, because my telegrams seemed to produce no effect. And I told you to get up and dress because I want you to get up and dress. I've come to take you back with me. I like your crust, wiring that you would come next year or whenever it was. You're coming now. I've got a job for you.'

'But I don't want a job.'

'What you want, my lad, and what you're going to get are two very different things. There is man's work for you to do at Brinkley Court. Be ready to the last button in twenty minutes.'

'But I can't possibly be ready to any buttons in twenty minutes. I'm feeling awful.'

She seemed to consider.

'Yes,' she said. 'I suppose it's only humane to give you a day or two to recover. All right, then, I shall expect you on the thirtieth at the latest.'

'But, dash it, what is all this? How do you mean, a job? Why a job? What sort of a job?'

'I'll tell you if you'll only stop talking for a minute. It's quite an easy, pleasant job. You will enjoy it. Have you ever heard of Market Snodsbury Grammar School?'

'Never.'

'It's a grammar school at Market Snodsbury.'

I told her a little frigidly that I had divined as much.

'Well, how was I to know that a man with a mind like yours would grasp it so quickly?' she protested. 'All right, then. Market Snodsbury Grammar School is, as you have guessed, the grammar school at Market Snodsbury. I'm one of the governors.'

'You mean one of the governesses.'

'I don't mean one of the governesses. Listen, ass. There was a board of governors at Eton, wasn't there? Very well. So there is at Market Snodsbury Grammar School, and I'm a member of it. And they left the arrangements for the summer prize giving to me. This prize giving takes place on the last – or thirty-first – day of this month. Have you got that clear?'

I took another oz. of the life-saving and inclined my head. Even after a Pongo Twistleton birthday party, I was capable of grasping simple facts like these.

'I follow you, yes. I see the point you are trying to make, certainly. Market . . . Snodsbury . . . Grammar School . . . Board of governors . . . Prize giving . . . Quite. But what's it got to do with me?'

'You're going to give away the prizes.'

I goggled. Her words did not appear to make sense.

They seemed the mere aimless vapouring of an aunt who has been sitting out in the sun without a hat.

'Me?'

'You.'

I goggled again.

'You don't mean me?'

'I mean you in person.'

I goggled a third time.

'You're pulling my leg.'

'I am not pulling your leg. Nothing would induce me to touch your beastly leg. The vicar was to have officiated, but when I got home I found a letter from him saying that he had strained a fetlock and must scratch his nomination. You can imagine the state I was in. I telephoned all over the place. Nobody would take it on. And then suddenly I thought of you.'

I decided to check all this rot at the outset. Nobody is more eager to oblige deserving aunts than Bertram Wooster, but there are limits, and sharply defined limits, at that.

'So you think I'm going to strew prizes at this bally Dotheboys Hall of yours?'

'I do.'

'And make a speech?'

'Exactly.'

I laughed derisively.

'For goodness' sake, don't start gargling now. This is serious.'

'I was laughing.'

'Oh, were you?' Well, I'm glad to see you taking it in this merry spirit.'

'Derisively,' I explained. 'I won't do it. That's final. I simply will not do it.'

'You will do it, young Bertie, or never darken my doors again. And you know what that means. No more of Anatole's dinners for you.'

A strong shudder shook me. She was alluding to her *chef*, that superb artist. A monarch of his profession, unsurpassed – nay, unequalled – at dishing up the raw material so that it melted in the mouth of the ultimate consumer, Anatole had always been a magnet that drew me to Brinkley Court with my tongue hanging out. Many of my happiest moments had been those which I had spent champing this great man's roasts and ragouts, and the prospect of being barred from digging into them in the future was a numbing one.

'No, I say, dash it!'

'I thought that would rattle you. Greedy young pig.'

'Greedy young pigs have nothing to do with it,' I said with a touch of hauteur. 'One is not a greedy young pig because one appreciates the cooking of a genius.'

'Well, I will say I like it myself,' conceded the relative. 'But not another bite of it do you get, if you refuse to do this simple, easy, pleasant job. No, not so much as another sniff. So put that in your twelve-inch cigarette holder and smoke it.'

I began to feel like some wild thing caught in a snare.

'But why do you want me? I mean, what am I? Ask yourself that.'

'I often have.'

'I mean to say, I'm not the type. You have to have some terrific nib to give away prizes. I seem to remember, when I was at school, it was generally a prime minister or somebody.'

'Ah, but that was at Eton. At Market Snodsbury we aren't nearly so choosy. Anybody in spats impresses us.'

'Why don't you get Uncle Tom?'

'Uncle Tom!'

'Well, why not? He's got spats.'

'Bertie,' she said, 'I will tell you why not Uncle Tom. You remember me losing all that money at baccarat at Cannes? Well, very shortly I shall have to sidle up to

Tom and break the news to him. If, right after that, I ask him to put on lavender gloves and a topper and distribute the prizes at Market Snodsbury Grammar School, there will be a divorce in the family. He would pin a note to the pincushion and be off like a rabbit. No, my lad, you're for it, so you may as well make the best of it.'

'But, Aunt Dahlia, listen to reason. I assure you, you've got hold of the wrong man. I'm hopeless at a game like that. Ask Jeeves about the time I got lugged in to address a girls' school. I made the most colossal ass of myself.'

'And I confidently anticipate that you will make an equally colossal ass of yourself on the thirty-first of this month. That's why I want you. The way I look at it is that, as the thing is bound to be a frost, anyway, one may as well get a hearty laugh out of it. I shall enjoy seeing you distribute those prizes, Bertie. Well, I won't keep you, as, no doubt, you want to do your Swedish exercises. I shall expect you in a day or two.'

And with these heartless words she beetled off, leaving me a prey to the gloomiest emotions. What with the natural reaction after Pongo's party and this stunning blow, it is not too much to say that the soul was seared.

And I was still writhing in the depths, when the door opened and Jeeves appeared.

'Mr Fink-Nottle to see you, sir,' he announced.

5

I gave him one of my looks.

'Jeeves,' I said, 'I had scarcely expected this of you. You are aware that I was up to an advanced hour last night. You know that I have barely had my tea. You cannot be ignorant of the effect of that hearty voice of Aunt Dahlia's on a man with a headache. And yet you come bringing me Fink-Nottles. Is this a time for Fink or any other kind of Nottle?'

'But did you not give me to understand, sir, that you wished to see Mr Fink-Nottle to advise him on his affairs?'

This, I admit, opened up a new line of thought. In the stress of my emotions, I had clean forgotten about having taken Gussie's interests in hand. It altered things. One can't give the raspberry to a client. I mean, you didn't find Sherlock Holmes refusing to see clients just because he had been out late the night before at Doctor Watson's birthday party. I could have wished that the man had selected some more suitable hour for approaching me, but as he appeared to be a sort of human lark, leaving his watery nest at daybreak, I supposed I had better give him an audience.

'True,' I said. 'All right. Bung him in.'

'Very good, sir.'

'But before doing so, bring me one of those pick-me-ups of yours.'

'Very good, sir.'

And presently he returned with the vital essence.

I have had occasion, I fancy, to speak before now of these pick-me-ups of Jeeves's and their effect on a fellow who is hanging to life by a thread on the morning after. What they consist of, I couldn't tell you. He says some kind of sauce, the yolk of a raw egg and a dash of red pepper, but nothing will convince me that the thing doesn't go much deeper than that. Be that as it may, however, the results of swallowing one are amazing.

For perhaps the split part of a second nothing happens. It is as though all Nature waited breathless. Then, suddenly, it is as if the Last Trump had sounded and Judgment Day set in with unusual severity.

Bonfires burst out in all parts of the frame. The abdomen becomes heavily charged with molten lava. A great wind seems to blow through the world, and the subject is aware of something resembling a steam hammer striking the back of the head. During this phase, the ears ring loudly, the eyeballs rotate and there is a tingling about the brow.

And then, just as you are feeling that you ought to ring up your lawyer and see that your affairs are in order before it is too late, the whole situation seems to clarify. The wind drops. The ears cease to ring. Birds twitter. Brass bands start playing. The sun comes up over the horizon with a jerk.

And a moment later all you are conscious of is a great peace.

As I drained the glass now, new life seemed to burgeon within me. I remember Jeeves, who, however much he may go off the rails at times in the matter of dress clothes and in his advice to those in love, has always had a neat turn of phrase, once speaking of someone rising on stepping-stones of his dead self to higher things. It was that way with me now. I felt that the Bertram Wooster who lay propped up against the pillows had become a better, stronger, finer Bertram.

'Thank you, Jeeves,' I said.

'Not at all, sir.'

'That touched the exact spot. I am now able to cope with life's problems.'

'I am gratified to hear it, sir.'

'What madness not to have had one of those before tackling Aunt Dahlia! However, too late to worry about that now. Tell me of Gussie. How did he make out at the fancy-dress ball?'

'He did not arrive at the fancy-dress ball, sir.'

I looked at him a bit austerely.

'Jeeves,' I said, 'I admit that after that pick-me-up of yours I feel better, but don't try me too high. Don't stand by my sick bed talking absolute rot. We shot Gussie into a cab and he started forth, headed for wherever this fancy-dress ball was. He must have arrived.'

'No, sir. As I gather from Mr Fink-Nottle, he entered the cab convinced in his mind that the entertainment to which he had been invited was to be held at No. 17, Suffolk Square, whereas the actual rendezvous was No. 71, Norfolk Terrace. These aberrations of memory are not uncommon with those who, like Mr Fink-Nottle, belong essentially to what one might call the dreamer-type.'

'One might also call it the fatheaded type.'

'Yes, sir.'

'Well?'

'On reaching No. 17, Suffolk Square, Mr Fink-Nottle endeavoured to produce money to pay the fare.'

'What stopped him?'

'The fact that he had no money, sir. He discovered that he had left it, together with his ticket of invitation, on the mantelpiece of his bedchamber in the house of his uncle, where he was residing. Bidding the cabman to wait, accordingly, he rang the doorbell, and when the butler appeared, requested him to pay the cab, adding that it was all right, as he was one of the guests invited to the dance. The butler then disclaimed all knowledge of a dance on the premises.'

'And declined to unbelt?'

'Yes, sir.'

'Upon which – '

'Mr Fink-Nottle directed the cabman to drive him back to his uncle's residence.'

'Well, why wasn't that the happy ending? All he had to do was go in, collect cash and ticket, and there he would have been, on velvet.'

'I should have mentioned, sir, that Mr Fink-Nottle had also left his latchkey on the mantelpiece of his bedchamber.'

'He could have rung the bell.'

'He did ring the bell, sir, for some fifteen minutes. At the expiration of that period he recalled that he had given permission to the caretaker – the house was officially closed and all the staff on holiday – to visit his sailor son at Portsmouth.'

'Golly, Jeeves!'

'Yes, sir.'

'These dreamer types do live, don't they?'

'Yes, sir.'

'What happened then?'

'Mr Fink-Nottle appears to have realized at this point that his position as regards the cabman had become equivocal. The figures on the clock had already reached a substantial sum, and he was not in a position to meet his obligations.'

'He could have explained.'

'You cannot explain to cabmen, sir. On endeavouring to do so, he found the fellow sceptical of his bona fides.'

'I should have legged it.'

'That is the policy which appears to have commended itself to Mr Fink-Nottle. He darted rapidly away, and the cabman, endeavouring to detain him, snatched at his overcoat. Mr Fink-Nottle contrived to extricate himself from the coat, and it would seem that his appearance in the masquerade costume beneath it came as something of a shock to the cabman. Mr Fink-Nottle informs me that he heard a species of whistling gasp, and, looking round, observed the man crouching against the railings with his hands over his face. Mr Fink-Nottle thinks he was praying. No doubt an uneducated, superstitious fellow, sir. Possibly a drinker.'

'Well, if he hadn't been one before, I'll bet he started being one shortly afterwards. I expect he could scarcely wait for the pubs to open.'

'Very possibly, in the circumstances he might have found a restorative agreeable, sir.'

'And so, in the circumstances, might Gussie too, I should think. What on earth did he do after that? London late at night – or even in the daytime, for that matter – is no place for a man in scarlet tights.'

'No, sir.'

'He invites comment.'

'Yes, sir.'

'I can see the poor old bird ducking down side streets, skulking in alleyways, diving into dustbins.'

'I gathered from Mr Fink-Nottle's remarks, sir, that something very much on those lines was what occurred. Eventually, after a trying night, he found his way to Mr Sipperley's residence, where he was able to secure lodging and a change of costume in the morning.'

I nestled against the pillows, the brow a bit drawn. It is all very well to try to do old school friends a spot of good, but I could not but feel that in espousing the cause of a lunkhead capable of mucking things up as Gussie had done, I had taken on a contract almost too big for human consumption. It seemed to me that what Gussie needed was not so much the advice of a seasoned man of the world as a padded cell in Colney Hatch and a couple of good keepers to see that he did not set the place on fire.

Indeed, for an instant I had half a mind to withdraw from the case and hand it back to Jeeves. But the pride of the Woosters restrained me. When we Woosters put our hands to the plough, we do not readily sheathe the sword. Besides, after that business of the mess jacket, anything resembling weakness would have been fatal.

'I suppose you realize, Jeeves,' I said, for though one dislikes to rub it in, these things have to be pointed out, 'that all this was your fault?'

'Sir?'

'It's no good saying "Sir?" You know it was. If you had not insisted on his going to that dance – a mad project, as I spotted from the first – this would not have happened.'

'Yes, sir, but I confess I did not anticipate – '

'Always anticipate everything, Jeeves,' I said, a little sternly. 'It is the only way. Even if you had allowed him to wear a Pierrot costume, things would not have panned out as they did. A Pierrot costume has pockets. However,' I went on more kindly, 'we need not go into that now. If all this has shown you what comes of going about the place in scarlet tights, that is something gained. Gussie waits without, you say?'

'Yes, sir.'

'Then shoot him in, and I will see what I can do for him.'

6

Gussie, on arrival, proved to be still showing traces of his grim experience. The face was pale, the eyes gooseberry-like, the ears drooping, and the whole aspect that of a man who has passed through the furnace and been caught in the machinery. I hitched myself up a bit higher on the pillows and gazed at him narrowly. It was a moment, I could see, when first aid was required, and I prepared to get down to cases.

'Well, Gussie.'

'Hullo, Bertie.'

'What ho.'

'What ho.'

These civilities concluded, I felt that the moment had come to touch delicately on the past.

'I hear you've been through it a bit.'

'Thanks to Jeeves.'

'It wasn't Jeeves's fault.'

'Entirely Jeeves's fault.'

'I don't see that. I forgot my money and latchkey – '

'And now you'd better forget Jeeves. For you will be interested to hear, Gussie,' I said, deeming it best to put him in touch with the position of affairs right away, 'that he is no longer handling your little problem.'

This seemed to slip it across him properly. The jaws fell, the ears drooped more limply. He had been looking like a dead fish. He now looked like a deader fish, one of the last year's, cast up on some lonely beach and left there at the mercy of the wind and tides.

'What!'

'Yes.'

'You don't mean that Jeeves isn't going to – '

'No.'

'But, dash it – '

I was kind, but firm.

'You will be much better off without him. Surely your terrible experiences of that awful night have told you that Jeeves needs a rest. The keenest of thinkers strikes a bad patch occasionally. That is what has happened to Jeeves. I have seen it coming on for some time. He has lost his form. He wants his plugs decarbonized. No doubt this is a shock to you. I suppose you came here this morning to seek his advice?'

'Of course I did.'

'On what point?'

'Madeline Bassett has gone to stay with these people in the country, and I want to know what he thinks I ought to do.'

'Well, as I say, Jeeves is off the case.'

'But, Bertie, dash it – '

'Jeeves,' I said with a certain asperity, 'is no longer on the case. I am now in sole charge.'

'But what on earth can you do?'

I curbed my resentment. We Woosters are fair-minded. We can make allowances for men who have been parading London all night in scarlet tights.

'That,' I said quietly, 'we shall see. Sit down and let us confer. I am bound to say the thing seems quite simple to me. You say this girl has gone to visit friends in the country. It would appear obvious that you must get there too, and flock round her like a poultice. Elementary.'

'But I can't plant myself on a lot of perfect strangers.'

'Don't you know these people?'

'Of course I don't. I don't know anybody.'

I pursed the lips. This did seem to complicate matters somewhat.

'All that I know is that their name is Travers, and it's a place called Brinkley Court down in Worcestershire.'

I unpursed my lips.

'Gussie,' I said, smiling paternally, 'it was a lucky day for you when Bertram Wooster interested himself in your affairs. As I foresaw from the start, I can fix everything. This afternoon you shall go to Brinkley Court, an honoured guest.'

He quivered like a mousse. I suppose it must always be rather a thrilling experience for the novice to watch me taking hold.

'But, Bertie, you don't mean you know these Traverses?'

'They are my Aunt Dahlia.'

'My gosh!'

'You see now,' I pointed out, 'how lucky you were to get me behind you. You go to Jeeves, and what does he do? He dresses you up in scarlet tights and one of the foulest false beards of my experience, and sends you off to fancy-dress balls. Result, agony of spirit and no progress. I then take over and put you on the right lines. Could Jeeves have got you into Brinkley Court? Not a chance. Aunt Dahlia isn't his aunt. I merely mention these things.'

'By Jove, Bertie, I don't know how to thank you.'

'My dear chap!'

'But, I say.'

'Now what?'

'What do I do when I get there?'

'If you knew Brinkley Court, you would not ask that question. In those romantic surroundings you can't miss. Great lovers through the ages have fixed up the preliminary formalities at Brinkley. The place is simply ill with atmosphere. You will stroll with the girl in the shady walks. You will sit with her in the shady lawns. You will row on the lake with her. And gradually you will find yourself working up to a point where – '

'By Jove, I believe you're right.'

'Of course, I'm right. I've got engaged three times at Brinkley. No business resulted, but the fact remains. And I went there without the foggiest idea of indulging in the tender pash. I hadn't the slightest intention of proposing to anybody. Yet no sooner had I entered those romantic grounds than I found myself reaching out for the nearest girl in sight and slapping my soul down in front of her. It's something in the air.'

'I see exactly what you mean. That's just what I want to be able to do – work up to it. And in London – curse the place – everything's in such a rush that you don't get a chance.'

'Quite. You see a girl alone for about five minutes a day, and if you want to ask her to be your wife, you've got to charge into it as if you were trying to grab the gold ring on a merry-go-round.'

'That's right. London rattles one. I shall be a different man altogether in the country. What a bit of luck this Travers woman turning out to be your aunt.'

'I don't know what you mean, turning out to be my aunt. She has been my aunt all along.'

'I mean, how extraordinary that it should be your aunt that Madeline's going to stay with.'

'Not at all. She and my Cousin Angela are close friends. At Cannes she was with us all the time.'

'Oh, you met Madeline at Cannes, did you? By Jove, Bertie,' said the poor lizard devoutly, 'I wish I could have seen her at Cannes. How wonderful she must have looked in beach pyjamas! Oh, Bertie – '

'Quite,' I said, a little distantly. Even when restored by one of Jeeves's depth bombs, one doesn't want this sort of thing after a hard night. I touched the bell and, when Jeeves appeared, requested him to bring me telegraph form and pencil. I then wrote a well-worded communication to Aunt Dahlia, informing her that I was sending my friend, Augustus Fink-Nottle, down to Brinkley today to enjoy her hospitality, and handed it to Gussie.

'Push that in at the first post office you pass,' I said. 'She will find it waiting for her on her return.'

Gussie popped along, flapping the telegram and looking like a close-up of Joan Crawford, and I turned to Jeeves and gave him a precis of my operations.

'Simple, you observe, Jeeves. Nothing elaborate.'

'No, sir.'

'Nothing far-fetched. Nothing strained or bizarre. Just Nature's remedy.'

'Yes, sir.'

'This is the attack as it should have been delivered. What do you call it when two people of opposite sexes are bunged together in close association in a secluded spot, meeting each other every day and seeing a lot of each other?'

'Is "propinquity" the word you wish, sir?'

'It is. I stake everything on propinquity, Jeeves. Propinquity, in my opinion is what will do the trick. At the moment, as you are aware, Gussie is a mere jelly when in the presence. But ask yourself how he will feel in a week or so, after he and she have been helping themselves to sausages out of the same dish day after day at the breakfast sideboard. Cutting the same ham, ladling out communal kidneys and bacon – why – '

I broke off abruptly. I had had one of my ideas.

'Golly, Jeeves!'

'Sir?'

'Here's an instance of how you have to think of everything. You heard me mention sausages, kidneys and bacon and ham.'

'Yes, sir.'

'Well, there must be nothing of that. Fatal. The wrong note entirely. Give me that telegraph form and pencil. I must warn Gussie without delay. What he's got to do is to create in this girl's mind the impression that he is pining away for love of her. This cannot be done by wolfing sausages.'

'No, sir.'

'Very well, then.'

And, taking form and p., I drafted the following:

Fink-Nottle
Brinkley Court
Market Snodsbury
Worcestershire
Lay off the sausages. Avoid the ham. Bertie.

'Send that off, Jeeves, instanter.'

'Very good, sir.'

I sank back on the pillows.

'Well, Jeeves,' I said, 'you see how I am taking hold. You notice the grip I am getting on this case. No doubt you realize now that it would pay you to study my methods.'

'No doubt, sir.'

'And even now you aren't on to the full depths of the extraordinary sagacity I've shown. Do you know what brought Aunt Dahlia up here this morning? She came to tell me I'd got to distribute the prizes at some beastly seminary she's a governor of down at Market Snodsbury.'

'Indeed, sir? I fear you will scarcely find that a congenial task.'

'Ah, but I'm not going to do it. I'm going to shove it off on to Gussie.'

'Sir?'

'I propose, Jeeves, to wire to Aunt Dahlia saying that I can't get down, and suggesting that she unleashes him on these young Borstal inmates of hers in my stead.'

'But if Mr Fink-Nottle should decline, sir?'

'Decline? Can you see him declining? Just conjure up the picture in your mind, Jeeves. Scene, the drawing room at Brinkley; Gussie wedged into a corner, with Aunt Dahlia standing over him making hunting noises. I put it to you, Jeeves, can you see him declining?'

'Not readily, sir, I agree. Mrs Travers is a forceful personality.'

'He won't have a hope of declining. His only way out would be to slide off. And he can't slide off, because he wants to be with Miss Bassett. No, Gussie will have to toe the line, and I shall be saved from a job at which I confess the soul shuddered. Getting up on a platform and delivering a short, manly speech to a lot of foul schoolkids! Golly, Jeeves. I've been through that sort of thing once, what? You remember that time at the girls' school?'

'Very vividly, sir.'

'What an ass I made of myself!'

'Certainly I have seen you to better advantage, sir.'

'I think you might bring me just one more of those dynamite specials of yours, Jeeves. This narrow squeak has made me come over all faint.'

I suppose it must have taken Aunt Dahlia three hours or so to get back to Brinkley, because it wasn't till well after lunch that her telegram arrived. It read like a telegram that had been dispatched in white-hot surge of emotion some two minutes after she had read mine.

As follows:

Am taking legal advice to ascertain whether strangling an idiot nephew counts as murder. If it doesn't, look out for yourself. Consider your conduct frozen limit. What do you mean by planting your loathsome friends on me like this? Do you think Brinkley Court is a leper colony or what is it? Who is this Spink-Bottle? Love. Travers.

I had expected some such initial reaction. I replied in temperate vein:

Not Bottle. Nottle. Regards. Bertie.

Almost immediately after she had despatched the above heart cry, Gussie must have arrived, for it wasn't twenty minutes later when I received the following:

Cipher telegram signed by you has reached me here. Runs 'Lay off the sausages. Avoid the ham.' Wire key immediately. Fink-Nottle.

I replied:

Also kidneys. Cheerio. Bertie.

I had staked all on Gussie making a favourable impression on his hostess, basing my confidence on the fact that he was one of those timid, obsequious, teacup-passing, thin-bread-and-butter-offering yes-men whom women of my Aunt Dahlia's type nearly always like at first sight. That I had not overrated my acumen was proved by her next in order, which, I was pleased to note, assayed a markedly larger percentage of the milk of human kindness.

As follows:

Well, this friend of yours has got here, and I must say that for a friend of yours he seems less sub-human than I had expected. A bit of a pop-eyed bleater, but on the whole clean and civil, and certainly most informative about newts. Am considering arranging series of lectures for him in neighbourhood. All the same I like your nerve using my house as a summer-hotel resort and shall have much to say to you on subject when you come down. Expect you thirtieth. Bring spats. Love. Travers.

To this I riposted:

On consulting engagement book find impossible come Brinkley Court. Deeply regret. Toodle-oo. Bertie.

Hers in reply struck a sinister note:

Oh, so it's like that, is it? You and your engagement book, indeed. Deeply regret my foot. Let me tell you, my lad, that you will regret it a jolly sight more deeply if you don't come down. If you imagine for one moment that you are going to get out of distributing those prizes, you are very much mistaken. Deeply regret Brinkley Court hundred miles from London, as unable hit you with a brick. Love Travers.

I then put my fortune to the test, to win or lose it all. It was not a moment for petty economies. I let myself go regardless of expense:

No, but dash it, listen. Honestly, you don't want me. Get Fink-Nottle distribute prizes. A born distributor, who will do you credit. Confidently anticipate Augustus Fink-Nottle as Master of Revels on thirty-first inst. would make genuine sensation. Do not miss this great chance, which may never occur again. Tinkerty-tonk. Bertie.

There was an hour of breathless suspense, and then the joyful tidings arrived:

Well, all right. Something in what you say, I suppose. Consider you treacherous worm and contemptible, spineless cowardly custard, but have booked Spink-

Bottle. Stay where you are, then, and I hope you get run over by an omnibus. Love. Travers.

The relief, as you may well imagine, was stupendous. A great weight seemed to have rolled off my mind. It was as if somebody had been pouring Jeeves's pick-me-ups into me through a funnel. I sang as I dressed for dinner that night. At the Drones I was so gay and cheery that there were several complaints. And when I got home and turned into the old bed, I fell asleep like a little child within five minutes of inserting the person between the sheets. It seemed to me that the whole distressing affair might now be considered definitely closed.

Conceive my astonishment, therefore, when waking on the morrow and sitting up to dig into the morning tea cup, I beheld on the tray another telegram.

My heart sank. Could Aunt Dahlia have slept on it and changed her mind? Could Gussie, unable to face the ordeal confronting him, have legged it during the night down a water-pipe? With these speculations racing through the bean, I tore open the envelope and as I noted contents I uttered a startled yip.

'Sir?' said Jeeves, pausing at the door.

I read the thing again. Yes, I had got the gist all right. No, I had not been deceived in the substance.

'Jeeves,' I said, 'do you know what?'

'No, sir.'

'You know my cousin Angela?'

'Yes, sir.'

'You know young Tuppy Glossop?'

'Yes, sir.'

'They've broken off their engagement.'

'I am sorry to hear that, sir.'

'I have here a communication from Aunt Dahlia,

specifically stating this. I wonder what the row was about.'

'I could not say, sir.'

'Of course you couldn't. Don't be an ass, Jeeves.'

'No, sir.'

I brooded. I was deeply moved.

'Well, this means that we shall have to go down to Brinkley today. Aunt Dahlia is obviously all of a twitter, and my place is by her side. You had better pack this morning, and catch that 12.45 train with the luggage. I have a lunch engagement, so will follow in the car.'

'Very good, sir.'

I brooded some more.

'I must say this has come as a great shock to me, Jeeves.'

'No doubt, sir.'

'A very great shock. Angela and Tuppy . . . Tut, tut! Why, they seemed like the paper on the wall. Life is full of sadness, Jeeves.'

'Yes, sir.'

'Still, there it is.'

'Undoubtedly, sir.'

'Right ho, then. Switch on the bath.'

'Very good, sir.'

7

I meditated pretty freely as I drove down to Brinkley in the old two-seater that afternoon. The news of this rift or rupture of Angela's and Tuppy's had disturbed me greatly.

The projected match, you see, was one on which I had always looked with kindly approval. Too often, when a chap of your acquaintance is planning to marry a girl you know, you find yourself knitting the brow a bit and chewing the lower lip dubiously, feeling that he or she, or both, should be warned while there is yet time.

But I have never felt anything of this nature about Tuppy and Angela. Tuppy, when not making an ass of himself, is a soundish sort of egg. So is Angela a soundish sort of egg. And, as far as being in love was concerned, it had always seemed to me that you wouldn't have been far out in describing them as two hearts that beat as one.

True, they had had their little tiffs, notably on the occasion when Tuppy – with what he said was fearless honesty and I considered thorough goofiness – had told Angela that her new hat made her look like a Pekingese. But in every romance you have to budget for the occasional dust-up, and after that incident I had supposed that he had learned his lesson and that from then on life would be one grand, sweet song.

And now this wholly unforeseen severing of diplomatic relations had popped up through a trap.

I gave the thing the cream of the Wooster brain all the way down, but it continued to beat me what could have caused the outbreak of hostilities, and I bunged my foot sedulously on the accelerator in order to get to Aunt Dahlia with the greatest possible speed and learn the inside history straight from the horse's mouth. And what with all six cylinders hitting nicely, I made good time and found myself closeted with the relative shortly before the hour of the evening cocktail.

She seemed glad to see me. In fact, she actually said she was glad to see me – a statement no other aunt on the list would have committed herself to, the customary reaction of these near and dear ones to the spectacle of Bertram arriving for a visit being a sort of sick horror.

'Decent of you to rally round, Bertie,' she said.

'My place was by your side, Aunt Dahlia,' I responded.

I could see at a g. that the unfortunate affair had got in amongst her in no uncertain manner. Her usually cheerful map was clouded, and the genial smile conspic. by its a. I pressed her hand sympathetically, to indicate that my heart bled for her.

'Bad show this, my dear old flesh and blood,' I said. 'I'm afraid you've been having a sticky time. You must be worried.'

She snorted emotionally. She looked like an aunt who has just bitten into a bad oyster.

'Worried is right. I haven't had a peaceful moment since I got back from Cannes. Ever since I put my foot across this blasted threshold,' said Aunt Dahlia, returning for the nonce to the hearty *argot* of the hunting field, 'everything's been at sixes and sevens. First there was that mix up about the prize giving.'

She paused at this point and gave me a look. 'I had been meaning to speak freely to you about your behaviour in that matter, Bertie,' she said. 'I had some good things all stored up. But, as you've rallied round like this, I suppose I shall have to let you off. And, anyway, it is probably all for the best that you evaded your obligations in that sickeningly craven way. I have an idea that this Spink-Bottle of yours is going to be good. If only he can keep off newts.'

'Has he been talking about newts?'

'He has. Fixing me with a glittering eye, like the Ancient Mariner. But if that was the worst I had to bear, I wouldn't mind. What I'm worrying about is what Tom says when he starts talking.'

'Uncle Tom?'

'I wish there was something else you could call him except "Uncle Tom",' said Aunt Dahlia a little testily. 'Every time you do it, I expect to see him turn black and start playing the banjo. Yes, Uncle Tom, if you must have it. I shall have to tell him soon about losing all that money at baccarat, and, when I do, he will go up like a rocket.'

'Still, no doubt Time, the great healer – '

'Time, the great healer, be blowed. I've got to get a cheque for five hundred pounds out of him for *Milady's Boudoir* by August the third at the latest.'

I was concerned. Apart from a nephew's natural interest in an aunt's refined weekly paper, I had always had a soft spot in my heart for *Milady's Boudoir* ever since I contributed that article to it on What the Well-Dressed Man is Wearing. Sentimental, possibly, but we old journalists do have these feelings.

'Is the *Boudoir* on the rocks?'

'It will be if Tom doesn't cough up. It needs help till it has turned the corner.'

'But wasn't it turning the corner two years ago?'

'It was. And it's still at it. Till you've run a weekly paper for women, you don't know what corners are.'

'And you think the chances of getting into Uncle – into my uncle my marriage's ribs are slight?'

'I'll tell you, Bertie. Up till now, when these subsidies were required, I have always been able to come to Tom in the gay, confident spirit of an only child touching an indulgent father for chocolate cream. But he's just had a demand from the income-tax people for an additional fifty-eight pounds, one and threepence, and all he's been talking about since I got back has been ruin and the sinister trend of socialistic legislation and what will become of us all.'

I could readily believe it. This Tom has a peculiarity I've noticed in other very oofy men. Nick him for the paltriest sum, and he lets out a squawk you can hear at Land's End. He has the stuff in gobs, but he hates giving up.

'If it wasn't for Anatole's cooking, I doubt if he would bother to carry on. Thank God for Anatole, I say.'

I bowed my head reverently.

'Good old Anatole,' I said.

'Amen,' said Aunt Dahlia.

Then the look of holy ecstasy, which is always the result of letting the mind dwell, however briefly, on Anatole's cooking, died out of her face.

'But don't let me wander from the subject,' she resumed. 'I was telling you of the way hell's foundations have been quivering since I got home. First the prize giving, then Tom, and now, on top of everything else, this infernal quarrel between Angela and young Glossop.'

I nodded gravely. 'I was frightfully sorry to hear of that. Terrible shock. What was the row about?'

'Sharks.'

'Eh?'

'Sharks. Or, rather, one individual shark. The brute

that went for the poor child when she was aquaplaning at Cannes. You remember Angela's shark?'

Certainly I remembered Angela's shark. A man of sensibility does not forget about a cousin nearly being chewed by monsters of the deep. The episode was still green in my memory.

In a nutshell, what had occurred was this: You know how you aquaplane. A motorboat nips on ahead, trailing a rope. You stand on a board, holding the rope, and the boat tows you along. And every now and then you lose your grip on the rope and plunge into the sea and have to swim to your board again.

A silly process it has always seemed to me, though many find it diverting.

Well, on the occasion referred to, Angela had just regained her board after taking a toss, when a great beastly shark came along and cannoned into it, flinging her into the salty once more. It took her quite a bit of time to get on again and make the motorboat chap realize what was up and haul her to safety, and during that interval you can readily picture her embarrassment.

According to Angela, the finny denizen kept snapping at her ankles virtually without cessation, so that by the time help arrived, she was feeling more like a salted almond at a public dinner than anything human. Very shaken the poor child had been, I recall, and had talked of nothing else for weeks.

'I remember the whole incident vividly,' I said. 'But how did that start the trouble?'

'She was telling him the story last night.'

'Well?'

'Her eyes shining and her little hands clasped in girlish excitement.'

'No doubt.'

'And instead of giving her the understanding and sympathy to which she was entitled, what do you think this blasted Glossop did? He sat listening like a lump of dough, as if she had been talking about the weather, and when she had finished, he took his cigarette holder out of his mouth and said, "I expect it was only a floating log"!'

'He didn't!'

'He did. And when Angela described how the thing had jumped and snapped at her, he took his cigarette holder out of his mouth again, and said, "Ah! Probably a flatfish. Quite harmless. No doubt it was just trying to play." Well, I mean! What would you have done if you had been Angela? She has pride, sensibility, all the natural feelings of a good woman. She told him he was an ass and a fool and an idiot, and didn't know what he was talking about.'

I must say I saw the girl's viewpoint. It's only about once in a lifetime that anything sensational ever happens to one, and when it does, you don't want people taking all the colour out of it. I remember at school having to read that stuff where that chap, Othello, tells the girl what a hell of a time he'd been having among the cannibals and what not. Well, imagine his feelings if, after he had described some particularly sticky passage with a cannibal chief and was waiting for the awestruck 'Oh-h! Not really?', she had said that the whole thing had no doubt been greatly exaggerated and that the man had probably really been a prominent local vegetarian.

Yes, I saw Angela's point of view.

'But don't tell me that when he saw how shirty she was about it, the chump didn't back down?'

'He didn't. He argued. And one thing led to another until, by easy stages, they had arrived at the point where she was saying that she didn't know if he was aware of it, but if he didn't knock off starchy foods and do exercises every morning, he would be getting as fat as a pig, and he was talking about this modern habit of girls putting make-up on their faces, of which he had always disapproved. This continued for a while, and then there was a loud pop and the air was full of mangled fragments of their engagement. I'm distracted about it. Thank goodness you've come, Bertie.'

'Nothing could have kept me away,' I replied, touched. 'I felt you needed me.'

'Yes.'

'Quite.'

'Or, rather,' she said, 'not you, of course, but Jeeves. The minute all this happened, I thought of him. The situation obviously cries out for Jeeves. If ever in the whole history of human affairs there was a moment when that lofty brain was required about the home, this is it.'

I think, if I had been standing up, I would have staggered. In fact, I'm pretty sure I would. But it isn't so dashed easy to stagger when you're sitting in an armchair. Only my face, therefore, showed how deeply I had been stung by these words.

Until she spoke them, I had been all sweetness and light – the sympathetic nephew prepared to strain every nerve to do his bit. I now froze, and the face became hard and set.

'Jeeves!' I said, between clenched teeth.

'Oom beroofen,' said Aunt Dahlia.

I saw that she had got the wrong angle.

'I was not sneezing. I was saying "Jeeves!" '

'And well you may. What a man! I'm going to put the whole thing up to him. There's nobody like Jeeves.'

My frigidity became more marked.

'I venture to take issue with you, Aunt Dahlia.'

'You take what?'

'Issue.'

'You do, do you?'

'I emphatically do. Jeeves is hopeless.'

'What?'

'Quite hopeless. He has lost his grip completely. Only a couple of days ago I was compelled to take him off a case because his handling of it was so footling. And, anyway, I resent this assumption, if assumption is the word I want, that Jeeves is the only fellow with brain. I object to the way everybody puts things up to him without consulting me and letting me have a stab at them first.'

She seemed about to speak, but I checked her with a gesture.

'It is true that in the past I have sometimes seen fit to seek Jeeves's advice. It is possible that in the future I may seek it again. But I claim the right to have a pop at these problems, as they arise, in person, without having everybody behave as if Jeeves was the only onion in the hash. I sometimes feel that Jeeves, though admittedly not unsuccessful in the past, has been lucky rather than gifted.'

'Have you and Jeeves had a row?'

'Nothing of the kind.'

'You seem to have it in for him.'

'Not at all.'

And yet I must admit that there was a modicum of truth in what she said. I had been feeling pretty austere about the man all day, and I'll tell you why.

You remember that he caught that 12.45 train with the luggage, while I remained on in order to keep a luncheon engagement. Well, just before I started out to the tryst, I was pottering about the flat, and suddenly – I don't know what put the suspicion into my head, possibly the fellow's manner had been furtive – something seemed to whisper to me to go and have a look in the wardrobe.

And it was as I had suspected. There was the mess jacket still on its hanger. The hound hadn't packed it.

Well, as anybody at the Drones will tell you, Bertram Wooster is a pretty hard chap to outgeneral. I shoved the thing in a brown-paper parcel and put it in the back of the car, and it was on a chair in the hall now. But that didn't alter the fact that Jeeves had attempted to do the dirty on me, and I suppose a certain what-d'you-call-it had crept into my manner during the above remarks.

'There has been no breach,' I said. 'You might describe it as a passing coolness, but no more. We did not happen to see eye to eye with regard to my white mess jacket with the brass buttons and I was compelled to assert my personality. But – '

'Well, it doesn't matter, anyway. The thing that matters is that you are talking piffle, you poor fish. Jeeves lost his grip? Absurd. Why, I saw him for a moment when he arrived, and his eyes were absolutely glittering with intelligence. I said to myself "Trust Jeeves", and I intend to.'

'You would be far better advised to let me see what I can accomplish, Aunt Dahlia.'

'For heaven's sake, don't you start butting in. You'll only make matters worse.'

'On the contrary, it may interest you to know that while driving here I concentrated deeply on this trouble of Angela's and was successful in formulating a plan, based on the psychology of the individual, which I am proposing to put into effect at an early moment.'

'Oh, my God!'

'My knowledge of human nature tells me it will work.'

'Bertie,' said Aunt Dahlia, and her manner struck me as febrile, 'lay off, lay off! For pity's sake, lay off. I know these plans of yours. I suppose you want to shove Angela into the lake and push young Glossop in after her to save her life, or something like that.'

'Nothing of the kind.'

'It's the sort of thing you would do.'

'My scheme is far more subtle. Let me outline it for you.'

'No, thanks.'

'I say to myself – '

'But not to me.'

'Do listen for a second.'

'I won't.'

'Right ho, then. I am dumb.'

'And have been from a child.'

I perceived that little good could result from continuing the discussion. I waved a hand and shrugged a shoulder.

'Very well, Aunt Dahlia,' I said, with dignity, 'if you don't want to be in on the ground floor, that is your affair. But you are missing an intellectual treat. And, anyway, no matter how much you may behave like the deaf adder of Scripture which, as you are doubtless aware, the more one piped, the less it danced, or words to that effect, I shall carry on as planned. I am extremely fond of Angela, and I shall spare no effort to bring the sunshine back into her heart.'

'Bertie, you abysmal chump, I appeal to you once more. Will you please lay off? You'll only make things ten times as bad as they are already.'

I remember reading in one of those historical novels once about a chap – a buck he would have been, no doubt, or a macaroni or some such bird as that – who, when people said the wrong thing, merely laughed down from lazy eyelids and flicked a speck of dust from the irreproachable Mechlin lace at his wrists. This was practically what I did now. At least, I straightened my tie and smiled one of those inscrutable smiles of mine. I then withdrew and went out for a saunter in the garden.

And the first chap I ran into was young Tuppy. His brow was furrowed, and he was moodily bunging stones at a flowerpot.

8

I think I have told you before about young Tuppy Glossop. He was a fellow, if you remember, who, callously ignoring the fact that we had been friends since boyhood, betted me one night at the Drones that I could swing myself across the swimming bath by the rings – a childish feat for one of my lissomness – and then, having seen me well on the way, looped back the last ring, thus rendering it necessary for me to drop into the deep end in formal evening costume.

To say that I had not resented this foul deed, which seemed to me deserving of the title of the crime of the century, would be paltering with the truth. I had resented it profoundly, chafing not a little at the time and continuing to chafe for some weeks.

But you know how it is with these things. The wound heals. The agony abates.

I am not saying, mind you, that had the opportunity presented itself of dropping a wet sponge on Tuppy from some high spot or of putting an eel in his bed or finding some other form of self-expression of a like nature, I would not have embraced it eagerly; but that let me out. I mean to say, grievously injured though I had been, it gave me no pleasure to feel that the fellow's bally life was being ruined by the loss of a girl whom, despite all that had passed, I was convinced he still loved like the dickens.

On the contrary, I was heart and soul in favour of healing the breach and rendering everything hotsy-totsy once more between these two young sundered blighters. You will have gleaned that from my remarks to Aunt Dahlia, and if you had been present at this moment and had seen the kindly commiserating look I gave Tuppy, you would have gleaned it still more.

It was one of those searching, melting looks, and was accompanied by the hearty clasp of the right hand and the gentle laying of the left on the collarbone.

'Well, Tuppy, old man,' I said. 'How are you, old man?'

My commiseration deepened as I spoke the words, for there had been no lighting up of the eye, no answering pressure of the palm, no sign whatever, in short, of any disposition on his part to do spring dances at the sight of an old friend. The man seemed sandbagged. Melancholy, as I remember Jeeves saying once about Pongo Twistleton when he was trying to knock off smoking, had marked him for her own. Not that I was surprised, of course. In the circs., no doubt, a certain moodiness was only natural.

I released the hand, ceased to knead the shoulder, and, producing the old case, offered him a cigarette.

He took it dully.

'Are you here, Bertie?' he asked.

'Yes, I'm here.'

'Just passing through, or come to stay?'

I thought for a moment. I might have told him that I had arrived at Brinkley Court with the express intention of bringing Angela and himself together once more, of knitting up the severed threads, and so on and so forth; and for perhaps half the time required for the lighting of a gasper I had almost decided to do so. Then, I reflected, better, on the whole, perhaps not. To broadcast the fact that I proposed to take him and Angela and play on them as on a couple of stringed instruments might have been injudicious. Chaps don't always like being played on as on a stringed instrument.

'It all depends,' I said. 'I may remain. I may push on. My plans are uncertain.'

He nodded listlessly, rather in the manner of a man who did not give a damn what I did, and stood gazing out over the sunlit garden. In build and appearance, Tuppy somewhat resembles a bulldog, and his aspect now was that of one of these fine animals who has just been refused a slice of cake. It was not difficult for a man of my discernment to read what was in his mind, and it occasioned me no surprise, therefore, when his next words had to do with the subject marked with a cross on the agenda paper.

'You've heard of this business of mine, I suppose? Me and Angela?'

'I have, indeed, Tuppy, old man.'

'We've bust up.'

'I know. Some little friction, I gather, *in re* Angela's shark.'

'Yes. I said it must have been a flatfish.'

'So my informant told me.'

'Who did you hear it from?'

'Aunt Dahlia.'

'I suppose she cursed me properly?'

'Oh, no. Beyond referring to you in one passage as "this blasted Glossop", she was, I thought, singularly temperate in her language for a woman who at one time hunted regularly with the Quorn. All the same, I could see, if you don't mind me saying so, old man, that she felt you might have behaved with a little more tact.'

'Tact!'

'And I must admit I rather agreed with her. Was it nice, Tuppy, was it quite kind to take the bloom off Angela's shark like that? You must remember that

Angela's shark is very dear to her. Could you not see what a sock on the jaw it would be for the poor child to hear it described by the man to whom she had given her heart as a flatfish?'

I saw that he was struggling with some powerful emotion.

'And what about my side of the thing?' he demanded, in a voice choked with feeling.

'Your side?'

'You don't suppose,' said Tuppy, with rising vehemence, 'that I would have exposed this dashed synthetic shark for the flatfish it undoubtedly was if there had not been causes that led up to it. What induced me to speak as I did was the fact that Angela, the little squirt, had just been most offensive, and I seized the opportunity to get a bit of my own back.'

'Offensive?'

'Exceedingly offensive. Purely on the strength of my having let fall some casual remark – simply by way of saying something and keeping the conversation going – to the effect that I wondered what Anatole was going to give us for dinner, she said that I was too material and ought not always to be thinking of food. Material, my elbow! As a matter of fact, I'm particularly spiritual.'

'Quite.'

'I don't see any harm in wondering what Anatole was going to give us for dinner. Do you?'

'Of course not. A mere ordinary tribute of respect to a great artist.'

'Exactly.'

'All the same – '

'Well?'

'I was only going to say that it seems a pity that the frail craft of love should come a stinker like this when a few manly words of contrition – '

He stared at me.

'You aren't suggesting that I should climb down?'

'It would be the fine, big thing, old egg.'

'I wouldn't dream of climbing down.'

'But, Tuppy – '

'No. I wouldn't do it.'

'But you love her, don't you?'

This touched the spot. He quivered noticeably, and his mouth twisted. Quite the tortured soul.

'I'm not saying I don't love the little blighter,' he said, obviously moved. 'I love her passionately. But that doesn't alter the fact that I consider that what she needs most in this world is a swift kick in the pants.'

A Wooster could scarcely pass this. 'Tuppy, old man!'

'It's no good saying "Tuppy, old man".'

'Well, I do say "Tuppy, old man". Your tone shocks me. One raises the eyebrows. Where is the fine, old, chivalrous spirit of the Glossops?'

'That's all right about the fine, old, chivalrous spirit of the Glossops. Where is the sweet, gentle, womanly spirit of the Angelas? Telling a fellow he was getting a double chin!'

'Did she do that?'

'She did.'

'Oh, well, girls will be girls. Forget it, Tuppy. Go to her and make it up.'

He shook his head.

'No. It is too late. Remarks have been passed about my tummy which it is impossible to overlook.'

'But, Tummy – Tuppy, I mean – be fair. You once told her her new hat made her look like a Pekingese.'

'It did make her look like a Pekingese. That was not vulgar abuse. It was sound, constructive criticism, with no motive behind it but the kindly desire to keep her from making an exhibition of herself in public. Wantonly to accuse a man of puffing when he goes up a flight of stairs is something very different.'

I began to see that the situation would require all my address and ingenuity. If the wedding bells were ever to ring out in the little church of Market Snodsbury, Bertram had plainly got to put in some shrewdish work. I had gathered, during my conversation with Aunt Dahlia, that there had been a certain amount of frank speech between the two contracting parties, but I had not realized till now that matters had gone so far.

The pathos of the thing gave me the pip. Tuppy had admitted in so many words that love still animated the Glossop bosom, and I was convinced that, even after all that had occurred, Angela had not ceased to love him. At the moment, no doubt, she might be wishing that she could hit him with a bottle, but deep down in her I was prepared to bet that there still lingered all the old affection and tenderness. Only injured pride was keeping these two apart, and I felt that if Tuppy would make the first move, all would be well.

I had another whack at it.

'She's broken-hearted about this rift, Tuppy.'

'How do you know? Have you seen her?'

'No, but I'll bet she is.'

'She doesn't look it.'

'Wearing the mask, no doubt. Jeeves does that when I assert my authority.'

'She wrinkles her nose at me as if I were a drain that had got out of order.'

'Merely the mask. I feel convinced she loves you still, and that a kindly word from you is all that is required.'

I could see that this had moved him. He plainly wavered. He did a sort of twiddly on the turf with his foot. And, when he spoke, one spotted the tremolo in the voice:

'You really think that?'

'Absolutely.'

'H'm.'

'If you were to go to her – '

He shook his head.

'I can't do that. It would be fatal. Bing, instantly, would go my prestige. I know girls. Grovel, and the best of them get uppish.' He mused. 'The only way to work the thing would be by tipping her off in some indirect way that I am prepared to open negotiations. Should I sigh a bit when we meet, do you think?'

'She would think you were puffing.'

'That's true.'

I lit another cigarette and gave my mind to the matter. And first crack out of the box, as is so often the way with the Woosters, I got an idea. I remembered the counsel I had given Gussie in the matter of the sausages and ham.

'I've got it, Tuppy. There is one infallible method of indicating to a girl that you love her, and it works just as well when you've had a row and want to make it up. Don't eat any dinner tonight. You can see how impressive that would be. She knows how devoted you are to food.'

He started violently.

'I am not devoted to food!'

'No, no.'

'I am not devoted to food at all.'

'Quite. All I meant – '

'This rot about me being devoted to food,' said Tuppy warmly, 'has got to stop. I am young and healthy and have a good appetite, but that's not the same as being devoted to food. I admire Anatole as a master of his craft, and am always willing to consider anything he may put before me, but when you say I am devoted to food – '

'Quite, quite. All I meant was that if she sees you

push away your dinner untasted, she will realize that your heart is aching, and will probably be the first to suggest blowing the all clear.'

Tuppy was frowning thoughtfully.

'Push my dinner away, eh?'

'Yes.'

'Push away a dinner cooked by Anatole?'

'Yes.'

'Push it away untasted?'

'Yes.'

'Let us get this straight. Tonight, at dinner, when the butler offers me a *ris de veau à la financière*, or whatever it may be, hot from Anatole's hands, you wish me to push it away untasted?'

'Yes.'

He chewed his lip. One could sense the struggle going on within. And then suddenly a sort of glow came into his face. The old martyrs probably used to look like that.

'All right.'

'You'll do it?'

'I will.'

'Fine.'

'Of course, it will be agony.'

I pointed out the silver lining.

'Only for the moment. You could slip down tonight, after everyone is in bed, and raid the larder.'

He brightened.

'That's right. I could, couldn't I?'

'I expect there would be something cold there.'

'There is something cold there,' said Tuppy, with growing cheerfulness. 'A steak-and-kidney pie. We had it for lunch today. One of Anatole's ripest. The thing I admire about that man,' said Tuppy reverently, 'the thing that I admire so enormously about Anatole is that, though a Frenchman, he does not, like so many of these chefs, confine himself exclusively to French dishes, but is always willing and ready to weigh in with some good old simple English fare such as this steak-and-kidney pie to which I have alluded. A masterly pie, Bertie, and it wasn't more than half finished. It will do me nicely.'

'And at dinner you will push, as arranged?'

'Absolutely as arranged.'

'Fine.'

'It's an excellent idea. One of Jeeves's best. You can tell him from me, when you see him, that I'm much obliged.'

The cigarette fell from my fingers. It was as though somebody had slapped Bertram Wooster across the face with a wet dishrag.

'You aren't suggesting that you think this scheme I have been sketching out is Jeeves's?'

'Of course it is. It's no good trying to kid me, Bertie. You wouldn't have thought of a wheeze like that in a million years.'

There was a pause. I drew myself up to my full height; then, seeing that he wasn't looking at me, lowered myself again.

'Come, Glossop,' I said coldly, 'we had better be going. It is time we were dressing for dinner.'

9

Tuppy's fatheaded words were still rankling in my bosom as I went up to my room. They continued rankling as I shed the form-fitting, and had not ceased to rankle when, clad in the old dressing-gown, I made my way along the corridor to the *salle de bain.*

It is not too much to say that I was piqued to the tonsils.

I mean to say, one does not court praise. The adulation of the multitude means very little to one. But, all the same, when one has taken the trouble to whack out a highly juicy scheme to benefit an in-the-soup friend in his hour of travail, it's pretty foul to find him giving the credit to one's personal attendant, particularly if that personal attendant is a man who goes about the place not packing mess jackets.

But after I had been splashing about in the porcelain for a bit, composure began to return. I have always found that in moments of heart-bowed-downness there is nothing that calms the bruised spirit like a good go at the soap and water. I don't say I actually sing in the tub, but there were times when it was a mere spin of the coin whether I would do so or not.

The spiritual anguish induced by that tactless speech had become noticeably lessened.

The discovery of a toy duck in the soap dish, presumably the property of some former juvenile visitor, contributed not a little to this new and happier frame of mind. What with one thing and another, I hadn't played with toy ducks in my bath for years, and I found the novel experience most invigorating. For the benefit of those interested, I may mention that if you shove the thing under the surface with the sponge and then let it go, it shoots out of the water in a manner calculated to divert the most careworn. Ten minutes of this and I was enabled to return to the bed-chamber much more the old merry Bertram.

Jeeves was there, lying out the dinner disguise. He greeted the young master with his customary suavity.

'Good evening, sir.'

I responded in the same affable key.

'Good evening, Jeeves.'

'I trust you had a pleasant drive, sir.'

'Very pleasant, thank you, Jeeves. Hand me a sock or two, will you?'

He did so, and I commenced to don.

'Well, Jeeves,' I said, reaching for the underlinen, 'here we are again at Brinkley Court in the county of Worcestershire.'

'Yes, sir.'

'A nice mess things seem to have gone and got themselves into in this rustic joint.'

'Yes, sir.'

'The rift between Tuppy Glossop and my cousin Angela would appear to be serious.'

'Yes, sir. Opinion in the servants' hall is inclined to take a grave view of the situation.'

'And the thought that springs to your mind, no doubt, is that I shall have my work cut out to fix things up?'

'Yes, sir.'

'You are wrong, Jeeves. I have the thing well in hand.'

'You surprise me, sir.'

'I thought I should. Yes, Jeeves, I pondered on the matter most of the way down here, and with the happiest results. I have just been in conference with Mr Glossop, and everything is taped out.'

'Indeed, sir? Might I inquire – '

'You know my methods, Jeeves. Apply them. Have you,' I asked, slipping into the shirt and starting to adjust the cravat, 'been gnawing on the thing at all?'

'Oh, yes, sir. I have always been much attached to Miss Angela, and I felt that it would afford me great pleasure were I to be able to be of service to her.'

'A laudable sentiment. But I suppose you drew blank?'

'No, sir. I was rewarded with an idea.'

'What was it?'

'It occurred to me that a reconciliation might be effected between Mr Glossop and Miss Angela by appealing to that instinct which prompts gentlemen in time of peril to hasten to the rescue of – '

I had to let go of the cravat in order to raise a hand. I was shocked.

'Don't tell me you were contemplating descending to that old he-saved-her-from-drowning gag? I am surprised, Jeeves. Surprised and pained. When I was discussing the matter with Aunt Dahlia on my arrival, she said in a sniffy sort of way that she supposed I was going to shove my cousin Angela into the lake and push Tuppy in to haul her out, and I let her see pretty clearly that I considered the suggestion an insult to my intelligence. And now, if your words have the meaning I read into them, you are mooting precisely the same drivelling scheme. Really, Jeeves!'

'No, sir. Not that. But the thought did cross my mind, as I walked in the grounds and passed the building where the fire bell hangs, that a sudden alarm of fire in the night might result in Mr Glossop endeavouring to assist Miss Angela to safety.'

I shivered.

'Rotten, Jeeves.'

'Well, sir – '

'No good. Not a bit like it.'

'I fancy, sir – '

'No, Jeeves. No More. Enough has been said. Let us drop the subj.'

I finished tying the tie in silence. My emotions were too deep for speech. I knew, of course, that this man had for the time being lost his grip, but I had never suspected that he had gone absolutely to pieces like this. Remembering some of the swift ones he had pulled in the past, I shrank with horror from the spectacle of his present ineptitude. Or is it ineptness? I mean this frightful disposition of his to stick straws in his hair and talk like a perfect ass. It was the old, old story, I supposed. A man's brain whizzes along for years exceeding the speed limit, and something suddenly goes wrong with the steering gear and it skids and comes a smeller in the ditch.

'A bit elaborate,' I said, trying to put the thing in as kindly a light as possible. 'Your old failing. You can see that it's a bit elaborate.'

'Possibly the plan I suggested might be considered open to that criticism, sir, but *faute de mieux* – '

'I don't get you, Jeeves.'

'A French expression, sir, signifying "for want of anything better".'

A moment before, I had been feeling for this wreck of a once fine thinker nothing but a gentle pity. These words jarred the Wooster pride, inducing asperity.

'I understand perfectly well what *faute de mieux* means, Jeeves. I did not recently spend two months among our Gallic neighbours for nothing. Besides, I remember that one from school. What caused my bewilderment was that you should be employing the expression, well knowing there is no bally *faute de mieux* about it at all. Where do you get that *faute de mieux* stuff? Didn't I tell you I had everything taped out?'

'Yes, sir, but – '

'What do you mean – but?'

'Well, sir – '

'Push on, Jeeves. I am ready, even anxious, to hear your views.'

'Well, sir, if I may take the liberty of reminding you of it, your plans in the past have not always been uniformly successful.

There was a silence – rather a throbbing one – during which I put on my waistcoat in a marked manner. Not till I had got the buckle at the back satisfactorily adjusted did I speak.

'It is true, Jeeves,' I said formally, 'that once or twice in the past I may have missed the bus. This, however, I attribute purely to bad luck.'

'Indeed, sir?'

'On the present occasion I shall not fail, and I'll tell you why I shall not fail. Because my scheme is rooted in human nature.'

'Indeed, sir?'

'It is simple. Not elaborate. And, furthermore, based on the psychology of the individual.'

'Indeed, sir?'

'Jeeves,' I said, 'don't keep saying "Indeed, sir?" No doubt nothing is further from your mind than to convey such a suggestion, but you have a way of stressing the "in" and then coming down with a thud on the "deed" which makes it virtually tantamount to "Oh, yeah?" Correct this, Jeeves.'

'Very good, sir.'

'I tell you I have everything nicely lined up. Would you care to hear what steps I have taken?'

'Very much, sir.'

'Then listen. Tonight at dinner I have recommended Tuppy to lay off the food.'

'Sir?'

'Tut, Jeeves, surely you can follow the idea, even though it is one that would never have occurred to yourself. Have you forgotten that telegram I sent to Gussie Fink-Nottle, steering him away from the sausages and ham? This is the same thing. Pushing the food away untasted is a universally recognized sign of love. It cannot fail to bring home the gravy. You must see that?'

'Well, sir – '

I frowned.

'I don't want to seem always to be criticizing your methods of voice production, Jeeves,' I said, 'but I must inform you that that "Well, sir" of yours is in many respects fully as unpleasant as your "Indeed, sir?" Like the latter, it seems to be tinged with a definite scepticism. It suggests a lack of faith in my vision. The impression I retain after hearing you shoot it at me a couple of times is that you consider me to be talking through the back of my neck, and that only a feudal sense of what is fitting restrains you from substituting for it the words, "Says you!" '

'Oh, no, sir.'

'Well, that's what it sounds like. Why don't you think this scheme will work?'

'I fear Miss Angela will merely attribute Mr Glossop's abstinence to indigestion, sir.'

I hadn't thought of that, and I must confess it shook me for a moment. Then I recovered myself. I saw what was at the bottom of all this. Mortified by the consciousness of his own ineptness – or ineptitude – the fellow was simply trying to hamper and obstruct. I decided to knock the stuffing out of him without further preamble.

'Oh?' I said. 'You do, do you? Well, be that as it may, it doesn't alter the fact that you've put out the wrong coat. Be so good, Jeeves,' I said, indicating with a gesture the gent's ordinary dinner jacket, or *smoking*, as we call it on the Côte d'Azur, which was suspended from the hanger on the knob of the wardrobe, 'as to shove that bally black thing in the cupboard and bring out my white mess jacket with the brass buttons.'

He looked at me in a meaning manner. And when I say a meaning manner, I mean there was a respectful but at the same time uppish glint in his eye and a sort of muscular spasm flickered across his face which wasn't quite a quiet smile and yet wasn't quite not a quiet smile. Also the soft cough.

'I regret to say, sir, that I inadvertently omitted to pack the garment to which you refer.'

The vision of that parcel in the hall seemed to rise before my eyes, and I exchanged a merry wink with it. I may even have hummed a bar or two. I'm not quite sure.

'I know you did, Jeeves,' I said, laughing down from lazy eyelids and flicking a speck of dust from the irreproachable Mechlin lace at my wrists. 'But I didn't. You will find it on a chair in the hall in a brown-paper parcel.'

The information that his low manœuvres had been rendered null and void and that the thing was on the strength after all, must have been the nastiest of jars, but there was no play of expression on his finely chiselled to indicate it. There very seldom is on Jeeves's f-c. In moments of discomfort, as I had told Tuppy, he wears a mask, preserving throughout the quiet stolidity of a stuffed moose.

'You might just slide down and fetch it, will you?'

'Very good, sir.'

'Right ho, Jeeves.'

And presently I was sauntering towards the drawing room with the good old j. nestling snugly abaft the shoulder blades.

Aunt Dahlia was in the drawing room. She glanced up at my entrance.

'Hullo, eyesore,' she said. 'What do you think you're made up as?'

I did not get the purport.

'The jacket, you mean?' I queried, groping.

'I do. You look like one of the chorus of male guests at Abernethy Towers in Act 2 of a touring musical comedy.'

'You do not admire this jacket?'

'I do not.'

'You did at Cannes.'

'Well, this isn't Cannes.'

'But, dash it – '

'Oh, never mind. Let it go. If you want to give my butler a laugh, what does it matter? What does anything matter now?'

There was a death-where-is-thy-sting-fullness about her manner which I found distasteful. It isn't often that I score off Jeeves in the devastating fashion just described, and when I do I like to see happy, smiling faces about me.

'Tails up, Aunt Dahlia,' I urged buoyantly.

'Tails up be dashed,' was her sombre response. 'I've just been talking to Tom.'

'Telling him?'

'No, listening to him. I haven't had the nerve to tell him yet.'

'Is he still upset about that income-tax money?'

'Upset is right. He says that Civilization is in the melting-pot and that all thinking men can read the writing on the wall.'

'What wall?'

'Old Testament, ass. Belshazzar's feast.'

'Oh, that, yes. I've often wondered how that gag was worked. With mirrors, I expect.'

'I wish I could use mirrors to break it to Tom about this baccarat business.'

I had a word of comfort to offer here. I had been turning the thing over in my mind since our last meeting, and I thought I saw where she had got twisted. Where she made her error, it seemed to me, was in feeling she had got to tell Uncle Tom. To my way of thinking, the matter was one on which it would be better to continue to exercise a quiet reserve.

'I don't see why you need mention that you lost that money at baccarat.'

'What do you suggest, then? Letting *Milady's Boudoir* join Civilization in the melting-pot? Because that is what it will infallibly do unless I get a cheque by next week. The printers have been showing a nasty spirit for months.'

'You don't follow. Listen. It's an understood thing, I take it, that Uncle Tom foots the *Boudoir* bills. If the bally sheet has been turning the corner for two years, he must have got used to forking out by this time. Well, simply ask him for the money to pay the printers.'

'I did. Just before I went to Cannes.'

'Wouldn't he give it to you?'

'Certainly he gave it to me. He brassed up like an officer and a gentleman. That was the money I lost at baccarat.'

'Oh? I didn't know that.'

'There isn't much you do know.'

A nephew's love made me overlook the slur.

'Tut!' I said.

'What did you say?'

'I said "Tut!" '

'Say it once again, and I'll biff you where you stand. I've enough to endure without being tutted at.'

'Quite.'

'Any tutting that's required, I'll attend to myself. And the same applies to clicking the tongue, if you were thinking of doing that.'

'Far from it.'

'Good.'

I stood awhile in thought. I was concerned to the core. My heart, if you remember, had already bled once for Aunt Dahlia this evening. It now bled again. I knew how deeply attached she was to this paper of hers. Seeing it go down the drain would be for her like watching a loved child sink for the third time in some pond or mere.

And there was no question that, unless carefully prepared for the touch, Uncle Tom would see a hundred *Milady's Boudoirs* go phut rather than take the rap.

Then I saw how the thing could be handled. This aunt, I perceived, must fall into line with my other clients. Tuppy Glossop was knocking off dinner to melt Angela. Gussie Fink-Nottle was knocking off dinner to impress the Bassett. Aunt Dahlia must knock off dinner to soften Uncle Tom. For the beauty of this scheme of mine was that there was no limit to the number of entrants. Come one, come all, the more the merrier, and satisfaction guaranteed in every case.

'I've got it,' I said. 'There is only one course to pursue. Eat less meat.'

She looked at me in a pleading sort of way. I wouldn't swear that her eyes were wet with unshed tears, but I rather think they were. Certainly she clasped her hands in piteous appeal.

'Must you drivel, Bertie? Won't you stop it just this once? Just for tonight, to please Aunt Dahlia?'

'I'm not drivelling.'

'I dare say that to a man of your high standards it doesn't come under the head of drivel, but – '

I saw what had happened. I hadn't made myself quite clear.

'It's all right,' I said. 'Have no misgivings This is the real Tabasco. When I said "Eat less meat", what I meant was that you must refuse your oats at dinner tonight. Just sit there, looking blistered, and wave away each course as it comes with a weary gesture of resignation. You see what will happen. Uncle Tom will notice your loss of appetite, and I am prepared to bet that at the conclusion of the meal he will come to you and say "Dahlia, darling" – I take it he calls you "Dahlia" – "Dahlia darling," he will say, "I noticed at dinner tonight that you were a bit off your feed. Is anything the matter, Dahlia, darling?" "Why, yes, Tom, darling," you will reply. "It is kind of you to ask, darling. The fact is, darling. I am terribly worried." "My darling," he will say – '

Aunt Dahlia interrupted at this point to observe that these Traverses seemed to be a pretty soppy couple of blighters, to judge by their dialogue. She also wished to know when I was going to get to the point.

I gave her a look.

' "My darling," he will say tenderly, "is there anything I can do?" To which your reply will be that there jolly well is – viz. reach for his cheque book and start writing.'

I was watching her closely as I spoke, and was pleased to note respect suddenly dawn in her eyes.

'But, Bertie, this is positively bright.'

'I told you Jeeves wasn't the only fellow with brain.'

'I believe it would work.'

'It's bound to work. I've recommended it to Tuppy.'

'Young Glossop?'

'In order to soften Angela.'

'Splendid!'

'And to Gussie Fink-Nottle, who wants to make a hit with the Bassett.'

'Well, well, well! What a busy little brain it is.'

'Always working, Aunt Dahlia, always working.'

'You're not the chump I took you for, Bertie.'

'When did you ever take me for a chump?'

'Oh, some time last summer. I forget what gave me the idea. Yes, Bertie, this scheme is bright. I suppose, as a matter of fact, Jeeves suggested it.'

'Jeeves did not suggest it. I resent these implications. Jeeves had nothing to do with it whatsoever.'

'Well, all right, no need to get excited about it. Yes, I think it will work. Tom's devoted to me.'

'Who wouldn't be?'

'I'll do it.'

And then the rest of the party trickled in, and we toddled down to dinner.

Conditions being as they were at Brinkley Court – I mean to say, the place being loaded down above the plimsoll mark with aching hearts and standing room only as regarded tortured souls – I hadn't expected the evening meal to be particularly effervescent. Nor was it. Silent. Sombre. The whole thing more than a bit like Christmas dinner on Devil's Island.

I was glad when it was over.

What with having, on top of her other troubles, to rein herself back from the trough, Aunt Dahlia was a total loss as far as anything in the shape of brilliant badinage was concerned. The fact that he was fifty quid in the red and expecting Civilization to take a toss at any moment had caused Uncle Tom, who always looked a bit like a pterodactyl with a secret sorrow, to take on a deeper melancholy. The Bassett was a silent bread crumbler. Angela might have been hewn from the living rock. Tuppy had the air of a condemned murderer refusing to make the usual hearty breakfast before tooling off to the execution shed.

And as for Gussie Fink-Nottle, many an experienced undertaker would have been deceived by his appearance and started embalming him on sight.

This was the first glimpse I had had of Gussie since we parted at my flat, and I must say his demeanour disappointed me. I had been expecting something a great deal more sparkling.

At my flat, on the occasion alluded to, he had, if you recall, practically given me a signed guarantee that all he needed to touch him off was a rural setting. Yet in this aspect now I could detect no indication whatsoever that he was about to round into mid-season form. He still looked like a cat in an adage, and it did not take me long to realize that my very first act on escaping this morgue must be to draw him aside to give him a pep talk.

If ever a chap wanted the clarion note, it looked as if it was this Fink-Nottle.

In the general exodus of mourners, however, I lost sight of him, and, owing to the fact that Aunt Dahlia roped me in for a game of backgammon, it was not immediately that I was able to institute a search. But after we had been playing for a while, the butler came in and asked her if she would speak to Anatole, so I managed to get away. And some ten minutes later, having failed to find scent in the house, I started to throw out the drag net through the grounds, and flushed him in the rose garden.

He was smelling a rose at the moment in a limp sort of way, but removed the beak as I approached.

'Well, Gussie,' I said.

I had beamed genially upon him as I spoke, such being my customary policy on meeting an old pal; but instead of beaming back genially, he gave me a most unpleasant look. His attitude perplexed me. It was as if he were not glad to see Bertram. For a moment he stood letting this unpleasant look play upon me, as it were, and then he spoke.

'You and your "Well, Gussie"!'

He said this between clenched teeth, always an unmatey thing to do, and I found myself more fogged than ever.

'How do you mean – me and my "Well, Gussie"?'

'I like your nerve, coming, bounding about the place, saying "Well, Gussie." That's about all the "Well, Gussie" I shall require from you, Wooster. And it's no good looking like that. You know what I mean. That damned prize giving! It was a dastardly act to crawl out as you did and shove it off on to me. I will not mince my words. It was the act of a hound and a stinker.'

Now, though, as I have shown, I had devoted most of the time on the journey down to meditating upon the case of Angela and Tuppy, I had not neglected to give a thought or two to what I was going to say when I encountered Gussie. I had foreseen that there might be some little temporary unpleasantness when we met, and when a difficult interview is in the offing Bertram Wooster likes to have his story ready.

So now I was able to reply with a manly, disarming frankness. The sudden introduction of the topic had given me a bit of a jolt, it is true, for in the stress of recent happenings I had rather let that prize-giving business slide to the back of my mind; but I had speedily recovered and, as I say, was able to reply with a manly d.f.

'But, my dear chap,' I said, 'I took it for granted that you would understand that that was all part of my schemes.'

He said something about my schemes which I did not catch.

'Absolutely. "Crawling out" is entirely the wrong way to put it. You don't suppose I didn't want to distribute those prizes, do you? Left to myself, there is nothing I would find a greater treat. But I saw that the square, generous thing to do was to step aside and let you take it on, so I did so. I felt that your need was greater than mine. You don't mean to say you aren't looking forward to it?'

He uttered a coarse expression which I wouldn't have thought he would have known. It just shows that you can bury yourself in the country and still somehow acquire a vocabulary. No doubt one picks up things from the neighbours – the vicar, the local doctor, the man who brings the milk, and so on.

'But, dash it,' I said, 'can't you see what this is going to do for you? It will send your stock up with a jump. There you will be, up on that platform, a romantic, impressive figure, the star of the whole proceedings, and what-d'you-call-it of all eyes. Madeline Bassett will be all over you. She will see you in a totally new light.'

'She will, will she?'

'Certainly she will. Augustus Fink-Nottle, the newts' friend, she knows. She is acquainted with Augustus Fink-Nottle, the dogs' chiropodist. But Augustus Fink-Nottle, the orator – that'll knock her sideways, or I know nothing of the female heart. Girls go potty over a public man. If ever anyone did anyone else a kindness, it was I when I gave this extraordinarily attractive assignment to you.'

He seemed impressed by my eloquence. Couldn't have helped himself, of course. The fire faded from behind his horn-rimmed spectacles, and in its place appeared the old fish-like goggle.

'M' yes,' he said meditatively. 'Have you ever made a speech, Bertie?'

'Dozens of times. It's pie. Nothing to it. Why, I once addressed a girls' school.'

'You weren't nervous?'

'Not a bit.'

'How did you go?'

'They hung on my lips. I held them in the hollow of my hand.'

'They didn't throw eggs, or anything.'

'Not a thing.'

He expelled a deep breath, and for a space stood staring in silence at a passing slug.

'Well,' he said, at length, 'it may be all right. Possibly I am letting the thing prey on my mind too much. I may be wrong in supposing it the fate that is worse than death. But I'll tell you this much: The prospect of that prize giving on the thirty-first of this month has been turning my existence into a nightmare. I haven't been able to sleep or think or eat . . . By the way, that reminds me. You never explained that cipher telegram about the sausages and ham.'

'It wasn't a cipher telegram. I wanted you to go light on the food, so that she would realize you were in love.'

He laughed hollowly.

'I see. Well, I've been doing that, all right.'

'Yes, I was noticing at dinner. Splendid.

'I don't see what's splendid about it, it's not going to get me anywhere. I shall never be able to ask her to marry me. I couldn't find nerve to do that if I lived on wafer biscuits for the rest of my life.'

'But, dash it, Gussie. In these romantic surroundings. I should have thought the whispering trees alone – '

'I don't care what you would have thought. I can't do it.'

'Oh, come!'

'I can't. She seems so aloof, so remote.

'She doesn't.'

'Yes, she does. Especially when you see her sideways. Have you seen her sideways, Bertie? That cold, pure profile. It just takes all the heart out of one.'

'It doesn't.'

'I tell you it does. I catch sight of it, and the words freeze on my lips.'

He spoke with a sort of dull despair, and so manifest was his lack of ginger and the spirit that wins to success that for an instant, I confess, I felt a bit stymied. It seemed hopeless to go on trying to steam up such a human jellyfish. Then I saw the way. With that extraordinary quickness of mine, I realized exactly what must be done if this Fink-Nottle was to be enabled to push his nose past the judges' box.

'She must be softened up,' I said.

'Be what?'

'Softened up. Sweetened. Worked on. Preliminary spade-work must be put in. Here, Gussie, is the procedure I propose to adopt: I shall now return to the house and lug this Bassett out for a stroll. I shall talk to her of hearts that yearn, intimating that there is one actually on the premises. I shall pitch it strong, sparing no effort. You, meanwhile, will lurk on the outskirts, and in about a quarter of an hour you will come along and carry on from there. By that time, her emotions having been stirred, you ought to be able to do the rest on your head. It will be like leaping on to a moving bus.'

I remember when I was a kid at school having to learn a poem of sorts about a fellow named Pig-something – a sculptor he would have been, no doubt – who made a statue of a girl, and what should happen one morning but that the bally thing suddenly came to life. A pretty nasty shock for the chap, of course, but the point I'm working round to is that there were a couple of lines that went, if I remember correctly:

She starts. She moves. She seems to feel
The stir of life along her keel.

And what I'm driving at is that you couldn't get a better description of what happened to Gussie as I spoke these heartening words. His brow cleared, his eyes brightened, he lost that fishy look, and he gazed at the slug, which was still on the long, long trail, with something approaching bonhomie. A marked improvement.

'I see what you mean. You will sort of pave the way, as it were.'

'That's right. Spadework.'

'It's a terrific idea, Bertie. It will make all the difference.'

'Quite. But don't forget that after that it will be up to you. You will have to haul up your slacks and give her the old oil, or my efforts will have been in vain.'

Something of his former Gawd-help-us-ness seemed to return to him. He gasped a bit.

'That's true. What the dickens shall I say?'

I restrained my impatience with an effort. The man had been at school with me.

'Dash it, there are hundreds of things you can say. Talk about the sunset.'

'The sunset?'

'Certainly. Half the married men you meet began by talking about the sunset.'

'But what can I say about the sunset?'

'Well, Jeeves got off a good one the other day. I met him airing the dog in the park one evening, and he said, "Now fades the glimmering landscape on the sight, sir, and all the air a solemn stillness holds." You might use that.'

'What sort of landscape?'

'Glimmering. *G* for "gastritis," *l* for "lizard" – '

'Oh, glimmering? Yes, that's not bad. Glimmering landscape . . . solemn stillness . . . Yes, I call that pretty good.'

'You could then say that you have often thought that the stars are God's daisy chain.'

'But I haven't.'

'I dare say not. But she has. Hand her that one, and I don't see how she can help feeling that you're a twin soul.'

'God's daisy chain?'

'God's daisy chain. And then you go on about how twilight always makes you sad. I know you're going to say it doesn't, but on this occasion it has jolly well got to.'

'Why?'

'That's just what she will ask, and you will then have got her going. Because you will reply that it is because yours is such a lonely life. It wouldn't be a bad idea to give her a brief description of a typical home evening at your Lincolnshire residence, showing how you pace the meadows with a heavy tread.'

'I generally sit indoors and listen to the wireless.'

'No, you don't. You pace the meadows with a heavy tread, wishing that you had someone to love you. And then you speak of the day when she came into your life.'

'Like a fairy princess.'

'Absolutely,' I said with approval. I hadn't expected such a hot one from such a quarter. 'Like a fairy princess. Nice work, Gussie.'

'And then?'

'Well, after that it's easy. You say you have something you want to say to her, and then you snap into it. I don't see how it can fail. If I were you, I should do it in this rose garden. It is well established that there is no sounder move than to steer the adored object into rose gardens in the gloaming. And you had better have a couple of quick ones first.'

'Quick ones?'

'Snifters.'

'Drinks, do you mean? But I don't drink.'

'What?'

'I've never touched a drop in my life.'

This made me a bit dubious, I must confess. On these occasions it is generally conceded that a moderate skinful is of the essence.

However, if the facts were as he had stated, I supposed there was nothing to be done about it.

'Well, you'll have to make out as best you can on ginger pop.'

'I always drink orange juice.'

'Orange juice, then. Tell me, Gussie, to settle a bet, do you really like that muck?'

'Very much.'

'Then there is no more to be said. Now, let's just have a run through, to see that you've got the layout straight. Start off with the glimmering landscape.'

'Stars God's daisy chain.'

'Twilight makes you feel sad.'

'Because mine lonely life.'

'Describe life.'

'Talk about the day I met her.'

'Add fairy-princess gag. Say there's something you want to say to her. Heave a couple of sighs. Grab her hand. And give her the works. Right.'

And confident that he had grasped the scenario and that everything might now be expected to proceed through the proper channels, I picked up the feet and hastened back to the house.

It was not until I had reached the drawing room and was enabled to take a square look at the Bassett that I found the debonair gaiety with which I had embarked on this affair beginning to wane a trifle. Beholding her at close range like this, I suddenly became cognisant of what I was in for. The thought of strolling with this rummy specimen undeniably gave me a most unpleasant sinking feeling. I could not but remember how often, when in her company at Cannes, I had gazed dumbly at her, wishing that some kindly motorist in a racing car would ease the situation by coming along and ramming her amidships. As I have already made abundantly clear, this girl was not one of my most congenial buddies.

However, a Wooster's word is his bond. Woosters may quail, but they do not edge out. Only the keenest ear could have detected the tremor in the voice as I asked her if she would care to come out for half an hour.

'Lovely evening,' I said.

'Yes, lovely, isn't it?'

'Lovely. Reminds me of Cannes.'

'How lovely the evenings were there!'

'Lovely,' I said.

'Lovely,' said the Bassett.

'Lovely,' I agreed.

That completed the weather and news bulletin for the French Riviera. Another minute, and we were out in the great open spaces, she cooing a bit about the scenery, and self replying, 'Oh, rather, quite,' and wondering how best to approach the matter in hand.

10

How different it all would have been, I could not but reflect, if this girl had been the sort of girl one chirrups cheerily to over the telephone and takes for spins in the old two-seater. In that case, I would simply have said, 'Listen,' and she would have said, 'What?' and I would have said, 'You know Gussie Fink-Nottle,' and she would have said, 'Yes,' and I would have said, 'He loves you,' and she would have said either, 'What, that mutt? Well, thank heaven for one good laugh today,' or else, in more passionate vein, 'Hot dog! Tell me more.'

'I mean to say, in either event the whole thing would have been over and done with in under a minute.

But with the Bassett something less snappy and a good deal more glutinous was obviously indicated. What with all this daylight-saving stuff, we had hit the great open spaces at a moment when twilight had not yet begun to cheese it in favour of the shades of night. There was a fag-end of sunset still functioning. Stars were beginning to peep out, bats were fooling round, the garden was full of the aroma of those niffy white flowers which only start to put in their heavy work at the end of the day – in short, the glimmering landscape was fading on the sight and all the air held a solemn stillness, and it was plain that this was having the worst effect on her. Her eyes were enlarged, and her whole map a good deal too suggestive of the soul's awakening for comfort.

Her aspect was that of a girl who was expecting something fairly fruity from Bertram.

In these circs. conversation inevitably flagged a bit. I am never at my best when the situation seems to call for a certain soupiness, and I've heard other members of the Drones say the same thing about themselves. I remember Pongo Twistleton telling me that he was out in a gondola with a girl by moonlight once, and the only time he spoke was to tell her that old story about the chap who was so good at swimming that they made him a traffic cop in Venice.

Fell rather flat, he assured me, and it wasn't much later when the girl said she thought it was getting a little chilly and how about pushing back to the hotel.

So now, as I say, the talk rather hung fire. It had been all very well for me to promise Gussie that I would cut loose to this girl about aching hearts, but you want a cue for that sort of thing. And when, toddling along, we reached the edge of the lake and she finally spoke, conceive my chagrin when I discovered that what she was talking about was stars.

Not a bit of good to me.

'Oh, look,' she said. She was a confirmed Oh-looker. I had noticed this at Cannes, where she had drawn my attention in this manner on various occasions to such diverse objects as a French actress, a Provençal filling station, the sunset over the Estorels, Michael Arlen, a man selling coloured spectacles, the deep velvet blue of the Mediterranean, and the late mayor of New York in a striped one-piece bathing suit. 'Oh, look at that sweet little star up there all by itself.'

I saw the one she meant, a little chap operating in a detached sort of way above a spinney.

'Yes,' I said.

'I wonder if it feels lonely.'

'Oh, I shouldn't think so.'

'A fairy must have been crying.'

'Eh?'

'Don't you remember?' "Every time a fairy sheds a tear, a wee bit star is born in the Milky Way." Have you ever thought that, Mr Wooster?'

I never had. Most improbable, I considered, and it didn't seem to me to check up with her statement that the stars were God's daisy chain. I mean, you can't have it both ways.

However, I was in no mood to dissect and criticize. I saw that I had been wrong in supposing that the stars were not germane to the issue. Quite a decent cue they had provided, and I leaped on it promptly: 'Talking of shedding tears – '

But she was now on the subject of rabbits, several of which were messing about in the park to our right.

'Oh, look. The little bunnies!'

'Talking of shedding tears – '

Don't you love this time of the evening, Mr Wooster, when the sun has gone to bed and all the bunnies come out to have their little suppers? When I was a child, I used to think that rabbits were gnomes, and that if I held my breath and stayed quite still, I should see the fairy queen.'

Indicating with a reserved gesture that this was just the sort of loony thing I should have expected her to think as a child, I returned to the point.

'Talking of shedding tears,' I said firmly, 'it may interest you to know that there is an aching heart in Brinkley Court.'

This held her. She cheesed the rabbit theme. Her face, which had been aglow with what I supposed was a pretty animation, clouded. She unshipped a sigh that sounded like the wind going out of a rubber duck.

'Ah, yes. Life is very sad, isn't it?'

'It is for some people. This aching heart, for instance.'

'Those wistful eyes of hers! Drenched irises. And they used to dance like elves of delight. And all through a foolish misunderstanding about a shark. What a tragedy misunderstandings are. That pretty romance broken and over just because Mr Glossop would insist that it was a flatfish.'

I saw that she had got the wires crossed.

'I'm not talking about Angela.'

'But her heart is aching.'

'I know it's aching. But so is somebody else's.'

She looked at me, perplexed.

'Somebody else? Mr Glossop's, you mean?'

'No, I don't.'

'Mrs Travers's?'

The exquisite code of politeness of the Woosters prevented me clipping her one on the earhole, but I would have given a shilling to be able to do it. There seemed to me something deliberately fatheaded in the way she persisted in missing the gist.

'No, not Aunt Dahlia's, either.'

'I'm sure she is dreadfully upset.'

'Quite. But this heart I'm talking about isn't aching because of Tuppy's row with Angela. It's aching for a different reason altogether. I mean to say – dash it, you know why hearts ache!'

She seemed to shimmy a bit. Her voice, when she spoke, was whispery: 'You mean – for love?'

'Absolutely. Right on the bull's-eye. For love.'

'Oh, Mr Wooster!'

'I take it you believe in love at first sight?'

'I do, indeed.'

'Well, that's what happened to this aching heart. It fell in love at first sight, and ever since it's been eating itself out, as I believe the expression is.'

There was a silence. She had turned away and was watching a duck out on the lake. It was tucking into weeds, a thing I've never been able to understand anyone wanting to do. Though I suppose, if you face it squarely, they're no worse than spinach. She stood drinking it in for a bit, and then it suddenly stood on its head and disappeared, and this seemed to break the spell.

'Oh, Mr Wooster!' she said again, and from the tone of her voice, I could see that I had got her going.

'For you, I mean to say,' I proceeded, starting to put in the fancy touches. I dare say you have noticed on these occasions that the difficulty is to plant the main idea, to get the general outline of the thing well fixed. The rest is mere detail work. I don't say I became glib at this juncture, but I certainly became a dashed glibber than I had been.

'It's having the dickens of a time. Can't eat, can't sleep – all for love of you. And what makes it all so particularly rotten is that it – this aching heart – can't bring itself up to the scratch and tell you the position of affairs, because your profile has gone and given it cold feet. Just as it is about to speak, it catches sight of you sideways, and words fail it. Silly, of course, but there it is.'

I heard her give a gulp, and I saw that her eyes had become moistish. Drenched irises, if you care to put it that way.

'Lend you a handkerchief?'

'No, thank you. I'm quite all right.'

It was more than I could say for myself. My efforts had left me weak. I don't know if you suffer in the same way, but with me the act of talking anything in the nature of real mashed potatoes always induces a sort of prickly sensation and a hideous feeling of shame, together with a marked starting of the pores.

I remember at my Aunt Agatha's place in Hertfordshire once being put on the spot and forced to enact the rôle of King Edward III saying goodbye to that girl of his, Fair Rosamund, at some sort of pageant in aid of the Distressed Daughters of the Clergy. It involved some rather warmish mediaeval dialogue, I recall, racy of the days when they called a spade a spade, and by the time the whistle blew, I'll bet no Daughter of the Clergy was half as distressed as I was. Not a dry stitch.

My reaction now was very similar. It was a highly liquid Bertram who, hearing his *vis-à-vis* give a couple of hiccups and start to speak, bent an attentive ear.

'Please don't say any more, Mr Wooster.'

Well, I wasn't going to, of course.

'I understand.'

I was glad to hear this.

'Yes, I understand. I won't be so silly as to pretend not to know what you mean. I suspected this at Cannes, when you used to stand and stare at me without speaking a word, but with whole volumes in your eyes.'

If Angela's shark had bitten me in the leg, I couldn't have leaped more convulsively. So tensely had I been concentrating on Gussie's interests that it hadn't so much as crossed my mind that another and an unfortunate construction could be placed on those words of mine. The persp., already bedewing my brow, became a regular Niagara.

My whole fate hung upon a woman's word. I mean to say, I couldn't back out. If a girl thinks a man is proposing to her, and on that understanding books him up, he can't explain to her that she has got hold of entirely the wrong end of the stick and that he hadn't the smallest intention of suggesting anything of the kind. He must simply let it ride. And the thought of being engaged to a girl who talked openly about fairies being born because stars blew their noses, or whatever it was, frankly appalled me.

She was carrying on with her remarks, and as I listened I clenched my fists till I shouldn't wonder if the knuckles didn't stand out white under the strain. It seemed as if she would never get to the nub.

'Yes, all through those days at Cannes I could see what you were trying to say. A girl always knows. And then you followed me down here, and there was that same dumb, yearning look in your eyes when we met this evening. And then you were so insistent that I should come out and walk with you in the twilight. And now you stammer out those halting words. No, this does not come as a surprise. But I am sorry – '

The word was like one of Jeeves's pick-me-ups. Just as if a glassful of meat sauce, red pepper, and the yolk of an egg – though, as I say, I am convinced that these are not the sole ingredients – had been shot into me, I expanded like some lovely flower blossoming in the sunshine. It was all right, after all. My guardian angel had not been asleep at the switch.

' – but I am afraid it is impossible.'

She paused.

'Impossible,' she repeated.

I had been so busy feeling saved from the scaffold that I didn't get on to it for a moment that an early reply was desired.

'Oh, right ho,' I said hastily.

'I'm sorry.'

'Quite all right.'

'Sorrier than I can say.'

'Don't give it another thought.'

'We can still be friends.'

'Oh, rather.'

'Then shall we just say no more about it; keep what has happened as a tender little secret between ourselves?'

'Absolutely.'

'We will. Like something lovely and fragrant laid away in lavender.'

'In lavender – right.'

There was a longish pause. She was gazing at me in a divinely pitying sort of way, much as if I had been a snail she had happened accidentally to bring her short French vamp down on, and I longed to tell her that it was all right, and that Bertram, so far from being the victim of despair, had never felt fizzier in his life. But, of course, one can't do that sort of thing. I simply said nothing, and stood there looking brave.

'I wish I could,' she murmured.

'Could?' I said, for my attensh had been wandering.

'Feel towards you as you would like me to feel.'

'Oh, ah.'

'But I can't. I'm sorry.'

'Absolutely OK. Faults on both sides, no doubt.'

'Because I am fond of you, Mr – no, I think I must call you Bertie. May I?'

'Oh, rather.'

'Because we are real friends.'

'Quite.'

'I do like you, Bertie. And if things were different – I wonder – '

'Eh?'

'After all, we are real friends . . . We have this common memory . . . You have a right to know . . . I don't want you to think – Life is such a muddle, isn't it?'

To many men, no doubt, these broken utterances would have appeared mere drooling and would have been dismissed as such. But the Woosters are quicker-witted than the ordinary and can read between the lines. I suddenly divined what it was that she was trying to get off the chest.

'You mean there's someone else?'

She nodded.

'You're in love with some other bloke?'

She nodded.

'Engaged, what?'

This time she shook the pumpkin.

'No, not engaged.'

Well, that was something, of course. Nevertheless, from the way she spoke, it certainly looked as if poor old Gussie might as well scratch his name off the entry list, and I didn't at all like the prospect of having to break the bad news to him. I had studied the man closely, and it was my conviction that this would about be his finish.

Gussie, you see, wasn't like some of my pals – the name of Bingo Little is one that springs to the lips – who, if turned down by a girl, would simply say, 'Well, bung-ho!' and toddle off quite happily to find another. He was so manifestly a bird who, having failed to score in the first chukker, would turn the thing up and spend the rest of his life brooding over his newts and growing long grey whiskers, like one of those chaps you read about in novels, who live in the great white house you can just see over there through the trees and shut themselves off from the world and have pained faces.

'I'm afraid he doesn't care for me in that way. At least, he has said nothing. You understand that I am only telling you this because – '

'Oh, rather.'

'It's odd that you should have asked me if I believed in love at first sight.' She half closed her eyes. "Who ever loved that loved not at first sight?" she said in a rummy voice that brought back to me – I don't know why – the picture of my Aunt Agatha, as Boadicea, reciting at that pageant I was speaking of. 'It's a silly little story. I was staying with some friends in the country, and I had gone for a walk with my dog, and the poor wee mite got a nasty thorn in his little foot and I didn't know what to do. And then suddenly this man came along – '

Harking back once again to that pageant, in sketching out for you my emotions on that occasion, I showed you only the darker side of the picture. There was, I should now mention, a splendid aftermath when, having climbed out of my suit of chain mail and sneaked off to the local pub, I entered the saloon bar and requested mine host to start pouring. A moment later, a tankard of their special home-brewed was in my hand, and the ecstasy of that first gollop is still green in my memory. The recollection of the agony through which I had passed was just what was needed to make it perfect.

It was the same now. When I realized, listening to her words, that she must be referring to Gussie – I mean to say, there couldn't have been a whole platoon of men taking thorns out of her dog that day; the animal wasn't a pincushion – and became aware that Gussie, who an instant before had, to all appearances, gone so far back in the betting as not to be worth a quotation, was the big winner after all, a positive thrill permeated the frame and there escaped my lips a 'Wow!' so crisp and hearty that the Bassett leaped a liberal inch and a half from terra firma.

'I beg your pardon?' she said.

I waved a jaunty hand.

'Nothing,' I said. 'Nothing. Just remembered there's a letter I have to write tonight without fail. If you don't mind, I think I'll be going in. Here,' I said, 'comes Gussie Fink-Nottle. He will look after you.'

And, as I spoke, Gussie came sidling out from behind a tree.

I passed away and left them to it. As regards these two, everything was beyond a question absolutely in order. All Gussie had to do was keep his head down and not press. Already, I felt, as I legged it back to the house, the happy ending must have begun to function. I mean to say, when you leave a girl and a man, each of whom has admitted in set terms that she and he loves him and her, in close juxtaposition in the twilight, there doesn't seem much more to do but start pricing fish slices.

Something attempted, something done, seemed to me to have earned two-penn'orth of wassail, in the smoking room.

I proceeded thither.

—11—

The makings were neatly laid out on a side table, and to pour into a glass an inch or so of the raw spirit and shoosh some soda water on top of it was with me the work of a moment. This done, I retired to an armchair and put my feet up, sipping the mixture with carefree enjoyment, rather like Caesar having one in his tent the day he overcame the Nervii.

As I let the mind dwell on what must even now be taking place in that peaceful garden, I felt bucked and uplifted. Though never for an instant faltering in my opinion that Augustus Fink-Nottle was Nature's final word in cloth-headed guffins, I liked the man, wished him well, and could not have felt more deeply involved in the success of his wooing if I, and not he, had been under the ether.

The thought that by this time he might quite easily have completed the preliminary *pourparlers* and be deep in an informal discussion of honeymoon plans was very pleasant to me.

Of course, considering the sort of girl Madeline Bassett was – stars and rabbits and all that, I mean – you might say that a sober sadness would have been more fitting. But in these matters you have got to realize that tastes differ. The impulse of right-thinking men might be to run a mile when they saw the Bassett, but for some reason she appealed to the deeps in Gussie, so that was that.

I had reached this point in my meditations, when I

was aroused by the sound of the door opening. Somebody came in and started moving like a leopard toward the side table and, lowering the feet, I perceived that it was Tuppy Glossop.

The sight of him gave me a momentary twinge of remorse, reminding me, as it did, that in the excitement of getting Gussie fixed up I had rather forgotten about this other client. It is often that way when you're trying to run two cases at once.

However, Gussie now being off my mind, I was prepared to devote my whole attention to the Glossop problem.

I had been much pleased by the way he had carried out the task assigned him at the dinner table. No easy one, I can assure you, for the browsing and sluicing had been of the highest quality, and there had been one dish in particular – I allude to the *nonnettes de poulet Agnès Sorel* – which might well have broken down the most iron resolution. But he had passed it up like a professional fasting man, and I was proud of him.

'Oh, hallo, Tuppy,' I said, 'I wanted to see you.'

He turned, snifter in hand, and it was easy to see that his privations had tried him sorely. He was looking like a wolf on the steppes of Russia which has seen its peasant shin up a high tree.

'Yes?' he said, rather unpleasantly. 'Well, here I am.'

'Well?'

'How do you mean – well?'

'Make your report'

'What report?'

'Have you nothing to tell me about Angela?'

'Only that she's a blister.'

I was concerned.

'Hasn't she come clustering round you yet?'

'She has not.'

'Very odd.'

'Why odd?'

'She must have noted your lack of appetite.'

He barked raspingly, as if he were having trouble with the tonsils of the soul.

'Lack of appetite! I'm as hollow as the Grand Canyon.'

'Courage, Tuppy! Think of Gandhi.'

'What about Gandhi?'

'He hasn't had a square meal for years.'

'Nor have I. Or I could swear I hadn't. Gandhi, my left foot.'

I saw that it might be best to let the Gandhi motif slide. I went back to where we had started.

'She's probably looking for you now.'

'Who is? Angela?'

'Yes. She must have noticed your supreme sacrifice.'

'I don't suppose she noticed it at all, the little fathead. I'll bet it didn't register in any way whatsoever.'

'Come, Tuppy,' I urged, 'this is morbid. Don't take this gloomy view. She must at least have spotted that you refused those *nonnettes de poulet Agnès Sorel*. It was a sensational renunciation and stuck out like a sore thumb. And the *crêpes à la Rossini* – '

A hoarse cry broke from his twisted lips:

'Will you stop it, Bertie! Do you think I am made of marble? Isn't it bad enough to have sat watching one of Anatole's supremest dinners flit by, course after course, without having you making a song about it? Don't remind me of those *nonnettes*. I can't stand it.'

I endeavoured to hearten and console.

'Be brave, Tuppy. Fix your thoughts on that cold steak-and-kidney pie in the larder. As the Good Book says, it cometh in the morning.'

'Yes, in the morning. And it's now about half-past nine at night. You would bring that pie up, wouldn't you? Just when I was trying to keep my mind off it.'

I saw what he meant. Hours must pass before he could dig into that pie. I dropped the subject, and we sat for a pretty good time in silence. Then he rose and began to pace the room in an overwrought sort of way, like a zoo lion who has heard the dinner gong go and is hoping the keeper won't forget him in the general distribution. I averted my gaze tactfully, but I could hear him kicking chairs and things. It was plain that the man's soul was in travail and his blood pressure high.

Presently he returned to his seat, and I saw that he was looking at me intently. There was that about his demeanour that led me to think that he had something to communicate.

Nor was I wrong. He tapped me significantly on the knee and spoke:

'Bertie.'

'Hullo?'

'Shall I tell you something?'

'Certainly, old bird,' I said cordially. 'I was just beginning to feel that the scene could do with a bit more dialogue.'

'This business of Angela and me.'

'Yes?'

'I've been putting in a lot of solid thinking about it.'

'Oh, yes?'

'I have analysed the situation pitilessly, and one thing stands out as clear as dammit. There has been dirty work afoot.'

'I don't get you.'

'All right. Let me review the facts. Up to the time she went to Cannes Angela loved me. She was all over me. I was the blue-eyed boy in every sense of the term. You'll admit that?'

'Indisputably.'

'And directly she came back we had this bust-up.'

'Quite.'

'About nothing.'

'Oh, dash it, old man, nothing? You were a bit tactless, what, about her shark.'

'I was frank and candid about her shark. And that's my point. Do you seriously believe that a trifling disagreement about sharks would make a girl hand a man his hat, if her heart were really his?'

'Certainly.'

It beats me why he couldn't see it. But then poor old Tuppy has never been very hot on the finer shades. He's one of those large, tough, football-playing blokes who lack the more delicate sensibilities, as I've heard Jeeves call them. Excellent at blocking a punt or walking across an opponent's face in cleated boots, but not so good when it comes to understanding the highly-strung female temperament. It simply wouldn't occur to him that a girl might be prepared to give up her life's happiness rather than waive her shark.

'Rot! It was just a pretext.'

'What was?'

'This shark business. She wanted to get rid of me, and grabbed at the first excuse.'

'No, no.'

'I tell you she did.'

'But what on earth would she want to get rid of you for?'

'Exactly. That's the very question I asked myself. And here's the answer: because she has fallen in love with somebody else. It sticks out a mile. There's no other possible solution. She goes to Cannes all for me, she comes back all off me. Obviously during those two months, she must have transferred her affections to some foul blister she met out there.'

'No, no.'

'Don't keep saying "No, no". She must have done.

Well, I'll tell you one thing, and you can take this as official. If ever I find this slimy, slithery snake in the grass, he had better make all the necessary arrangements at his favourite nursing-home without delay, because I am going to be very rough with him. I propose, if and when found, to take him by his beastly neck, shake him till he froths, and pull him inside out and make him swallow himself.'

With which words he biffed off; and I, having given him a minute or two to get out of the way, rose and made for the drawing room. The tendency of females to roost in drawing rooms after dinner being well marked, I expected to find Angela there. It was my intention to have a word with Angela.

To Tuppy's theory that some insinuating bird had stolen the girl's heart from him at Cannes I had given, as I have indicated, little credence, considering it the mere unbalanced apple sauce of a bereaved man. It was, of course, the shark, and nothing but the shark, that had caused love's young dream to go temporarily off the boil, and I was convinced that a word or two with the cousin at this juncture would set everything right.

For, frankly, I thought it incredible that a girl of her natural sweetness and tender-heartedness should not have been moved to her foundations by what she had seen at dinner that night. Even Seppings, Aunt Dahlia's butler, a cold, unemotional man, had gasped and practically reeled when Tuppy waved aside those *nonnettes de poulet Agnès Sorel*, while the footman, standing by with the potatoes, had stared like one seeing a vision. I simply refused to consider the possibility of the significance of the thing having been lost on a nice girl like Angela. I fully expected to find her in the drawing room with her heart bleeding freely, all ripe for an immediate reconciliation.

In the drawing room, however, when I entered, only

Aunt Dahlia met the eye. It seemed to me that she gave me rather a jaundiced look as I hove in sight, but this, having so recently beheld Tuppy in his agony, I attributed to the fact that she, like him, had been going light on the menu. You can't expect an empty aunt to beam like a full aunt.

'Oh, it's you, is it?' she said.

Well, it was, of course.

'Where's Angela?' I asked.

'Gone to bed.'

'Already?'

'She said she had a headache.'

'H'm.'

I wasn't so sure that I liked the sound of that so much. A girl who has observed the sundered lover sensationally off his feed does not go to bed with headaches if love has been reborn in her heart. She sticks around and gives him the swift, remorseful glance from beneath the drooping eyelashes and generally endeavours to convey to him that, if he wants to get together across a round table and try to find a formula, she is all for it too. Yes, I am bound to say I found that going-to-bed stuff a bit disquieting.

'Gone to bed, eh?' I murmured musingly.

'What did you want her for?'

'I thought she might like a stroll and a chat.'

'Are you going for a stroll?' said Aunt Dahlia, with a sudden show of interest. 'Where?'

'Oh, hither and thither.'

'Then I wonder if you would mind doing something for me.'

'Give it a name.'

'It won't take you long. You know that path that runs past the greenhouses into the kitchen garden. If you go along it, you come to a pond.'

'That's right.'

'Well, will you get a good, stout piece of rope or cord and go down that path till you come to the pond – '

'To the pond. Right.'

'– and look about you till you find a nice, heavy stone. Or a fairly large brick would do.'

'I see,' I said, though I didn't, being still fogged. 'Stone or brick. Yes. And then?'

'Then,' said the relative, 'I want you, like a good boy, to fasten the rope to the brick and tie it around your damned neck and jump into the pond and drown yourself. In a few days I will send and have you fished up and buried because I shall need to dance on your grave.'

I was more fogged than ever. And not only fogged – wounded and resentful. I remember reading a book where a girl 'suddenly fled from the room, afraid to stay for fear dreadful things would come tumbling from her lips; determined that she would not remain another day in this house to be insulted and misunderstood.' I felt much about the same.

Then I reminded myself that one has got to make allowances for a woman with only about half a spoonful of soup inside her, and I checked the red-hot crack that rose to the lips.

'What,' I said gently, 'is this all about? You seem pipped with Bertram.'

'Pipped!'

'Noticeably pipped. Why this ill-concealed animus?'

A sudden flame shot from her eyes, singeing my hair.

'Who was the ass, who was the chump, who was the dithering idiot who talked me, against my better judgment, into going without my dinner? I might have guessed – '

I saw that I had divined correctly the cause of her strange mood.

'It's all right, Aunt Dahlia. I know just how you're feeling. A bit on the hollow side, what? But the agony-will pass. If I were you, I'd sneak down and raid the larder after the household have gone to bed. I am told there's a pretty good steak-and-kidney pie there which will repay inspection. Have faith, Aunt Dahlia,' I urged. 'Pretty soon Uncle Tom will be along, full of sympathy and anxious inquiries.'

'Will he? Do you know where he is now?'

'I haven't seen him.'

'He is in the study with his face buried in his hands, muttering about Civilization and melting pots.'

'Eh? Why?'

'Because it has just been my painful duty to inform him that Anatole has given notice.'

I own that I reeled.

'What?'

'Given notice. As the result of that drivelling scheme of yours. What did you expect a sensitive, temperamental French cook to do, if you went about urging everybody to refuse all food? I hear that when the first two courses came back to the kitchen practically untouched, his feelings were so hurt that he cried like a child. And when the rest of the dinner followed, he came to the conclusion that the whole thing was a studied and calculated insult, and decided to hand in his portfolio.'

'Golly.'

'You may well say "Golly!" Anatole, God's gift to the gastric juices, gone like the dew off the petal of a rose, all through your idiocy. Perhaps you understand now why I want you to go and jump in that pond. I might have known that some hideous disaster would strike this house like a thunderbolt if once you wriggled your way into it and started trying to be clever.'

Harsh words, of course, as from aunt to nephew, but I bore her no resentment. No doubt, if you looked at it from a certain angle, Bertram might be considered to have made something of a floater.

'I am sorry.'

'What's the good of being sorry?'

'I acted for what I deemed the best.'

'Another time try acting for the worst. Then we may possibly escape with a mere flesh wound.'

'Uncle Tom's not feeling too bucked about it all, you say?'

'He's groaning like a lost soul. And any chance I ever had of getting that money out of him has gone.'

I stroked the chin thoughtfully. There was, I had to admit, reason in what she said. None knew better than I how terrible a blow the passing of Anatole would be to Uncle Tom.

I have stated earlier in this chronicle that this curious object of the seashore with whom Aunt Dahlia has linked her lot is a bloke who habitually looks like a pterodactyl that has suffered, and the reason he does so is that all those years he spent in making millions in the Far East put his digestion on the blink, and the only cook that has ever been discovered capable of pushing food into him without starting something like Old Home Week in Moscow under the third waistcoat button is this uniquely gifted Anatole. Deprived of Anatole's services, all he was likely to give the wife of his b. was a dirty look. Yes, unquestionably, things seemed to have struck a somewhat rocky patch, and I must admit that I found myself, at moment of going to press, a little destitute of constructive ideas.

Confident, however, that these would come ere long, I kept the stiff upper lip.

'Bad,' I conceded. 'Quite bad, beyond a doubt. Certainly a nasty jar for one and all. But have no fear, Aunt Dahlia, I will fix everything.'

I have alluded earlier to the difficulty of staggering when you're sitting down, showing that it is a feat of which I, personally, am not capable. Aunt Dahlia, to my amazement, now did it apparently without an effort. She was well wedged into a deep armchair, but, nevertheless, she staggered like billy-o. A sort of spasm of horror and apprehension contorted her face.

'If you dare to try any more of your lunatic schemes – '

I saw that it would be fruitless to try to reason with her. Quite plainly, she was not in the vein. Contenting myself, accordingly, with a gesture of loving sympathy, I left the room. Whether she did or did not throw a handsomely-bound volume of the *Works of Alfred, Lord Tennyson*, at me, I am not in a position to say. I had seen it lying on the table beside her, and as I closed the door I remember receiving the impression that some blunt instrument had crashed against the woodwork, but I was feeling too preoccupied to note and observe.

I blame myself for not having taken into consideration the possible effect of a sudden abstinence on the part of virtually the whole strength of the company on one of Anatole's impulsive Provençal temperament. These Gauls, I should have remembered, can't take it. Their tendency to fly off the handle at the slightest provocation is well known. No doubt the man had put his whole soul into those *nonnettes de poulet*, and to see them come homing back to him must have gashed him like a knife.

However, spilt milk blows nobody any good, and it is useless to dwell upon it. The task now confronting Bertram was to put matters right, and I was pacing the lawn, pondering to this end, when I suddenly heard a groan so lost soulish that I thought it must have proceeded from Uncle Tom, escaped from captivity and come to groan in the garden.

Looking about me, however, I could discern no uncles. Puzzled, I was about to resume my meditations, when the sound came again. And peering into the shadows I observed a dim form seated on one of the rustic benches which so liberally dotted this pleasance and another dim form standing beside same. A second and more penetrating glance and I had assembled the facts.

These dim forms were, in the order named, Gussie Fink-Nottle and Jeeves. And what Gussie was doing, groaning all over the place like this, was more than I could understand.

Because, I mean to say, there was no possibility of error. He wasn't singing. As I approached, he gave an encore, and it was beyond question a groan. Moreover, I could now see him clearly, and his whole aspect was definitely sand bagged.

'Good evening, sir,' said Jeeves. 'Mr Fink-Nottle is not feeling well.'

Nor was I. Gussie had begun to make a low, bubbling noise, and I could no longer disguise it from myself that something must have gone seriously wrong with the works. I mean, I know marriage is a pretty solemn business and the realization that he is in for it frequently churns a chap up a bit, but I had never come across a case of a newly-engaged man taking it on the chin so completely as this.

Gussie looked up. His eye was dull. He clutched the thatch.

'Goodbye, Bertie,' he said, rising.

I seemed to spot an error.

'You mean "Hallo," don't you?'

'No, I don't. I mean goodbye. I'm off.'

'Off where?'

'To the kitchen garden. To drown myself.'

'Don't be an ass.'

'I'm not an ass . . . Am I an ass, Jeeves?'

'Possibly a little injudicious, sir.'

'Drowning myself, you mean?'

'Yes, sir.'

'You think, on the whole, not drown myself?'

'I should not advocate it, sir.'

'Very well, Jeeves. I accept your ruling. After all, it would be unpleasant for Mrs Travers to find a swollen body floating in her pond.'

'Yes, sir.'

'And she has been very kind to me.'

'Yes, sir.'

'And you have been very kind to me, Jeeves.'

'Thank you, sir.'

'So have you, Bertie. Very kind. Everybody has been very kind to me. Very, very kind. Very kind indeed. I have no complaints to make. All right, I'll go for a walk instead.'

I followed him with bulging eyes as he tottered off into the dark.

'Jeeves,' I said, and I am free to admit that in my emotion I bleated like a lamb drawing itself to the attention of the parent sheep, 'what the dickens is all this?'

'Mr Fink-Nottle is not quite himself, sir. He has passed through a trying experience.'

I endeavoured to put together a brief synopsis of previous events.

'I left him out here with Miss Bassett.'

'Yes, sir.'

'I had softened her up.'

'Yes, sir.'

'He knew exactly what he had to do. I had coached him thoroughly in lines and business.'

'Yes, sir. So Mr Fink-Nottle informed me.'

'Well, then – '

'I regret to say, sir, that there was a slight hitch.'

'You mean, something went wrong?'

'Yes, sir.'

I could not fathom. The brain seemed to be tottering on its throne.

'But how could anything go wrong? She loves him, Jeeves.'

'Indeed, sir?'

'She definitely told me so. All he had to do was propose.'

'Yes, sir.'

'Well, didn't he?'

'No, sir.'

'Then what the dickens did he talk about?'

'Newts, sir.'

'Newts?'

'Yes, sir.'

'Newts?'

'Yes, sir.'

'But why did he want to talk about newts?'

'He did not want to talk about newts, sir. As I gather from Mr Fink-Nottle, nothing could have been more alien to his plans.'

I simply couldn't grasp the trend.

'But you can't force a man to talk about newts.'

'Mr Fink-Nottle was the victim of a sudden unfortunate spasm of nervousness, sir. Upon finding himself alone with the young lady, he admits to having lost his morale. In such circumstances, gentlemen frequently talk at random, saying the first thing that chances to enter their heads. This, in Mr Fink-Nottle's case, would seem to have been the newt, its treatment in sickness and in health.'

The scales fell from my eyes. I understood. I had had the same sort of thing happen to me in moments of crisis. I remember once detaining a dentist with the drill at one of my lower bicuspids and holding him up for nearly ten minutes with a story about a Scotsman, an Irishman, and a Jew. Purely automatic. The more he tried to jab, the more I said 'Hoots, mon,' 'Begorrah,' and 'Oy, oy'. When one loses one's nerve, one simply babbles.

I could put myself in Gussie's place. I could envisage the scene. There he and the Bassett were, alone together in the evening stillness. No doubt, as I had advised, he had shot the works about sunsets and fairy princesses, and so forth, and then had arrived at the point where he had to say that bit about having something to say to her. At this, I take it, she lowered her eyes and said, 'Oh, yes?'

He then, I should imagine, said it was something very important; to which her response would, one assumes, have been something on the lines of 'Really?' or 'Indeed?' or possibly just the sharp intake of the breath. And then their eyes met, just as mine met the dentist's, and something suddenly seemed to catch him in the pit of the stomach and everything went black and he heard his voice starting to drool about newts. Yes, I could follow the psychology.

Nevertheless, I found myself blaming Gussie. On discovering that he was stressing the newt note in this manner, he ought, of course, to have tuned out, even if it had meant sitting there saying nothing. No matter how much of a twitter he was in, he should have had sense enough to see that he was throwing a spanner into the works. No girl, when she has been led to expect that a man is about to pour forth his soul in a fervour of passion, likes to find him suddenly shelving the whole topic in favour of an address on aquatic *Salamandridae*.

'Bad, Jeeves.'

'Yes, sir.'

'And how long did this nuisance continue?'

'For some not inconsiderable time, I gather, sir. According to Mr Fink-Nottle, he supplied Miss Bassett with very full and complete information not only with respect to the common newt, but also the crested and palmated varieties. He described to her how newts, during the breeding season, live in the water, subsisting upon tadpoles, insect larvae, and crustaceans; how, later, they make their way to the land and eat slugs and worms; and how the newly born newt has three pairs of long, plumlike, external gills. And he was just observing that newts differ from salamanders in the shape of the tail, which is compressed, and that a marked sexual dimorphism prevails in most species, when the young lady rose and said that she thought she would go back to the house.'

'And then – '

'She went, sir.'

I stood musing. More and more, it was beginning to be borne in upon me what a particular difficult chap Gussie was to help. He seemed to so marked an extent to lack snap and finish. With infinite toil, you manoeuvred him into a position where all he had to do was charge ahead, and he didn't charge ahead, but went off sideways, missing the objective completely.

'Difficult, Jeeves.'

'Yes, sir.'

In happier circs., of course, I would have canvassed his views on the matter. But after what had occurred in connection with that mess jacket, my lips were sealed.

'Well, I must think it over.'

'Yes, sir.'

'Burnish the brain a bit and endeavour to find the way out.'

'Yes, sir.'

'Well, good night, Jeeves.'

'Good night, sir.'

He shimmered off, leaving a pensive Bertram Wooster standing motionless in the shadows. It seemed to me that it was hard to know what to do for the best.

12

I don't know if it has happened to you at all, but a thing I've noticed with myself is that, when I'm confronted by a problem which seems for the moment to stump and baffle, a good sleep will often bring the solution in the morning.

It was so on the present occasion.

The nibs who study these matters claim, I believe, that this has got something to do with the subconscious mind, and very possibly they may be right. I wouldn't have said off-hand that I had a subconscious mind, but I suppose I must without knowing it, and no doubt it was there, sweating away diligently at the old stand, all the while the corporeal Wooster was getting his eight hours.

For directly I opened my eyes on the morrow, I saw daylight. Well, I don't mean that exactly, because naturally I did. What I mean is that I found I had the thing all mapped out. The good old subconscious m. had delivered the goods, and I perceived exactly what steps must be taken in order to put Augustus Fink-Nottle among the practising Romeos.

I should like you, if you can spare me a moment of your valuable time, to throw your mind back to that conversation he and I had had in the garden on the previous evening. Not the glimmering landscape bit, I don't mean that, but the concluding passages of it. Having done so, you will recall that when he informed me that he never touched alcoholic liquor, I shook the head a bit, feeling that this must inevitably weaken him as a force where proposing to girls was concerned.

And events had shown that my fears were well founded.

Put to the test, with nothing but orange juice inside him, he had proved a complete bust. In a situation calling for words of molten passion of a nature calculated to go through Madeline Bassett like a red-hot gimlet through half a pound of butter, he had said not a syllable that could bring a blush to the cheek of modesty, merely delivering a well-phrased but, in the circumstances, quite misplaced lecture on newts.

A romantic girl is not to be won by such tactics. Obviously, before attempting to proceed further, Augustus Fink-Nottle must be induced to throw off the shackling inhibitions of the past and fuel up. It must be primed, confident Fink-Nottle who squared up to the Bassett for Round No. 2.

Only so could the *Morning Post* make its ten bob, or whatever it is, for printing the announcement of the forth-coming nuptials.

Having arrived at this conclusion I found the rest easy, and by the time Jeeves brought me my tea I had evolved a plan complete in every detail. This I was about to place before him – indeed, I had got as far as the preliminary 'I say, Jeeves' – when we were interrupted by the arrival of Tuppy.

He came listlessly into the room, and I was pained to observe that a night's rest had effected no improvement in the unhappy wreck's appearance. Indeed, I should have said, if anything, that he was looking rather more moth-eaten than when I had seen him last. If you can visualize a bulldog which has just been kicked in the ribs and had its dinner sneaked by the cat, you will have Hildebrand Glossop as he now stood before me.

'Stap my vitals, Tuppy, old corpse,' I said, concerned, 'you're looking pretty blue round the rims.'

Jeeves slid from the presence in that tactful, eel-like way of his, and I motioned the remains to take a seat.

'What's the matter?' I said.

He came to anchor on the bed, and for a while sat picking at the coverlet in silence.

'I've been through hell, Bertie.'

'Through where?'

'Hell.'

'Oh, hell? And what took you there?'

Once more he became silent, staring before him with sombre eyes. Following his gaze, I saw that he was looking at an enlarged photograph of my Uncle Tom in some sort of Masonic uniform which stood on the mantelpiece. I've tried to reason with Aunt Dahlia about this photograph for years, placing before her two alternative suggestions: (*a*) To burn the beastly thing; or (*b*) if she must preserve it, to shove me in another room when I come to stay. But she declines to accede. She says it's good for me. A useful discipline, she maintains, teaching me that there is a darker side to life and that we were not put into this world for pleasure only.

'Turn it to the wall, if it hurts you, Tuppy,' I said gently.

'Eh?'

'That photograph of Uncle Tom as the bandmaster.'

'I didn't come here to talk about photographs. I came for sympathy.'

'And you shall have it. What's the trouble? Worrying about Angela, I suppose? Well, have no fear. I have another well-laid plan for encompassing that young shrimp. I'll guarantee that she will be weeping on your neck before yonder sun has set.'

He barked sharply.

'A fat chance!'

'Tup, Tushy!'

'Eh?'

'I mean "Tush, Tuppy." I tell you I will do it. I was just going to describe this plan of mine to Jeeves when you came in. Care to hear it?'

'I don't want to hear any of your beastly plans. Plans are no good. She's gone and fallen in love with this other bloke, and now hates my gizzard.'

'Rot.'

'It isn't rot.'

'I tell you, Tuppy, as one who can read the female heart, that this Angela loves you still.'

'Well, it didn't look much like it in the larder last night.'

'Oh, you went to the larder last night?'

'I did.'

'And Angela was there?'

'She was. And your aunt. Also your uncle.'

I saw that I should require footnotes. All this was new stuff to me. I had stayed at Brinkley Court quite a lot in my time, but I had no idea the larder was such a social vortex. More like a snack bar on a racecourse than anything else, it seemed to have become.

'Tell me the whole story in your own words,' I said, 'omitting no detail, however apparently slight, for one never knows how important the most trivial detail may be.'

He inspected the photograph for a moment with growing gloom.

'All right,' he said. 'This is what happened. You know my views about that steak-and-kidney pie.'

'Quite.'

'Well, round about one a.m. I thought the time was ripe. I stole from my room and went downstairs. The pie seemed to beckon me.'

I nodded. I knew how pies do.

'I got to the larder. I fished it out. I set it on the table. I found knife and fork. I collected salt, mustard, and pepper. There were some cold potatoes. I added those. And I was about to pitch in when I heard a sound behind me, and there was your aunt at the door. In a blue-and-yellow dressing gown.'

'Embarrassing.'

'Most.'

'I suppose you didn't know where to look.'

'I looked at Angela.'

'She came in with my aunt?'

'No. With your uncle, a minute or two later. He was wearing mauve pyjamas and carried a pistol. Have you ever seen your uncle in pyjamas and a pistol?'

'Never.'

'You haven't missed much.'

'Tell me, Tuppy,' I asked, for I was anxious to ascertain this, 'about Angela. Was there any momentary softening in her gaze as she fixed it on you?'

'She didn't fix it on me. She fixed it on the pie.'

'Did she say anything?'

'Not right away. Your uncle was the first to speak. He said to your aunt, "God bless my soul, Dahlia, what are you doing here?" To which she replied, "Well, if it comes to that, my merry somnambulist, what are you?" Your uncle then said that he thought there must be burglars in the house, as he had heard noises.'

I nodded again. I could follow the trend. Ever since the scullery window was found open the year Shining Light was disqualified in the Cesarewitch for boring, Uncle Tom has had a marked complex about burglars. I can still recall my emotions when, paying my first visit after he had bars put on all windows and attempting to thrust the head out in order to get a sniff of country air, I nearly fractured my skull on a sort of iron grille, as worn by the tougher kinds of mediaeval prison.

' "What sort of noises?" said your aunt. "Funny noises," said your uncle. Whereupon Angela – with a nasty, steely tinkle in her voice, the little buzzard – observed, "I expect it was Mr Glossop eating." And then she did give me a look. It was the sort of wondering, revolted look a very spiritual woman would give a fat man gulping soup in a restaurant. The kind of look that makes a fellow feel he's forty-six round the waist and has great rolls of superfluous flesh pouring down over the back of his collar. And, still speaking in the same unpleasant tone, she added, "I ought to have told you, Father, that Mr Glossop always likes to have a good meal three or four times during the night. It helps to keep him going till breakfast. He has the most amazing appetite. See, he has practically finished a large steak-and-kidney pie already".'

As he spoke these words, a feverish animation swept over Tuppy. His eyes glittered with a strange light, and he thumped the bed violently with his fist, nearly catching me a juicy one on the leg.

'That was what hurt, Bertie. That was what stung. I hadn't so much as started on that pie. But that's a woman all over.'

'The eternal feminine.'

'She continued her remarks. "You've no idea," she said, "how Mr Glossop loves food. He just lives for it. He always eats six or seven meals a day, and then starts in again after bedtime. I think it's rather wonderful." Your aunt seemed interested, and said it reminded her of a boa constrictor. Angela said, didn't she mean a python? And then they argued as to which of the two it was. Your uncle, meanwhile, poking about with that damned pistol of his till human life wasn't safe in the vicinity. And the pie lying there on the table, and me unable to touch it. You begin to understand why I said I had been through hell.'

'Quite. Can't have been at all pleasant.'

'Presently your aunt and Angela settled their discussion, deciding that Angela was right and that it was a python that I reminded them of. And shortly after that we all pushed back to bed, Angela warning me in a motherly voice not to take the stairs too quickly. After seven or eight solid meals, she said, a man of my build ought to be very careful, because of the danger of apoplectic fits. She said it was the same with dogs. When they became very fat and overfed, you had to see that they didn't hurry upstairs, as it made them puff and pant, and that was bad for their hearts. She asked your aunt if she remembered the late spaniel, Ambrose; and your aunt said, "Poor old Ambrose, you couldn't keep him away from the garbage pail"; and Angela said, "Exactly, so do please be careful, Mr Glossop." And you tell me she loves me still!'

I did my best to encourage.

'Girlish banter, what?'

'Girlish banter be dashed. She's right off me. Once her ideal, I am now less than the dust beneath her chariot wheels. She became infatuated with this chap, whoever he was, at Cannes, and now she can't stand the sight of me.'

I raised my eyebrows.

'My dear Tuppy, you are not showing your usual good sense in this Angela-chap-at-Cannes matter. If you will forgive me saying so, you have got an *idée fixe*.'

'A what?'

'An *idée fixe*. You know. One of those things fellows get. Like Uncle Tom's delusion that everybody who is known even slightly to the police is lurking in the garden, waiting for a chance to break into the house. You keep talking about this chap at Cannes, and there never was a chap at Cannes, and I'll tell you why I'm so sure about this. During those two months on the

Riviera, it so happens that Angela and I were practically inseparable. If there had been somebody nosing round her, I should have spotted it in a second.'

He started. I could see that this had impressed him.

'Oh, she was with you all the time at Cannes, was she?'

'I don't suppose she said two words to anybody else, except, of course, idle conv. at the crowded dinner table or a chance remark in a throng at the Casino.'

'I see. You mean that anything in the shape of mixed bathing and moonlight strolls she conducted solely in your company?'

'That's right. It was quite a joke in the hotel.'

'You must have enjoyed that.'

'Oh, rather. I've always been devoted to Angela.'

'Oh, yes?'

'When we were kids, she used to call herself my little sweetheart.'

'She did?'

'Absolutely.'

'I see.'

He sat plunged in thought, while I, glad to have set his mind at rest, proceeded with my tea. And presently there came the banging of a gong from the hall below, and he started like a war horse at the sound of the bugle.

'Breakfast!' he said, and was off to a flying start, leaving me to brood and ponder. And the more I brooded and pondered, the more did it seem to me that everything now looked pretty smooth. Tuppy, I could see, despite that painful scene in the larder, still loved Angela with all the old fervour.

This meant that I could rely on that plan to which I had referred to bring home the bacon. And as I had found the way to straighten out the Gussie-Bassett difficulty, there seemed nothing more to worry about.

It was with an uplifted heart that I addressed Jeeves as he came in to remove the tea tray.

13

'Jeeves,' I said.

'Sir?'

'I've just been having a chat with young Tuppy, Jeeves. Did you happen to notice that he wasn't looking very roguish this morning?'

'Yes, sir. It seemed to me that Mr Glossop's face was sicklied o'er with the pale cast of thought.'

'Quite. He met my cousin Angela in the larder last night, and a rather painful interview ensued.'

'I am sorry, sir.'

'Not half so sorry as he was. She found him closeted with a steak-and-kidney pie, and appears to have been a bit caustic about fat men who lived for food alone.'

'Most disturbing, sir.'

'Very. In fact, many people would say that things had gone so far between these two nothing now could bridge the chasm. A girl who could make cracks about human pythons who ate nine or ten meals a day and ought to be careful not to hurry upstairs because of the danger of apoplectic fits is a girl, many people would say, in whose heart love is dead. Wouldn't people say that, Jeeves?'

'Undeniably, sir.'

'They would be wrong.'

'You think so, sir?'

'I am convinced of it. I know these females. You can't go by what they say.'

'You feel that Miss Angela's strictures should not be taken too much *au pied de la lettre*, sir?'

'Eh?'

'In English, we should say "literally".'

'Literally. That's exactly what I mean. You know what girls are. A tiff occurs, and they shoot their heads off. But underneath it all the old love still remains. Am I correct?'

'Quite correct, sir. The poet Scott – '

'Right ho, Jeeves.'

'Very good, sir.'

'And in order to bring that old love whizzing to the surface once more, all that is required is the proper treatment.'

'By "proper treatment," sir, you mean – '

'Clever handling, Jeeves. A spot of the good old snaky work. I see what must be done to jerk my Cousin Angela back to normalcy. I'll tell you, shall I?'

'If you would be so kind, sir.'

I lit a cigarette, and eyed him keenly through the smoke. He waited respectfully for me to unleash the words of wisdom. I must say for Jeeves that – till, as he is so apt to do, he starts shoving his oar in and cavilling and obstructing – he makes a very good audience. I don't know if he is actually agog, but he looks agog, and that's the great thing.

'Suppose you were strolling through the illimitable jungle, Jeeves, and happened to meet a tiger cub.'

'The contingency is a remote one, sir.'

'Never mind. Let us suppose it.'

'Very good, sir.'

'Let us now suppose that you sloshed that tiger cub, and let us suppose further that word reached its mother that it was being put upon. What would you expect the attitude of that mother to be? In what frame of mind do you consider that that tigress would approach you?'

'I should anticipate a certain show of annoyance, sir.'

'And rightly. Due to what is known as the maternal instinct, what?'

'Yes, sir.'

'Very good, Jeeves. We will now suppose that there has recently been some little coolness between this tiger cub and this tigress. For some days, let us say, they have not been on speaking terms. Do you think that that would make any difference to the vim with which the latter would leap to the former's aid?'

'No, sir.'

'Exactly. Here, then, in brief, is my plan, Jeeves. I am going to draw my Cousin Angela aside to a secluded spot and roast Tuppy properly.'

'Roast, sir?'

'Knock. Slam. Tick off. Abuse. Denounce. I shall be very terse about Tuppy, giving it as my opinion that in all essentials he is more like a wart hog than an ex-member of a fine old English public school. What will ensue? Hearing him attacked, my Cousin Angela's womanly heart will be as sick as mud. The maternal tigress in her will awake. No matter what differences they may have had, she will remember only that he is the man she loves, and will leap to his defence. And from that to falling into his arms and burying the dead past will be but a step. How do you react to that?'

'The idea is an ingenious one, sir.'

'We Woosters are ingenious, Jeeves, exceedingly ingenious.'

'Yes, sir.'

'As a matter of fact, I am not speaking without a knowledge of the form book. I have tested this theory.'

'Indeed, sir?'

'Yes, in person. And it works. I was standing on the Eden rock at Antibes last month, idly watching the bathers disport themselves in the water, and a girl I knew slightly pointed at a male diver and asked me if I didn't think his legs were about the silliest-looking pair of props ever issued to human being. I replied that I did, indeed, and for the space of perhaps two minutes was extraordinarily witty and satirical about this bird's underpinning. At the end of that period, I suddenly felt as if I had been caught up in the tail of a cyclone.

'Beginning with a critique of my own limbs, which she said, justly enough, were nothing to write home about, this girl went on to dissect my manners, morals, intellect, general physique, and method of eating asparagus with such acerbity that by the time she had finished the best you could say of Bertram was that, so far as was known, he had never actually committed murder or set fire to an orphan asylum. Subsequent investigation proved that she was engaged to the fellow with the legs and had had a slight disagreement with him the evening before on the subject of whether she should or should not have made an original call of two spades, having seen, but without the ace. That night I saw them dining together with every indication of relish, their differences made up and the lovelight once more in their eyes. That shows you, Jeeves.'

'Yes, sir.'

'I expect precisely similar results from my Cousin Angela when I start roasting Tuppy, By lunchtime, I should imagine, the engagement will be on again and the diamond-and-platinum ring glittering as of yore on her third finger. Or is it the fourth?'

'Scarcely by luncheon time, sir. Miss Angela's maid informs me that Miss Angela drove off in her car early this morning with the intention of spending the day with friends in the vicinity.'

'Well, within half an hour of whatever time she comes back, then, These are mere straws, Jeeves. Do not let us chop them.'

'No, sir.'

'The point is that, as far as Tuppy and Angela are concerned, we may say with confidence that everything will shortly be hotsy-totsy once more. And what an agreeable thought that is, Jeeves.'

'Very true, sir.'

'If there is one thing that gives me the pip, it is two loving hearts being estranged.'

'I can readily appreciate the fact, sir.'

I placed the stub of my gasper in the ash tray and lit another, to indicate that that completed Chap. I.

'Right ho, then. So much for the western front. We now turn to the eastern.'

'Sir?'

'I speak in parables, Jeeves. What I mean is, we now approach the matter of Gussie and Miss Bassett.'

'Yes, sir.'

'Here, Jeeves, more direct methods are required. In handling the case of Augustus Fink-Nottle, we must keep always in mind the fact that we are dealing with a poop.'

'A sensitive plant would, perhaps, be a kinder expression, sir.'

'No, Jeeves, a poop. And with poops one has to employ the strong, forceful, straightforward policy. Psychology doesn't get you anywhere. You, if I may remind you without wounding your feelings, fell into the error of mucking about with psychology in connection with this Fink-Nottle, and the result was a wash-out. You attempted to push him over the line by rigging him out in a Mephistopheles costume and sending him off to a fancy-dress ball, your view being that scarlet tights would embolden him. Futile.'

'The matter was never actually put to the test, sir.'

'No. Because he didn't get to the ball. And that strengthens my argument. A man who can set out in a cab for a fancy-dress ball and not get there is manifestly a poop of no common order. I don't think I have ever known anybody else who was such a dashed silly ass that he couldn't even get to a fancy-dress ball. Have you, Jeeves?'

'No, sir.'

'But don't forget this, because it is the point I wish, above all, to make: even if Gussie had got to that ball; even if those scarlet tights, taken in conjunction with his horn-rimmed spectacles, hadn't given the girl a fit of some kind; even if she had rallied from the shock and he had been able to dance and generally hobnob with her; even then your efforts would have been fruitless, because, Mephistopheles costume or no Mephistopheles costume, Augustus Fink-Nottle would never have been able to summon up the courage to ask her to be his. All that would have resulted would have been that she would have got that lecture on newts a few days earlier. And why, Jeeves? Shall I tell you why?'

'Yes, sir.'

'Because he would have been attempting the hopeless task of trying to do the thing on orange juice.'

'Sir?'

'Gussie is an orange-juice addict. He drinks nothing else.'

'I was not aware of that, sir.'

'I have it from his own lips. Whether from some hereditary taint, or because he promised his mother he wouldn't or simply because he doesn't like the taste of the stuff, Gussie Fink-Nottle has never in the whole course of his career pushed so much as the simplest gin and tonic over the larynx. And he expects – this poop expects, Jeeves – this babbling, shrinking, diffident rabbit in human shape expects under these conditions to propose to the girl he loves. One hardly knows whether to smile or weep, what?'

'You consider total abstinence a handicap to a gentleman who wishes to make a proposal of marriage, sir?'

The question amazed me.

'Why, dash it,' I said, astounded, 'you must know it is. Use your intelligence, Jeeves. Reflect what proposing means. It means that a decent, self-respecting chap has got to listen to himself saying things which, if spoken on the silver screen, would cause him to dash to the box office and demand his money back. Let him attempt to do it on orange juice, and what ensues? Shame seals his lips, or, if it doesn't do that, makes him lose his morale and start to babble. Gussie, for example, as we have seen, babbles of syncopated newts.'

'Palmated newts, sir.'

'Palmated or syncopated, it doesn't matter which. The point is that he babbles and is going to babble again, if he has another try at it. Unless – and this is where I want you to follow me very closely, Jeeves – unless steps are taken at once through the proper channels. Only active measures, promptly applied, can provide this poor, pusillanimous poop with the proper pep. And that is why, Jeeves, I intend tomorrow to secure a bottle of gin and lace his luncheon orange juice with it liberally.'

'Sir?'

I clicked the tongue.

'I have already had occasion, Jeeves,' I said rebukingly, 'to comment on the way you say "Well, sir" and "Indeed, sir?" I take this opportunity of informing you that I object equally strongly to your "Sir?" pure and simple. The word seems to suggest that in your opinion I have made a statement or mooted a scheme so bizarre that your brain reels at it. In the present instance, there is absolutely nothing to say "Sir?" about. The plan I have put forward is entirely reasonable and icily logical, and should excite no stirring whatsoever. Or don't you think so?'

'Well, sir – '

'Jeeves!'

'I beg your pardon, sir. The expression escaped me inadvertently. What I intended to say, since you press me, was that the action which you propose does seem to me somewhat injudicious.'

'Injudicious? I don't follow you, Jeeves.'

'A certain amount of risk would enter into it, in my opinion, sir. It is not always a simple matter to gauge the effect of alcohol on a subject unaccustomed to such stimulant. I have known it to have distressing results in the case of parrots.'

'Parrots?'

'I was thinking of an incident of my earlier life, sir, before I entered your employment. I was in the service of the late Lord Brancaster at the time, a gentleman who owned a parrot to which he was greatly devoted, and one day the bird chanced to be lethargic, and his lordship, with the kindly intention of restoring it to its customary animation, offered it a portion of seed cake steeped in the '84 port. The bird accepted the morsel gratefully and consumed it with every indication of satisfaction. Almost immediately afterwards, however, its manner became markedly feverish. Having bitten his lordship in the thumb and sung part of a sea shanty, it fell to the bottom of the cage and remained there for a considerable period of time with its legs in the air, unable to move. I merely mention this, sir, in order to – '

I put my finger on the flaw. I had spotted it all along.

'But Gussie isn't a parrot.'

'No, sir, but – '

'It is high time, in my opinion, that this question of what young Gussie really is was threshed out and cleared up. He seems to think he is a male newt, and you now appear to suggest that he is a parrot. The truth of the matter being that he is just a plain, ordinary poop and needs a snootful as badly as ever man did. So no more discussion, Jeeves. My mind is made up. There is only one way of handling this difficult case, and that is the way I have outlined.'

'Very good, sir.'

'Right ho, Jeeves. So much for that, then. Now here's something else: You noticed that I said I was going to put this project through tomorrow, and no doubt you wondered why I said tomorrow. Why did I, Jeeves?'

'Because you feel that if it were done when 'tis done, then 'twere well it were done quickly, sir?'

'Partly, Jeeves, but not altogether. My chief reason for fixing the date as specified is that tomorrow, though you have doubtless forgotten, is the day of the distribution of prizes at Market Snodsbury Grammar School, at which, as you know, Gussie is to be the male star and master of the revels. So you see we shall, by lacing that juice, not only embolden him to propose to Miss Bassett, but also put him so into shape that he will hold that Market Snodsbury audience spellbound.'

'In fact, you will be killing two birds with one stone, sir.'

'Exactly. A very neat way of putting it. And now here is a minor point. On second thoughts, I think the best plan will be for you, not me, to lace the juice.'

'Sir?'

'Jeeves!'

'I beg your pardon, sir.'

'And I'll tell you why that will be the best plan. Because you are in a position to obtain ready access to the stuff. It is served to Gussie daily, I have noticed, in an individual jug. This jug will presumably be lying about the kitchen or somewhere before lunch tomorrow. It will be the simplest of tasks for you to slip a few fingers of gin in it.'

'No doubt, sir, but – '

'Don't say "but," Jeeves.'

'I fear, sir – '

' "I fear, sir" is just as bad.'

'What I am endeavouring to say, sir, is that I am sorry, but I am afraid I must enter an unequivocal *nolle prosequi.*'

'Do what?'

'The expression is a legal one, sir, signifying the resolve not to proceed with a matter. In other words, eager though I am to carry out your instructions, sir, as a general rule, on this occasion I must respectfully decline to cooperate.'

'You won't do it, you mean?'

'Precisely, sir.'

I was stunned. I began to understand how a general must feel when he has ordered a regiment to charge and has been told that it isn't in the mood.

'Jeeves,' I said, 'I had not expected this of you.'

'No, sir?'

'No, indeed. Naturally, I realize that lacing Gussie's orange juice is not one of those regular duties for which you receive the monthly stipend, and if you care to stand on the strict letter of the contract, I suppose there is nothing to be done about it. But you will permit me to observe that this is scarcely the feudal spirit.'

'I am sorry, sir.'

'It is quite all right, Jeeves, quite all right. I am not angry, only a little hurt.'

'Very good, sir.'

'Right ho, Jeeves.'

14

Investigation proved that the friends Angela had gone to spend the day with were some stately-home owners of the name of Stretchley-Budd, hanging out in a joint called Kingham Manor, about eight miles distant in the direction of Pershore. I didn't know these birds, but their fascination must have been considerable, for she tore herself away from them only just in time to get back and dress for dinner. It was, accordingly, not until coffee had been consumed that I was able to get matters moving. I found her in the drawing room and at once proceeded to put things in train.

It was with very different feelings from those which had animated the bosom when approaching the Bassett twenty-four hours before in the same manner in this same drawing room that I headed for where she sat. As I had told Tuppy, I have always been devoted to Angela, and there is nothing I like better than a ramble in her company.

And I could see by the look of her now how sorely in need she was of my aid and comfort.

Frankly, I was shocked by the unfortunate young prune's appearance. At Cannes she had been a happy, smiling English girl of the best type, full of beans and buck. Her face now was pale and drawn, like that of a hockey centreforward at a girls' school who, in addition to getting a fruity one on the shin, has just been penalized for 'sticks'. In any normal gathering, her demeanour would have excited instant remark, but the standard of gloom at Brinkley Court had become so high that it passed unnoticed. Indeed, I shouldn't wonder if Uncle Tom, crouched in his corner waiting for the end, didn't think she was looking indecently cheerful.

I got down to the agenda in my debonair way.

'What ho, Angela, old girl.'

'Hullo, Bertie, darling.'

'Glad you're back at last. I missed you.'

'Did you, darling?'

'I did, indeed. Care to come for a saunter?'

'I'd love it.'

'Fine. I have much to say to you that is not for the public ear.'

I think at this moment poor old Tuppy must have got a sudden touch of cramp. He had been sitting hard by, staring at the ceiling, and he now gave a sharp leap like a gaffed salmon and upset a small table containing a vase, a bowl of potpourri, two china dogs, and a copy of Omar Khayyam bound in limp leather.

Aunt Dahlia uttered a startled hunting cry. Uncle Tom, who probably imagined from the noise that this was civilization crashing at last, helped things along by breaking a coffee cup.

Tuppy said he was sorry. Aunt Dahlia, with a death-bed groan, said it didn't matter. And Angela, having stared haughtily for a moment like a princess of the old régime confronted by some notable example of gaucherie on the part of some particularly foul member of the underworld, accompanied me across the threshold. And presently I had deposited her and self on one of the rustic benches in the garden, and was ready to snap into the business of the evening.

I considered it best, however, before doing so, to ease things along with a little informal chitchat. You don't want to rush a delicate job like the one I had in hand. And so for a while we spoke of neutral topics. She said that what had kept her so long at the Stretchley-Budds was that Hilda Stretchley-Budd had made her stop on and help with the arrangements for their servants' ball tomorrow night, a task which she couldn't very well decline, as all the Brinkley Court domestic staff were to be present. I said that a jolly night's revelry might be just what was needed to cheer Anatole up and take his mind off things. To which she replied that Anatole wasn't going. On being urged to do so by Aunt Dahlia, she said, he had merely shaken his head sadly and gone on talking of returning to Provence, where he was appreciated.

It was after the sombre silence induced by this statement that Angela said the grass was wet and she thought she would go in.

This, of course, was entirely foreign to my policy.

'No, don't do that. I haven't had a chance to talk to you since you arrived.'

'I shall ruin my shoes.'

'Put your feet up on my lap.'

'All right. And you can tickle my ankles.'

'Quite.'

Matters were accordingly arranged on these lines, and for some minutes we continued chatting in desultory fashion. Then the conversation petered out. I made a few observations *in re* the scenic effects, featuring the twilight hush, the peeping stars, and the soft glimmer of the waters of the lake, and she said yes. Something rustled in the bushes in front of us, and I advanced the theory that it was possibly a weasel, and she said it might be. But it was plain that the girl was distrait, and I considered it was best to waste no more time.

'Well, old thing,' I said, 'I've heard all about your little dust-up. So those wedding bells are not going to ring out, what?'

'No.'

'Definitely over, is it?'

'Yes.'

'Well, if you want my opinion, I think that's a bit of goose for you, Angela, old girl. I think you're extremely well out of it. It's a mystery to me how you stood this Glossop so long. Take him for all in all, he ranks very low down among the wines and spirits. A wash-out, I should describe him as. A frightful oik, and a mass of side to boot. I'd pity the girl who was linked for life to a bargee like Tuppy Glossop.'

And I emitted a hard laugh – one of the sneering kind.

'I always thought you were such friends,' said Angela.

I let go another hard one, with a bit more top spin on it than the first time:

'Friends? Absolutely not. One was civil, of course, when one met the fellow, but it would be absurd to say one was a friend of his. A club acquaintance, and a mere one at that. And then one was at school with the man.'

'At Eton?'

'Good heavens, no. We wouldn't have a fellow like that at Eton. At a kid's school before I went there. A grubby little brute he was, I recollect. Covered with ink and mire generally, washing only on alternate Thursdays. In short, a notable outsider, shunned by all.'

I paused. I was more than a bit perturbed. Apart from the agony of having to talk in this fashion of one who, except when he was looping back rings and causing me to plunge into swimming baths in correct evening costume, had always been a very dear and esteemed crony, I didn't seem to be getting anywhere. Business was not resulting. Staring into the bushes without a yip, she appeared to be bearing these slurs and innuendos of mine with an easy calm.

I had another pop at it:

' "Uncouth" about sums it up. I doubt if I've ever seen an uncouther kid than this Glossop. Ask anyone who knew him in those days to describe him in a word, and the word they will use is "uncouth". And he's just the same today. It's the old story. The boy is the father of the man.'

She appeared not to have heard.

'The boy,' I repeated, not wishing her to miss that one, 'is the father of the man.'

'What are you talking about?'

'I'm talking about this Glossop.'

'I thought you said something about somebody's father.'

'I said the boy was the father of the man.'

'What boy?'

'The boy Glossop.'

'He hasn't got a father.'

'I never said he had. I said he was the father of the boy – or, rather, of the man.'

'What man?'

I saw that the conversation had reached a point where, unless care was taken, we should be muddled.

'The point I am trying to make,' I said, 'is that the boy Glossop is the father of the man Glossop. In other words, each loathsome fault and blemish that led the boy Glossop to be frowned upon by his fellows is present in the man Glossop, and causes him – I am speaking now of the man Glossop – to be a hissing and a byword at places like the Drones, where a certain standard of decency is demanded from the inmates. Ask anyone at the Drones, and they will tell you that it was a black day for the dear old club when this chap Glossop somehow wriggled into the list of members. Here you will find a man who dislikes his face; there one who could stand his face if it wasn't for his habits. But the universal consensus of opinion is that the fellow is a bounder and a tick, and that the moment he showed signs of wanting to get into the place he should have been met with a firm *nolle prosequi* and heartily blackballed.'

I had to pause again here, partly in order to take in a spot of breath, and partly to wrestle with the almost physical torture of saying these frightful things about poor old Tuppy.

'There are some chaps,' I resumed, forcing myself once more to the nauseous task, 'who, in spite of looking as if they had slept in their clothes, can get by quite nicely because they are amiable and suave. There are others who, for all that they excite adverse comment by being fat and uncouth, find themselves on the credit side of the ledger owing to their wit and sparkling humour. But this Glossop, I regret to say, falls into neither class. In addition to looking like one of those things that come out of hollow trees, he is universally admitted to be a dumb brick of the first water. No soul. No conversation. In short, any girl who, having been rash enough to get engaged to him, has managed at the eleventh hour to slide out is justly entitled to consider herself dashed lucky.'

I paused once more, and cocked an eye at Angela to see how the treatment was taking. All the while I had been speaking, she had sat gazing silently into the bushes, but it seemed to me incredible that she should not now turn on me like a tigress, according to specifications. It beat me why she hadn't done it already. It seemed to me that a mere tithe of what I had said, if said to a tigress about a tiger of which she was fond, would have made her – the tigress, I mean – hit the ceiling.

And the next moment you could have knocked me down with a toothpick.

'Yes,' she said, nodding thoughtfully, 'you're quite right.'

'Eh?'

'That's exactly what I've been thinking myself.'

'What!'

' "Dumb brick." It just describes him. One of the six silliest asses in England, I should think he must be.'

I did not speak. I was endeavouring to adjust the faculties, which were in urgent need of a bit of first-aid treatment.

I mean to say, all this had come as a complete surprise. In formulating the well-laid plan which I had just been putting into effect, the one contingency I had not budgeted for was that she might adhere to the sentiments which I expressed. I had braced myself for a gush of stormy emotion. I was expecting the tearful ticking off, the girlish recriminations and all the rest of the bag of tricks along those lines.

But this cordial agreement with my remarks I had not foreseen, and it gave me what you might call pause for thought.

She proceeded to develop her theme, speaking in ringing, enthusiastic tones, as if she loved the topic. Jeeves could tell you the word I want. I think it's 'ecstatic', unless that's the sort of rash you get on your face and have to use ointment for. But if that is the right word, then that's what her manner was as she ventilated the subject of poor old Tuppy. If you had been able to go simply by the sound of her voice, she might have been a court poet cutting loose about an Oriental monarch, or Gussie Fink-Nottle describing his last consignment of newts.

'It's so nice, Bertie, talking to somebody who really takes a sensible view about this man Glossop. Mother says he's a good chap, which is simply absurd. Anybody can see that he's absolutely impossible. He's conceited and opinionative and argues all the time, even when he knows perfectly well that he's talking through his hat, and he smokes too much and eats too much and drinks too much, and I don't like the colour of his hair. Not that he'll have any hair in a year or two, because he's pretty thin on the top already, and before he knows where he is he'll be as bald as an egg, and he's the last man who can afford to go bald. And I think it's simply disgusting, the way he gorges all the time. Do you know, I found him in the larder at one o'clock this morning, absolutely wallowing in a steak-and-kidney pie? There was hardly any of it left. And you remember what an enormous dinner he had. Quite disgusting, I call it. But I can't stop out here all night, talking about men who aren't worth wasting a word on and haven't even enough sense to tell sharks from flatfish. I'm going in.'

And gathering about her slim shoulders the shawl which she had put on as a protection against the evening dew, she buzzed off, leaving me alone in the silent night.

Well, as a matter of fact, not absolutely alone, because a few moments later there was a sort of upheaval in the bushes in front of me, and Tuppy emerged.

15

I gave him the eye. The evening had begun to draw in a bit by now and the visibility, in consequence, was not so hot, but there still remained ample light to enable me to see him clearly. And what I saw convinced me that I should be a lot easier in my mind with a stout rustic bench between us. I rose, accordingly, modelling my style on that of a rocketing pheasant, and proceeded to deposit myself on the other side of the object named.

My prompt agility was not without its effect. He seemed somewhat taken aback. He came to a halt, and, for about the space of time required to allow a bead of persp. to trickle from the top of the brow to the tip of the nose, stood gazing at me in silence.

'So!' he said at length, and it came as a complete surprise to me that fellows ever really do say 'So!' I had always thought it was just a thing you read in books. Like 'Quotha!' I mean to say, or 'Odds bodikins!' or even 'Eh, ba goom!'

Still, there it was. Quaint or not quaint, bizarre or not bizarre, he had said 'So!' and it was up to me to cope with the situation on those lines.

It would have been a duller man than Bertram Wooster who had failed to note that the dear old chap was a bit steamed up. Whether his eyes were actually shooting forth flame, I couldn't tell you, but there appeared to me to be a distinct incandescence. For the rest, his fists were clenched, his ears quivering, and the muscles of his jaw rotating rhythmically, as if he were making an early supper of something.

His hair was full of twigs, and there was a beetle hanging to the side of his head which would have interested Gussie Fink-Nottle. To this, however, I paid scant attention. There is a time for studying beetles and a time for not studying beetles.

'So!' he said again.

Now, those who know Bertram Wooster best will tell you that he is always at his shrewdest and most level-headed in moments of peril. Who was it who, when gripped by the arm of the law on boat-race night not so many years ago and hauled off to Vine Street police station, assumed in a flash the identity of Eustace H. Plimsoll, of The Laburnums, Alleyn Road, West Dulwich, thus saving the grand old name of Wooster from being dragged in the mire and avoiding wide publicity of the wrong sort? Who was it . . .

But I need not labour the point. My record speaks for itself. Three times pinched, but never once sentenced under the correct label. Ask anyone at the Drones about this.

So now, in a situation threatening to become every moment more scaly, I did not lose my head. I preserved the old sang-froid. Smiling a genial and affectionate smile, and hoping that it wasn't too dark for it to register, I spoke with a jolly cordiality:

'Why, hallo, Tuppy. You here?'

He said, yes, he was here.

'Been here long?'

'I have.'

'Fine. I wanted to see you.'

'Well, here I am. Come out from behind that bench.'

'No, thanks, old man. I like leaning on it. It seems to rest the spine.'

'In about two seconds,' said Tuppy, 'I'm going to kick your spine up through the top of your head.'

I raised the eyebrows. Not much good, of course, in that light, but it seemed to help the general composition.

'Is this Hildebrand Glossop speaking?' I said.

He replied that it was, adding that if I wanted to make sure I might move a few feet over in his direction. He also called me an opprobrious name.

I raised the eyebrows again.

'Come, come, Tuppy, don't let us let this little chat become acrid. Is "acrid" the word I want?'

'I couldn't say,' he replied, beginning to sidle round the bench.

I saw that anything I might wish to say must be said quickly. Already he had sidled some six feet. And though, by dint of sidling, too, I had managed to keep the bench between us, who could predict how long this happy state of affairs would last?

I came to the point, therefore.

'I think I know what's on your mind, Tuppy,' I said. 'If you were in those bushes during my conversation with the recent Angela, I dare say you heard what I was saying about you.'

'I did.'

'I see. Well, we won't go into the ethics of the thing. Eavesdropping, some people might call it, and I can imagine stern critics drawing in the breath to some extent. Considering it – I don't want to hurt your feelings, Tuppy – but considering it un-English. A bit un-English, Tuppy, old man, you must admit.'

'I'm Scottish.'

'Really?' I said. 'I never knew that before. Rummy how you don't suspect a man of being Scottish unless he's Mac-something and says "Och, aye" and things like that. I wonder,' I went on, feeling that an academic discussion on some neutral topic might ease the tension, 'if you can tell me something that has puzzled me a good deal. What exactly is it that they put into haggis? I've often wondered about that.'

From the fact that his only response to the question was to leap over the bench and make a grab at me, I gathered that his mind was not on haggis.

'However,' I said, leaping over the bench in my turn, 'that is a side issue. If, to come back to it, you were in those bushes and heard what I was saying about you – '

He began to move round the bench in a nor'-nor'-easterly direction. I followed his example, setting a course sou'-sou'-west.

'No doubt you were surprised at the way I was talking.'

'Not a bit'

'What? Did nothing strike you as odd in the tone of my remarks?'

'It was just the sort of stuff I should have expected a treacherous, sneaking hound like you to say.'

'My dear chap,' I protested, 'this is not your usual form. A bit slow in the uptake, surely? I should have thought you would have spotted right away that it was all part of a well-laid plan.'

'I'll get you in a jiffy,' said Tuppy, recovering his balance after a swift clutch at my neck. And so probable did this seem that I delayed no longer, but hastened to place all the facts before him.

Speaking rapidly and keeping moving, I related my emotions on receipt of Aunt Dahlia's telegram, my instant rush to the scene of the disaster, my meditations in the car, and the eventual framing of this well-laid plan of mine. I spoke clearly and well, and it was with considerable concern, consequently, that I heard him observe – between clenched teeth, which made it worse – that he didn't believe a damned word of it.

'But, Tuppy,' I said, 'why not? To me the thing rings

true to the last drop. What makes you sceptical? Confide in me, Tuppy.'

He halted and stood taking a breather. Tuppy, pungently though Angela might have argued to the contrary, isn't really fat. During the winter months you will find him constantly booting the football with merry shouts, and in the summer the tennis racket is seldom out of his hand.

But at the recently concluded evening meal, feeling, no doubt, that after that painful scene in the larder there was nothing to be gained by further abstinence, he had rather let himself go and, as it were, made up leeway; and after really immersing himself in one of Anatole's dinners, a man of his sturdy build tends to lose elasticity a bit. During the exposition of my plans for his happiness a certain animation had crept into this round-and-round-the-mulberry-bush jamboree of ours – so much so, indeed, that for the last few minutes we might have been a rather oversized greyhound and a somewhat slimmer electric hare doing their stuff on a circular track for the entertainment of the many-headed.

This, it appeared, had taken it out of him a bit, and I was not displeased. I was feeling the strain myself, and welcomed a lull.

'It absolutely beats me why you don't believe it,' I said. 'You know we've been pals for years. You must be aware that, except at the moment when you caused me to do a nose dive into the Drones's swimming bath, an incident which I long since decided to put out of my mind and let the dead past bury its dead about, if you follow what I mean – except on that one occasion, as I say, I have always regarded you with the utmost esteem. Why, then, if not for the motives I have outlined, should I knock you to Angela? Answer me that. Be very careful.'

'What do you mean, be very careful?'

Well, as a matter of fact, I didn't quite know myself. It was what the magistrate had said to me on the occasion when I stood in the dock as Eustace Plimsoll, of The Laburnums: and as it had impressed me a good deal of the time, I just bunged it in now by way of giving the conversation a tone.

'All right. Never mind about being careful, then. Just answer me that question. Why, if I had not your interests sincerely at heart, should I have ticked you off, as stated?'

A sharp spasm shook him from base to apex. The beetle, which, during the recent exchanges, had been clinging to his head, hoping for the best, gave it up at this and resigned office. It shot off and was swallowed in the night.

'Ah!' I said. 'Your beetle,' I explained. 'No doubt you were unaware of it, but all this while there has been a beetle of sorts parked on the side of your head. You have now dislodged it.'

He snorted.

'Beetles!'

'Not beetles. One beetle only.'

'I like your crust!' cried Tuppy, vibrating like one of Gussie's newts during the courting season. 'Talking of beetles, when all the time you know you're a treacherous, sneaking hound.'

It was a debatable point, of course, why treacherous, sneaking hounds should be considered ineligible to talk about beetles, and I dare say a good cross-examining counsel would have made quite a lot of it.

But I let it go.

'That's the second time you've called me that. And,' I said firmly, 'I insist on an explanation. I have told you that I acted throughout from the best and kindliest motives in roasting you to Angela. It cut me to the quick to have to speak like that, and only the recollection of our lifelong friendship would have made me do it. And now you say you don't believe me and call me names for which I am not sure I couldn't have you up before a beak and jury and mulct you in very substantial damages. I should have to consult my solicitor, of course, but it would surprise me very much if an action did not lie. Be reasonable, Tuppy. Suggest another motive I could have had. Just one.'

'I will. Do you think I don't know? You're in love with Angela yourself.'

'What?'

'And you knocked me in order to poison her mind against me and finally remove me from your path.'

I had never heard anything so absolutely loopy in my life. Why, dash it, I've known Angela since she was so high. You don't fall in love with close relations you've known since they were so high. Besides, isn't there something in the book of rules about a man may not marry his cousin? Or am I thinking of grandmothers?

'Tuppy, my dear old ass,' I cried, 'this is pure banana oil! You've come unscrewed.'

'Oh, yes?'

'Me in love with Angela? Ha-ha?'

'You can't get out of it with ha-has. She called you "darling".'

'I know. And I disapproved. This habit of the younger g. of scattering "darlings" about like birdseed is one that I deprecate. Lax, is how I should describe it.'

'You tickled her ankles.'

'In a purely cousinly spirit. It didn't mean a thing. Why, dash it, you must know that in the deeper and true sense I wouldn't touch Angela with a barge pole.'

'Oh? And why not? Not good enough for you?'

'You misunderstand me,' I hastened to reply. 'When I say I wouldn't touch Angela with a barge pole, I intend merely to convey that my feelings towards her are those of distant, though cordial, esteem. In other words, you may rest assured that between this young prune and myself there never has been and never could be any sentiment warmer and stronger than that of ordinary friendship.'

'I believe it was you who tipped her off that I was in the larder last night, so that she could find me there with that pie, thus damaging my prestige.'

'My dear Tuppy! A Wooster?' I was shocked. 'You think a Wooster would do that?'

He breathed heavily.

'Listen,' he said. 'It's no good your standing there arguing. You can't get away from the facts. Somebody stole her from me at Cannes. You told me yourself that she was with you all the time at Cannes and hardly saw anybody else. You gloated over the mixed bathing, and those moonlight walks you had together – '

'Not gloated. Just mentioned them.'

'So now you understand why, as soon as I can get you clear of this damned bench, I am going to tear you limb from limb. Why they have these bally benches in gardens,' said Tuppy discontentedly, 'is more than I can see. They only get in the way.'

He ceased, and, grabbing out, missed me by a hair's breadth.

It was a moment for swift thinking, and it is at such moments, as I have already indicated, that Bertram Wooster is at his best. I suddenly remembered the recent misunderstanding with the Bassett, and with a flash of clear vision saw that this was where it was going to come in handy.

'You've got it all wrong, Tuppy,' I said, moving to the left. 'True, I saw a lot of Angela, but my dealings with her were on a basis from start to finish of the purest and most wholesome camaraderie. I can prove it. During that sojourn in Cannes my affections were engaged elsewhere.'

'What?'

'Engaged elsewhere. My affections. During that sojourn.'

I had struck the right note. He stopped sidling. His clutching hand fell to his side.

'Is that true?'

'Quite official.'

'Who was she?'

'My dear Tuppy, does one bandy a woman's name?'

'One does if one doesn't want one's ruddy head pulled off.'

I saw that it was a special case.

'Madeline Bassett,' I said.

'Who?'

'Madeline Bassett.'

He seemed stunned

'You stand there and tell me you were in love with that Bassett disaster?'

'I wouldn't call her "that Bassett disaster", Tuppy. Not respectful.'

'Dash being respectful. I want the facts. You deliberately assert that you loved that weird Gawd-help-us?'

'I don't see why you should call her a weird Gawd-help-us, either. A very charming and beautiful girl. Odd in some of her views perhaps – one does not quite see eye to eye with her in the matter of stars and rabbits – but not a weird Gawd-help-us.'

'Anyway, you stick to it that you were in love with her?'

'I do.'

'It sounds thin to me, Wooster, very thin.'

I saw that it would be necessary to apply the finishing touch.

'I must ask you to treat this as entirely confidential,

Glossop, but I may as well inform you that it is not twenty-four hours since she turned me down.'

'Turned you down?'

'Like a bedspread. In this very garden.'

'Twenty-four hours?'

'Call it twenty-five. So you will readily see that I can't be the chap, if any, who stole Angela from you at Cannes.'

And I was on the brink of adding that I wouldn't touch Angela with a barge pole, when I remembered I had said it already and it hadn't gone frightfully well. I desisted, therefore.

My manly frankness seemed to be producing good results. The homicidal glare was dying out of Tuppy's eyes. He had the aspect of a hired assassin who had paused to think things over.

'I see,' he said, at length. 'All right, then. Sorry you were troubled.'

'Don't mention it, old man,' I responded courteously.

For the first time since the bushes had begun to pour forth Glossops, Bertram Wooster could be said to have breathed freely. I don't say I actually came out from behind the bench, but I did let go of it, and with something of the relief which those three chaps in the Old Testament must have experienced after sliding out of the burning fiery furnace, I even groped tentatively for my cigarette case.

The next moment a sudden snort made me take my fingers off it as if it had bitten me. I was distressed to note in the old friend a return of the recent frenzy.

'What the hell did you mean by telling her that I used to be covered with ink when I was a kid?'

'My dear Tuppy – '

'I was almost finickingly careful about my personal cleanliness as a boy. You could have eaten your dinner off me.'

'Quite. But – '

'And all that stuff about having no soul. I'm crawling with soul. And being looked on as outsider at the Drones – '

'But, my dear old chap, I explained that. It was all part of my ruse or scheme.'

'It was, was it? Well, in future do me a favour and leave me out of your foul ruses.'

'Just as you say, old boy.'

'All right, then. That's understood.'

He relapsed into silence, standing with folded arms, staring before him rather like a strong, silent man in a novel when he's just been given the bird by the girl and is thinking of looking in at the Rocky Mountains and bumping off a few bears. His manifest pippedness excited my compash, and I ventured a kindly word.

'I don't suppose you know what *au pied de la lettre* means, Tuppy, but that's how I don't think you ought to take all that stuff Angela was saying just now too much.'

He seemed interested.

'What the devil,' he asked, 'are you talking about?'

I saw that I should have to make myself clearer.

'Don't take all that guff of hers too literally, old man. You know what girls are like.'

'I do,' he said, with another snort that came straight up from his insteps. 'And I wish I'd never met one.'

'I mean to say, it's obvious that she must have spotted you in those bushes and was simply talking to score off you. There you were, I mean, if you follow the psychology, and she saw you, and in that impulsive way girls have, she seized the opportunity of ribbing you a bit – just told you a few home truths, I mean to say.'

'Home truths?'

'That's right.'

He snorted once more, causing me to feel rather like

royalty receiving a twenty-one gun salute from the fleet. I can't remember ever having met a better right-and-left hand snorter.

'What do you mean, "home truths"? I'm not fat.'

'No, no.'

'And what's wrong with the colour of my hair?'

'Quite in order, Tuppy, old man. The hair, I mean.'

'And I'm not a bit thin on top . . . What the dickens are you grinning about?'

'Not grinning. Just smiling slightly. I was conjuring up a sort of vision, if you know what I mean, of you as seen through Angela's eyes. Fat in the middle and thin on the top. Rather funny.'

'You think it funny, do you?'

'Not a bit.'

'You'd better not.'

'Quite.'

It seemed to me that the conversation was becoming difficult again. I wished it could be terminated. And so it was. For at this moment something came shimmering through the laurels in the quiet evenfall, and I perceived that it was Angela.

She was looking sweet and saintlike, and she had a plate of sandwiches in her hand. Ham, I was to discover later.

'If you see Mr Glossop anywhere, Bertie,' she said, her eyes resting dreamily on Tuppy's façade, 'I wish you would give him these. I'm so afraid he may be hungry, poor fellow. It's nearly ten o'clock, and he hasn't eaten a morsel since dinner. I'll just leave them on this bench.'

She pushed off, and it seemed to me that I might as well go with her. Nothing to keep me here, I mean. We moved towards the house, and presently from behind us there sounded in the night the splintering crash of a well-kicked plate of ham sandwiches, accompanied by the muffled oaths of a strong man in his wrath.

'How still and peaceful everything is,' said Angela.

16

Sunshine was gilding the grounds of Brinkley Court and the ear detected a marked twittering of birds in the ivy outside the window when I woke next morning to a new day. But there was no corresponding sunshine in Bertram Wooster's soul and no answering twitter in his heart as he sat up in bed, sipping his cup of strengthening tea. It could not be denied that to Bertram, reviewing the happenings of the previous night, the Tuppy-Angela situation seemed more or less to have slipped a cog. With every desire to look for the silver lining, I could not but feel that the rift between these two haughty spirits had now reached such impressive proportions that the task of bridging same would be beyond even my powers.

I am a shrewd observer, and there had been something in Tuppy's manner as he booted that plate of ham sandwiches that seemed to tell me that he would not lightly forgive.

In these circs., I deemed it best to shelve their problem for the nonce and turn the mind to the matter of Gussie, which presented a brighter picture.

With regard to Gussie, everything was in train. Jeeves's morbid scruples about lacing the chap's orange juice had put me to a good deal of trouble, but I had surmounted every obstacle in the old Wooster way. I had secured an abundance of the necessary spirit, and it was now lying in its flask in the drawer of the dressing table. I had also ascertained that the jug, duly filled, would be standing on a shelf in the butler's pantry round about the hour of one. To remove it from that shelf, sneak it up to my room, and return it, laced, in good time for the midday meal would be a task calling, no doubt, for address, but in no sense an exacting one.

It was with something of the emotions of one preparing a treat for a deserving child that I finished my tea and rolled over for that extra spot of sleep which just makes all the difference when there is man's work to be done and the brain must be kept clear for it.

And when I came downstairs an hour or so later, I knew how right I had been to formulate this scheme for Gussie's bucking up. I ran into him on the lawn, and I could see at a glance that if ever there was a man who needed a snappy stimulant, it was he. All nature, as I have indicated, was smiling, but not Augustus Fink-Nottle. He was walking round in circles, muttering something about not proposing to detain us long, but on this auspicious occasion feeling compelled to say a few words.

'Ah, Gussie,' I said, arresting him as he was about to start another lap. 'A lovely morning, is it not?'

Even if I had not been aware of it already, I could have divined from the abruptness with which he damned the lovely morning that he was not in merry mood. I addressed myself to the task of bringing the roses back to his cheeks.

'I've got good news for you, Gussie.'

He looked at me with a sudden sharp interest.

'Has Market Snodsbury Grammar School burned down?'

'Not that I know of.'

'Have mumps broken out? Is the place closed on account of measles?'

'No, no.'

'Then what do you mean you've got good news?'

I endeavoured to soothe.

'You mustn't take it so hard, Gussie. Why worry about a laughably simple job like distributing prizes at a school?'

'Laughably simple, eh? Do you realize I've been sweating for days and haven't been able to think of a thing to say yet, except that I won't detain them long. You bet I won't detain them long. I've been timing my speech, and it lasts five seconds. What the devil am I to say, Bertie? What do you say when you're distributing prizes?'

I considered. Once, at my private school, I had won a prize for Scripture knowledge, so I suppose I ought to have been full of inside stuff. But memory eluded me.

Then something emerged from the mists.

'You say the race is not always to the swift.'

'Why?'

'Well, it's a good gag. It generally gets a hand.'

'I mean, why isn't it? Why isn't the race to the swift?'

'Ah, there you have me. But the nibs say it isn't.'

'But what does it mean?'

'I take it it's supposed to console the chaps who haven't won prizes.'

'What's the good of that to me? I'm not worrying about them. It's the ones that have won prizes that I'm worrying about, the little blighters who will come up on the platform. Suppose they make faces at me.'

'They won't.'

'How do you know they won't? It's probably the first thing they'll think of. And even if they don't – Bertie, shall I tell you something?'

'What?'

'I've a good mind to take that tip of yours and have a drink.'

I smiled. He little knew, about summed up what I was thinking.

'Oh, you'll be all right,' I said again.

He became fevered again.

'How do you know I'll be all right? I'm sure to blow up in my lines.'

'Tush!'

'Or drop a prize.'

'Tut!'

'Or something. I can feel it in my bones. As sure as I'm standing here, something is going to happen this afternoon which will make everybody laugh themselves sick at me. I can hear them now. Like hyenas . . . Bertie!'

'Hullo?'

'Do you remember that kids' school we went to before Eton?'

'Quite. It was there I won my Scripture prize.'

'Never mind about your Scripture prize. I'm not talking about your Scripture prize. Do you recollect the Bosher incident?'

I did, indeed. It was one of the high spots of my youth.

'Major-General Sir Wilfred Bosher came to distribute the prizes at that school,' proceeded Gussie in a dull, toneless voice. 'He dropped a book. He stooped to pick it up. And, as he stooped, his trousers split up the back.'

'How we roared!'

Gussie's face twisted.

'We did, little swine that we were. Instead of remaining silent and exhibiting a decent sympathy for a gallant officer at a peculiarly embarrassing moment, we howled and yelled with mirth. I loudest of any. That is what will happen to me this afternoon, Bertie. It will be a judgment on me for laughing like that at Major-General Sir Wilfred Bosher.'

'No, no, Gussie, old man. Your trousers won't split.'

'How do you know they won't? Better men than I have split their trousers. General Bosher was a DSO, with a fine record of service on the north-western frontier of India, and his trousers split. I shall be a mockery and a scorn. I know it. And you, fully cognizant of what I am in for, come babbling about good news. What news could possibly be good to me at this moment except the information that bubonic plague had broken out among the scholars of Market Snodsbury Grammar School, and that they were all confined to their beds with spots?'

The moment had come for me to speak. I laid a hand gently on his shoulder. He brushed it off. I laid it on again. He brushed it off once more. I was endeavouring to lay it on for the third time, when he moved aside and desired, with a certain petulance, to be informed if I thought I was a ruddy osteopath.

I found his manner trying, but one has to make allowances. I was telling myself that I should be seeing a very different Gussie after lunch.

'When I said I had good news, old man, I meant about Madeline Bassett.'

The febrile gleam died out of his eyes, to be replaced by a look of infinite sadness.

'You can't have good news about her. I've dished myself there completely.'

'Not at all. I am convinced that if you take another whack at her, all will be well.'

And, keeping it snappy, I related what had passed between the Bassett and myself on the previous night.

'So all you have to do is play a return date, and you cannot fail to swing the voting. You are her dream man.'

He shook his head.

'No.'

'What?'

'No use.'

'What do you mean?'

'Not a bit of good trying.'

'But I tell you she said in so many words – '

'It doesn't make any difference. She may have loved me once. Last night will have killed all that.'

'Of course it won't.'

'It will. She despises me now.'

'Not a bit of it. She knows you simply got cold feet.'

'And I should get cold feet if I tried again. It's no good, Bertie. I'm hopeless, and there's an end of it. Fate made me the sort of chap who can't say "boo" to a goose.'

'It isn't a question of saying "boo" to a goose. The point doesn't arise at all. It is simply a matter of – '

'I know, I know. But it's no good. I can't do it. The whole thing is off. I am not going to risk a repetition of last night's fiasco. You talk in a light way of taking another whack at her, but you don't know what it means. You have not been through the experience of starting to ask the girl you love to marry you and then suddenly finding yourself talking about the plumlike external gills of the newly born newt. It's not a thing you can do twice. No, I accept my destiny. It's all over. And now, Bertie, like a good chap, shove off. I want to compose my speech. I can't compose my speech with you mucking around. If you are going to continue to muck around, at least give me a couple of stories. The little hell hounds are sure to expect a story or two.'

'Do you know the one about – '

'No good. I don't want any of your off-colour stuff from the Drones's smoking room. I need something clean. Something that will be a help to them in their after lives. Not that I care a damn about their after lives, except that I hope they'll all choke.'

'I heard a story the other day. I can't quite remember

it, but it was about a chap who snored and disturbed the neighbours, and it ended, "It was his adenoids that adenoid them." '

He made a weary gesture.

'You expect me to work that in, do you, into a speech to be delivered to an audience of boys, every one of whom is probably riddled with adenoids? Damn it, they'd rush the platform. Leave me, Bertie. Push off. That's all I ask you to do. Push off . . . Ladies and gentlemen,' said Gussie, in a low, soliloquizing sort of way, 'I do not propose to detain this auspicious occasion long – '

It was a thoughtful Wooster who walked away and left him at it. More than ever I was congratulating myself on having had the sterling good sense to make all my arrangements so that I could press a button and set things moving at an instant's notice.

Until now, you see, I had rather entertained a sort of hope that when I had revealed to him the Bassett's mental attitude, Nature would have done the rest, bracing him up to such an extent that artificial stimulants would not be required. Because, naturally, a chap doesn't want to have to spring about country houses lugging jugs of orange juice, unless it is absolutely essential.

But now I saw that I must carry on as planned. The total absence of pep, ginger, and the right spirit which the man had displayed during these conversational exchanges convinced me that the strongest measures would be necessary. Immediately upon leaving him, therefore, I proceeded to the pantry, waited till the butler had removed himself elsewhere, and nipped in and secured the vital jug. A few moments later, after a wary passage of the stairs, I was in my room. And the first thing I saw there was Jeeves, fooling about with trousers.

He gave the jug a look which – wrongly, as it was to turn out – I diagnosed as censorious. I drew myself up a bit. I intended to have no rot from the fellow.

'Yes, Jeeves?'

'Sir?'

'You have the air of one about to make a remark, Jeeves.'

'Oh, no, sir. I note that you are in possession of Mr Fink-Nottle's orange juice. I was merely about to observe that in my opinion it would be injudicious to add spirit to it.'

'That is a remark, Jeeves, and it is precisely – '

'Because I have already attended to the matter, sir.'

'What?'

'Yes, sir. I decided, after all, to acquiesce in your wishes.'

I stared at the man, astounded. I was deeply moved. Well, I mean, wouldn't any chap who had been going about thinking that the old feudal spirit was dead and then suddenly found it wasn't have been deeply moved?

'Jeeves,' I said, 'I am touched.'

'Thank you, sir.'

'Touched and gratified.'

'Thank you very much, sir.'

'But what caused this change of heart?'

'I chanced to encounter Mr Fink-Nottle in the garden, sir, while you were still in bed, and we had a brief conversation.'

'And you came away feeling that he needed a bracer?'

'Very much so, sir. His attitude struck me as defeatist.'

I nodded.

'I felt the same. "Defeatist" sums it up to a nicety. Did you tell him his attitude struck you as defeatist?'

'Yes, sir.'

'But it didn't do any good?'

'No, sir.'

'Very well, then, Jeeves. We must act. How much gin did you put in the jug?'

'A liberal tumblerful, sir.'

'Would that be a normal dose for an adult defeatist, do you think?'

'I fancy it should prove adequate, sir.'

'I wonder. We must not spoil the ship for a ha'porth of tar. I think I'll add just another fluid ounce or so.'

'I would not advocate it, sir. In the case of Lord Brancaster's parrot – '

'You are falling into your old error, Jeeves, of thinking that Gussie is a parrot. Fight against this. I shall add the oz.'

'Very good, sir.'

'And, by the way, Jeeves, Mr Fink-Nottle is in the market for bright, clean stories to use in his speech. Do you know any?'

'I know a story about two Irishmen, sir.'

'Pat and Mike?'

'Yes, sir.'

'Who were walking along Broadway?'

'Yes, sir.'

'Just what he wants. Any more?'

'No, sir.'

'Well, every little helps. You had better go and tell it to him.'

'Very good, sir.'

He passed from the room, and I unscrewed the flask and tilted into the jug a generous modicum of its contents. And scarcely had I done so, when there came to my ears the sound of footsteps without. I had only just time to shove the jug behind the photograph of Uncle Tom on the mantelpiece before the door opened and in came Gussie, curveting like a circus horse.

'What-ho, Bertie,' he said. 'What-ho, what-ho, what-ho, and again what-ho. What a beautiful world this is, Bertie. One of the nicest I ever met.'

I stared at him, speechless. We Woosters are as quick as lightning, and I saw at once that something had happened.

I mean to say, I told you about him walking round in circles. I recorded what passed between us on the lawn. And if I portrayed the scene with anything like adequate skill, the picture you will have retained of this Fink-Nottle will have been that of a nervous wreck, sagging at the knees, green about the gills, and picking feverishly at the lapels of his coat in an ecstasy of craven fear. In a word, defeatist. Gussie, during that interview, had, in fine, exhibited all the earmarks of one licked to a custard.

Vastly different was the Gussie who stood before me now. Self-confidence seemed to ooze from the fellow's every pore. His face was flushed, there was a jovial light in his eyes, the lips were parted in a swashbuckling smile. And when with a genial hand he sloshed me on the back before I could sidestep, it was as if I had been kicked by a mule.

'Well, Bertie,' he proceeded, as blithely as a linnet without a thing on his mind, 'you will be glad to hear that you were right. Your theory has been tested and proved correct. I feel like a fighting cock.'

My brain ceased to reel. I saw all.

'Have you been having a drink?'

'I have. As you advised. Unpleasant stuff. Like medicine. Burns your throat, too, and makes one as thirsty as the dickens. How anyone can mop it up, as you do, for pleasure, beats me. Still, I would be the last to deny that it tunes up the system. I could bite a tiger.'

'What did you have?'

'Whisky. At least, that was the label on the decanter, and I have no reason to suppose that a woman like your aunt – staunch, true-blue, British – would deliberately deceive the public. If she labels her decanters Whisky, then I consider that we know where we are.'

'A whisky and soda, eh? You couldn't have done better.'

'Soda?' said Gussie thoughtfully. 'I knew there was something I had forgotten.'

'Didn't you put any soda in it?'

'It never occurred to me. I just nipped into the dining room and drank out of the decanter.'

'How much?'

'Oh, about ten swallows. Twelve, maybe. Or fourteen. Say sixteen medium-sized gulps. Gosh, I'm thirsty.'

He moved over to the washstand and drank deeply out of the water bottle. I cast a covert glance at Uncle Tom's photograph behind his back. For the first time since it had come into my life, I was glad that it was so large. It hid its secret well. If Gussie had caught sight of that jug of orange juice, he would unquestionably have been on to it like a knife.

'Well, I'm glad you're feeling braced,' I said.

He moved buoyantly from the washstand, and endeavoured to slosh me on the back again. Foiled by my nimble footwork, he staggered to the bed and sat down upon it.

'Braced? Did I say I could bite a tiger?'

'You did.'

'Make it two tigers. I could chew holes in a steel door. What an ass you must have thought me out there in the garden. I see now you were laughing in your sleeve.

'No, no.'

'Yes,' insisted Gussie. 'That very sleeve,' he said, pointing. 'And I don't blame you. I can't imagine why I made all that fuss about a potty job like distributing prizes at a rotten little country grammar school. Can you imagine, Bertie?'

'No.'

'Exactly. Nor can I imagine. There's simply nothing to it. I just shin up on the platform, drop a few gracious words, hand the little blighters their prizes, and hop down again, admired by all. Not a suggestion of split trousers from start to finish. I mean, why should anybody split his trousers? I can't imagine. Can you imagine?'

'No.'

'Nor can I imagine. I shall be a riot. I know just the sort of stuff that's needed – simple, manly, optimistic stuff straight from the shoulder. This shoulder,' said Gussie, tapping. 'Why I was so nervous this morning I can't imagine. For anything simpler than distributing a few footling books to a bunch of grimy-faced kids I can't imagine. Still, for some reason I can't imagine, I was feeling a little nervous, but now I feel fine, Bertie – fine, fine, fine – and I say this to you as an old friend. Because that's what you are, old man, when all the smoke has cleared away – an old friend. I don't think I've ever met an older friend. How long have you been an old friend of mine, Bertie?'

'Oh, years and years.'

'Imagine! Though, of course, there must have been a time when you were a new friend . . . Hallo, the luncheon gong. Come on, old friend.'

And, rising from the bed like a performing flea, he made for the door.

I followed rather pensively. What had occurred was, of course, so much velvet, as you might say. I mean, I had wanted a braced Fink-Nottle – indeed, all my plans had had a braced Fink-Nottle as their end and aim – but I found myself wondering a little whether the Fink-Nottle now sliding down the banister wasn't, perhaps, a shade too braced. His demeanour seemed to me that of a man who might quite easily throw bread about at lunch.

Fortunately, however, the settled gloom of those round him exercised a restraining effect upon him at the table. It would have needed a far more plastered man to have been rollicking at such a gathering. I had told the Bassett that there were aching hearts in Brinkley Court, and it now looked probable that there would shortly be aching tummies. Anatole, I learned, had retired to his bed with a fit of the vapours, and the meal now before us had been cooked by the kitchen maid – as C3 a performer as ever wielded a skillet.

This, coming on top of their other troubles, induced in the company a pretty unanimous silence – a solemn stillness, as you might say – which even Gussie did not seem prepared to break. Except, therefore, for one short snatch of song on his part, nothing untoward marked the occasion, and presently we rose, with instructions from Aunt Dahlia to put on festal raiment and be at Market Snodsbury not later than 3.30. This leaving me ample time to smoke a gasper or two in a shady bower beside the lake, I did so, repairing to my room round about the hour of three.

Jeeves was on the job, adding the final polish to the old topper, and I was about to apprise him of the latest developments in the matter of Gussie, when he forestalled me by observing that the latter had only just concluded an agreeable visit to the Wooster bedchamber.

'I found Mr Fink-Nottle seated here when I arrived to lay out your clothes, sir.'

'Indeed, Jeeves? Gussie was in here, was he?'

'Yes, sir. He left only a few moments ago. He is driving to the school with Mr and Mrs Travers in the large car.'

'Did you give him your story of the two Irishmen?'

'Yes, sir. He laughed heartily.'

'Good. Had you any other contributions for him?'

'I ventured to suggest that he might mention to the young gentlemen that education is a drawing out, not a putting in. The late Lord Brancaster was much addicted to presenting prizes at schools, and he invariably employed this dictum.'

'And how did he react to that?'

'He laughed heartily, sir.'

'This surprised you, no doubt? This practically incessant merriment, I mean.'

'Yes, sir.'

'You thought it odd in one who, when you last saw him, was well up in Group A of the defeatists.'

'Yes, sir.'

'There is a ready explanation, Jeeves. Since you last saw him, Gussie has been on a bender. He's as tight as an owl.'

'Indeed, sir?'

'Absolutely. His nerve cracked under the strain, and he sneaked into the dining room and started mopping the stuff up like a vacuum cleaner. Whisky would seem to be what he filled the radiator with. I gather that he used up most of the decanter. Golly, Jeeves, it's lucky he didn't get at that laced orange juice on top of that, what?'

'Extremely, sir.'

I eyed the jug. Uncle Tom's photograph had fallen into the fender, and it was standing there right out in the open, where Gussie couldn't have helped seeing it. Mercifully, it was empty now.

'It was a most prudent act on your part, if I may say so, sir, to dispose of the orange juice.'

I stared at the man.

'What? Didn't you?'

'No, sir.'

'Jeeves, let us get this clear. Was it not you who threw away that o.j.?'

'No, sir. I assumed, when I entered the room and found the pitcher empty, that you had done so.'

We looked at each other, awed. Two minds with but a single thought.

'I very much fear, sir – '

'So do I, Jeeves.'

'It would seem almost certain – '

'Quite certain. Weigh the facts. Sift the evidence. The jug was standing on the mantelpiece, for all eyes to behold. Gussie had been complaining of thirst. You found him in here, laughing heartily. I think that there can be little doubt, Jeeves, that the entire contents of that jug are at this moment reposing on top of the existing cargo in that already brilliantly lit man's interior. Disturbing, Jeeves.'

'Most disturbing, sir.'

'Let us face the position, forcing ourselves to be calm. You inserted in that jug – shall we say a tumblerful of the right stuff?'

'Fully a tumblerful, sir.'

'And I added of my plenty about the same amount.'

'Yes, sir.'

'And in two shakes of a duck's tail Gussie, with all that lapping about inside him, will be distributing the prizes at Market Snodsbury Grammar School before an audience of all that is fairest and most refined in the county.'

'Yes, sir.'

'It seems to me, Jeeves, that the ceremony may be one fraught with considerable interest.'

'Yes, sir.'

'What, in your opinion, will the harvest be?'

'One finds it difficult to hazard a conjecture, sir.'

'You mean imagination boggles?'

'Yes, sir.'

I inspected my imagination. He was right. It boggled.

17

'And yet, Jeeves,' I said, twiddling a thoughtful steering wheel, 'there is always the bright side.'

Some twenty minutes had elapsed, and, having picked the honest fellow up outside the front door, I was driving in the two-seater to the picturesque town of Market Snodsbury. Since we had parted – he to go to his lair and fetch his hat, I to remain in my room and complete the formal costume – I had been doing some close thinking.

The results of this I now proceeded to hand on to him.

'However dark the prospect may be, Jeeves, however murkily the storm clouds may seem to gather, a keen eye can usually discern the blue bird. It is bad, no doubt, that Gussie should be going, some ten minutes from now, to distribute prizes in a state of advanced intoxication, but we must never forget that these things cut both ways.'

'You imply, sir – '

'Precisely. I am thinking of him in his capacity as wooer. All this ought to have put him in rare shape for offering his hand in marriage. I shall be vastly surprised if it won't turn him into a sort of caveman. Have you ever seen James Cagney in the movies?'

'Yes, sir.'

'Something on those lines.'

I heard him cough, and sniped him with a sideways glance. He was wearing that informative look of his.

'Then you have not heard, sir?'

'Eh?'

'You are not aware that a marriage has been arranged and will shortly take place between Mr Fink-Nottle and Miss Bassett?'

'What?'

'Yes, sir.'

'When did this happen?'

'Shortly after Mr Fink-Nottle had left your room, sir.'

'Ah! In the post-orange-juice era?'

'Yes, sir.'

'But are you sure of your facts? How do you know?'

'My informant was Mr Fink-Nottle himself, sir. He appeared anxious to confide in me. His story was somewhat incoherent, but I had no difficulty in apprehending its substance. Prefacing his remarks with the statement that this was a beautiful world, he laughed heartily and said that he had become formally engaged.'

'No details?'

'No, sir.'

'But one can picture the scene.'

'Yes, sir.'

'I mean, imagination doesn't boggle.'

'No, sir.'

And it didn't. I could see exactly what must have happened. Insert a liberal dose of mixed spirits in a normally abstemious man, and he becomes a force. He does not stand around, twiddling his fingers and stammering. He acts. I had no doubt that Gussie must have reached for the Bassett and clasped her to him like a stevedore handling a sack of coals. And one could readily envisage the effect of that sort of thing on a girl of romantic mind.

'Well, well, well, Jeeves.'

'Yes, sir.'

'This is splendid news.'

'Yes, sir.'

'You see now how right I was.'

'Yes, sir.'

'It must have been rather an eye-opener for you, watching me handle this case.'

'Yes, sir.'

'The simple, direct method never fails.'

'No, sir.'

'Whereas the elaborate does.'

'Yes, sir.'

'Right ho, Jeeves.'

We had arrived at the main entrance of Market Snodsbury Grammar School. I parked the car, and went in, well content. True, the Tuppy-Angela problem still remained unsolved and Aunt Dahlia's five hundred quid seemed as far off as ever, but it was gratifying to feel that good old Gussie's troubles were over, at any rate.

The Grammar School at Market Snodsbury had, I understood, been built somewhere in the year 1416, and, as with so many of these ancient foundations, there still seemed to brood over its Great Hall, where the afternoon's festivities were to take place, not a little of the fug of the centuries. It was the hottest day of the summer, and though somebody had opened a tentative window or two, the atmosphere remained distinctive and individual.

In this hall the youth of Market Snodsbury had been eating its daily lunch for a matter of five hundred years, and the flavour lingered. The air was sort of heavy and languorous, if you know what I mean, with the scent of Young England and boiled beef and carrots.

Aunt Dahlia, who was sitting with a bevy of the local nibs in the second row, sighted me as I entered and waved to me to join her, but I was too smart for that.

I wedged myself in among the standees at the back, leaning up against a chap who from the aroma, might have been a corn chandler or something of that order. The essence of strategy on these occasions is to be as near the door as possible.

The hall was gaily decorated with flags and coloured paper, and the eye was further refreshed by the spectacle of a mixed drove of boys, parents, and what not, the former running a good deal to shiny faces and Eton collars, the latter stressing the black-satin note rather when female, and looking as if their coats were too tight, if male. And presently there was some applause – sporadic, Jeeves has since told me it was – and I saw Gussie being steered by a bearded bloke in a gown to a seat in the middle of the platform.

And I confess that as I beheld him and felt that there but for the grace of God went Bertram Wooster, a shudder ran through the frame. It all reminded me so vividly of the time I had addressed that girls' school.

Of course, looking at it dispassionately, you may say that for horror and peril there is no comparison between an almost human audience like the one before me and a mob of small girls with pigtails down their backs, and this, I concede, is true. Nevertheless, the spectacle was enough to make me feel like a fellow watching a pal going over Niagara Falls in a barrel, and the thought of what I had escaped caused everything for a moment to go black and swim before my eyes.

When I was able to see clearly once more, I perceived that Gussie was now seated. He had his hands on his knees, with his elbows out at right angles, like a negro minstrel of the old school about to ask Mr Bones why a chicken crosses the road, and he was staring before him with a smile so fixed and pebble-beached that I should have thought that anybody could have guessed that there sat one in whom the old familiar juice was splashing up against the back of the front teeth.

In fact, I saw Aunt Dahlia, who, having assisted at so many hunting dinners in her time, is second to none as a judge of the symptoms, give a start and gaze long and earnestly. And she was just saying something to Uncle Tom on her left when the bearded bloke stepped to the footlights and started making a speech. From the fact that he spoke as if he had a hot potato in his mouth without getting the raspberry from the lads in the ringside seats, I deduced that he must be the headmaster.

With his arrival in the spotlight, a sort of perspiring resignation seemed to settle on the audience. Personally, I snuggled up against the chandler and let my attention wander. The speech was on the subject of the doings of the school during the past term, and this part of a prize giving is always apt rather to fail to grip the visiting stranger. I mean, you know how it is. You're told that J. B. Brewster has won an Exhibition for Classics at Cat's, Cambridge, and you feel that it's one of those stories where you can't see how funny it is unless you really know the fellow. And the same applies to G. Bullett being awarded the Lady Jane Wix Scholarship at the Birmingham College of Veterinary Science.

In fact, I and the corn chandler, who was looking a bit fagged I thought, as if he had had a hard morning chandling the corn, were beginning to doze lightly when things suddenly brisked up, bringing Gussie into the picture for the first time.

'Today,' said the bearded bloke, 'we are all happy to welcome as the guest of the afternoon Mr Fitz-Wattle – '

At the beginning of the address, Gussie had subsided into a sort of daydream, with his mouth hanging open. About halfway through, faint signs of life had begun to show. And for the last few minutes he had been trying to cross one leg over the other and failing and having another shot and failing again. But only now did he exhibit any real animation. He sat up with a jerk.

'Fink-Nottle,' he said, opening his eyes.

'Fitz-Nottle.'

'Fink-Nottle.'

'I should say Fink-Nottle.'

'Of course you should, you silly ass,' said Gussie genially. 'All right, get on with it.'

And closing his eyes, he began trying to cross his legs again.

I could see that this little spot of friction had rattled the bearded bloke a bit. He stood for a moment fumbling at the fungus with a hesitating hand. But they make these headmasters of tough stuff. The weakness passed. He came back nicely and carried on.

'We are all happy, I say, to welcome as the guest of the afternoon Mr Fink-Nottle, who has kindly consented to award the prizes. This task, as you know, is one that should have devolved upon that well-beloved and vigorous member of our board of governors, the Rev. William Plomer, and we are all, I am sure, very sorry that illness at the last moment should have prevented him from being here today. But, if I may borrow a familiar metaphor from the – if I may employ a homely metaphor familiar to you all – what we lose on the swings we gain on the roundabouts.'

He paused, and beamed rather freely, to show that this was comedy. I could have told the man it was no use. Not a ripple. The corn chandler leaned against me and muttered 'Whoddidesay?' but that was all.

It's always a nasty jar to wait for the laugh and find that the gag hasn't got across. The bearded bloke was visibly discomposed. At that, however, I think he would have got by, had he not, at this juncture, unfortunately stirred Gussie up again.

'In other words, though deprived of Mr Plomer, we have with us this afternoon Mr Fink-Nottle. I am sure that Mr Fink-Nottle's name is one that needs no introduction to you. It is, I venture to assert, a name that is familiar to us all.'

'Not to you,' said Gussie.

And the next moment I saw what Jeeves had meant when he had described him as laughing heartily. 'Heartily' was absolutely the *mot juste*. It sounded like a gas explosion.

'You didn't seem to know it so dashed well, what, what?' said Gussie. And, reminded apparently by the word 'what' of the word 'Wattle,' he repeated the latter some sixteen times with a rising inflection.

'Wattle, Wattle, Wattle,' he concluded. 'Right-ho. Push on.'

But the bearded bloke had shot his bolt. He stood there, licked at last; and, watching him closely, I could see that he was now at the crossroads. I could spot what he was thinking as clearly as if he had confided it to my personal ear. He wanted to sit down and call it a day, I mean, but the thought that gave him pause was that, if he did, he must then either uncork Gussie or take the Fink-Nottle speech as read and get straight on to the actual prize giving.

It was a dashed tricky thing, of course, to have to decide on the spur of the moment. I was reading in the paper the other day about those birds who are trying to split the atom, the nub being that they haven't the foggiest as to what will happen if they do. It may be all right. On the other hand, it may not be all right. And pretty silly a chap would feel, no doubt, if, having split the atom, he suddenly found the house going up in smoke and himself torn limb from limb.

So with the bearded bloke. Whether he was abreast of the inside facts in Gussie's case, I don't know, but it was obvious to him by this time that he had run into something pretty hot. Trial gallops had shown that Gussie had his own way of doing things. Those interruptions had been enough to prove to the perspicacious that here, seated on the platform at the big binge of the season, was one who, if pushed forward to make a speech, might let himself go in a rather epoch-making manner.

On the other hand, chain him up and put a green-baize cloth over him, and where were you? The proceedings would be over about half an hour too soon.

It was, as I say, a difficult problem to have to solve, and, left to himself, I don't know what conclusion he would have come to. Personally, I think he would have played it safe. As it happened, however, the thing was taken out of his hands, for at this moment, Gussie, having stretched his arms and yawned a bit, switched on that pebble-beached smile again and tacked down to the edge of the platform.

'Speech,' he said affably.

He then stood with his thumbs in the armholes of his waistcoat, waiting for the applause to die down.

It was some time before this happened, for he had got a very fine hand indeed. I suppose it wasn't often that the boys of Market Snodsbury Grammar School came across a man public-spirited enough to call their headmaster a silly ass, and they showed their appreciation in no uncertain manner. Gussie may have been one over the eight, but as far as the majority of those present were concerned he was sitting on top of the world.

'Boys,' said Gussie, 'I mean ladies and gentlemen and boys, I do not detain you long, but I suppose on this occasion to feel compelled to say a few auspicious words. Ladies – and boys and gentlemen – we have all listened with interest to the remarks of our friend here who forgot to shave this morning – I don't know his name, but then he didn't know mine – Fitz-Wattle, I mean, absolutely absurd – which squares things up a bit – and we are all sorry that the Reverend What-ever-he-was-called should be dying of adenoids, but after all, here today, gone tomorrow, and all flesh is as grass, and what not, but that wasn't what I wanted to say. What I wanted to say was this – and I say it confidently – without fear of contradiction – I say, in short, I am happy to be here on this auspicious occasion, and I take much pleasure in kindly awarding the prizes, consisting of the handsome books you see laid out on that table. As Shakespeare says, there are sermons in books, stones in the running brooks, or, rather, the other way about, and there you have it in a nutshell.'

It went well, and I wasn't surprised. I couldn't quite follow some of it, but anybody could see that it was real ripe stuff, and I was amazed that even the course of treatment he had been taking could have rendered so normally tongue-tied a dumb brick as Gussie capable of it.

It just shows, what any Member of Parliament will tell you, that if you want real oratory, the preliminary noggin is essential. Unless pie-eyed, you cannot hope to grip.

'Gentlemen,' said Gussie, 'I mean ladies and gentlemen and, of course, boys, what a beautiful world this is. A beautiful world, full of happiness on every side. Let me tell you a little story. Two Irishmen, Pat and Mike, were walking along Broadway, and one said to the other, "Begorrah, the race is not always to the swift," and the other replied, "Faith and begob, education is a drawing out, not a putting in." '

I must say it seemed to me the rottenest story I had

ever heard, and I was surprised that Jeeves should have considered it worth while shoving into a speech. However, when I taxed him with this later, he said that Gussie had altered the plot a good deal, and I dare say that accounts for it.

At any rate, that was the *conte* as Gussie told it, and when I say that it got a very fair laugh, you will understand what a popular favourite he had become with the multitude. There might be a bearded bloke or so on the platform and a small section in the second row who were wishing the speaker would conclude his remarks and resume his seat, but the audience as a whole was for him solidly.

There was applause, and a voice cried: 'Hear, hear!'

'Yes,' said Gussie, 'it is a beautiful world. The sky is blue, the birds are singing, there is optimism everywhere. And why not, boys and ladies and gentlemen? I'm happy, you're happy, we're all happy, even the meanest Irishman that walks along Broadway. Though, as I say, there were two of them – Pat and Mike, one drawing out, the other putting in. I should like you boys, taking the time from me, to give three cheers for this beautiful world. All together now.'

Presently the dust settled down and the plaster stopped falling from the ceiling, and he went on.

'People who say it isn't a beautiful world don't know what they are talking about. Driving here in the car today to award the kind prizes, I was reluctantly compelled to tick off my host on this very point. Old Tom Travers. You will see him sitting there in the second row next to the large lady in beige.'

He pointed helpfully, and the hundred or so Market Snodsburyians who craned their necks in the direction indicated were able to observe Uncle Tom blushing prettily.

'I ticked him off properly, the poor fish. He expressed

the opinion that the world was in a deplorable state. I said, "Don't talk rot, old Tom Travers". "I am not accustomed to talk rot," he said. "Then, for a beginner," I said, "you do it dashed well." And I think you will admit, boys and ladies and gentlemen, that that was telling him.'

The audience seemed to agree with him. The point went big. The voice that had said, 'Hear, hear' said 'Hear, hear' again, and my corn chandler hammered the floor vigorously with a large-size walking stick.

'Well, boys,' resumed Gussie, having shot his cuffs and smirked horribly, 'this is the end of the summer term, and many of you, no doubt, are leaving the school. And I don't blame you, because there's a froust in here you could cut with a knife. You are going out into the great world. Soon many of you will be walking along Broadway. And what I want to impress upon you is that, however much you may suffer from adenoids, you must all use every effort to prevent yourselves becoming pessimists and talking rot like old Tom Travers. There in the second row. The fellow with a face rather like a walnut.'

He paused to allow those wishing to do so to refresh themselves with another look at Uncle Tom, and I found myself musing in some little perplexity. Long association with the members of the Drones has put me pretty well in touch with the various ways in which an overdose of the blushful Hippocrene can take the individual, but I had never seen anyone react quite as Gussie was doing.

There was a snap about his work which I had never witnessed before, even in Barmy Fotheringay-Phipps on New Year's Eve.

Jeeves, when I discussed the matter with him later, said it was something to do with inhibitions, if I caught the word correctly, and the suppression of, I think he said, the ego. What he meant, I gathered, was that, owing to the fact that Gussie had just completed a five-year-stretch of blameless seclusion among the newts, all the goofiness which ought to have been spread out thin over those five years and had been bottled up during that period came to the surface on this occasion in a lump – or, if you prefer to put it that way, like a tidal wave.

There may be something in this. Jeeves generally knows.

Anyway, be that as it may, I was dashed glad I had had the shrewdness to keep out of that second row. It might be unworthy of the prestige of a Wooster to squash in among the proletariat in the standing-room-only section, but at least, I felt, I was out of the danger zone. So thoroughly had Gussie got it up his nose by now that it seemed to me that had he sighted me he might have become personal about even an old school friend.

'If there's one thing in the world I can't stand,' proceeded Gussie, 'it's a pessimist. Be optimists, boys. You all know the difference between an optimist and a pessimist. An optimist is a man who – well, take the case of two Irishmen walking along Broadway. One is an optimist and one is a pessimist, just as one's name is Pat and the other's Mike . . . Why, hullo, Bertie; I didn't know you were here.'

Too late, I endeavoured to go to earth behind the chandler, only to discover that there was no chandler there. Some appointment, suddenly remembered – possibly a promise to his wife that he would be home to tea – had caused him to ooze away while my attention was elsewhere, leaving me right out in the open.

Between me and Gussie, who was now pointing in an offensive manner, there was nothing but a sea of interested faces looking up at me.

'Now, there,' boomed Gussie, continuing to point, 'is an instance of what I mean. Boys and ladies and gentlemen, take a good look at that object standing up there at the back – morning-coat, trousers as worn, quiet grey tie, and carnation in buttonhole – you can't miss him. Bertie Wooster, that is, and as foul a pessimist as ever bit a tiger. I tell you I despise that man. And why do I despise him? Because, boys and ladies and gentlemen, he is a pessimist. His attitude is defeatist. When I told him I was going to address you this afternoon, he tried to dissuade me. And do you know why he tried to dissuade me? Because he said my trousers would split up the back.'

The cheers that greeted this were the loudest yet. Anything about splitting trousers went straight to the simple hearts of the young scholars of Market Snodsbury Grammar School. Two in the row in front of me turned purple, and a small lad with freckles seated beside them asked me for my autograph.

'Let me tell you a story about Bertie Wooster.'

A Wooster can stand a good deal, but he cannot stand having his name bandied in a public place. Picking my feet up softly, I was in the very process of executing a quiet sneak for the door, when I perceived that the bearded bloke had at last decided to apply the closure.

Why he hadn't done so before is beyond me. Spellbound, I take it. And, of course, when a chap is going like a breeze with the public, as Gussie had been, it's not so dashed easy to chip in. However, the prospect of hearing another of Gussie's anecdotes seemed to have done the trick. Rising rather as I had risen from my bench at the beginning of that painful scene with Tuppy in the twilight, he made a leap for the table, snatched up a book and came bearing down on the speaker.

He touched Gussie on the arm, and Gussie, turning sharply and seeing a large bloke with a beard apparently about to bean him with a book, sprang back in an attitude of self-defence.

'Perhaps, as time is getting on, Mr Fink-Nottle, we had better – '

'Oh, ah,' said Gussie, getting the trend. He relaxed. 'The prizes, eh? Of course, yes. Right ho. Yes, might as well be shoving along with it. What's this one?'

'Spelling and dictation – P. K. Purvis,' announced the bearded bloke.

'Spelling and dictation – P. K. Purvis,' echoed Gussie, as if he were calling coals. 'Forward, P. K. Purvis.'

Now that the whistle had been blown on his speech, it seemed to me that there was no longer any need for the strategic retreat which I had been planning. I had no wish to tear myself away unless I had to. I mean, I had told Jeeves that this binge would be fraught with interest, and it was fraught with interest. There was a fascination about Gussie's methods which gripped and made one reluctant to pass the thing up provided personal innuendoes were steered clear of. I decided, accordingly, to remain, and presently there was a musical squeaking and P. K. Purvis climbed the platform.

The spelling-and-dictation champ was about three foot six in his squeaking shoes, with a pink face and sandy hair. Gussie patted his hair. He seemed to have taken an immediate fancy to the lad.

'You P. K. Purvis?'

'Sir, yes, sir.'

'It's a beautiful world, P. K. Purvis.'

'Sir, yes, sir.'

'Ah, you've noticed it, have you? Good. You married, by any chance?'

'Sir, no, sir.'

'Get married, P. K. Purvis,' said Gussie earnestly. 'It's the only life . . . Well, here's your book. Looks rather bilge to me from a glance at the title page, but, such as it is, here you are.'

P. K. Purvis squeaked off amidst sporadic applause, but one could not fail to note that the sporadic was followed by a rather strained silence. It was evident that Gussie was striking something of a new note in Market Snodsbury scholastic circles. Looks were exchanged between parent and parent. The bearded bloke had the air of one who has drained the bitter cup. As for Aunt Dahlia, her demeanour now told only too clearly that her last doubts had been resolved and her verdict was in. I saw her whisper to the Bassett, who sat on her right, and the Bassett nodded sadly and looked like a fairy about to shed a tear and add another star to the Milky Way.

Gussie, after the departure of P. K. Purvis, had fallen into a sort of daydream and was standing with his mouth open and his hands in his pockets. Becoming abruptly aware that a fat kid in knickerbockers was at his elbow, he started violently.

'Hullo!' he said, visibly shaken. 'Who are you?'

'This,' said the bearded bloke, 'Is R. V. Smethurst.'

'What's he doing here?' asked Gussie suspiciously.

'You are presenting him with the drawing prize, Mr Fink-Nottle.'

This apparently struck Gussie as a reasonable explanation. His face cleared.

'That's right, too,' he said . . . 'Well, here it is, cocky. You off?' he said, as the kid prepared to withdraw.

'Sir, yes, sir.'

'Wait, R. V. Smethurst. Not so fast. Before you go, there is a question I wish to ask you.'

But the bearded bloke's aim now seemed to be to rush the ceremonies a bit. He hustled R. V. Smethurst off stage rather like a chucker-out in a pub regretfully ejecting an old and respected customer, and started paging G. G. Simmons. A moment later the latter was up and coming, and conceive my emotion when it was announced that the subject on which he had clicked was Scripture knowledge. One of us, I mean to say.

G. G. Simmons was an unpleasant, perky-looking stripling, mostly front teeth and spectacles, but I gave him a big hand. We Scripture-knowledge sharks stick together.

Gussie, I was sorry to see, didn't like him. There was in his manner, as he regarded G. G. Simmons, none of the chumminess which had marked it during his interview with P. K. Purvis or, in a somewhat lesser degree, with R. V. Smethurst. He was cold and distant.

'Well, G. G. Simmons.'

'Sir, yes, sir.'

'What do you mean – sir, yes, sir? Dashed silly thing to say. So you've won the Scripture-knowledge prize, have you?'

'Sir, yes, sir.'

'Yes,' said Gussie, 'you look just the sort of little tick who would. And yet,' he said, pausing and eyeing the child keenly, 'how are we to know that this has all been open and above board? Let me test you, G. G. Simmons. What was What's-His-Name – the chap who begat Thingummy? Can you answer me that, Simmons?'

'Sir, no, sir.'

Gussie turned to the bearded bloke.

'Fishy,' he said. 'Very fishy. This boys appears to be totally lacking in Scripture knowledge.'

The bearded bloke passed a hand across his forehead.

'I can assure you, Mr Fink-Nottle, that every care was taken to ensure a correct marking and that Simmons outdistanced his competitors by a wide margin.'

'Well, if you say so,' said Gussie doubtfully. 'All right, G. G. Simmons, take your prize.'

'Sir, thank you, sir.'

'But let me tell you that there's nothing to stick on side about in winning a prize for Scripture knowledge. Bertie Wooster – '

I don't know when I've had a nastier shock. I had been going on the assumption that, now that they had stopped him making his speech, Gussie's fangs had been drawn, as you might say. To duck my head down and resume my edging toward the door was with me the work of a moment.

'Bertie Wooster won the Scripture-knowledge prize at a kids' school we were at together, and you know what he's like. But, of course, Bertie frankly cheated. He succeeded in scrounging that Scripture-knowledge trophy over the heads of better men by means of some of the rawest and most brazen swindling methods ever witnessed even at a school where such things were common. If that man's pockets, as he entered the examination room, were not stuffed to bursting point with lists of the kings of Judah – '

I heard no more. A moment later I was out in God's air, fumbling with a fevered foot at the self-starter of the old car.

The engine raced. The clutch slid into position. I tooted and drove off.

My ganglions were still vibrating as I ran the car into the stables of Brinkley Court, and it was a much shaken Bertram who tottered up to his room to change into something loose. Having donned flannels, I lay down on the bed for a bit, and I suppose I must have dozed off, for the next thing I remember is finding Jeeves at my side.

I sat up. 'My tea, Jeeves?'

'No, sir. It is nearly dinnertime.'

The mists cleared away.

'I must have been asleep.'

'Yes, sir.'

'Nature taking its toll of the exhausted frame.'

'Yes, sir.'

'And enough to make it.'

'Yes, sir.'

'And now it's nearly dinnertime, you say? All right. I am in no mood for dinner, but I suppose you had better lay out the clothes.'

'It will not be necessary, sir. The company will not be dressing tonight. A cold collation has been set out in the dining room.'

'Why's that?'

'It was Mrs Travers's wish that this should be done in order to minimize the work for the staff, who are attending a dance at Sir Percival Stretchley-Budd's residence tonight.'

'Of course, yes. I remember. My cousin Angela told me. Tonight's the night, what? You going, Jeeves?'

'No, sir. I am not very fond of this form of entertainment in the rural districts, sir.'

'I know what you mean. These country binges are all the same. A piano, one fiddle, and a floor like sandpaper. Is Anatole going? Angela hinted not.'

'Miss Angela was correct, sir. Monsieur Anatole is in bed.'

'Temperamental blighters, these Frenchmen.'

'Yes, sir.'

There was a pause.

'Well, Jeeves,' I said, 'it was certainly one of those afternoons, what?'

'Yes, sir.'

'I cannot recall one more packed with incident. And I left before the finish.'

'Yes, sir. I observed your departure.'

'You couldn't blame me for withdrawing.'

'No, sir. Mr Fink-Nottle had undoubtedly become embarrassingly personal.'

'Was there much more of it after I went?'

'No, sir. The proceedings were terminated very shortly. Mr Fink-Nottle's remarks with reference to Master G. G. Simmons brought about an early closure.'

'But he had finished his remarks about G. G. Simmons.'

'Only temporarily, sir. He resumed them immediately after your departure. If you recollect, sir, he had already proclaimed himself suspicious of Master Simmons's bona fides, and he now proceeded to deliver a violent verbal attack upon the young gentleman, asserting that it was impossible for him to have won the Scripture-knowledge prize without systematic cheating on an impressive scale. He went so far as to suggest that Master Simmons was well known to the police.'

'Golly, Jeeves!'

'Yes, sir. The words did create a considerable sensation. The reaction of those present to this accusation I should describe as mixed. The young students appeared pleased and applauded vigorously, but Master Simmons's mother rose from her seat and addressed Mr Fink-Nottle in terms of strong protest.'

'Did Gussie seem taken aback? Did he recede from his position?'

'No, sir. He said that he could see it all now, and hinted at a guilty liaison between Master Simmons's mother and the headmaster, accusing the latter of having cooked the marks, as his expression was, in order to gain favour with the former.'

'You don't mean that?'

'Yes, sir.'

'Egad, Jeeves! And then – '

'They sang the national anthem, sir,'

'Surely not?'

'Yes, sir.'

'At a moment like that?'

'Yes, sir.'

'Well, you were there and you know, of course, but I should have thought the last thing Gussie and this woman would have done in the circs. would have been to start singing duets.'

'You misunderstand me, sir. It was the entire company who sang. The headmaster turned to the organist and said something to him in a low tone. Upon which the latter began to play the national anthem, and the proceedings terminated.'

'I see. About time, too.'

'Yes, sir. Mrs Simmons's attitude had become unquestionably menacing.'

I pondered. What I had heard was, of course, of a nature to excite pity and terror, not to mention alarm and despondency, and it would be paltering with the truth to say that I was pleased about it. On the other hand, it was all over now, and it seemed to me that the thing to do was not to mourn over the past but to fix the mind on the bright future. I mean to say, Gussie might have lowered the existing Worcestershire record for goofiness and definitely forfeited all chance of becoming Market Snodsbury's favourite son, but you couldn't get away from the fact that he had proposed to Madeline Bassett, and you had to admit that she had accepted him.

I put this to Jeeves.

'A frightful exhibition,' I said, 'and one which will very possibly ring down history's pages. But we must not forget, Jeeves, that Gussie, though now doubtless looked upon in the neighbourhood as the world's worst freak, is all right otherwise.'

'No, sir.'

I did not quite get this.

'When you say "No, sir," do you mean "Yes, sir"?'

'No, sir. I mean "No, sir." '

'He is not all right otherwise?'

'No, sir.'

'But he is betrothed.'

'No longer, sir. Miss Bassett has severed the engagement.'

'You don't mean that.'

'Yes, sir.'

I wonder if you have noticed a rather peculiar thing about this chronicle. I allude to the fact that at one time or another practically everybody playing a part in it has had occasion to bury his or her face in his or her hands. I have participated in some pretty glutinous affairs in my time, but I think that never before or since have I been mixed up with such a solid body of brow clutchers.

Uncle Tom did it, if you remember. So did Gussie. So did Tuppy. So, probably, though I have no data, did Anatole, and I wouldn't put it past the Bassett. And Aunt Dahlia, I have no doubt, would have done it, too, but for the risk of disarranging the carefully fixed coiffure.

Well, what I am trying to say is that at this juncture I did it myself. Up went the hands and down went the head, and in another jiffy I was clutching as energetically as the best of them.

And it was while I was still massaging the coconut and wondering what the next move was that something barged up against the door like the delivery of a ton of coals.

'I think this may very possibly be Mr Fink-Nottle himself, sir,' said Jeeves.

His intuition, however, had led him astray. It was not Gussie but Tuppy. He came in and stood breathing asthmatically. It was plain that he was deeply stirred.

18

I eyed him narrowly. I didn't like his looks. Mark you, I don't say I ever had, much, because Nature, when planning this sterling fellow, shoved in a lot more lower jaw than was absolutely necessary and made the eyes a bit too keen and piercing for one who was neither an Empire builder nor a traffic policeman. But on the present occasion, in addition to offending the aesthetic sense, this Glossop seemed to me to be wearing a distinct air of menace, and I found myself wishing that Jeeves wasn't always so dashed tactful.

I mean, it's all very well to remove yourself like an eel sliding into mud when the employer has a visitor, but there are moments – and it looked to me as if this was going to be one of them – when the truer tact is to stick around and stand ready to lend a hand in the free-for-all.

For Jeeves was no longer with us. I hadn't seen him go, and I hadn't heard him go, but he had gone. As far as the eye could reach, one noted nobody but Tuppy. And in Tuppy's demeanour, as I say, there was a certain something that tended to disquiet. He looked to me very much like a man who had come to reopen that matter of my tickling Angela's ankles.

However, his opening remark told me that I had been alarming myself unduly. It was of a pacific nature, and came as a great relief.

'Bertie,' he said, 'I owe you an apology. I have come to make it.'

My relief on hearing these words, containing as they did no reference to any sort of tickled ankles, was, as I say, great. But I don't think it was any greater than my surprise. Months had passed since that painful episode at the Drones, and until now he hadn't given a sign of remorse and contrition. Indeed, word had reached me through private sources that he frequently told the story at dinners and other gatherings and, when doing so, laughed his silly head off.

I found it hard to understand, accordingly, what could have caused him to abase himself at this later date. Presumably he had been given the elbow by his better self, but why?

Still, there it was.

'My dear chap,' I said, gentlemanly to the gills, 'don't mention it.'

'What's the sense of saying, "Don't mention it"? I have mentioned it.'

'I mean, don't mention it any more. Don't give the matter another thought. We all of us forget ourselves sometimes and do things which, in our calmer moments, we regret. No doubt you were a bit tight at the time.'

'What the devil do you think you're talking about?'

I didn't like his tone. Brusque.

'Correct me if I am wrong,' I said, with a certain stiffness, 'but I assumed that you were apologizing for your foul conduct in looping back the last ring that night in the Drones, causing me to plunge into the swimming b. in the full soup and fish.'

'Ass! Not that, at all.'

'Then what?'

'This Bassett business.'

'What Bassett business?'

'Bertie,' said Tuppy, 'when you told me last night that you were in love with Madeline Bassett, I gave you the impression that I believed you, but I didn't. The thing seemed too incredible. However, since then I have made inquiries, and the facts appear to square with your statement. I have now come to apologize for doubting you.'

'Made inquiries?'

'I asked her if you had proposed to her, and she said, yes, you had.'

'Tuppy! You didn't?'

'I did.'

'Have you no delicacy, no proper feeling?'

'No.'

'Oh? Well, right ho, of course, but I think you ought to have.'

'Delicacy be dashed. I wanted to be certain that it was not you who stole Angela from me. I now know it wasn't.'

So long as he knew that, I didn't so much mind him having no delicacy.

'Ah,' I said. 'Well, that's fine. Hold that thought.'

'I have found out who it was.'

'What?'

He stood brooding for a moment. His eyes were smouldering with a dull fire. His jaw stuck out like the back of Jeeves's head.

'Bertie,' he said, 'do you remember what I swore I would do to the chap who stole Angela from me?'

'As nearly as I recall, you planned to pull him inside out – '

'– and make him swallow himself. Correct. The programme still holds good.'

'But, Tuppy, I keep assuring you, as a competent eyewitness, that nobody snitched Angela from you during that Cannes trip.'

'No. But they did after she got back.'

'What?'

'Don't keep saying "What?" You heard.'

'But she hasn't seen anybody since she got back.'

'Oh, no? How about that newt bloke?'

'Gussie?'

'Precisely. The serpent Fink-Nottle.'

This seemed to me absolute gibbering.

'But Gussie loves the Bassett.'

'You can't all love this blighted Bassett. What astonishes me is that anyone can do it. He loves Angela, I tell you. And she loves him.'

'But Angela handed you her hat before Gussie ever got here.'

'No, she didn't. Couple of hours after.'

'He couldn't have fallen in love with her in a couple of hours.'

'Why not? I fell in love with her in a couple of minutes. I worshipped her immediately we met, the pop-eyed little excrescence.'

'But, dash it – '

'Don't argue, Bertie. The facts are all docketed. She loves this newt-nuzzling blister.'

'Quite absurd, laddie – quite absurd.'

'Oh?' He ground a heel into the carpet – a thing I've often read about, but had never seen done before. 'Then perhaps you will explain how it is that she happens to come to be engaged to him?'

You could have knocked me down with a f.

'Engaged to him?'

'She told me herself.'

'She was kidding you.'

'She was not kidding me. Shortly after the conclusion of this afternoon's binge at Market Snodsbury Grammar School he asked her to marry him, and she appears to have right-hoed without a murmur.'

'There must be some mistake.'

'There was. The snake Fink-Nottle made it, and by

now I bet he realizes it. I've been chasing him since 5.30.'

'Chasing him?'

'All over the place. I want to pull his head off.'

'I see. Quite.'

'You haven't seen him, by any chance?'

'No.'

'Well, if you do, say goodbye to him quickly and put in your order for lilies . . . Oh, Jeeves.'

'Sir?'

I hadn't heard the door open, but the man was on the spot once more. My private belief, as I think I have mentioned before, is that Jeeves doesn't have to open doors. He's like one of those birds in India who bung their astral bodies about – the chaps, I mean, who having gone into thin air in Bombay, reassemble the parts and appear two minutes later in Calcutta. Only some such theory will account for the fact that he's not there one moment and is there the next. He just seems to float from Spot A to Spot B like some form of gas.

'Have you seen Mr Fink-Nottle, Jeeves?'

'No, sir.'

'I'm going to murder him.'

'Very good, sir.'

Tuppy withdrew, banging the door behind him, and I put Jeeves abreast.

'Jeeves,' I said, 'do you know what? Mr Fink-Nottle is engaged to my Cousin Angela.'

'Indeed, sir?'

'Well, how about it? Do you grasp the psychology? Does it make sense? Only a few hours ago he was engaged to Miss Bassett.'

'Gentlemen who have been discarded by one young lady are often apt to attach themselves without delay to another, sir. It is what is know as a gesture.'

I began to grasp.

'I see what you mean. Defiant stuff.'

'Yes, sir.'

'A sort of "Oh, right ho, please yourself, but if you don't want me, there are plenty who do." '

'Precisely, sir. My Cousin George – '

'Never mind about your Cousin George, Jeeves.'

'Very good, sir.'

'Keep him for the long winter evenings, what?'

'Just as you wish, sir.'

'And, anyway, I bet your Cousin George wasn't a shrinking, non-goose-boo-ing jellyfish like Gussie. That is what astounds me, Jeeves – that it should be Gussie who has been putting in all this heavy gesture-making stuff.'

'You must remember, sir, that Mr Fink-Nottle is in a somewhat inflamed cerebral condition.'

'That's true. A bit above par at the moment, as it were?'

'Exactly, sir.'

'Well, I'll tell you one thing – he'll be in a jolly sight more inflamed cerebral condition if Tuppy gets hold of him . . . What's the time?'

'Just on eight o'clock, sir.'

'Then Tuppy has been chasing him for two hours and a half. We must save the unfortunate blighter, Jeeves.'

'Yes, sir.'

'A human life is a human life, what?'

'Exceedingly true, sir.'

'The first thing, then, is to find him. After that we can discuss plans and schemes. Go forth, Jeeves, and scour the neighbourhood.'

'It will not be necessary, sir. If you will glance behind you, you will see Mr Fink-Nottle coming out from beneath your bed.'

And, by Jove, he was absolutely right.

There was Gussie, emerging as stated. He was

covered with fluff and looked like a tortoise popping forth for a bit of a breather.

'Gussie!' I said.

'Jeeves,' said Gussie.

'Sir?' said Jeeves.

'Is that door locked, Jeeves?'

'No, sir, but I will attend to the matter immediately.'

Gussie sat down on the bed, and I thought for a moment that he was going to be in the mode by burying his face in his hands. However, he merely brushed a dead spider from his brow.

'Have you locked the door, Jeeves?'

'Yes, sir.'

'Because you can never tell that that ghastly Glossop may not take it into his head to come – '

The word 'back' froze on his lips. He hadn't got any further than a b-ish sound, when the handle of the door began to twist and rattle. He sprang from the bed, and for an instant stood looking exactly like a picture my Aunt Agatha has in her dining room – The Stag at Bay – Landseer. Then he made a dive for the cupboard and was inside it before one really got on to it that he had started leaping. I have seen fellows late for the 9.15 move less nippily.

I shot a glance at Jeeves. He allowed his right eyebrow to flicker slightly, which is as near as he ever gets to a display of the emotions.

'Hullo?' I yipped.

'Let me in, blast you!' responded Tuppy's voice from without. 'Who locked this door?'

I consulted Jeeves once more in the language of the eyebrow. He raised one of his. I raised one of mine. He raised his other. I raised my other. Then we both raised both. Finally, there seeming to be no other policy to pursue, I flung wide the gates and Tuppy came shooting in.

'Now what?' I said, as nonchalantly as I could manage.

'Why was the door locked?' demanded Tuppy.

I was in pretty good eyebrow-raising form by now, so I gave him a touch of it.

'Is one to have no privacy, Glossop?' I said coldly. 'I instructed Jeeves to lock the door because I was about to disrobe.'

'A likely story!' said Tuppy, and I'm not sure he didn't add 'Forsooth!' 'You needn't try to make me believe that you're afraid people are going to run excursion trains to see you in your underwear. You locked that door because you've got the snake Fink-Nottle concealed in here. I suspected it the moment I'd left, and I decided to come back and investigate. I'm going to search this room from end to end. I believe he's in that cupboard . . . What's in this cupboard?'

'Just clothes,' I said, having another stab at the nonchalant, though extremely dubious as to whether it would come off. 'The usual wardrobe of the English gentleman paying a country-house visit.'

'You're lying!'

Well, I wouldn't have been if he had only waited a minute before speaking, because the words were hardly out of his mouth before Gussie was out of the cupboard. I have commented on the speed with which he had gone in. It was as nothing to the speed with which he emerged. There was a sort of whir and blur, and he was no longer with us.

I think Tuppy was surprised. In fact, I'm sure he was. Despite the confidence with which he had stated his view that the cupboard contained Fink-Nottles, it plainly disconcerted him to have the chap fizzing out at him like this. He gargled sharply, and jumped back about five feet. The next moment, however, he had recovered his poise and was galloping down the corridor in pursuit. It only needed Aunt Dahlia after them, shouting 'Yoicks!' or whatever is customary on these occasions, to complete the resemblance to a brisk run with the Quorn.

I sank into a handy chair. I am not a man whom it is easy to discourage, but it seemed to me that things had at last begun to get too complex for Bertram.

'Jeeves,' I said, 'all this is a bit thick.'

'Yes, sir.'

'The head rather swims.'

'Yes, sir.'

'I think you had better leave me, Jeeves. I shall need to devote the very closest thought to the situation which has arisen.'

'Very good, sir.'

The door closed. I lit a cigarette and began to ponder.

—19—

Most chaps in my position, I imagine, would have pondered all the rest of the evening without getting a bite, but we Woosters have an uncanny knack of going straight to the heart of things, and I don't suppose it was much more than ten minutes after I had started pondering before I saw what had to be done.

What was needed to straighten matters out, I perceived, was a heart-to-heart talk with Angela. She had caused all the trouble by her mutton-headed behaviour in saying 'Yes' instead of 'No' when Gussie, in the grip of mixed drinks and cerebral excitement, had suggested teaming up. She must obviously be properly ticked off and made to return him to store. A quarter of an hour later, I had tracked her down to the summerhouse in which she was taking a cooler and was seating myself by her side.

'Angela,' I said, and if my voice was stern, well, whose wouldn't have been, 'this is all perfect drivel.'

She seemed to come out of a reverie. She looked at me inquiringly.

'I'm sorry, Bertie, I didn't hear. What were you talking drivel about?'

'I was not talking drivel.'

'Oh, sorry, I thought you said you were.'

'Is it likely that I would come out here in order to talk drivel?'

'Very likely.'

I thought it best to haul off and approach the matter from another angle.

'I've just been seeing Tuppy.'

'Oh?'

'And Gussie Fink-Nottle.'

'Oh, yes?'

'It appears that you have gone and got engaged to the latter.'

'Quite right.'

'Well, that's what I meant when I said it was all perfect drivel. You can't possibly love a chap like Gussie.'

'Why not?'

'You simply can't.'

Well, I mean to say, of course she couldn't. Nobody could love a freak like Gussie except a similar freak like the Bassett. The shot wasn't on the board. A splendid chap, of course, in many ways – courteous, amiable, and just the fellow to tell you what to do till the doctor came, if you had a sick newt on your hands – but quite obviously not of Mendelssohn's March timber. I have no doubt that you could have flung bricks by the hour in England's most densely populated districts without endangering the safety of a single girl capable of becoming Mrs Augustus Fink-Nottle without an anaesthetic.

I put this to her, and she was forced to admit the justice of it.

'All right, then. Perhaps I don't.'

'Then what,' I said keenly, 'did you want to go and get engaged to him for, you unreasonable young fathead?'

'I thought it would be fun.'

'Fun!'

'And so it has been. I've had a lot of fun out of it. You should have seen Tuppy's face when I told him.'

A sudden bright light shone upon me.

'Ha! A gesture!'

'What?'

'You got engaged to Gussie just to score off Tuppy?'

'I did.'

'Well, then, that was what I was saying. It was a gesture.'

'Yes, I suppose you could call it that.'

'And I'll tell you something else I'll call it – viz. a dashed low trick. I'm surprised at you, young Angela.'

'I don't see why.'

I curled the lip about half an inch. 'Being a female, you wouldn't. You gentler sexes are like that. You pull off the rawest stuff without a pang. You pride yourselves on it. Look at Jael, the wife of Heber.'

'Where ever did you hear of Jael, the wife of Heber?'

'Possibly you are not aware that I once won a Scripture-knowledge prize at school?'

'Oh, yes. I remember Augustus mentioning it in his speech.'

'Quite,' I said, a little hurriedly. I had no wish to be reminded of Augustus's speech. 'Well, as I say, look at Jael, the wife of Heber. Dug spikes into the guest's coconut while he was asleep, and then went swanking about the place like a Girl Guide. No wonder they say, "Oh, woman, woman!" '

'Who?'

'The chaps who do. Coo, what a sex! But you aren't proposing to keep this up, of course?'

'Keep what up?'

'This rot of being engaged to Gussie.'

'I certainly am.'

'Just to make Tuppy look silly.'

'Do you think he looks silly?'

'I do.'

'So he ought to.'

I began to get the idea that I wasn't making real

headway. I remember when I won that Scripture-knowledge prize, having to go into the facts about Balaam's ass. I can't quite recall what they were, but I still retain a sort of general impression of something digging its feet in and putting its ears back and refusing to cooperate; and it seemed to me that this was what Angela was doing now. She and Balaam's ass were, so to speak, sisters under the skin. There's a word beginning with r – 're' something – 'recal' something – No, it's gone. But what I am driving at is that this is what Angela was showing herself.

'Silly young geezer,' I said.

She pinkened.

'I'm not a silly young geezer.'

'You are a silly young geezer. And, what's more, you know it.'

'I don't know anything of the kind.'

'Here you are, wrecking Tuppy's life, wrecking Gussie's life, all for the sake of a cheap score.'

'Well, it's no business of yours.'

I sat on this promptly.

'No business of mine when I see two lives I used to go to school with wrecked? Ha! Besides, you know you're potty about Tuppy.'

'I'm not!'

'Is that so? If I had a quid for every time I've seen you gaze at him with the lovelight in your eyes – '

She gazed at me, but without the lovelight.

'Oh, for goodness sake, go away and boil your head, Bertie!'

I drew myself up.

'That,' I replied, with dignity, 'is just what I am going to go away and boil. At least, I mean, I shall now leave you. I have said my say.'

'Good.'

'But permit me to add – '

'I won't.'

'Very good,' I said coldly. 'In that case, tinkerty tonk.'

And I meant it to sting.

'Moody' and 'discouraged' were about the two adjectives you would have selected to describe me as I left the summer-house. It would be idle to deny that I had expected better results from this little chat.

I was surprised at Angela. Odd how you never realize that every girl is at heart a vicious specimen until something goes wrong with her love affair. This cousin and I had been meeting freely since the days when I wore sailor suits and she hadn't any front teeth, yet only now was I beginning to get onto her hidden depths. A simple, jolly, kindly young pimple she had always struck me as – the sort you could more or less rely on not to hurt a fly. But here she was now laughing heartlessly – at least, I seemed to remember hearing her laugh heartlessly – like something cold and callous out of a sophisticated talkie, and fairly spitting on her hands in her determination to bring Tuppy's grey hairs in sorrow to the grave.

I've said it before, and I'll say it again – girls are rummy. Old Pop Kipling never said a truer word than when he made that crack about the f. of the s. being more d. than the m.

It seemed to me in the circs. that there was but one thing to do – that is, head for the dining room and take a slash at the cold collation of which Jeeves had spoken. I felt in urgent need of sustenance, for the recent interview had pulled me down a bit. There is no gainsaying the fact that this naked-emotion stuff reduces a chap's vitality and puts him in the vein for a good whack at the beef and ham.

To the dining room, accordingly, I repaired, and had barely crossed the threshold when I perceived Aunt

Dahlia at the sideboard, tucking into salmon mayonnaise.

The spectacle drew from me a quick 'Oh, ah,' for I was somewhat embarrassed. The last time this relative and I had enjoyed a *tête-à-tête*, it will be remembered, she had sketched out plans for drowning me in the kitchen-garden pond, and I was not quite sure what my present standing with her was.

I was relieved to find her in genial mood. Nothing could have exceeded the cordiality with which she waved her fork.

'Hallo, Bertie, you old ass,' was her very matey greeting. 'I thought I shouldn't find you far away from the food. Try some of this salmon. Excellent.'

'Anatole's?' I queried.

'No. He's still in bed. But the kitchen maid has struck an inspired streak. It suddenly seems to have come home to her that she isn't catering for a covey of buzzards in the Sahara Desert, and she has put out something quite fit for human consumption. There is good in the girl, after all, and I hope she enjoys herself at the dance.'

I ladled out a portion of salmon, and we fell into pleasant conversation, chatting of this servants' ball at the Stretchley-Budds and speculating idly, I recall, as to what Seppings, the butler, would look like doing the rumba.

It was not till I had cleaned up the first platter and was embarking on a second that the subject of Gussie came up. Considering what had passed at Market Snodsbury that afternoon, it was one which I had been expecting her to touch on earlier. When she did touch on it, I could see that she had not yet been informed of Angela's engagement.

'I say, Bertie,' she said, meditatively chewing fruit salad, 'this Spink-Bottle.'

'Nottle.'

'Bottle,' insisted the aunt firmly. 'After that exhibition of his this afternoon, Bottle, and nothing but Bottle, is how I shall always think of him. However, what I was going to say was that, if you see him, I wish you would tell him that he has made an old woman very, very happy. Except for the time when the curate tripped over a loose shoelace and fell down the pulpit steps, I don't think I have ever had a more wonderful moment than when good old Bottle suddenly started ticking Tom off from the platform. In fact, I thought his whole performance in the most perfect taste.'

I could not but demur.

'Those references to myself – '

'Those were what I liked next best. I thought they were fine. Is it true that you cheated when you won that Scripture-knowledge prize?'

'Certainly not. My victory was the outcome of the most strenuous and unremitting efforts.'

'And how about this pessimism we hear of? Are you a pessimist, Bertie?'

I could have told her that what was occurring in this house was rapidly making me one, but I said no, I wasn't.

'That's right. Never be a pessimist. Everything is for the best in this best of all possible worlds. It's a long lane that has no turning. It's always darkest before the dawn. Have patience and all will come right. The sun will shine, although the day's a grey one . . . Try some of this salad.'

I followed her advice, but even as I plied the spoon my thoughts were elsewhere. I was perplexed. It may have been the fact that I had recently been hobnobbing with so many bowed-down hearts that made this cheeriness of hers seem so bizarre, but bizarre was certainly what I found it.

'I thought you might have been a trifle peeved,' I said.

'Peeved?'

'By Gussie's manoeuvres on the platform this afternoon. I confess that I had rather expected the tapping foot and the drawn brow.'

'Nonsense. What was there to be peeved about? I took the whole thing as a great compliment, proud to feel that any drink from my cellars could have produced such a majestic jag. It restores one's faith in post-war whisky. Besides, I couldn't be peeved at anything tonight. I am like a little child clapping its hands and dancing in the sunshine. For though it has been some time getting a move on, Bertie, the sun has at last broken through the clouds. Ring out those joy bells. Anatole has withdrawn his notice.'

'What? Oh, very hearty congratulations.'

'Thanks. Yes, I worked on him like a beaver after I got back this afternoon, and finally, vowing he would ne'er consent, he consented. He stays on, praises be, and the way I look at it now is that God's in His heaven and all's right with – '

She broke off. The door had opened, and we were plus a butler.

'Hello, Seppings,' said Aunt Dahlia. 'I thought you had gone.'

'Not yet, madam.'

'Well, I hope you will all have a good time.'

'Thank you, madam.'

'Was there something you wanted to see me about?'

'Yes, madam. It is with reference to Monsieur Anatole. Is it by your wish, madam, that Mr Fink-Nottle is making faces at Monsieur Anatole through the skylight of his bedroom?'

20

There was one of those long silences. Pregnant, I believe, is what they're generally called. Aunt looked at butler. Butler looked at aunt. I looked at both of them. An eerie silence seemed to envelop the room like a linseed poultice. I happened to be biting on a slice of apple in my fruit salad at the moment, and it sounded as if Carnera had jumped off the top of the Eiffel Tower on to a cucumber frame.

Aunt Dahlia steadied herself against the sideboard, and spoke in a low, husky voice:

'Faces?'

'Yes, madam.'

'Through the skylight?'

'Yes, madam.'

'You mean he's sitting on the roof?'

'Yes, madam. It had upset Monsieur Anatole very much.'

I suppose it was that word 'upset' that touched Aunt Dahlia off. Experience has taught her what happened when Anatole got upset. I had always known her as a woman who was quite active on her pins, but I had never suspected her of being capable of the magnificent burst of speed which she now showed. Pausing merely to get a rich hunting-field expletive off her chest, she was out of the room and making for the stairs before I could swallow a sliver of – I think – banana. And feeling, as I had felt when I got that telegram of hers about Angela and Tuppy, that my place was by her side,

I put down my plate and hastened after her, Seppings following at a loping gallop.

I say that my place was by her side, but it was not so dashed easy to get there, for she was setting a cracking pace. At the top of the first flight she must have led by a matter of half a dozen lengths, and was still shaking off my challenge when she rounded into the second. At the next landing, however, the gruelling going appeared to tell on her, for she slackened off a trifle and showed symptoms of roaring, and by the time we were in the straight we were running practically neck and neck. Our entry into Anatole's room was as close a finish as you could have wished to see.

Result:

1. *Aunt Dahlia.*
2. *Bertram.*
3. *Seppings.*

Won by a short head. Half a staircase separated second and third.

The first thing that met the eye on entering was Anatole. This wizard of the cooking stove is a tubby little man with a moustache of the outsize or soup-strainer type, and you can generally take a line through it as to the state of his emotions. When all is well, it turns up at the ends like a sergeant-major's. When the soul is bruised, it droops.

It was drooping now, striking a sinister note. And if any shadow of doubt had remained as to how he was feeling, the way he was carrying on would have dispelled it. He was standing by the bed in pink pyjamas, waving his fists at the skylight. Through the glass, Gussie was staring down. His eyes were bulging and his mouth was open, giving him so striking a resemblance to some rare fish in an aquarium that one's primary impulse was to offer him an ant's egg.

Watching this fist-waving cook and this goggling guest, I must say that my sympathies were completely with the former. I considered him thoroughly justified in waving all the fists he wanted to.

Review the facts, I mean to say. There he had been, lying in bed, thinking idly of whatever French cooks do think about when in bed, and he had suddenly become aware of that frightful face at the window. A thing to jar the most phlegmatic. I know I should hate to be lying in bed and have Gussie popping up like that. A chap's bedroom – you can't get away from it – is his castle, and he has every right to look askance if gargoyles come glaring in at him.

While I stood musing thus, Aunt Dahlia, in her practical way, was coming straight to the point:

'What's all this?'

Anatole did a sort of Swedish exercise, starting at the base of the spine, carrying on through the shoulder blades and finishing up among the back hair.

Then he told her.

In the chats I have had with this wonder man, I have always found his English fluent, but a bit on the mixed side. If you remember, he was with Mrs Bingo Little for a time before coming to Brinkley, and no doubt he picked up a good deal from Bingo. Before that, he had been a couple of years with an American family at Nice and had studied under their chauffeur, one of the Maloneys of Brooklyn. So, what with Bingo and what with Maloney, he is, as I say, fluent but a bit mixed.

He spoke, in part, as follows:

'Hot dog! You ask me what is it? Listen. Make some attention a little. Me, I have hit the hay, but I do not sleep so good, and presently I wake and up I look, and there is one who makes faces against me through the dashed window. Is that a pretty affair? Is that convenient? If you think I like it, you jolly well mistake yourself. I am so mad as a wet hen. And why not? I am somebody, isn't it? This is a bedroom, what-what, not a house for some apes? Then for what do blighters sit on my window so cool as a few cucumbers, making some faces?'

'Quite,' I said. Dashed reasonable, was my verdict.

He threw another look up at Gussie, and did Exercise 2 – the one where you clutch the moustache, give it a tug and then start catching flies.

'Wait yet a little. I am not finish. I say I see this type on my window, making a few faces. But what then? Does he buzz off when I shout a cry, and leave me peaceable? Not on your life. He remain planted there, not giving any damns, and sit regarding me like a cat watching a duck. He make faces against me and again he make faces against me, and the more I command that he should get to hell out of here, the more he do not get to hell out of here. He cry something towards me, and I demand what is his desire, but he do not explain. Oh, no, that arrives never. He does but shrug his head. What damn silliness! Is this amusing for me? You think I like it? I am not content with such folly. I think the poor mutt's loony. *Je me fiche de ce type infect. C'est idiot de faire comme ça l'oiseau . . . Allez-vous-en, louffier . . .* Tell the boob to go away. He is mad as some March hatters.'

I must say I thought he was making out a jolly good case, and evidently Aunt Dahlia felt the same. She laid a quivering hand on his shoulder.

'I will, Monsieur Anatole, I will,' she said, and I couldn't have believed that robust voice capable of sinking to such an absolute coo. More like a turtle dove calling to its mate than anything else. 'It's quite all right.'

She had said the wrong thing. He did Exercise 3.

'All right? *Nom d'un nom d'un nom!* The hell you

say it's all right! Of what use to pull stuff like that? Wait one half-moment. Not yet quite so quick, my old sport. It is by no means all right. See yet again a little. It is some very different dishes of fish. I can take a few smooths with a rough, it is true, but I do not find it agreeable when one play larks against me on my windows. Than cannot do. A nice thing, no. I am a serious man. I do not wish a few larks on my windows. I enjoy larks on my windows worse as any. It is very little all right. If such rannygazoo is to arrive, I do not remain any longer in this house no more. I buzz off and do not stay planted.'

Sinister words, I had to admit, and I was not surprised that Aunt Dahlia, hearing them, should have uttered a cry like the wail of a master of hounds seeing a fox shot. Anatole had begun to wave his fists again at Gussie, and she now joined him. Seppings, who was puffing respectfully in the background, didn't actually wave his fists, but he gave Gussie a pretty austere look. It was plain to the thoughtful observer that this Fink-Nottle, in getting on to that skylight, had done a mistaken thing. He couldn't have been more unpopular in the home of G. G. Simmons.

'Go away, you crazy loon!' cried Aunt Dahlia, in that ringing voice of hers which had once caused nervous members of the Quorn to lose stirrups and take tosses from the saddle.

Gussie's reply was to waggle his eyebrows. I could read the message he was trying to convey.

'I think he means,' I said – reasonable old Bertram, always trying to throw oil on troubled w. – 'that if he does he will fall down the side of the house and break his neck.'

'Well, why not?' said Aunt Dahlia.

I could see her point, of course, but it seemed to me that there might be a nearer solution. This skylight happened to be the only window in the house which Uncle Tom had not festooned with his bally bars. I suppose he felt that if a burglar had the nerve to climb up as far as this, he deserved what was coming to him.

'If you opened the skylight, he could jump in.'

The idea got across.

'Seppings, how does this skylight open?'

'With a pole, madam.'

'Then get a pole. Get two poles. Ten.'

And presently Gussie was mixing with the company. Like one of those chaps you read about in the papers, the wretched man seemed deeply conscious of his position.

I must say Aunt Dahlia's bearing and demeanour did nothing to assist toward a restored composure. Of the amiability which she had exhibited when discussing this unhappy chump's activities with me over the fruit salad, no trace remained, and I was not surprised that speech more or less froze on the Fink-Nottle lips. It isn't often that Aunt Dahlia, normally as genial a bird as ever encouraged a gaggle of hounds to get their noses down to it, lets her angry passions rise, but when she does, strong men climb trees and pull them up after them.

'Well?' she said.

In answer to this, all that Gussie could produce was a sort of strangled hiccough.

'Well?'

Aunt Dahlia's face grew darker. Hunting, if indulged in regularly over a period of years, is a pastime that seldom fails to lend a fairly deepish tinge to the patient's complexion, and her best friends could not have denied that even at normal times the relative's map tended a little toward the crushed strawberry. But never had I seen it take on so pronounced a richness as now. She looked like a tomato struggling for self-expression.

'Well?'

Gussie tried hard. And for a moment it seemed as if something was going to come through. But in the end it turned out nothing more than a sort of death-rattle.

'Oh, take him away, Bertie, and put ice on his head,' said Aunt Dahlia, giving the thing up. And she turned to tackle what looked like the rather man's-size job of soothing Anatole, who was now carrying on a muttered conversation with himself in a rapid sort of way.

Seeming to feel that the situation was one to which he could not do justice in Bingo-cum-Maloney Anglo-American, he had fallen back on his native tongue. Words like *'marmiton de Domange,' 'pignouf,' 'hurluberlu,'* and *'roustisseur'* were fluttering from him like bats out of a barn. Lost on me, of course, because, though I sweated a bit at the Gallic language during that Cannes visit, I'm still more or less in the Esker-vous-avez stage. I regretted this, for they sounded good.

I assisted Gussie down the stairs. A cooler thinker than Aunt Dahlia, I had already guessed the hidden springs and motives which had led him to the roof. Where she had seen only a cockeyed reveller indulging himself in a drunken prank or whimsy, I had spotted the hunted fawn.

'Was Tuppy after you?' I asked sympathetically.

What I believe is called a *frisson* shook him.

'He nearly got me on the top landing. I shinned out through a passage window and scrambled along a sort of ledge.'

'That baffled him, what?'

'Yes. But then I found I had stuck. The roof sloped down in all directions. I couldn't go back. I had to go on, crawling along this ledge. And then I found myself looking down the skylight. Who was that chap?'

'That was Anatole, Aunt Dahlia's chef.'

'French?'

'To the core.'

'That explains why I couldn't make him understand. What asses these Frenchmen are. They don't seem able to grasp the simplest thing. You'd have thought if a chap saw a chap on a skylight, the chap would realize the chap wanted to be let in. But no, he just stood there.'

'Waving a few fists.'

'Yes. Silly idiot. Still, here I am.'

'Here you are, yes – for the moment.'

'Eh?'

'I was thinking that Tuppy is probably lurking somewhere.'

He leaped like a lamb in springtime.

'What shall I do?'

I considered this.

'Sneak back to your room and barricade the door. That is the manly policy.'

'Suppose that's where he's lurking?'

'In that case, move elsewhere.'

But on arrival at the room, it transpired that Tuppy, if anywhere, was infesting some other portion of the house. Gussie shot in, and I heard the key turn. And feeling that there was no more that I could do in that quarter, I returned to the dining room for further fruit salad and a quiet think. And I had barely filled my plate when the door opened and Aunt Dahlia came in. She sank into a chair, looking a bit shopworn.

'Give me a drink, Bertie.'

'What sort?'

'Any sort, so long as it's strong.'

Approach Bertram Wooster along these lines, and you catch him at his best. St Bernard dogs doing the square thing by Alpine travellers could not have bustled about more assiduously. I filled the order, and for some moments nothing was to be heard but the sloshing sound of an aunt restoring her tissues.

'Shove it down, Aunt Dahlia,' I said sympathetically. 'These things take it out of one, don't they? You've had a toughish time, no doubt, soothing Anatole,' I proceeded, helping myself to anchovy paste on toast. 'Everything pretty smooth now, I trust?'

She gazed at me in a long, lingering sort of way, her brow wrinkled as if in thought.

'Attila,' she said at length. 'That's the name, Attila, the Hun.'

'Eh?'

'I was trying to think who you reminded me of. Somebody who went about strewing ruin and desolation and breaking up homes which, until he came along, had been happy and peaceful. Attila is the man. It's amazing,' she said, drinking me in once more. 'To look at you, one would think you were just an ordinary sort of amiable idiot – certifiable, perhaps, but quite harmless. Yet, in reality, you are a worse scourge than the Black Death. I tell you, Bertie, when I contemplate you I seem to come up against all the underlying sorrow and horror of life with such a thud that I feel as if I had walked into a lamp post.'

Pained and surprised, I would have spoken, but the stuff I had thought was anchovy paste had turned out to be something far more gooey and adhesive. It seemed to wrap itself round the tongue and impede utterance like a gag. And while I was still endeavouring to clear the vocal cords for action, she went on:

'Do you realize what you started when you sent that Spink-Bottle man down here? As regards his getting blotto and turning the prize-giving ceremonies at Market Snodsbury Grammar School into a sort of two-reel comic film, I will say nothing, for frankly I enjoyed it. But when he comes leering at Anatole through skylights, just after I had with infinite pains and tact induced him to withdraw his notice, and makes him so temperamental that he won't hear of staying on after tomorrow – '

The paste stuff gave way. I was able to speak.

'What?'

'Yes. Anatole goes tomorrow, and I suppose poor old Tom will have indigestion for the rest of his life. And that is not all. I have just seen Angela, and she tells me she is engaged to this Bottle.'

'Temporarily, yes,' I had to admit.

'Temporarily be blowed. She's definitely engaged to him and talks with a sort of hideous coolness of getting married in October. So there it is. If the prophet Job were to walk into the room at this moment, I could sit swapping hard-luck stories with him till bedtime. Not that Job was in my class.'

'He had boils.'

'Well, what are boils?'

'Dashed painful, I understand.'

'Nonsense. I'd take all the boils on the market in exchange for my troubles. Can't you realize the position? I've lost the best cook in England. My husband, poor soul, will probably die of dyspepsia. And my only daughter, for whom I had dreamed such a wonderful future, is engaged to be married to an inebriated newt fancier. And you talk about boils!'

I corrected her on a small point:

'I don't absolutely talk about boils. I merely mentioned that Job had them. Yes, I agree with you, Aunt Dahlia, that things are not looking too oojah-cum-spiff at the moment, but be of good cheer. A Wooster is seldom baffled for more than the nonce.'

'You rather expect to be coming along shortly with another of your schemes?'

'At any minute.'

She sighed resignedly.

'I thought as much. Well, it needed but this. I don't

see how things could possibly be worse than they are, but no doubt you will succeed in making them so. Your genius and insight will find the way. Carry on, Bertie. Yes, carry on. I am past caring now. I shall even find a faint interest in seeing into what darker and profounder abysses of hell you can plunge this home. Go to it, lad . . . What's that stuff you're eating?'

'I find it a little difficult to classify. Some sort of paste on toast. Rather like glue flavoured with beef extract.'

'Gimme,' said Aunt Dahlia listlessly.

'Be careful how you chew,' I advised. 'It sticketh closer than a brother . . . Yes, Jeeves?'

The man had materialized on the carpet. Absolutely noiseless, as usual.

'A note for you, sir.'

'A note for me, Jeeves?'

'A note for you, sir.'

'From whom, Jeeves?'

'From Miss Bassett, Sir.'

'From whom, Jeeves?'

'From Miss Bassett, sir.'

'From Miss Bassett, Jeeves?'

'From Miss Bassett, sir,'

At this point, Aunt Dahlia, who had taken one nibble at her whatever-it-was-on-toast and laid it down, begged us – a little fretfully, I thought – for heaven's sake to cut out the cross-talk vaudeville stuff, as she had enough to bear already without having to listen to us doing our imitation of the Two Macs. Always willing to oblige, I dismissed Jeeves with a nod, and he flickered for a moment and was gone. Many a spectre would have been less slippy.

'But what,' I mused, toying with the envelope, 'can this female be writing to me about?'

'Why not open the damn thing and see?'

'A very excellent idea,' I said, and did so.

'And if you are interested in my movements,' proceeded Aunt Dahlia, heading for the door, 'I propose to go to my room, do some Yogi deep breathing, and try to forget.'

'Quite,' I said absently, skimming p. 1. And then, as I turned over, a sharp howl broke from my lips, causing Aunt Dahlia to shy like a startled mustang.

'Don't do it!' she exclaimed, quivering in every limb.

'Yes, but dash it – '

'What a pest you are, you miserable object,' she sighed. 'I remember years ago, when you were in your cradle, being left alone with you for one day and you nearly swallowed your rubber comforter and started turning purple. And I, ass that I was, took it out and saved your life. Let me tell you, young Bertie, it will go very hard with you if you ever swallow a rubber comforter again when only I am by to aid.'

'But, dash it!' I cried. 'Do you know what's happened? Madeline Bassett says she's going to marry me!'

'I hope it keeps fine for you,' said the relative, and passed from the room looking like something out of an Edgar Allan Poe story.

—21—

I don't suppose I was looking so dashed unlike something out of an Edgar Allen Poe story myself, for, as you can readily imagine, the news item which I have just recorded had got in amongst me properly. If the Bassett, in the belief that the Wooster heart had long been hers and was waiting ready to be scooped in on demand, had decided to take up her option, I should, as a man of honour and sensibility, have no choice but to come across and kick in. The matter was obviously not one that could be straightened out with a curt *nolle prosequi*. All the evidence, therefore, seemed to point to the fact that the doom had come upon me and, what was more, had come to stay.

And yet, though it would be idle to pretend that my grip on the situation was quite the grip I would have liked it to be, I did not despair of arriving at a solution. A lesser man, caught in this awful snare, would no doubt have thrown in the towel at once and ceased to struggle; but the whole point about the Woosters is that they are not lesser men.

By way of a start, I read the note again. Not that I had any hope that a second perusal would enable me to place a different construction on its contents, but it helped to fill in while the brain was limbering up. I then, to assist thought, had another go at the fruit salad, and in addition ate a slice of sponge cake. And it was as I passed on to the cheese that the machinery started working. I saw what had to be done.

To the question which had been exercising the mind – viz., can Bertram cope? – I was now able to reply with a confident 'Absolutely'.

The great wheeze on these occasions of dirty work at the crossroads is not to lose your head but to keep cool and try to find the ringleaders. Once find the ringleaders, and you know where you are.

The ringleader here was plainly the Bassett. It was she who had started the whole imbroglio by chucking Gussie, and it was clear that before anything could be done to solve and clarify, she must be induced to revise her views and take him on again. This would put Angela back into circulation, and that would cause Tuppy to simmer down a bit, and then we could begin to get somewhere.

I decided that as soon as I had had another morsel of cheese I would seek this Bassett out and be pretty eloquent.

And at this moment in she came. I might have foreseen that she would be turning up shortly. I mean to say, hearts may ache, but if they know that there is a cold collation set out in the dining-room, they are pretty sure to come popping in sooner or later.

Her eyes, as she entered the room, were fixed on the salmon mayonnaise, and she would no doubt have made a beeline for it and started getting hers, had I not, in the emotion of seeing her, dropped a glass of the best with which I was endeavouring to bring about a calmer frame of mind. The noise caused her to turn, and for an instant, embarrassment supervened. A slight flush mantled the cheek, and the eyes popped a bit.

'Oh!' she said.

I have always found that there is nothing that helps to ease you over one of these awkward moments like a spot of stage business. Find something to do with your hands, and it's half the battle. I grabbed a plate and hastened forward.

'A touch of salmon?'

'Thank you.'

'With a suspicion of salad?'

'If you please.'

'And to drink? Name the poison.'

'I think I would like a little orange juice.'

She gave a gulp. Not at the orange juice, I don't mean, because she hadn't got it yet, but at all the tender associations those two words provoked. It was as if someone had mentioned spaghetti to the relict of an Italian organ-grinder. Her face flushed a deeper shade, she registered anguish, and I saw that it was no longer within the sphere of practical politics to try to confine the conversation to neutral topics like cold boiled salmon.

So did she, I imagine, for when I, as a preliminary to getting down to brass tacks, said 'Er,' she said 'Er,' too, simultaneously, the brace of 'Ers' clashing in mid-air.

'I'm sorry.'

'I beg your pardon.'

'You were saying – '

'You were saying – '

'No, please go on.'

'Oh, right ho.'

I straightened the tie, my habit when in this girl's society, and had at it:

'With reference to yours of even date – '

She flushed again, and took a rather strained forkful of salmon.

'You got my note?'

'Yes, I got your note.'

'I gave it to Jeeves to give it to you.'

'Yes, he gave it to me. That's how I got it.'

There was another silence. And as she was plainly

shrinking from talking turkey, I was reluctantly compelled to do so. I mean, somebody had got to. Too dashed silly, a male and female in our position simply standing eating salmon and cheese at one another without a word.

'Yes, I got it all right.'

'I see. You got it.'

'Yes, I got it. I've just been reading it. And what I was rather wanting to ask you, if we happened to run into each other, was – well, what about it?'

'What about it?'

'That's what I say: What about it?'

'But it was quite clear.'

'Oh, quite. Perfectly clear. Very well expressed and all that. But – I mean – Well, I mean, deeply sensible of the honour, and so forth – but – Well, dash it!'

She had polished off her salmon, and now put the plate down.

'Fruit salad?'

'No, thank you.'

'Spot of pie?'

'No, thanks.'

'One of those glue things on toast?'

'No, thank you.'

She took a cheese straw. I found myself a cold egg which I had overlooked. Then I said 'I mean to say' just as she said 'I think I know', and there was another collision.

'I beg your pardon.'

'I'm sorry.'

'Do go on.'

'No, you go on.'

I waved my cold egg courteously, to indicate that she had the floor, and she started again.

'I think I know what you are trying to say. You are surprised.'

'Yes.'

'You are thinking of – '

'Exactly.'

'– Mr Fink-Nottle.'

'The very man.'

'You find what I have done hard to understand.'

'Absolutely.'

'I don't wonder.'

'I do.'

'And yet it is quite simple.'

She took another cheese straw. She seemed to like cheese straws.

'Quite simple, really. I want to make you happy.'

'Dashed decent of you.'

'I am going to devote the rest of my life to making you happy.'

'A very matey scheme.'

'I can at least do that. But – may I be quite frank with you, Bertie?'

'Oh, rather.'

'Then I must tell you this. I am fond of you. I will marry you. I will do my best to make you a good wife. But my affection for you can never be the flamelike passion I felt for Augustus.'

'Just the very point I was working round to. There, as you say, is the snag. Why not chuck the whole idea of hitching up with me? Wash it out altogether. I mean, if you love old Gussie – '

'No longer.'

'Oh, come.'

'No. What happened this afternoon has killed my love. A smear of ugliness has been drawn across a thing of beauty, and I can never feel towards him as I did.'

I saw what she meant, of course. Gussie had bunged his heart at her feet; she had picked it up, and, almost immediately after doing so, had discovered that he had been stewed to the eyebrows all the time. The shock must have been severe. No girl likes to feel that a chap has got to be thoroughly plastered before he can ask her to marry him. It wounds the pride.

Nevertheless, I persevered.

'But have you considered,' I said, 'that you may have got a wrong line on Gussie's performance this afternoon? Admitted that all the evidence points to a more sinister theory, what price him simply having got a touch of the sun? Chaps do get touches of the sun, you know, especially when the weather's hot.'

She looked at me, and I saw that she was putting in a bit of the old drenched-irises stuff.

'It was like you to say that, Bertie. I respect you for it.'

'Oh, no.'

'Yes. You have a splendid, chivalrous soul.'

'Not a bit.'

'Yes, you have. You remind me of Cyrano.'

'Who?'

'Cyrano de Bergerac.'

'The chap with the nose?'

'Yes.'

I can't say I was any too pleased. I felt the old beak furtively. It was a bit on the prominent side, perhaps, but dash it, not in the Cyrano class. It began to look as if the next thing this girl would do would be to compare me to Schnozzle Durante.

'He loved, but pleaded another's cause.'

'Oh, I see what you mean now.'

'I like you for that, Bertie. It was fine of you – fine and big. But it is no use. There are things which kill love. I can never forget Augustus, but my love for him is dead. I will be your wife.'

Well, one has to be civil.

'Right ho,' I said. 'Thanks awfully.'

Then the dialogue sort of poofed out once more, and we stood eating cheese straws and cold eggs respectively in silence. There seemed to exist some little uncertainty as to what the next move was.

Fortunately, before embarrassment could do much more supervening, Angela came in, and this broke up the meeting. The Bassett announced our engagement, and Angela kissed her and said she hoped she would be very, very happy, and the Bassett kissed her and said she hoped she would be very, very happy with Gussie, and Angela said she was sure she would, because Augustus was such a dear, and the Bassett kissed her again, and Angela kissed her again, and, in a word, the whole thing got so bally feminine that I was glad to edge away.

I would have been glad to do so, of course, in any case, for if ever there was a moment when it was up to Bertram to think, and think hard, this moment was that moment.

It was, it seemed to me, the end. Not even on the occasion, some years earlier, when I had inadvertently become betrothed to Tuppy's frightful Cousin Honoria, had I experienced a deeper sense of being waist high in the gumbo and about to sink without trace. I wandered out into the garden, smoking a tortured gasper, with the iron well embedded in the soul. And I had fallen into a sort of trance, trying to picture what it would be like having the Bassett on the premises for the rest of my life and at the same time, if you follow me, trying not to picture what it would be like, when I charged into something which might have been a tree, but was not – being, in point of fact, Jeeves.

'I beg your pardon, sir,' he said. 'I should have moved to one side.'

I did not reply. I stood looking at him in silence. For the sight of him had opened up a new line of thought.

This Jeeves, now, I reflected. I had formed the opinion

that he had lost his grip and was no longer the force he had been, but was it not possible, I asked myself, that I might be mistaken? Start him off exploring avenues and might he not discover one through which I would be enabled to sneak off to safety, leaving no hard feelings behind? I found myself answering that it was quite on the cards that he might.

After all, his head still bulged out at the back as of old. One noted in the eyes the same intelligent glitter.

Mind you, after what had passed between us in the matter of that white mess jacket with the brass buttons, I was not prepared absolutely to hand over to the man. I would, of course, merely take him into consultation. But, recalling some of his earlier triumphs – the Sipperley Case, the Episode of My Aunt Agatha and the Dog McIntosh, and the smoothly handled Affair of Uncle George and the Barmaid's Niece were a few that sprang to my mind – I felt justified at least in offering him the opportunity of coming to the aid of the young master in his hour of peril.

But before proceeding further there was one thing that had got to be understood between us, and understood clearly.

'Jeeves,' I said, 'a word with you.'

'Sir?'

'I am up against it a bit, Jeeves.'

'I am sorry to hear that, sir. Can I be of any assistance?'

'Quite possibly you can, if you have not lost your grip. Tell me frankly, Jeeves, are you in pretty good shape mentally?'

'Yes, sir.'

'Still eating plenty of fish?'

'Yes, sir.'

'Then it may be all right. But there is just one point before I begin. In the past, when you have contrived to extricate self or some pal from some little difficulty, you have frequently shown a disposition to take advantage of my gratitude to gain some private end. Those purple socks, for instance. Also the plus fours and the Old Etonian spats. Choosing your moment with subtle cunning, you came to me when I was weakened by relief and got me to get rid of them. And what I am saying now is that if you are successful on the present occasion there must be no rot of that description about that mess jacket of mine.'

'Very good, sir.'

'You will not come to me when all is over and ask me to jettison the jacket?'

'Certainly not, sir.'

'On that understanding then, I will carry on. Jeeves, I'm engaged.'

'I hope you will be very happy, sir.'

'Don't be an ass. I'm engaged to Miss Bassett.'

'Indeed, sir? I was not aware – '

'Nor was I. It came as a complete surprise. However, there it is. The official intimation was in that note you brought me.'

'Odd, sir.'

'What is?'

'Odd, sir, that the contents of that note should have been as you describe. It seemed to me that Miss Bassett, when she handed me the communication, was far from being in a happy frame of mind.'

'She is far from being in a happy frame of mind. You don't suppose she really wants to marry me, do you? Pshaw, Jeeves! Can't you see that this is simply another of those bally gestures which are rapidly rendering Brinkley Court a hell for man and beast? Dash all gestures, is my view.'

'Yes, sir.'

'Well, what's to be done?'

'You feel that Miss Bassett, despite what has occurred, still retains a fondness for Mr Fink-Nottle, sir?'

'She's pining for him.'

'In that case, sir, surely the best plan would be to bring about a reconciliation between them.'

'How? You see. You stand silent and twiddle the fingers. You are stumped.'

'No, sir. If I twiddled my fingers, it was merely to assist thought.'

'Then continue twiddling.'

'It will not be necessary, sir.'

'You don't mean you've got a bite already?'

'Yes, sir.'

'You astound me, Jeeves. Let's have it.'

'The device which I have in mind is one that I have already mentioned to you, sir.'

'When did you ever mention any device to me?'

'If you will throw your mind back to the evening of our arrival, sir. You were good enough to inquire of me if I had any plan to put forward with a view to bringing Miss Angela and Mr Glossop together, and I ventured to suggest – '

'Good Lord! Not the old fire-alarm thing?'

'Precisely, sir.'

'You're still sticking to that?'

'Yes, sir.'

It shows how much the ghastly blow I had received had shaken me when I say that, instead of dismissing the proposal with a curt 'Tchah!' or anything like that, I found myself speculating as to whether there might not be something in it, after all.

When he had first mooted this fire-alarm scheme of his, I had sat upon it, if you remember, with the maximum of promptitude and vigour. 'Rotten' was the adjective I had employed to describe it, and you may recall that I mused a bit sadly, considering the idea conclusive proof of the general breakdown of a once fine mind. But now it somehow began to look as if it might have possibilities. The fact of the matter was that I had about reached the stage where I was prepared to try anything once, however goofy.

'Just run through that wheeze again, Jeeves,' I said thoughtfully. 'I remember thinking it cuckoo, but it may be that I missed some of the finer shades.'

'Your criticism of it at the time, sir, was that it was too elaborate, but I do not think it is so in reality. As I see it, sir, the occupants of the house, hearing the fire bell ring, will suppose that a conflagration has broken out.'

I nodded. One could follow the train of thought.

'Yes, that seems reasonable.'

'Whereupon Mr Glossop will hasten to save Miss Angela, while Mr Fink-Nottle performs the same office for Miss Bassett.'

'Is that based on psychology?'

'Yes, sir. Possibly you may recollect that it was an axiom of the late Sir Arthur Conan Doyle's fictional detective, Sherlock Holmes, that the instinct of everyone, upon an alarm of fire, is to save the object dearest to them.'

'It seems to me that there is a grave danger of seeing Tuppy come out carrying a steak-and-kidney pie, but resume, Jeeves, resume. You think that this would clean everything up.'

'The relations of the two young couples could scarcely continue distant after such an occurrence, sir.'

'Perhaps you're right. But, dash it, if we go ringing fire bells in the night watches, shan't we scare half the domestic staff into fits? There is one of the housemaids – Jane, I believe – who already skips like the high hills if I so much as come on her unexpectedly round a corner.'

'A neurotic girl, sir, I agree. I have noticed her. But by acting promptly we should avoid such a contingency. The entire staff, with the exception of Monsieur Anatole, will be at the ball at Kingham Manor tonight.'

'Of course. That just shows the condition this thing has reduced me to. Forget my own name next. Well, then, let's just try to envisage. Bong goes the bell. Gussie rushes and grabs the Bassett . . . Wait. Why shouldn't she simply walk downstairs?'

'You are overlooking the effect of sudden alarm on the feminine temperament, sir.'

'That's true.'

'Miss Bassett's impulse, I would imagine, sir, would be to leap from her window.'

'Well, that's worse. We don't want her spread out in a sort of *purée* on the lawn. It seems to me that the flaw in this scheme of yours, Jeeves, is that it's going to litter the garden with mangled corpses.'

'No, sir. You will recall that Mr Travers's fear of burglars has caused him to have stout bars fixed to all the windows.'

'Of course, yes. Well, it sounds all right,' I said, though still a bit doubtfully. 'Quite possibly it may come off. But I have a feeling that it will slip up somewhere. However, I am in no position to cavil at even a 100 to 1 shot. I will adopt this policy of yours, Jeeves, though, as I say, with misgivings. At what hour would you suggest bonging the bell?'

'Not before midnight, sir.'

'That is to say, some time after midnight.'

'Yes, sir.'

'Right ho, then. At 12.30 on the dot, I will bong.'

'Very good, sir.'

22

I don't know why it is, but there's something about the rural districts after dark that always has a rummy effect on me. In London I can stay out till all hours and come home with the milk without a tremor, but put me in the garden of a country house after the strength of the company has gone to roost and the place is shut up, and a sort of goose-fleshy feeling steals over me. The night wind stirs the tree tops, twigs crack, bushes rustle, and before I know where I am, the morale has gone phut and I'm expecting the family ghost to come sneaking up behind me, making groaning noises.

Dashed unpleasant, the whole thing, and if you think it improves matters to know that you are shortly about to ring the loudest fire bell in England and start an all-hands-to-the-pumps panic in that quiet, darkened house, you err.

I knew all about the Brinkley Court fire bell. The dickens of a row it makes. Uncle Tom, in addition to not liking burglars, is a bloke who has always objected to the idea of being cooked in his sleep, so when he bought the place he saw to it that the fire bell should be something that might give you heart failure, but which you couldn't possibly mistake for the drowsy chirping of a sparrow in the ivy.

When I was a kid and spent my holidays at Brinkley, we used to have fire drills after closing time, and many is the night I've had it jerk me out of the dreamless like the Last Trump.

I confess that the recollection of what this bell could do when it buckled down to it gave me pause as I stood that night at 12.30 p.m. prompt beside the outhouse where it was located. The sight of the rope against the whitewashed wall and the thought of the bloodsome uproar which was about to smash the peace of the night into hash served to deepen that rummy feeling to which I have alluded.

Moreover, now that I had had time to meditate upon it, I was more than ever defeatist about this scheme of Jeeves's.

Jeeves seemed to take it for granted that Gussie and Tuppy, faced with a hideous fate, would have no thought beyond saving the Bassett and Angela.

I could not bring myself to share his sunny confidence.

I mean to say, I know how moments when they're faced with a hideous fate affect chaps. I remember Freddie Widgeon, one of the most chivalrous birds in the Drones, telling me how there was an alarm of fire once at a seaside hotel where he was staying and, far from rushing about saving women, he was down the escape within ten seconds of the kick-off, his mind concerned with but one thing – viz., the personal well-being of F. Widgeon.

As far as any idea of doing the delicately nurtured a bit of good went, he tells me, he was prepared to stand underneath and catch them in blankets, but no more.

Why, then, should this not be so with Augustus Fink-Nottle and Hildebrand Glossop?

Such were my thoughts as I stood toying with the rope, and I believe I should have turned the whole thing up, had it not been at this juncture there floated into my mind a picture of the Bassett hearing that bell for the first time. Coming as a wholly new experience, it would probably startle her into a decline.

And so agreeable was this reflection that I waited no longer, but seized the rope, braced the feet and snapped into it.

Well, as I say, I hadn't been expecting that bell to hush things up to any great extent. Nor did it. The last time I had heard it, I had been in my room on the other side of the house, and even so it had hoiked me out of bed as if something had exploded under me. Standing close to it like this, I got the full force and meaning of the thing, and I've never heard anything like it in my puff.

I rather enjoy a bit of noise, as a general rule. I remember Catsmeat Potter-Pirbright bringing a police rattle into the Drones one night and loosing it off behind my chair, and I just lay back and closed my eyes with a pleasant smile, like someone in a box at the opera. And the same applies to the time when my Aunt Agatha's son, young Thos., put a match to the parcel of Guy Fawkes' Day fireworks to see what would happen.

But the Brinkley Court fire bell was too much for me. I gave about half a dozen tugs, and then, feeling that enough was enough, sauntered round to the front lawn to ascertain what solid results had been achieved.

Brinkley Court had given of its best. A glance told me that we were playing to capacity. The eye, roving to and fro, noted here Uncle Tom in a purple dressing gown, there Aunt Dahlia in the old blue and yellow. It also fell upon Anatole, Tuppy, Gussie, Angela, the Bassett and Jeeves, in the order named. There they all were, present and correct.

But – and this was what caused me immediate concern – I could detect no sign whatever that there had been any rescue work going on.

What I had been hoping, of course, was to see Tuppy bending solicitously over Angela in one corner, while Gussie fanned the Bassett with a towel in the other.

Instead of which, the Bassett was one of the group which included Aunt Dahlia and Uncle Tom and seemed to be busy trying to make Anatole see the bright side, while Angela and Gussie were, respectively, leaning against the sundial with a peeved look and sitting on the grass rubbing a barked shin. Tuppy was walking up and down the path, all by himself.

A disturbing picture, you will admit. It was with a rather imperious gesture that I summoned Jeeves to my side.

'Well, Jeeves?'

'Sir?'

I eyed him sternly. 'Sir?' forsooth!

'It's no good saying "Sir?" Jeeves. Look round you. See for yourself. Your scheme has proved a bust.'

'Certainly it would appear that matters have not arranged themselves quite as we anticipated, sir.'

'We?'

'As I had anticipated, sir.'

'That's more like it. Didn't I tell you it would be a flop?'

'I remember that you did seem dubious, sir.'

'Dubious is no word for it, Jeeves. I hadn't a scrap of faith in the idea from the start. When you first mooted it, I said it was rotten, and I was right. I'm not blaming you, Jeeves. It is not your fault that you have sprained your brain. But after this – forgive me if it hurts your feelings, Jeeves – I shall know better than to allow you to handle any but the simplest and most elementary problems. It is best to be candid about this, don't you think? Kindest to be frank and straightforward?'

'Certainly, sir.'

'I mean, the surgeon's knife, what?'

'Precisely, sir.'

'I consider – '

'If you will pardon me for interrupting you, sir, I fancy Mrs Travers is endeavouring to attract your attention.'

And at this moment a ringing 'Hoy!' which could have proceeded only from the relative in question, assured me that his view was correct.

'Just step this way a moment, Attila, if you don't mind,' boomed that well-known – and under certain conditions, well-loved – voice, and I moved over.

I was not feeling unmixedly at my ease. For the first time it was beginning to steal upon me that I had not prepared a really good story in support of my questionable behaviour in ringing fire bells at such an hour, and I have known Aunt Dahlia to express herself with a hearty freedom upon far smaller provocation.

She exhibited, however, no signs of violence. More a sort of frozen calm, if you know what I mean. You could see that she was a woman who had suffered.

'Well, Bertie, dear,' she said, 'here we all are.'

'Quite,' I replied guardedly.

'Nobody missing, is there?'

'I don't think so.'

'Splendid. So much healthier for us out in the open like this than frowsting in bed. I had just dropped off when you did your bell-ringing act. For it was you, my sweet child, who rang that bell, was it not?'

'I did ring the bell, yes.'

'Any particular reason, or just a whim?'

'I thought there was a fire.'

'What gave you that impression, dear?'

'I thought I saw flames.'

'Where, darling? Tell Aunt Dahlia.'

'In one of the windows.'

'I see. So we have all been dragged out of bed and scared rigid because you have been seeing things.'

Here Uncle Tom made a noise like a cork coming out

of a bottle, and Anatole, whose moustache had hit a new low, said something about 'some apes' and, if I am not mistaken, a *'rogommier'* – whatever that is.

'I admit I was mistaken. I am sorry.'

'Don't apologize, ducky. Can't you see how pleased we all are? What were you doing out here, anyway?'

'Just taking a stroll.'

'I see. And are you proposing to continue your stroll?'

'No, I think I'll go in now.'

'That's fine. Because I was thinking of going in, too, and I don't believe I could sleep knowing you were out here giving rein to that powerful imagination of yours. The next thing that would happen would be that you would think you saw a pink elephant sitting on the drawing-room windowsill and start throwing bricks at it . . . Well, come on, Tom, the entertainment seems to be over . . . But wait. The newt king wishes a word with us . . . Yes, Mr Fink-Nottle?'

Gussie, as he joined our little group, seemed upset about something.

'I say!'

'Say on, Augustus.'

'I say, what are we going to do?'

'Speaking for myself, I intend to return to bed.'

'But the door's shut.'

'What door?'

'The front door. Somebody must have shut it.'

'Then I shall open it.'

'But it won't open.'

'Then I shall try another door.'

'But all the other doors are shut.'

'What? Who shut them?'

'I don't know.'

I advanced a theory.

'The wind?'

Aunt Dahlia's eyes met mine.

'Don't try me too high,' she begged. 'Not now, precious.' And, indeed, even as I spoke, it did strike me that the night was pretty still.

Uncle Tom said we must get in through a window. Aunt Dahlia sighed a bit.

'How? Could Lloyd George do it, could Winston do it, could Baldwin do it? No. Not since you had those bars of yours put on.'

'Well, well, well. God bless my soul, ring the bell, then.'

'The fire bell?'

'The door bell.'

'To what end, Thomas? There's nobody in the house. The servants are all at Kingham.'

'But, confound it all, we can't stop out here all night.'

'Can't we? You just watch us. There is nothing – literally nothing – which a country house party can't do with Attila here operating on the premises. Seppings presumably took the back-door key with him. We must just amuse ourselves till he comes back.'

Tuppy made a suggestion:

'Why not take out one of the cars and drive over to Kingham and get the key from Seppings?'

It went well. No question about that. For the first time, a smile lit up Aunt Dahlia's drawn face. Uncle Tom grunted approvingly. Anatole said something in Provençal that sounded complimentary. And I thought I detected even on Angela's map a slight softening.

'A very excellent idea,' said Aunt Dahlia. 'One of the best. Nip round to the garage at once.'

After Tuppy had gone, some extremely flattering things were said about his intelligence and resource, and there was a disposition to draw rather invidious comparisons between him and Bertram. Painful for me, of course, but the ordeal didn't last long, for it couldn't have been more than five minutes before he was with us again.

Tuppy seemed perturbed.

'I say, it's all off.'

'Why?'

'The garage is locked.'

'Unlock it.'

'I haven't the key.'

'Shout, then, and wake Waterbury.'

'Who's Waterbury?'

'The chauffeur, ass. He sleeps over the garage.'

'But he's gone to the dance at Kingham.'

It was the final wallop. Until this moment, Aunt Dahlia had been able to preserve her frozen calm. The dam now burst. The years rolled away from her, and she was once more the Dahlia Wooster of the old yoicks-and-tantivy days – the emotional, free-speaking girl who had so often risen in her stirrups to yell derogatory personalities at people who were heading hounds.

'Curse all dancing chauffeurs! What on earth does a chauffeur want to dance for? I mistrusted that man from the start. Something told me he was a dancer. Well, this finishes it. We're out here till breakfast-time. If those blasted servants come back before eight o'clock, I shall be vastly surprised. You won't get Seppings away from a dance till you throw him out. I know him. The jazz'll go to his head, and he'll stand clapping and demanding encores till his hands blister. Damn all dancing butlers! What is Brinkley Court? A respectable English country house or a crimson dancing school? One might as well be living in the middle of the Russian Ballet. Well, all right. If we must stay out here, we must. We shall all be frozen stiff, except' – here she directed at me not one of her friendliest glances – 'Except dear old Attila, who is, I observe, well and warmly clad. We will resign ourselves to the prospect of freezing to death like the Babes in the Wood, merely expressing a dying wish that our pal Attila will see that we are covered with leaves. No doubt he will also toll that fire bell of his as a mark of respect – And what might you want, my good man?'

She broke off, and stood glaring at Jeeves. During the latter portion of her address, he had been standing by in a respectful manner, endeavouring to catch the speaker's eye.

'If I might make a suggestion, madam.'

I am not saying that in the course of our long association I have always found myself able to view Jeeves with approval. There are aspects of his character which have frequently caused coldness to arise between us. He is one of those fellows who, if you give them a thingummy, take a what-d'you-call it. His work is often raw, and he has been known to allude to me as 'mentally negligible'. More than once, as I have shown, it has been my painful task to squelch in him a tendency to get uppish and treat the young master as a serf or peon.

These are grave defects.

But one thing I have never failed to hand the man. He is magnetic. There is about him something that seems to soothe and hypnotize. To the best of my knowledge, he has never encountered a charging rhinoceros, but should this contingency occur, I have no doubt that the animal, meeting his eye, would check itself in midstride, roll over and lie purring with its legs in the air.

At any rate he calmed down Aunt Dahlia, the nearest thing to a charging rhinoceros, in under five seconds. He just stood there looking respectful, and though I didn't time the thing – not having a stopwatch on me – I should say it wasn't more than three seconds and a quarter before her whole manner underwent an astounding change for the better. She melted before one's eyes.

'Jeeves! You haven't got an idea?'

'Yes, madam.'

'That great brain of yours has really clicked as ever in the hour of need?'

'Yes, madam.'

'Jeeves,' said Aunt Dahlia in a shaking voice, 'I am sorry I spoke so abruptly. I was not myself. I might have known that you would not come simply trying to make conversation. Tell us this idea of yours, Jeeves. Join our little group of thinkers and let us hear what you have to say. Make yourself at home, Jeeves, and give us the good word. Can you really get us out of this mess?'

'Yes, madam, if one of the gentlemen would be willing to ride a bicycle.'

'A bicycle?'

'There is a bicycle in the gardener's shed in the kitchen garden, madam. Possibly one of the gentlemen might feel disposed to ride over to Kingham Manor and procure the back-door key from Mr Seppings.'

'Splendid, Jeeves!'

'Thank you, madam.'

'Wonderful!'

'Thank you, madam.'

'Attila!' said Aunt Dahlia, turning and speaking in a quiet, authoritative manner.

I had been expecting it. From the very moment those ill-judged words had passed the fellow's lips, I had had a presentiment that a determined effort would be made to elect me as the goat, and I braced myself to resist and obstruct.

And as I was about to do so, while I was in the very act of summoning up all my eloquence to protest that I didn't know how to ride a bike and couldn't possibly learn in the brief time at my disposal, I'm dashed if the man didn't go and nip me in the bud.

'Yes, madam, Mr Wooster would perform the task admirably. He is an expert cyclist. He has often boasted to me of his triumphs on the wheel.'

I hadn't. I hadn't done anything of the sort. It's simply monstrous how one's words get twisted. All I had ever done was to mention to him – casually, just as an interesting item of information, one day in New York when we were watching the six-day bicycle race – that at the age of fourteen, while spending my holidays with a vicar of sorts who had been told off to teach me Latin, I had won the Choir Boys' Handicap at the local school treat.

A different thing from boasting of one's triumphs on the wheel.

I mean, he was a man of the world and must have known that the form of school treats is never of the hottest. And, if I'm not mistaken, I had specifically told him that on the occasion referred to I had received half a lap start and that Willie Punting, the odds-on favourite to whom the race was expected to be a gift, had been forced to retire, owing to having pinched his elder brother's machine without asking the elder brother, and the elder brother coming along just as the pistol went and giving him one on the side of the head and taking it away from him, thus rendering him a scratched-at-the-post non-starter. Yet, from the way he talked, you would have thought I was one of those chaps in sweaters with medals all over them, whose photographs bob up from time to time in the illustrated press on the occasion of their having ridden from Hyde Park to Glasgow in three seconds under the hour, or whatever it is.

And as if this were not bad enough, Tuppy had to shove his oar in.

'That's right,' said Tuppy. 'Bertie has always been a great cyclist. I remember at Oxford he used to take all his clothes off on bump-supper nights and ride around the quad, singing comic songs. Jolly fast he used to go too.'

'Then he can go jolly fast now,' said Aunt Dahlia with animation. 'He can't go too fast for me. He may also sing comic songs, if he likes . . . And if you wish to take your clothes off, Bertie, my lamb, by all means do so. But whether clothed or in the nude, whether singing comic songs or not singing comic songs, get a move on.'

I found speech.

'I haven't ridden for years.'

'Then it's high time you began again.'

'I've probably forgotten how to ride.'

'You'll soon get the knack after you've taken a toss or two. Trial and error. The only way.'

'But it's miles to Kingham.'

'So the sooner you're off, the better.'

'But – '

'Bertie, dear.'

'But, dash it – '

'Bertie, darling.'

'Yes, but dash it – '

'Bertie, my sweet.'

And so it was arranged. Presently I was moving sombrely off through the darkness, Jeeves at my side, Aunt Dahlia calling after me something about trying to imagine myself the man who brought the good news from Ghent to Aix. The first I had heard of the chap.

'So, Jeeves,' I said, as we reached the shed, and my voice was cold and bitter, 'this is what your great scheme has accomplished! Tuppy, Angela, Gussie and the Bassett not on speaking terms, and self faced with an eight-mile ride – '

'Nine, I believe, sir.'

'- a nine-mile ride, and another nine-mile ride back.'

'I am sorry, sir.'

'No good being sorry now. Where is this foul boneshaker?'

'I will bring it out, sir.'

He did so. I eyed it sourly.'

'Where's the lamp?'

'I fear there is no lamp, sir.'

'No lamp?'

'No, sir.'

'But I may come a fearful stinker without a lamp. Suppose I barge into something?'

I broke off and eyed him frigidly.

'You smile, Jeeves. The thought amuses you?'

'I beg your pardon, sir. I was thinking of a tale my Uncle Cyril used to tell me as a child. An absurd little story, sir, though I confess that I have always found it droll. According to my Uncle Cyril, two men named Nicholls and Jackson set out to ride to Brighton on a tandem bicycle, and were so unfortunate as to come into collision with a brewer's van. And when the rescue party arrived on the scene of the accident, it was discovered that they had been hurled together with such force that it was impossible to sort them out at all adequately. The keenest eye could not discern which portion of the fragments was Nicholls and which Jackson. So they collected as much as they could, and called it Nixon. I was remembering laughing very much at that story when I was a child, sir.'

I had to pause a moment to master my feelings.

'You did, eh?'

'Yes, sir.'

'You thought it funny?'

'Yes, sir.'

'And your Uncle Cyril thought it funny?'

'Yes, sir.'

'Golly, what a family! Next time you meet your Uncle Cyril, Jeeves, you can tell him from me that his sense of humour is morbid and unpleasant.'

'He is dead, sir.'

'Thank heaven for that . . . Well, give me the blasted machine.'

'Very good, sir.'

'Are the tyres inflated?'

'Yes, sir.'

'The nuts firm, the brakes in order, the sprockets running true with the differential gear?'

'Yes, sir.'

'Right ho, Jeeves.'

In Tuppy's statement that, when at the University of Oxford, I had been known to ride a bicycle in the nude about the quadrangle of our mutual college, there had been, I cannot deny, a certain amount of substance. Correct, however, though his facts were, so far as they went, he had not told all. What he had omitted to mention was that I had invariably been well oiled at the time, and when in that condition a chap is capable of feats at which in cooler moments his reason would rebel.

Stimulated by the juice, I believe, men have even been known to ride alligators.

As I started now to pedal out into the great world, I was icily sober, and the old skill, in consequence, had deserted me entirely. I found myself wobbling badly, and all the stories I had ever heard of nasty bicycle accidents came back to me with a rush, headed by Jeeves's Uncle Cyril's cheery little anecdote about Nicholls and Jackson.

Pounding wearily through the darkness, I found myself at a loss to fathom the mentality of men like Jeeves's Uncle Cyril. What on earth he could see funny in a disaster which had apparently involved the complete extinction of a human creature – or, at any rate, of half a human creature and half another human creature – was more than I could understand. To me, the thing was one of the most poignant tragedies that had ever been brought to my attention, and I have no doubt that I should have continued to brood over it for quite a time, had my thoughts not been diverted by the sudden necessity of zigzagging sharply in order to avoid a pig in the fairway.

For a moment it looked like being real Nicholls-and-Jackson stuff, but, fortunately, a quick zig on my part coinciding with an adroit zag on the part of the pig, enabled me to win through, and I continued to ride safe, but with the heart fluttering like a captive bird.

The effect of this narrow squeak upon me was to shake the nerve to the utmost. The fact that pigs were abroad in the night seemed to bring home to me the perilous nature of my enterprise. It set me thinking of all the other things that could happen to a man out and about on a velocipede without a lamp after lighting-up time. In particular, I recalled the statement of a pal of mine that in certain sections of the rural districts goats were accustomed to stray across the road to the extent of their chains, thereby forming about as sound a booby trap as one could well wish.

He mentioned, I remember, the case of a friend of his whose machine got entangled with a goat chain and who was dragged seven miles – like skijoring in Switzerland – so that he was never the same man again. And there was one chap who ran into an elephant, left over from a travelling circus.

Indeed, taking it for all in all, it seemed to me that, with the possible exception of being bitten by sharks, there was virtually no front-page disaster that could not happen to a fellow, once he had allowed his dear ones to override his better judgment and shove him out into the great unknown on a push-bike, and I am not ashamed to confess that, taking it by and large, the amount of quailing I did from this point on was pretty considerable.

However, in respect to goats and elephants, I must say things panned out unexpectedly well.

Oddly enough, I encountered neither. But when you have said that you have said everything, for in every other way the conditions could scarcely have been fouler.

Apart from the ceaseless anxiety of having to keep an eye skinned for elephants, I found myself much depressed by barking dogs, and once I received a most unpleasant shock when, alighting to consult a signpost, I saw sitting on top of it an owl that looked exactly like my Aunt Agatha. So agitated, indeed, had my frame of mind become by this time that I thought at first it was Aunt Agatha, and only when reason and reflection told me how alien to her habits it would be to climb signposts and sit on them, could I pull myself together and overcome the weakness.

In short, what with all this mental disturbance added to the more purely physical anguish in the billowy portions and the calves and ankles, the Bertram Wooster who eventually toppled off at the door of Kingham Manor was a very different Bertram from the gay and insouciant *boulevardier* of Bond Street and Piccadilly.

Even to one unaware of the inside facts, it would have been evident that Kingham Manor was throwing its weight about a bit tonight. Lights shone in the windows, music was in the air, and as I drew nearer my ear detected the sibilant shuffling of the feet of butlers, footmen, chauffeurs, parlour maids, house maids, tweenies and, I have no doubt, cooks, who were busily treading the measure. I suppose you couldn't sum it up much better than by saying that there was a sound of revelry by night.

The orgy was taking place in one of the ground-floor rooms which had french windows opening on to the drive, and it was to these french windows that I now made my way. An orchestra was playing something with a good deal of zip to it, and under happier conditions I dare say my feet would have started twitching in time to the melody. But I had sterner work before me than to stand hoofing it by myself on gravel drives. I wanted that back-door key, and I wanted it instanter.

Scanning the throng within, I found it difficult for a while to spot Seppings. Presently, however, he hove in view, doing fearfully lissom things in midfloor. I 'Hi-Seppings!'-ed a couple of times, but his mind was too much on his job to be diverted, and it was only when the swirl of the dance had brought him within prodding distance of my forefinger that a quick one to the lower ribs enabled me to claim his attention.

The unexpected buffet caused him to trip over his partner's feet, and it was with marked austerity that he turned. As he recognized Bertram, however, coldness melted, to be replaced by astonishment.

'Mr Wooster!'

I was in no mood for bandying words.

'Less of the "Mr Wooster" and more back-door keys,' I said curtly. 'Give me the key of the back door, Seppings.'

He did not seem to grasp the gist.

'The key of the back door, sir?'

'Precisely. The Brinkley Court back-door key.'

'But it is at the Court, sir.'

I clicked the tongue, annoyed.

'Don't be frivolous, my dear old butler,' I said. 'I haven't ridden nine miles on a push-bike to listen to you trying to be funny. You've got it in your trousers pocket.'

'No, sir. I left it with Mr Jeeves.'

'You did – what?'

'Yes, sir. Before I came away. Mr Jeeves said that he wished to walk in the garden before retiring for the night. He was to place the key on the kitchen windowsill.'

I stared at the man dumbly. His eye was clear, his hand steady. He had none of the appearance of a butler who has had a couple.

'You mean that all this while the key has been in Jeeves's possession?'

'Yes, sir.'

I could speak no more. Emotion had overmastered my voice. I was at a loss and not abreast; but of one thing, it seemed to me, there could be no doubt. For some reason, not to be fathomed now, but most certainly to be gone well into as soon as I had pushed this infernal sewing-machine of mine over those nine miles of lonely country road and got within striking distance of him, Jeeves had been doing the dirty. Knowing that at any given moment he could have solved the whole situation, he had kept Aunt Dahlia and others roosting out on the front lawn *en déshabille* and, worse still, had stood calmly by and watched his young employer set out on a wholly unnecessary eighteen-mile bicycle ride.

I could scarcely believe such a thing of him. Of his Uncle Cyril, yes. With that distorted sense of humour of his, Uncle Cyril might quite conceivably have been capable of such conduct. But that it should be Jeeves –

I leaped into the saddle and, stifling the cry of agony which rose to the lips as the bruised person touched the hard leather, set out on the homeward journey.

23

I remember Jeeves saying on one occasion – I forget how the subject had arisen – he may simply have thrown the observation out, as he does sometimes, for me to take or leave – that hell hath no fury like a woman scorned. And until tonight I had always felt that there was a lot in it. I had never scorned a woman myself, but Pongo Twistleton once scorned an aunt of his, flatly refusing to meet her son Gerald at Paddington and give him lunch and see him off to school at Waterloo, and he never heard the end of it. Letters were written, he tells me, which had to be seen to be believed. Also two very strong telegrams and a bitter picture postcard with a view of the Little Chilbury War Memorial on it.

Until tonight, therefore, as I say, I had never questioned the accuracy of the statement. Scorned women first and the rest nowhere, was how it had always seemed to me.

But tonight I revised my views. If you want to know what hell can really do in the way of furies, look for the chap who has been hornswoggled into taking a long and unnecessary bicycle ride in the dark without a lamp.

Mark that word 'unnecessary'. That was the part of it that really jabbed the iron into the soul. I mean, if it was a case of riding to the doctor's to save the child with croup, or going off to the local pub to fetch supplies in the event of the cellar having run dry, no one would leap to the handlebars more readily than I. Young Lochinvar, absolutely. But this business of being put through it merely to gratify one's personal attendant's diseased sense of the amusing was a bit too thick, and I chafed from start to finish.

So, what I mean to say, although the providence which watches over good men saw to it that I was enabled to complete the homeward journey unscathed except in the billowy portions, removing from my path all goats, elephants, and even owls that looked like my Aunt Agatha, it was a frowning and jaundiced Bertram who finally came to anchor at the Brinkley Court front door. And when I saw a dark figure emerging from the porch to meet me, I prepared to let myself go and uncork all that was fizzing in the mind.

'Jeeves!' I said.

'It is I, Bertie.'

The voice which spoke sounded like warm treacle, and even if I had not recognized it immediately as that of the Bassett, I should have known that it did not proceed from the man I was yearning to confront. For this figure before me was wearing a simple tweed dress and had employed my first name in its remarks. And Jeeves, whatever his moral defects, would never go about in skirts calling me Bertie.

The last person, of course, whom I would have wished to meet after a long evening in the saddle, but I vouchsafed a courteous 'What ho!'

There was a pause, during which I massaged the calves. Mine, of course, I mean.

'You got in, then?' I said, in allusion to the change of costume.

'Oh, yes. About a quarter of an hour after you left Jeeves went searching about and found the back-door key on the kitchen windowsill.'

'Ha!'

'What?'

'Nothing.'

'I thought you said something.'

'No, nothing.'

And I continued to do so. For at this juncture, as had so often happened when this girl and I were closeted, the conversation once more went blue on us. The night breeze whispered, but not the Bassett. A bird twittered, but not so much as a chirp escaped Bertram. It was perfectly amazing, the way her mere presence seemed to wipe speech from my lips – and mine, for that matter, from hers. It began to look as if our married life together would be rather like twenty years among the Trappist monks.

'Seen Jeeves anywhere?' I asked, eventually coming through.

'Yes, in the dining room.'

'The dining room?'

'Waiting on everybody. They are having eggs and bacon and champagne . . . What did you say?'

I had said nothing – merely snorted. There was something about the thought of these people carelessly revelling at a time when, for all they knew, I was probably being dragged about the countryside by goats or chewed by elephants, that struck home at me like a poisoned dart. It was the sort of thing you read about as having happened just before the French Revolution – the haughty nobles in their castles callously digging in and quaffing while the unfortunate blighters outside were suffering frightful privations.

The voice of the Bassett cut in on these mordant reflections:

'Bertie.'

'Hallo!'

Silence.

'Hallo!' I said again.

No response. Whole thing rather like one of those telephone conversations where you sit at your end of the wire saying: 'Hallo! Hallo!' unaware that the party of the second part has gone off to tea.

Eventually, however, she came to the surface again:

'Bertie, I have something to say to you.'

'What?'

'I have something to say to you.'

'I know. I said "What?" '

'Oh, I thought you didn't hear what I said.'

'Yes, I heard what you said, all right, but not what you were going to say.'

'Oh, I see.'

'Right ho.'

So that was straightened out. Nevertheless, instead of proceeding she took time off once more. She stood twisting the fingers and scratching the gravel with her foot. When finally she spoke, it was to deliver an impressive boost:

'Bertie, do you read Tennyson?'

'Not if I can help.'

'You remind me so much of those Knights of the Round Table in the "Idylls of the King".'

Of course I had heard of them – Lancelot, Galahad and all that lot, but I didn't see where the resemblance came in. It seemed to me that she must be thinking of a couple of other fellows.

'How do you mean?'

'You have such a great heart, such a fine soul. You are so generous, so unselfish, so chivalrous. I have always felt that about you – that you are one of the few really chivalrous men I have ever met.'

Well, dashed difficult, of course, to know what to say when someone is giving you the old oil on a scale like that. I muttered an 'Oh, yes?' or something on those lines, and rubbed the billowy portions in some embarrassment. And there was another silence, broken only by a sharp howl as I rubbed a bit too hard.

'Bertie.'

'Hallo?'

I heard her give a sort of gulp.

'Bertie, will you be chivalrous now?'

'Rather. Only too pleased. How do you mean?'

'I am going to try you to the utmost. I am going to test you as few men have ever been tested. I am going – '

I didn't like the sound of this.

'Well,' I said doubtfully, 'always glad to oblige, you know, but I've just had the dickens of a bicycle ride, and I'm a bit stiff and sore, especially in the – as I say, a bit stiff and sore. If it's anything to be fetched from upstairs – '

'No, no, you don't understand.'

'I don't, quite, no.'

'Oh, it's so difficult . . . How can I say it? . . . Can't you guess?'

'No. I'm dashed if I can.'

'Bertie – let me go!'

'But I haven't got hold of you.'

'Release me!'

'Re – '

And then I suddenly got it. I suppose it was fatigue that had made me so slow to apprehend the nub.

'What?'

I staggered, and the left pedal came up and caught me on the shin. But such was the ecstasy in the soul that I didn't utter a cry.

'Release you?'

'Yes.'

I didn't want any confusion on the point.

'You mean you want to call it all off? You're going to hitch up with Gussie, after all?'

'Only if you are fine and big enough to consent.'

'Oh, I am.'

'I gave you my promise.'

'Dash promises.'

'Then you really – '

'Absolutely.'

'Oh, Bertie!'

She seemed to sway like a sapling. It is saplings that sway, I believe.

'A very parfait knight!' I heard her murmur, and there not being much to say after that, I excused myself on the ground that I had got about two pecks of dust down my back and would like to go and get my maid to put me into something loose.

'You go back to Gussie,' I said, 'and tell him that all is well.'

She gave a sort of hiccup and, darting forward, kissed me on the forehead. Unpleasant, of course, but, as Anatole would say, I can take a few smooths with a rough. The next moment she was legging it for the dining room, while I, having bunged the bicycle into a bush, made for the stairs.

I need not dwell upon my buckedness. It can be readily imagined. Talk about chaps with the noose round their necks and the hangman about to let her go and somebody galloping up on a foaming horse, waving the reprieve – not in it. Absolutely not in it at all. I don't know that I can give you a better idea of the state of my feelings than by saying that as I started to cross the hall I was conscious of so profound a benevolence toward all created things that I found myself thinking kindly thoughts even of Jeeves.

I was about to mount the stairs when a sudden 'What ho!' from my rear caused me to turn. Tuppy was standing in the hall. He had apparently been down to the cellar for reinforcements, for there were a couple of bottles under his arm.

'Hullo, Bertie,' he said. 'You back?' He laughed

amusedly. 'You look like the Wreck of the Hesperus. Get run over by a steamroller or something?'

At any other time I might have found his coarse badinage hard to bear. But such was my uplifted mood that I waved it aside and slipped him the good news.

'Tuppy, old man, the Bassett's going to marry Gussie Fink-Nottle.'

'Tough luck on both of them, what?'

'But don't you understand? Don't you see what this means? It means that Angela is once more out of pawn, and you have only to play your cards properly – '

He bellowed rollickingly. I saw now that he was in the pink. As a matter of fact, I had noticed something of the sort directly I met him, but had attributed it to alcoholic stimulant.

'Good Lord! You're right behind the times, Bertie. Only to be expected, of course, if you will go riding bicycles half the night. Angela and I made it up hours ago.'

'What?'

'Certainly. Nothing but a passing tiff. All you need in these matters is a little give and take, a bit of reasonableness on both sides. We got together and talked things over. She withdrew my double chin. I conceded her shark. Perfectly simple. All done in minutes.'

'But – '

'Sorry, Bertie. Can't stop chatting with you all night. There is a rather impressive beano in progress in the dining room, and they are waiting for supplies.'

Endorsement was given to this statement by a sudden shout from the apartment named. I recognized – as who would not – Aunt Dahlia's voice:

'Glossop!'

'Hallo?'

'Hurry up with that stuff.'

'Coming, coming.'

'Well, come, then. Yoicks! Hard for-rard!'

'Tallyho, not to mention tantivy. Your aunt,' said Tuppy, 'is a bit above herself. I don't know all the facts of the case, but it appears that Anatole gave notice and has now consented to stay on, and also your uncle has given her a cheque for that paper of hers. I didn't get the details, but she is much braced. See you later. I must rush.'

To say that Bertram was now definitely nonplussed would be but to state the simple truth. I could make nothing of this. I had left Brinkley Court a stricken home, with hearts bleeding wherever you looked, and I had returned to find it a sort of earthly paradise. It baffled me.

I bathed bewilderedly. The toy duck was still in the soap dish, but I was too preoccupied to give it a thought. Still at a loss, I returned to my room, and there was Jeeves. And it is proof of my fogged condish that my first words to him were words not of reproach and stern recrimination but of inquiry:

'I say, Jeeves!'

'Good evening, sir. I was informed that you had returned. I trust you had an enjoyable ride.'

At any other moment, a crack like that would have woken the fiend in Bertram Wooster. I barely noticed it. I was intent on getting to the bottom of this mystery.

'But I say, Jeeves, what?'

'Sir?'

'What does all this mean?'

'You refer, sir – '

'Of course I refer. You know what I'm talking about. What has been happening here since I left? The place is positively stiff with happy endings.'

'Yes, sir. I am glad to say that my efforts have been rewarded.'

'What do you mean, your efforts? You aren't going

to try to make out that that rotten fire-bell scheme of yours had anything to do with it?'

'Yes, sir.'

'Don't be an ass, Jeeves. It flopped.'

'Not altogether, sir. I fear, sir, that I was not entirely frank with regard to my suggestion of ringing the fire bell. I had not really anticipated that it would in itself produce the desired results. I had intended it merely as a preliminary to what I might describe as the real business of the evening.'

'You gibber, Jeeves.'

'No, sir. It was essential that the ladies and gentlemen should be brought from the house, in order that, once out of doors, I could ensure that they remained there for the necessary period of time.'

'How do you mean?'

'My plan was based on psychology, sir.'

'How?'

'It is a recognized fact, sir, that there is nothing that so satisfactorily unites individuals who have been so unfortunate as to quarrel amongst themselves as a strong mutual dislike for some definite person. In my own family, if I may give a homely illustration, it was a generally accepted axiom that in times of domestic disagreement it was necessary only to invite my Aunt Annie for a visit to heal all breaches between the other members of the household. In the mutual animosity excited by Aunt Annie, those who had become estranged were reconciled almost immediately. Remembering this, it occurred to me that were you, sir, to be established as the person responsible for the ladies and gentlemen being forced to spend the night in the garden, everybody would take so strong a dislike to you that in this common sympathy they would sooner or later come together.'

I would have spoken, but he continued:

'And such proved to be the case. All, as you see, sir, is now well. After your departure on the bicycle, the various estranged parties agreed so heartily in their abuse of you that the ice, if I may use the expression, was broken, and it was not long before Mr Glossop was walking beneath the trees with Miss Angela, telling her anecdotes of your career at the university in exchange for hers regarding your childhood; while Mr Fink-Nottle, leaning against the sun-dial, held Miss Bassett enthralled with stories of your schooldays. Mrs Travers, meanwhile, was telling Monsieur Anatole – '

I found speech.

'Oh?' I said. 'I see. And now, I suppose, as the result of this dashed psychology of yours, Aunt Dahlia is so sore with me that it will be years before I can dare to show my face here again – years, Jeeves, during which, night after night, Anatole will be cooking those dinners of his – '

'No, sir. It was to prevent any such contingency that I suggested that you should bicycle to Kingham Manor. When I informed the ladies and gentlemen that I had found the key, and it was borne in upon them that you were having that long ride for nothing, their animosity vanished immediately, to be replaced by cordial amusement. There was much laughter.'

'There was, eh?'

'Yes, sir. I fear you may possibly have to submit to a certain amount of good-natured chaff, but nothing more. All, if I may say so, is forgiven, sir.'

'Oh?'

'Yes, sir.'

I mused awhile.

'You certainly seem to have fixed things.'

'Yes, sir.'

'Tuppy and Angela are once more betrothed. Also Gussie and the Bassett. Uncle Tom appears to have coughed up that money for *Milady's Boudoir*. And Anatole is staying on.

'Yes, sir.'

'I suppose you might say that all's well that ends well.'

'Very apt, sir.'

I mused again.

'All the same, your methods are a bit rough, Jeeves.'

'One cannot make an omelette without breaking eggs, sir.'

I started.

'Omelette! Do you think you could get me one?'

'Certainly, sir.'

'Together with half a bot. of something?'

'Undoubtedly, sir.'

'Do so, Jeeves, and with all speed.'

I climbed into bed and sank back against the pillows. I must say that my generous wrath had ebbed a bit. I was aching the whole length of my body, particularly toward the middle, but against this you had to set the fact that I was no longer engaged to Madeline Bassett. In a good cause one is prepared to suffer. Yes, looking at the things from every angle, I saw that Jeeves had done well, and it was with an approving beam that I welcomed him as he returned with the needful.

He did not check up with this beam. A bit grave, he seemed to me to be looking, and I probed the matter with a kindly query:

'Something on our mind, Jeeves?'

'Yes, sir. I should have mentioned it earlier, but in the evening's disturbance it escaped my memory. I fear I have been remiss, sir.'

'Yes, Jeeves?' I said, champing contentedly.

'In the matter of your mess jacket, sir.'

A nameless fear shot through me, causing me to swallow a mouthful of omelette the wrong way.

'I am sorry to say, sir, that while I was ironing it this afternoon I was careless enough to leave the hot instrument upon it. I very much fear that it will be impossible for you to wear it again, sir.'

One of those pregnant silences filled the room.

'I am extremely sorry, sir.'

For a moment, I confess, that generous wrath of mine came bounding back, hitching up its muscles and snorting a bit through the nose, but, as we say on the Riviera, *à quoi sert-il?* There was nothing to be gained by g. w. now.

We Woosters can bite the bullet. I nodded moodily and speared another slab of omelette.

'Right ho, Jeeves.'

'Very good, sir.'

P. G. Wodehouse

SHORT STORIES

To Bernard le Strange
and
E. Phillips Oppenheim

1
JEEVES TAKES CHARGE

Now, touching this business of old Jeeves – my man, you know – how do we stand? Lots of people think I'm much too dependent on him. My Aunt Agatha, in fact, has even gone so far as to call him my keeper. Well, what I say is: Why not? The man's a genius. From the collar upward he stands alone. I gave up trying to run my own affairs within a week of his coming to me. That was about half a dozen years ago, directly after the rather rummy business of Florence Craye, my Uncle Willoughby's book, and Edwin, the Boy Scout.

The thing really began when I got back to Easeby, my uncle's place in Shropshire. I was spending a week or so there, as I generally did in the summer; and I had had to break my visit to come back to London to get a new valet. I had found Meadowes, the fellow I had taken to Easeby with me, sneaking my silk socks, a thing no bloke of spirit could stick at any price. It transpiring, moreover, that he had looted a lot of other things here and there about the place. I was reluctantly compelled to hand the misguided blighter the mitten and go to London to ask the registry office to dig up another specimen for my approval. They sent me Jeeves.

I shall always remember the morning he came. It so happened that the night before I had been present at a rather cheery little supper, and I was feeling pretty rocky. On top of this I was trying to read a book Florence Craye had given me. She had been one of the house-party at Easeby, and two or three days before I left we had got engaged. I was due back at the end of the week, and I knew she would expect me to have finished the book by then. You see, she was particularly keen on boosting me up a bit nearer her own plane of intellect. She was a girl with a wonderful profile, but steeped to the gills in serious purpose. I can't give you a better idea of the way things stood than by telling you that the book she'd given me to read was called *Types of Ethical Theory*, and that when I opened it at random I struck a page beginning:

> The postulate or common understanding involved in speech is certainly co-extensive, in the obligation it carries, with the social organism of which language is the instrument, and the ends of which it is an effort to subserve.

All perfectly true, no doubt; but not the sort of thing to spring on a lad with a morning head.

I was doing my best to skim through this bright little volume when the bell rang. I crawled off the sofa and opened the door. A kind of darkish sort of respectful Johnnie stood without.

'I was sent by the agency, sir,' he said. 'I was given to understand that you require a valet.'

I'd have preferred an undertaker; but I told him to stagger in, and he floated noiselessly through the doorway like a healing zephyr. That impressed me from the start. Meadowes had had flat feet and used to clump. This fellow didn't seem to have any feet at all. He just streamed in. He had a grave, sympathetic face, as if he, too, knew what it was to sup with the lads.

'Excuse me, sir,' he said gently.

Then he seemed to flicker, and wasn't there any

longer. I heard him moving about in the kitchen, and presently he came back with a glass on a tray.

'If you would drink this, sir,' he said, with a kind of bedside manner, rather like the royal doctor shooting the bracer into the sick prince. 'It is a little preparation of my own invention. It is the Worcester Sauce that gives it colour. The raw egg makes it nutritious. The red pepper gives it its bite. Gentlemen have told me they have found it extremely invigorating after a late evening.'

I would have clutched at anything that looked like a lifeline that morning. I swallowed the stuff. For a moment I felt as if somebody had touched off a bomb inside the old bean and was strolling down my throat with a lighted torch, and then everything seemed suddenly to get all right. The sun shone in through the window; birds twittered in the tree-tops; and, generally speaking, hope dawned once more.

'You're engaged!' I said, as soon as I could say anything.

I perceived clearly that this cove was one of the world's workers, the sort no home should be without.

'Thank you, sir. My name is Jeeves.'

'You can start in at once?'

'Immediately, sir.'

'Because I'm due down at Easeby, in Shropshire, the day after tomorrow.'

'Very good, sir.' He looked past me at the mantelpiece. 'That is an excellent likeness of Lady Florence Craye, sir. It is two years since I saw her ladyship. I was at one time in Lord Worplesdon's employment. I tendered my resignation because I could not see eye to eye with his lordship in his desire to dine in dress trousers, a flannel shirt, and a shooting coat.'

He couldn't tell me anything I didn't know about

the old boy's eccentricity. This Lord Worplesdon was Florence's father. He was the old buster who, a few years later, came down to breakfast one morning, lifted the first cover he saw, said "Eggs! Eggs! Eggs! Damn all eggs!" in an overwrought sort of voice, and instantly legged it for France, never to return to the bosom of his family. This, mind you, being a bit of luck for the bosom of the family, for old Worplesdon had the worst temper in the county.

I had known the family ever since I was a kid, and from boyhood up this old boy had put the fear of death into me. Time, the great healer, could never remove from my memory the occasion when he found me – then a stripling of fifteen – smoking one of his special cigars in the stables. He got after me with a hunting-crop just at the moment when I was beginning to realize that what I wanted most on earth was solitude and repose, and chased me more than a mile across difficult country. If there was a flaw, so to speak, in the pure joy of being engaged to Florence, it was the fact that she rather took after her father, and one was never certain when she might erupt. She had a wonderful profile, though.

'Lady Florence and I are engaged, Jeeves,' I said.

'Indeed, sir?'

You know, there was a kind of rummy something about his manner. Perfectly all right and all that, but not what you'd call chirpy. It somehow gave me the impression that he wasn't keen on Florence. Well, of course, it wasn't my business. I supposed that while he had been valeting old Worplesdon she must have trodden on his toes in some way. Florence was a dear girl, and, seen sideways, most awfully good-looking; but if she had a fault it was a tendency to be a bit imperious with the domestic staff.

At this point in the proceedings there was another ring at the front door. Jeeves shimmered out and came back with a telegram. I opened it. It ran:

Return immediately. Extremely urgent. Catch first train. Florence.

'Rum!' I said.

'Sir?'

'Oh, nothing!'

It shows how little I knew Jeeves in those days that I didn't go a bit deeper into the matter with him. Nowadays I would never dream of reading a rummy communication without asking him what he thought of it. And this one was devilish odd. What I mean is, Florence knew I was going back to Easeby the day after tomorrow, anyway; so why the hurry call? Something must have happened, of course; but I couldn't see what on earth it could be.

'Jeeves,' I said, 'we shall be going down to Easeby this afternoon. Can you manage it?'

'Certainly, sir.'

'You can get your packing done and all that?'

'Without any difficulty, sir. Which suit will you wear for the journey?'

'This one.'

I had on a rather sprightly young check that morning, to which I was a good deal attached; I fancied it, in fact, more than a little. It was perhaps rather sudden till you got used to it, but, nevertheless, an extremely sound effort, which many lads at the club and elsewhere had admired unrestrainedly.

'Very good, sir.'

Again there was that kind of rummy something in his manner. It was the way he said it, don't you know. He didn't like the suit. I pulled myself together to assert myself. Something seemed to tell me that, unless I was jolly careful and nipped this lad in the bud, he would be starting to boss me. He had the aspect of a distinctly resolute blighter.

Well, I wasn't going to have any of that sort of thing, by Jove! I'd seen so many cases of fellows who had become perfect slaves to their valets. I remember poor old Aubrey Fothergill telling me – with absolute tears in his eyes, poor chap! – one night at the club, that he had been compelled to give up a favourite pair of brown shoes simply because Meekyn, his man, disapproved of them. You have to keep these fellows in their place, don't you know. You have to work the good old iron-hand-in-the-velvet-glove wheeze. If you give them a what's-its-name, they take a thingummy.

'Don't you like this suit, Jeeves?' I said coldly.

'Oh, yes, sir.'

'Well, what don't you like about it?'

'It is a very nice suit, sir.'

'Well, what's wrong with it? Out with it, dash it!'

'If I might make the suggestion, sir, a simple brown or blue, with a hint of some quiet twill – '

'What absolute rot!'

'Very good, sir.'

'Perfectly blithering, my dear man!'

'As you say, sir.'

I felt as if I had stepped on the place where the last stair ought to have been, but wasn't. I felt defiant, if you know what I mean, and there didn't seem anything to defy.

'All right, then,' I said.

'Yes, sir.'

And then he went away to collect his kit, while I started in again on *Types of Ethical Theory* and took a stab at a chapter headed "Idiopsychological Ethics".

Most of the way down in the train that afternoon, I was wondering what could be up at the other end. I simply couldn't see what could have happened. Easeby wasn't one of those country houses you read about in the society novels, where young girls are lured on to play baccarat and then skinned to the bone of their jewellery, and so on. The house-party I had left had consisted entirely of law-abiding birds like myself.

Besides, my uncle wouldn't have let anything of that kind go on in his house. He was a rather stiff, precise sort of old boy, who liked a quiet life. He was just finishing a history of the family or something, which he had been working on for the last year, and didn't stir much from the library. He was rather a good instance of what they say about its being a good scheme for a fellow to sow his wild oats. I'd been told that in his youth Uncle Willoughby had been a bit of a bounder. You would never have thought it to look at him now.

When I got to the house, Oakshott, the butler, told me that Florence was in her room, watching her maid pack. Apparently there was a dance on at a house about twenty miles away that night, and she was motoring over with some of the Easeby lot and would be away some nights. Oakshott said she had told him to tell her the moment I arrived; so I trickled into the smoking-room and waited, and presently in she came. A glance showed me that she was perturbed, and even peeved. Her eyes had a goggly look, and altogether she appeared considerably pipped.

'Darling!' I said, and attempted the good old embrace; but she side-stepped like a bantam-weight.

'Don't!'

'What's the matter?'

'Everything's the matter! Bertie, you remember asking

me, when you left, to make myself pleasant to your uncle?'

'Yes.'

The idea being, of course, that as at the time I was more or less dependent on Uncle Willoughby I couldn't very well marry without his approval. And though I knew he wouldn't have any objection to Florence, having known her father since they were at Oxford together, I hadn't wanted to take any chances; so I had told her to make an effort to fascinate the old boy.

'You told me it would please him particularly if I asked him to read me some of his history of the family.'

'Wasn't he pleased.'

'He was delighted. He finished writing the thing yesterday afternoon, and read me nearly all of it last night. I have never had such a shock in my life. The book is an outrage. It is impossible. It is horrible!'

'But, dash it, the family weren't so bad as all that.'

'It is not a history of the family at all. Your uncle has written his reminiscences! He calls them *Recollections of a Long Life*!'

I began to understand. As I say, Uncle Willoughby had been somewhat on the tabasco side as a young man, and it began to look as if he might have turned out something pretty fruity if he had started recollecting his long life.

'If half of what he has written is true,' said Florence, 'your uncle's youth must have been perfectly appalling. The moment we began to read he plunged straight into a most scandalous story of how he and my father were thrown out of a music-hall in 1887!'

'Why?'

'I decline to tell you why.'

It must have been something pretty bad. It took a lot to make them chuck people out of music-halls in 1887.

'Your uncle specifically states that father had drunk a quart and a half of champagne before beginning the evening,' she went on. 'The book is full of stories like that. There is a dreadful one about Lord Emsworth.'

'Lord Emsworth? Not the one we know? Not the one at Blandings?'

A most respectable old Johnnie, don't you know. Doesn't do a thing nowadays but dig in the garden with a spud.

'The very same. That is what makes the book so unspeakable. It is full of stories about people one knows who are the essence of propriety today, but who seem to have behaved, when they were in London in the eighties, in a manner that would not have been tolerated in the fo'c'sle of a whaler. Your uncle seems to remember everything disgraceful that happened to anybody when he was in his early twenties. There is a story about Sir Stanley Gervase-Gervase at Rosherville Gardens which is ghastly in its perfection of detail. It seems that Sir Stanley – but I can't tell you!'

'Have a dash!'

'No!'

'Oh, well, I shouldn't worry. No publisher will print the book if it's as bad as all that.'

'On the contrary, your uncle told me that all negotiations are settled with Riggs and Ballinger, and he's sending off the manuscript tomorrow for immediate publication. They make a special thing of that sort of book. They published Lady Carnaby's *Memories of Eighty Interesting Years*.'

'I read 'em!'

'Well, then, when I tell you that Lady Carnaby's *Memories* are simply not to be compared with your uncle's *Recollections*, you will understand my state of mind. And father appears in nearly every story in the book! I am horrified at the things he did when he was a young man!'

'What's to be done?'

'The manuscript must be intercepted before it reaches Riggs and Ballinger, and destroyed!'

I sat up.

This sounded rather sporting.

'How are you going to do it?' I inquired.

'How can I do it? Didn't I tell you the parcel goes off tomorrow? I am going to the Murgatroyds' dance tonight and shall not be back till Monday. You must do it. That is why I telegraphed to you.'

'What!'

She gave me a look.

'Do you mean to say you refuse to help me, Bertie?'

'No; but – I say!'

'It's quite simple.'

'But even if I – What I mean is – Of course, anything I can do – but – if you know what I mean – '

'You say you want to marry me, Bertie?'

'Yes, of course; but still – '

For a moment she looked exactly like her old father.

'I will never marry you if those *Recollections* are published.'

'But, Florence, old thing!'

'I mean it. You may look on it as a test, Bertie. If you have the resource and courage to carry this thing through, I will take it as evidence that you are not the vapid and shiftless person most people think you. If you fail, I shall know that your Aunt Agatha was right when she called you a spineless invertebrate and advised me strongly not to marry you. It will be perfectly simple for you to intercept the manuscript, Bertie. It only requires a little resolution.'

'But suppose Uncle Willoughby catches me at it? He'd cut me off with a bob.'

'If you care more for your uncle's money than for me – '

'No, no! Rather not!'

'Very well, then. The parcel containing the manuscript will, of course, be placed on the hall table tomorrow for Oakshott to take to the village with the letters. All you have to do is to take it away and destroy it. Then your uncle will think it has been lost in the post.'

It sounded thin to me.

'Hasn't he got a copy of it?'

'No; it has not been typed. He is sending the manuscript just as he wrote it.'

'But he could write it over again.'

'As if he would have the energy!'

'But – '

'If you are going to do nothing but make absurd objections, Bertie – '

'I was only pointing things out.'

'Well, don't! Once and for all, will you do me this quite simple act of kindness?'

The way she put it gave me an idea.

'Why not get Edwin to do it? Keep it in the family, kind of, don't you know. Besides, it would be a boon to the kid.'

A jolly bright idea it seemed to me. Edwin was her young brother, who was spending his holidays at Easeby. He was a ferret-faced kid, whom I had disliked since birth. As a matter of fact, talking of Recollections and Memories, it was young blighted Edwin who, nine years before, had led his father to where I was smoking his cigar and caused all the unpleasantness. He was fourteen now and had just joined the Boy Scouts. He was one of those thorough kids, and took his responsibilities pretty seriously. He was always in a sort of fever because he was dropping behind schedule with his daily acts of kindness. However hard he tried, he'd fall behind; and then you would find him prowling about the house, setting such a clip to try and catch up with himself that Easeby was rapidly becoming a perfect hell for man and beast.

The idea didn't seem to strike Florence.

'I shall do nothing of the kind, Bertie. I wonder you can't appreciate the compliment I am paying you – trusting you like this.'

'Oh, I see that all right, but what I mean is, Edwin would do it so much better than I would. These Boy Scouts are up to all sorts of dodges. They spoor, don't you know, and take cover and creep about, and what not.'

'Bertie, will you or will you not do this perfectly trivial thing for me? If not, say so now, and let us end this farce of pretending that you care a snap of the fingers for me.'

'Dear old soul, I love you devotedly!'

'Then will you or will you not – '

'Oh, all right,' I said. 'All right! All right! All right!'

And then I tottered forth to think it over. I met Jeeves in the passage just outside.

'I beg your pardon, sir. I was endeavouring to find you.'

'What's the matter?'

'I felt that I should tell you, sir, that somebody has been putting black polish on our brown walking shoes.'

'What! Who? Why?'

'I could not say, sir.'

'Can anything be done with them?'

'Nothing, sir.'

'Damn!'

'Very good, sir.'

I've wondered since then how these murderer fellows manage to keep in shape while they're contemplating their next effort. I had a much simpler sort of job on hand, and the thought of it rattled me to such an extent in the night watches that I was a perfect wreck next day. Dark circles under the eyes – I give you my word! I had to call on Jeeves to rally round with one of those lifesavers of his.

From breakfast on I felt like a bag-snatcher at a railway station. I had to hang about waiting for the parcel to be put on the hall table, and it wasn't put. Uncle Willoughby was a fixture in the library, adding the finishing touches to the great work, I supposed, and the more I thought the thing over the less I liked it. The chances against my pulling it off seemed about three to two, and the thought of what would happen if I didn't gave me cold shivers down the spine. Uncle Willoughby was a pretty mild sort of old boy, as a rule, but I've known him to cut up rough, and, by Jove, he was scheduled to extend himself if he caught me trying to get away with his life work.

It wasn't till nearly four that he toddled out of the library with the parcel under his arm, put it on the table, and toddled off again. I was hiding a bit to the south-east at the moment, behind a suit of armour. I bounded out and legged it for the table. Then I nipped upstairs to hide the swag. I charged in like a mustang and nearly stubbed my toe on young blighted Edwin, the Boy Scout. He was standing at the chest of drawers, confound him, messing about with my ties.

'Hallo!' he said.

'What are you doing here?'

'I'm tidying your room. It's my last Saturday's act of kindness.'

'Last Saturday's.'

'I'm five days behind. I was six till last night, but I polished your shoes.'

'Was it you – '

'Yes. Did you see them? I just happened to think of it. I was in here, looking round. Mr Berkeley had this room while you were away. He left this morning. I thought perhaps he might have left something in it that I could have sent on. I've often done acts of kindness that way.'

'You must be a comfort to one and all!'

It became more and more apparent to me that this infernal kid must somehow be turned out eftsoons or right speedily. I had hidden the parcel behind my back, and I didn't think he had seen it; but I wanted to get at that chest of drawers quick, before anyone else came along.

'I shouldn't bother about tidying the room,' I said.

'I like tidying it. It's not a bit of trouble – really.'

'But it's quite tidy now.'

'Not so tidy as I shall make it.'

This was getting perfectly rotten. I didn't want to murder the kid, and yet there didn't seem any other way of shifting him. I pressed down the mental accelerator. The old lemon throbbed fiercely. I got an idea.

'There's something much kinder than that which you could do,' I said. 'You see that box of cigars? Take it down to the smoking-room and snip off the ends for me. That would save me no end of trouble. Stagger along, laddie.'

He seemed a bit doubtful; but he staggered. I shoved the parcel into a drawer, locked it, trousered the key, and felt better. I might be a chump, but, dash it, I could out-general a mere kid with a face like a ferret. I went downstairs again. Just as I was passing the smoking-room door out curveted Edwin. It seemed to me that if he wanted to do a real act of kindness he would commit suicide.

'I'm snipping them,' he said.

'Snip on! Snip on!'

'Do you like them snipped much, or only a bit?'

'Medium.'

'All right. I'll be getting on, then'.

'I should.'

And we parted.

Fellows who know all about that sort of thing – detectives, and so on – will tell you that the most difficult thing in the world is to get rid of the body. I remember, as a kid, having to learn by heart a poem about a bird by the name of Eugene Aram, who had the deuce of a job in this respect. All I can recall of the actual poetry is the bit that goes:

Tum-tum, tum-tum, tum-tumty-tum,
I slew him, tum-tum tum!

But I recollect that the poor blighter spent much of his valuable time dumping the corpse into ponds and burying it, and what not, only to have it pop out at him again. It was about an hour after I had shoved the parcel into the drawer when I realized that I had let myself in for just the same sort of thing.

Florence had talked in an airy sot of way about destroying the manuscript; but when one came down to it, how the deuce can a chap destroy a great chunky mass of paper in somebody else's house in the middle of summer? I couldn't ask to have a fire in my bedroom, with the thermometer in the eighties. And if I didn't burn the thing, how else could I get rid of it? Fellows on the battlefield eat dispatches to keep them from falling into the hands of the enemy, but it would have taken me a year to eat Uncle Willoughby's *Recollections*.

I'm bound to say the problem absolutely baffled me. The only thing seemed to be to leave the parcel in the drawer and hope for the best.

I don't know whether you have ever experienced it, but it's a dashed unpleasant thing having a crime on one's conscience. Towards the end of the day the mere sight of the drawer began to depress me. I found myself getting all on edge; and once when Uncle Willoughby trickled silently into the smoking-room when I was alone there and spoke to me before I knew he was there, I broke the record for the sitting high jump.

I was wondering all the time when Uncle Willoughby would sit up and take notice. I didn't think he would have time to suspect that anything had gone wrong till Saturday morning, when he would be expecting, of course, to get the acknowledgement of the manuscript from the publishers. But early on Friday evening he came out of the library as I was passing and asked me to step in. He was looking considerably rattled.

'Bertie,' he said – he always spoke in a precise sort of pompous kind of way – 'an exceedingly disturbing thing has happened. As you know, I dispatched the manuscript of my book to Messrs Riggs and Ballinger, the publishers, yesterday afternoon. It should have reached them by the first post this morning. Why I should have been uneasy I cannot say, but my mind was not altogether at rest respecting the safety of the parcel. I therefore telephoned to Messrs Riggs and Ballinger a few moments back to make inquiries. To my consternation they informed me that they were not yet in receipt of my manuscript.'

'Very rum!'

'I recollect distinctly placing it myself on the hall table in good time to be taken to the village. But here is a sinister thing. I have spoken to Oakshott, who took the rest of the letters to the post office, and he cannot recall seeing it there. He is, indeed, unswerving in his assertions that when he went to the hall to collect the letters there was no parcel among them.'

'Sounds funny!'

'Bertie, shall I tell you what I suspect?'

'What's that?'

'The suspicion will no doubt sound to you incredible, but it alone seems to fit the facts as we know them. I incline to the belief that the parcel has been stolen.'

'Oh, I say! Surely not!'

'Wait! Hear me out. Though I have said nothing to you before, or to anyone else, concerning the matter, the fact remains that during the past few weeks a number of objects – some valuable, others not – have disappeared in this house. The conclusion to which one is irresistibly impelled is that we have a kleptomaniac in our midst. It is a peculiarity of kleptomania, as you are no doubt aware, that the subject is unable to differentiate between the intrinsic values of objects. He will purloin an old coat as readily as a diamond ring, or a tobacco pipe costing but a few shillings with the same eagerness as a purse of gold. The fact that this manuscript of mine could be of no possible value to any outside person convinces me that – '

'But, uncle, one moment; I know all about those things that were stolen. It was Meadowes, my man, who pinched them. I caught him snaffling my silk socks. Right in the act, by Jove!'

He was tremendously impressed.

'You amaze me, Bertie! Send for the man at once and question him.'

'But he isn't here. You see, directly I found that he was a sock-sneaker I gave him the boot. That's why I went to London – to get a new man.'

'Then, if the man Meadowes is no longer in the house it could not be he who purloined my manuscript. The whole thing is inexplicable.'

After which we brooded for a bit. Uncle Willoughby pottered about the room, registering baffledness, while I sat sucking at a cigarette, feeling rather like a chappie I'd once read about in a book, who murdered another cove and hid the body under the dining-room table, and then had to be the life and soul of a dinner party, with it there all the time. My guilty secret oppressed me to such an extent that after a while I couldn't stick it any longer. I lit another cigarette and started for a stroll in the grounds, by way of cooling off.

It was one of those still evenings you get in the summer, when you can hear a snail clear its throat a mile away. The sun was sinking over the hills and the gnats were fooling about all over the place, and everything smelled rather topping – what with the falling dew and so on – and I was just beginning to feel a little soothed by the peace of it all when suddenly I heard my name spoken.

'It's about Bertie.'

It was the loathsome voice of young blighted Edwin! For a moment I couldn't locate it. Then I realized that it came from the library. My stroll had taken me within a few yards of the open window.

I had often wondered how those Johnnies in books did it – I mean the fellows with whom it was the work of a moment to do about a dozen things that ought to have taken them about ten minutes. But, as a matter of fact, it was the work of a moment with me to chuck away my cigarette, swear a bit, leap about ten yards, dive into a bush that stood near the library window, and stand there with my ears flapping. I was as certain as I've ever been of anything that all sorts of rotten things were in the offing.

'About Bertie?' I heard Uncle Willoughby say.

'About Bertie and your parcel. I heard you talking to him just now. I believe he's got it.'

When I tell you that just as I heard these frightful words a fairly substantial beetle of sorts dropped from the bush down the back of my neck, and I couldn't even stir to squash the same, you will understand that I felt pretty rotten. Everything seemed against me.

'What do you mean, boy? I was discussing the disappearance of my manuscript with Bertie only a moment back, and he professed himself as perplexed by the mystery as myself.'

'Well, I was in his room yesterday afternoon, doing him an act of kindness, and he came in with a parcel. I could see it, though he tried to keep it behind his back. And then he asked me to go to the smoking-room and snip some cigars for him; and about two minutes afterwards he came down – and he wasn't carrying anything. So it must be in his room.

I understand they deliberately teach these dashed Boy Scouts to cultivate their powers of observation and education and what not. Devilish thoughtless and inconsiderate of them, I call it. Look at the trouble it causes.

'It sounds incredible,' said Uncle Willoughby, thereby bucking me up a trifle.

'Shall I go and look in his room?' asked young blighted Edwin. 'I'm sure the parcel's there.'

'But what could be his motive for perpetrating this extraordinary theft?'

'Perhaps he's a – what you said just now.'

'A kleptomaniac! Impossible!'

'It might have been Bertie who took all those things from the very start,' suggested the little brute hopefully. 'He may be like Raffles.'

'Raffles?'

'He's a chap in a book who went about pinching things.'

'I cannot believe that Bertie would – ah – go about pinching things.'

'Well, I'm sure he's got the parcel. I'll tell you what you might do. You might say that Mr Berkeley wired that he had left something here. He had Bertie's room, you know. You might say you wanted to look for it.'

'That would be possible. I – '

I didn't wait to hear any more. Things were getting too hot. I sneaked softly out of my bush and raced for the front door. I sprinted up to my room and made for the drawer where I had put the parcel. And then I found I hadn't the key. It wasn't for the deuce of a time that I recollected I had shifted it to my evening trousers the night before and must have forgotten to take it out again.

Where the dickens were my evening things? I had looked all over the place before I remembered that Jeeves must have taken them away to brush. To leap at the bell and ring it was, with me, the work of a moment. I had just rung it when there was a footstep outside, and in came Uncle Willoughby.

'Oh, Bertie,' he said, without a blush, 'I have – ah – received a telegram from Berkeley, who occupied this room in your absence, asking me to forward him his – er – his cigarette-case, which, it would appear, he inadvertently omitted to take with him when he left the house. I cannot find it downstairs; and it has, therefore, occurred to me that he may have left it in this room. I will – er – just take a look round.'

It was one of the most disgusting spectacles I've ever seen – this white-haired old man, who should have been thinking of the hereafter, standing there lying like an actor.

'I haven't seen it anywhere,' I said.

'Nevertheless, I will search. I must – ah – spare no effort.'

'I should have seen it if it had been here – what?'

'It may have escaped your notice. It is – er – possibly in one of the drawers.'

He began to nose about. He pulled out drawer after drawer, pottering round like an old bloodhound, and babbling from time to time about Berkeley and his cigarette-case in a way that struck me as perfectly ghastly. I just stood there, losing weight every moment.

Then he came to the drawer where the parcel was.

'This appears to be locked,' he said, rattling the handle.

'Yes; I shouldn't bother about that one. It – it's – er – locked, and all that sort of thing.'

'You have not the key?'

A soft, respectable voice spoke behind me.

'I fancy, sir, that this must be the key you require. It was in the pocket of your evening trousers.'

It was Jeeves. He had shimmered in, carrying my evening things, and was standing there holding out the key. I could have massacred the man.

'Thank you,' said my uncle.

'Not at all, sir.'

The next moment Uncle Willoughby had opened the drawer. I shut my eyes.

'No,' said Uncle Willoughby, 'there is nothing here. The drawer is empty. Thank you, Bertie. I hope I have not disturbed you. I fancy – er – Berkeley must have taken his case with him after all.'

When he had gone I shut the door carefully. Then I turned to Jeeves. The man was putting my evening things out on a chair.

'Er – Jeeves!'

'Sir?'

'Oh, nothing.'

It was deuced difficult to know how to begin.

'Er – Jeeves!'

'Sir?'

'Did you – Was there – Have you by chance–'

'I removed the parcel this morning, sir.'

'Oh – ah – why?'

'I considered it more prudent, sir.'

I mused for a while.

'Of course, I suppose all this seems tolerably rummy to you, Jeeves?'

'Not at all, sir. I chanced to overhear you and Lady Florence speaking of the matter the other evening, sir.'

'Did you, by Jove?'

'Yes, sir.'

'Well – er – Jeeves, I think that, on the whole, if you were to – as it were – freeze on to that parcel until we get back to London–'

'Exactly, sir.'

'And then we might – er – so to speak – chuck it away somewhere – what?'

'Precisely, sir.'

'I'll leave it in your hands.'

'Entirely, sir.'

'You know, Jeeves, you're by way of being rather a topper.'

'I endeavour to give satisfaction, sir.'

'One in a million, by Jove!'

'It is very kind of you to say so, sir.'

'Well, that's about all, then, I think.'

'Very good, sir.'

Florence came back on Monday. I didn't see her till we were all having tea in the hall. It wasn't till the crowd had cleared away a bit that we got a chance of having a word together.

'Well, Bertie?' she said.

'It's all right.'

'You have destroyed the manuscript?'

'Not exactly; but – '

'What do you mean?'

'I mean I haven't absolutely – '

'Bertie, your manner is furtive!'

'It's all right. It's this way – '

And I was just going to explain how things stood when out of the library came leaping Uncle Willoughby, looking as braced as a two-year-old. The old boy was a changed man.

'A most remarkable thing, Bertie! I have just been speaking with Mr Riggs on the telephone, and he tells me he received my manuscript by the first post this morning. I cannot imagine what can have caused the delay. Our postal facilities are extremely inadequate in the rural districts. I shall write to headquarters about it. It is insufferable if valuable parcels are to be delayed in this fashion.'

I happened to be looking at Florence's profile at the moment, and at this juncture she swung round and gave me a look that went right through me like a knife. Uncle Willoughby meandered back to the library, and there was a silence that you could have dug bits out of with a spoon.

'I can't understand it,' I said at last. 'I can't understand it, by Jove!'

'I can. I can understand it perfectly, Bertie. Your heart failed you. Rather than risk offending your uncle you – '

'No, no! Absolutely!'

'You preferred to lose me rather than risk losing the money. Perhaps you did not think I meant what I said. I meant every word. Our engagement is ended.'

'But – I say!'

'Not another word!'

'But, Florence, old thing!'

'I do not wish to hear any more. I see now that your Aunt Agatha was perfectly right. I consider that I have had a very lucky escape. There was a time when I thought that, with patience, you might be moulded into something worth while. I see now that you are impossible!'

And she popped off, leaving me to pick up the pieces. When I had collected the debris to some extent I went to my room and rang for Jeeves. He came in looking as if nothing had happened or was ever going to happen. He was the calmest thing in captivity.

'Jeeves!' I yelled. 'Jeeves, that parcel has arrived in London!'

'Yes, sir?'

'Did you send it?'

'Yes, sir. I acted for the best, sir. I think that both you and Lady Florence overestimated the danger of people being offended at being mentioned in Sir Willoughby's *Recollections*. It has been my experience, sir, that the normal person enjoys seeing his or her name in print, irrespective of what is said about them. I have an aunt, sir, who a few years ago was a martyr to swollen limbs. She tried Walkinshaw's Supreme Ointment and obtained considerable relief – so much so that she sent them an unsolicited testimonial. Her pride at seeing her photograph in the daily papers in connexion with descriptions of her lower limbs before taking, which were nothing less than revolting, was so intense that it led me to believe that publicity, of whatever sort, is what nearly everybody desires. Moreover, if you have ever studied psychology, sir, you will know that respectable old gentlemen are by no means averse to having it advertised that they were extremely wild in their youth. I have an uncle–'

I cursed his aunts and his uncles and him and all the rest of the family.

'Do you know that Lady Florence has broken off her engagement with me?'

'Indeed, sir?'

Not a bit of sympathy! I might have been telling him it was a fine day.

'You're sacked!'

'Very good, sir.'

He coughed gently.

'As I am no longer in your employment, sir, I can speak freely without appearing to take a liberty. In my opinion you and Lady Florence were quite unsuitably matched. Her ladyship is of a highly determined and arbitrary temperament, quite opposed to your own. I was in Lord Worplesdon's service for nearly a year, during which time I had ample opportunities of studying her ladyship. The opinion of the servants' hall was far from favourable to her. Her ladyship's temper caused a good deal of adverse comment among us. It was at times quite impossible. You would not have been happy, sir!'

'Get out!'

'I think you would also have found her educational methods a little trying, sir. I have glanced at the book her ladyship gave you – it has been lying on your table since our arrival – and it is, in my opinion, quite unsuitable. You would not have enjoyed it. And I have it from her ladyship's own maid, who happened to overhear a conversation between her ladyship and one of the gentlemen staying here – Mr Maxwell, who is employed in an editorial capacity by one of the reviews – that it was her intention to start you almost immediately upon Nietzsche. You would not enjoy Nietzsche, sir. He is fundamentally unsound.'

'Get out!'

'Very good, sir.'

It's rummy how sleeping on a thing often makes you feel quite different about it. It's happened to me over and over again. Somehow or other, when I woke next morning the old heart didn't feel half so broken as it had done. It was a perfectly topping day, and there was something about the way the sun came in at the window and the row the birds were kicking up in the ivy that made me half wonder whether Jeeves wasn't right. After all, though she had a wonderful profile, was it such a catch being engaged to Florence Craye as the casual observer might imagine? Wasn't there something in what Jeeves had said about her character? I began to realize that my ideal wife was something quite different, something a lot more clinging and drooping and prattling, and what not.

I had got as far as this in thinking the thing out when that *Types of Ethical Theory* caught my eye. I opened it, and I give you my honest word this was what hit me:

> Of the two antithetic terms in the Greek philosophy one only was real and self-subsisting; and that one was Ideal Thought as opposed to that which it has to penetrate and mould. The other, corresponding to our Nature, was in itself phenomenal, unreal, without any permanent footing, having no predicates that held true for two moments together; in short, redeemed from negation only by including indwelling realities appearing through.

Well – I mean to say – what? And Nietzsche, from all accounts, a lot worse than that!

'Jeeves,' I said, when he came in with my morning tea, 'I've been thinking it over. You're engaged again.'

'Thank you, sir.'

I sucked down a cheerful mouthful. A great respect for this bloke's judgement began to soak through me.

'Oh, Jeeves,' I said: 'about that check suit.'

'Yes, sir?'

'Is it really a frost?'

'A trifle too bizarre, sir, in my opinion.'

'But lots of fellows have asked me who my tailor is.'

'Doubtless in order to avoid him, sir.'

'He's supposed to be one of the best men in London.'

'I am saying nothing against his moral character, sir.'

I hesitated a bit. I had a feeling that I was passing into this chappie's clutches, and that if I gave in now I should become just like poor old Aubrey Fothergill, unable to call my soul my own. On the other hand, this was obviously a cove of rare intelligence, and it would be a comfort in a lot of ways to have him doing the thinking for me. I made up my mind.

'All right, Jeeves,' I said. 'You know! Give the bally thing away to somebody!'

He looked down at me like a father gazing tenderly at the wayward child.

'Thank you, sir. I gave it to the under-gardener last night. A little more tea, sir?'

—2—

THE PRIDE OF THE WOOSTERS IS WOUNDED

If there's one thing I like, it's a quiet life. I'm not one of those fellows who get all restless and depressed if things aren't happening to them all the time. You can't make it too placid for me. Give me regular meals, a good show with decent music every now and then, and one or two pals to totter round with, and I ask no more.

That is why the jar, when it came, was such a particularly nasty jar. I mean, I'd returned from Roville with a sort of feeling that from now on, nothing could occur to upset me. Aunt Agatha, I imagined, would require at least a year to recover from the Hemmingway affair; and apart from Aunt Agatha there isn't anybody who really does much in the way of harrying me. It seemed to me that the skies were blue, so to speak, and no clouds in sight.

I little thought . . . Well, look here, what happened was this, and I ask you if it wasn't enough to rattle anybody.

Once a year Jeeves takes a couple of weeks' vacation and biffs off to the sea or somewhere to restore his tissues. Pretty rotten for me, of course, while he's away. But it has to be stuck, so I stick it; and I must admit that he usually manages to get hold of a fairly decent fellow to look after me in his absence.

Well, the time had come round again, and Jeeves was in the kitchen giving the understudy a few tips about his duties. I happened to want a stamp or something, and I toddled down the passage to ask him for it. The silly ass had left the kitchen door open, and I hadn't gone two steps when his voice caught me squarely in the eardrum.

'You will find Mr Wooster,' he was saying to the substitute chappie, 'an exceedingly pleasant and amiable young gentleman, but not intelligent. By no means intelligent. Mentally he is negligible – quite negligible!'

Well, I mean to say, what!

I suppose, strictly speaking, I ought to have charged in and ticked the blighter off properly in no uncertain voice. But I doubt whether it's humanly possible to tick Jeeves off. Personally, I didn't even have a dash at it. I merely called for my hat and stick in a marked manner and legged it. But the memory rankled, if you know what I mean. We Woosters do not lightly forget. At least, we do – some things – appointments, and people's birthdays, and letters to post, and all that – but not an absolute bally insult like the above. I brooded like the dickens.

I was still brooding when I dropped in at the oyster-bar at Buck's for a quick bracer. I needed a bracer rather particularly at the moment, because I was on my way to lunch with Aunt Agatha. A pretty frightful ordeal, believe me or believe me not, even though I took it that after what had happened at Roville she would be in a fairly subdued and amiable mood. I had just had one quick and another rather slower, and was feeling about as cheerio as was possible under the circs, when a muffled voice hailed me from the north-east, and, turning round, I saw young Bingo Little propped up in a corner, wrapping himself round a sizeable chunk of bread and cheese.

'Hallo-allo-allo!' I said. 'Haven't seen you for ages. You've not been in here lately, have you?'

'No. I've been living out in the country.'

'Eh?' I said, for Bingo's loathing for the country was well known. 'Whereabouts?'

'Down in Hampshire, at a place called Ditteredge.'

'No, really? I know some people who've got a house there. The Glossops. Have you met them?'

'Why, that's where I'm staying!' said young Bingo. 'I'm tutoring the Glossop kid.'

'What for?' I said. I couldn't seem to see young Bingo as a tutor. Though, of course, he did get a degree of sorts at Oxford, and I suppose you can always fool some of the people some of the time.

'What for? For money, of course! An absolute sitter came unstitched in the second race at Haydock Park,' said young Bingo, with some bitterness, 'and I dropped my entire month's allowance. I hadn't the nerve to touch my uncle for any more, so it was a case of buzzing round to the agents and getting a job. I've been down there three weeks.'

'I haven't met the Glossop kid.'

'Don't!' advised Bingo, briefly.

'The only one of the family I really know is the girl.' I had hardly spoken these words when the most extraordinary change came over young Bingo's face. His eyes bulged, his cheeks flushed, and his Adam's apple hopped about like one of those india-rubber balls on the top of the fountain in a shooting-gallery.

'Oh, Bertie!' he said, in a strangled sort of voice.

I looked at the poor fish anxiously. I knew that he was always falling in love with someone, but it didn't seem possible that even he could have fallen in love with Honoria Glossop. To me the girl was simply nothing more nor less than a pot of poison. One of those dashed large, brainy, strenuous, dynamic girls you see so many of these days. She had been at Girton, where, in addition to enlarging her brain to the most frightful extent, she had gone in for every kind of sport and developed the physique of a middle-weight catch-as-catch-can wrestler. I'm not sure she didn't box for the Varsity while she was up. The effect she had on me whenever she appeared was to make me want to slide into a cellar and lie low till they blew the All-Clear.

Yet here was young Bingo obviously all for her. There was no mistaking it. The love-light was in the blighter's eyes.

'I worship her, Bertie! I worship the very ground she treads on!' continued the patient, in a loud, penetrating voice. Fred Thompson and one or two fellows had come in, and McGarry, the chappie behind the bar, was listening with his ears flapping. But there's no reticence about Bingo. He always reminds me of the hero of a musical comedy who takes the centre of the stage, gathers the boys round him in a circle, and tells them all about his love at the top of his voice.

'Have you told her?'

'No. I haven't the nerve. But we walk together in the garden most evenings, and it sometimes seems to me that there is a look in her eyes.'

'I know that look. Like a sergeant-major.'

'Nothing of the kind! Like a tender goddess.'

'Half a second, old thing,' I said. 'Are you sure we're talking about the same girl? The one I mean is Honoria. Perhaps there's a younger sister or something I've not heard of?'

'Her name is Honoria,' bawled Bingo reverently.

'And she strikes you as a tender goddess?'

'She does.'

'God bless you!' I said.

'She walks in beauty like the night of cloudless climes and starry skies; and all that's best of dark and bright meet in her aspect and her eyes. Another bit of bread and cheese,' he said to the lad behind the bar.

'You're keeping your strength up,' I said.

'This is my lunch. I've got to meet Oswald at Waterloo at one-fifteen, to catch the train back. I brought him up to town to see the dentist.'

'Oswald? Is that the kid?'

'Yes. Pestilential to a degree.'

'Pestilential! That reminds me, I'm lunching with my Aunt Agatha. I'll have to pop off now, or I'll be late.'

I hadn't seen Aunt Agatha since that little affair of the pearls; and, while I didn't anticipate any great pleasure from gnawing a bone in her society, I must say that there was one topic of conversation I felt pretty confident she wouldn't touch on, and that was the subject of my matrimonial future. I mean, when a woman's made a bloomer like the one Aunt Agatha made at Roville, you'd naturally think that a decent shame would keep her off it for, at any rate, a month or two.

But women beat me. I mean to say, as regards nerve. You'll hardly credit it, but she actually started in on me with the fish. Absolutely with the fish, I give you my solemn word. We'd hardly exchanged a word about the weather, when she let me have it without a blush.

'Bertie,' she said. 'I've been thinking again about you and how necessary it is that you should get married. I quite admit that I was dreadfully mistaken in my opinion of that terrible, hypocritical girl at Roville, but this time there is no danger of an error. By great good luck I have found the very wife for you, a girl whom I have only recently met, but whose family is above suspicion. She has plenty of money, too, though that does not matter in your case. The great point is that she is strong, self-reliant and sensible, and will counterbalance the deficiencies and weaknesses of your character. She has met you; and, while there is naturally much in you of which she disapproves, she does not dislike you. I know this, for I have sounded her – guardedly, of course – and I am sure that you have only to make the first advances – '

'Who is it?' I would have said it long before, but the shock had made me swallow a bit of roll the wrong way, and I had only just finished turning purple and trying to get a bit of air back into the old windpipe. 'Who is it?'

'Sir Roderick Glossop's daughter, Honoria.'

'No, no!' I cried, paling beneath the tan.

'Don't be silly, Bertie. She is just the wife for you.'

'Yes, but look here – '

'She will mould you.'

'But I don't want to be moulded.'

Aunt Agatha gave me the kind of look she used to give me when I was a kid and had been found in the jam cupboard.

'Bertie! I hope you are not going to be troublesome.'

'Well, but I mean – '

'Lady Glossop has very kindly invited you to Ditteredge Hall for a few days. I told her you would be delighted to come down tomorrow.'

'I'm sorry, but I've got a dashed important engagement tomorrow.'

'What engagement?'

'Well – er – '

'You have no engagement. And, even if you had, you must put it off. I shall be very seriously annoyed, Bertie, if you do not go to Ditteredge Hall tomorrow.'

'Oh, right-o!' I said.

It wasn't two minutes after I had parted from Aunt Agatha before the old fighting spirit of the Woosters reasserted itself. Ghastly as the peril was which loomed before me, I was conscious of a rummy sort of exhilaration. It was a tight corner, but the tighter the corner, I felt, the more juicily should I score off Jeeves when I got myself out of it without a bit of help from him. Ordinarily, of course, I should have consulted him and trusted to him to solve the difficulty; but after what I had heard him saying in the kitchen, I was dashed if I was going to demean myself. When I got home I addressed the man with light abandon.

'Jeeves,' I said, 'I'm in a bit of a difficulty.'

'I'm sorry to hear that, sir.'

'Yes, quite a bad hole. In fact, you might say on the brink of a precipice, and faced by an awful doom.'

'If I could be of any assistance, sir – '

'Oh, no. No, no. Thanks very much, but no, no. I won't trouble you. I've no doubt I shall be able to get out of it by myself.'

'Very good, sir.'

So that was that. I'm bound to say I'd have welcomed a bit more curiosity from the fellow, but that is Jeeves all over. Cloaks his emotions, if you know what I mean.

Honoria was away when I got to Ditteredge on the following afternoon. Her mother told me that she was staying with some people named Braythwayt in the neighbourhood, and would be back next day, bringing the daughter of the house with her for a visit. She said I would find Oswald out in the grounds, and such is a mother's love that she spoke as if that were a bit of a boost for the grounds and an inducement to go there.

Rather decent, the grounds at Ditteredge. A couple of terraces, a bit of lawn with a cedar on it, a bit of shrubbery, and finally a small but goodish lake with a stone bridge running across it. Directly I'd worked my way round the shrubbery I spotted young Bingo leaning against the bridge smoking a cigarette. Sitting on the stonework, fishing, was a species of kid whom I took to be Oswald the Plague-Spot.

Bingo was both surprised and delighted to see me, and introduced me to the kid. If the latter was surprised and delighted too, he concealed it like a diplomat. He just looked at me, raised his eyebrows slightly, and went on fishing. He was one of those supercilious striplings who give you the impression that you went to the wrong school and that your clothes don't fit.

'This is Oswald,' said Bingo.

'What,' I replied cordially, 'could be sweeter? How are you?'

'Oh, all right,' said the kid.

'Nice place, this.'

'Oh, all right,' said the kid.

'Having a good time fishing?'

'Oh, all right,' said the kid.

Young Bingo led me off to commune apart.

'Doesn't jolly old Oswald's incessant flow of prattle make your head ache sometimes?' I asked.

Bingo sighed.

'It's a hard job.'

'What's a hard job?'

'Loving him.'

'Do you love him?' I asked, surprised. I shouldn't have thought it could be done.

'I try to,' said young Bingo, 'for Her sake. She's coming back tomorrow, Bertie.'

'So I heard.'

'She is coming, my love, my own – '

'Absolutely,' I said. 'But touching on young Oswald

once more. Do you have to be with him all day? How do you manage to stick it?'

'Oh, he doesn't give much trouble. When we aren't working he sits on that bridge all the time, trying to catch tiddlers.'

'Why don't you shove him in?'

'Shove him in?'

'It seems to me distinctly the thing to do,' I said, regarding the stripling's back with a good deal of dislike. 'It would wake him up a bit, and make him take an interest in things.'

Bingo shook his head a bit wistfully.

'Your proposition attracts me,' he said, 'but I'm afraid it can't be done. You see, She would never forgive me. She is devoted to the little brute.'

'Great Scott!' I cried. 'I've got it!' I don't know if you know that feeling when you get an inspiration, and tingle all down your spine from the soft collar as now worn to the very soles of the old Waukeesis? Jeeves, I suppose, feels that way more or less all the time, but it isn't often it comes to me. But now all Nature seemed to be shouting at me. 'You've clicked!' and I grabbed young Bingo by the arm in a way that must have made him feel as if a horse had bitten him. His finely-chiselled features were twisted with agony and what not, and he asked me what the dickens I thought I was playing at.

'Bingo,' I said, 'what would Jeeves have done?'

'How do you mean, what would Jeeves have done?'

'I mean what would he have advised in a case like yours? I mean you wanting to make a hit with Honoria Glossop and all that. Why, take it from me, laddie, he would have shoved you behind that clump of bushes over there; he would have got me to lure Honoria on to the bridge somehow; then, at the proper time, he would have told me to give the kid a pretty hefty jab in the small of the back, so as to shoot him into the water; and then you would have dived in and hauled him out. How about it?'

'You didn't think that out by yourself, Bertie?' said young Bingo, in a hushed sort of voice.

'Yes, I did. Jeeves isn't the only fellow with ideas.'

'But it's absolutely wonderful.'

'Just a suggestion.'

'The only objection I can see is that it would be so dashed awkward for you. I mean to say, suppose the kid turned round and said you had shoved him in, that would make you frightfully unpopular with Her.'

'I don't mind risking that.'

The man was deeply moved.

'Bertie, this is noble.'

'No, no.'

He clasped my hand silently, then chuckled like the last drop of water going down the waste-pipe in a bath.

'Now what?' I said.

'I was only thinking,' said young Bingo, 'how fearfully wet Oswald will get. Oh, happy day!'

3

THE HERO'S REWARD

I don't know if you've noticed it, but it's rummy how nothing in this world ever seems to be absolutely perfect. The drawback to this otherwise singularly fruity binge was, of course, the fact that Jeeves wouldn't be on the spot to watch me in action. Still, apart from that there wasn't a flaw. The beauty of the thing was, you see, that nothing could possibly go wrong. You know how it is, as a rule, when you want to get Chappie A on Spot B at exactly the same moment when Chappie C is on Spot D. There's always a chance of a hitch. Take the case of a general, I mean to say, who's planning out a big movement. He tells one regiment to capture the hill with the windmill on it at the exact moment when another regiment is taking the bridgehead or something down in the valley; and everything gets all messed up. And then, when they're chatting the thing over in camp that night, the colonel of the first regiment says, "Oh, sorry! Did you say the hill with the windmill? I thought you said the one with the flock of sheep." And there you are! But in this case, nothing like that could happen, because Oswald and Bingo would be on the spot right along, so that all I had to worry about was getting Honoria there in due season. And I managed that all right, first shot, by asking her if she would come for a stroll in the grounds with me, as I had something particular to say to her.

She had arrived shortly after lunch in the car with

the Braythwayt girl. I was introduced to the latter, a tallish girl with blue eyes and fair hair. I rather took to her – she was so unlike Honoria – and, if I had been able to spare the time, I shouldn't have minded talking to her for a bit. But business was business – I had fixed it up with Bingo to be behind the bushes at three sharp, so I got hold of Honoria and steered her out through the grounds in the direction of the lake.

'You're very quiet, Mr Wooster,' she said.

Made me jump a bit. I was concentrating pretty tensely at the moment. We had just come in sight of the lake, and I was casting a keen eye over the ground to see that everything was in order. Everything appeared to be as arranged. The kid Oswald was hunched up on the bridge; and, as Bingo wasn't visible, I took it that he had got into position. My watch made it two minutes after the hour.

'Eh?' I said. 'Oh, ah, yes. I was just thinking.'

'You said you had something important to say to me.'

'Absolutely!' I had decided to open the proceedings by sort of paving the way for young Bingo. I mean to say, without actually mentioning his name, I wanted to prepare the girl's mind for the fact that, surprising as it might seem, there was someone who had long loved her from afar and all that sort of rot. 'It's like this,' I said. 'It may sound rummy and all that, but there's somebody who's frightfully in love with you and so forth – a friend of mine, you know.'

'Oh, a friend of yours?'

'Yes.'

She gave a kind of a laugh.

'Well, why doesn't he tell me so?'

'Well, you see, that's the sort of chap he is. Kind of shrinking, diffident kind of fellow. Hasn't got the nerve.

Thinks you so much above him, don't you know. Looks on you as a sort of goddess. Worships the ground you tread on, but can't whack up the ginger to tell you so.'

'This is very interesting.'

'Yes. He's not a bad chap, you know, in his way. Rather an ass, perhaps, but well-meaning. Well, that's the posish. You might just bear it in mind, what?'

'How funny you are!'

She chucked back her head and laughed with considerable vim. She had a penetrating sort of laugh. Rather like a train going into a tunnel. It didn't sound over-musical to me, and on the kid Oswald it appeared to jar not a little. He gazed at us with a good deal of dislike.

'I wish the dickens you wouldn't make that row,' he said. 'Scaring all the fish away.'

It broke the spell a bit. Honoria changed the subject.

'I do wish Oswald wouldn't sit on the bridge like that,' she said. 'I'm sure it isn't safe. He might easily fall in.'

'I'll go and tell him,' I said.

I suppose the distance between the kid and me at this juncture was about five yards, but I got the impression that it was nearer a hundred. And, as I started to toddle across the intervening space, I had a rummy feeling that I'd done this very thing before. Then I remembered. Years ago, at a country-house party, I had been roped in to play the part of a butler in some amateur theatricals in aid of some ghastly charity or other; and I had had to open the proceedings by walking across the empty stage from left upper entrance and shoving a tray on a table down right. They had impressed it on me at rehearsals that I mustn't take the course at a quick heel-and-toe, like a chappie finishing strongly in a walking-race; and the result was that I kept the brakes on to such an extent that it seemed to me as if I was never going to get to the bally table at all. The stage seemed to stretch out in front of me like a trackless desert, and there was a kind of breathless hush as if all Nature had paused to concentrate its attention on me personally. Well, I felt just like that now. I had a kind of dry gulping in my throat, and the more I walked the farther away the kid seemed to get, till suddenly I found myself standing just behind him without quite knowing how I'd got there.

'Hallo!' I said, with a sickly sort of grin – wasted on the kid, because he didn't bother to turn round and look at me. He merely wiggled his left ear in a rather peevish manner. I don't know when I've met anybody in whose life I appeared to mean so little.

'Hallo!' I said. 'Fishing?'

I laid my hand in a sort of elderly-brotherly way on his shoulder.

'Here, look out!' said the kid, wobbling on his foundations.

It was one of those things that want doing quickly or not at all. I shut my eyes and pushed. Something seemed to give. There was a scrambling sound, a kind of yelp, a scream in the offing, and a splash. And so the long day wore on, so to speak.

I opened my eyes. The kid was just coming to the surface.

'Help!' I shouted, cocking an eye on the bush from which young Bingo was scheduled to emerge.

Nothing happened. Young Bingo didn't emerge to the slightest extent whatever.

'I say! Help!' I shouted again.

I don't want to bore you with reminiscences of my theatrical career, but I must touch once more on that appearance of mine as the butler. The scheme on that occasion had been that when I put the tray on the table the heroine would come on and say a few words to get me off. Well, on the night the misguided female forgot to stand by, and it was a full minute before the search-party located her and shot her on to the stage. And all that time I had to stand there, waiting. A rotten sensation, believe me, and this was just the same, only worse. I understood what these writer-chappies mean when they talk about time standing still.

Meanwhile, the kid Oswald was presumably being cut off in his prime, and it began to seem to me that some sort of steps ought to be taken about it. What I had seen of the lad hadn't particularly endeared him to me, but it was undoubtedly a bit thick to let him pass away. I don't know when I have seen anything more grubby and unpleasant than the lake as viewed from the bridge; but the thing apparently had to be done. I chucked off my coat and vaulted over.

It seems rummy that water should be so much wetter when you go into it with your clothes on than when you're just bathing, but take it from me that it is. I was only under about three seconds, I suppose, but I came up feeling like the bodies you read of in the paper which "had evidently been in the water several days". I felt clammy and bloated.

At this point the scenario struck another snag. I had assumed that directly I came to the surface I should get hold of the kid and steer him courageously to shore. But he hadn't waited to be steered. When I had finished getting the water out of my eyes and had time to look round, I saw him about ten yards away, going strongly and using, I think, the Australian crawl. The spectacle took all the heart out of me. I mean to say, the whole essence of rescue, if you know what I mean, is that the party of the second part shall keep fairly still and in one spot. If he starts swimming off on his own account and can obviously give you at least forty yards in the hundred, where are you? The whole thing falls through. It didn't seem to me that there was much to be done except get ashore, so I got ashore. By the time I had landed, the kid was half-way to the house. Look at it from whatever angle you like, the thing was a wash-out.

I was interrupted in my meditations by a noise like the Scotch express going under a bridge. It was Honoria Glossop laughing. She was standing at my elbow, looking at me in a rummy manner.

'Oh, Bertie, you are funny!' she said. And even in that moment there seemed to me something sinister in the words. She had never called me anything except "Mr Wooster" before. 'How wet you are!'

'Yes, I am wet.'

'You had better hurry into the house and change.'

'Yes.'

I wrung a gallon or two of water out of my clothes.

'You *are* funny!' she said again. 'First proposing in that extraordinary roundabout way, and then pushing poor little Oswald into the lake so as to impress me by saving him.'

I managed to get the water out of my throat sufficiently to try to correct this fearful impression.

'No, no!'

'He said you pushed him in, and I saw you do it. Oh, I'm not angry, Bertie. I think it was too sweet of you. But I'm quite sure it's time that I took you in hand. You certainly want someone to look after you. You've been seeing too many moving-pictures. I suppose the next thing you would have done would have been to set the house on fire so as to rescue me.' She looked at me in a proprietary sort of way. 'I think,' she said, 'I shall be able to make something of you, Bertie. It is true yours has been a wasted life up to the present, but you are still young, and there is a lot of good in you.'

'No, really there isn't.'

'Oh, yes, there is. It simply wants bringing out. Now you run straight up to the house and change your wet clothes, or you will catch cold.'

And, if you know what I mean, there was a sort of motherly note in her voice which seemed to tell me, even more than her actual words, that I was for it.

As I was coming downstairs after changing, I ran into young Bingo, looking festive to a degree.

'Bertie!' he said. 'Just the man I wanted to see. Bertie, a wonderful thing has happened.'

'You blighter!' I cried. 'What became of you? Do you know -?'

'Oh, you mean about being in those bushes? I hadn't time to tell you about that. It's all off.'

'All off?'

'Bertie, I was actually starting to hide in those bushes when the most extraordinary thing happened. Walking across the lawn I saw the most radiant, the most beautiful girl in the world. There is none like her, none. Bertie, do you believe in love at first sight? You do believe in love at first sight, don't you, Bertie, old man? Directly I saw her she seemed to draw me like a magnet. I seemed to forget everything. We two were alone in a world of music and sunshine. I joined her. I got into conversation. She is a Miss Braythwayt, Bertie – Daphne Braythwayt. Directly our eyes met, I realized that what I had imagined to be my love for Honoria Glossop had been a mere passing whim. Bertie, you do believe in love at first sight, don't you? She is so wonderful, so sympathetic. Like a tender goddess – '

At this point I left the blighter.

Two days later I got a letter from Jeeves.

'. . . The weather,' it ended, 'continues fine. I have had one exceedingly enjoyable bathe.'

I gave one of those hollow, mirthless laughs, and went downstairs to join Honoria. I had an appointment with her in the drawing-room. She was going to read Ruskin to me.

4

INTRODUCING CLAUDE AND EUSTACE

The blow fell precisely at one forty-five (summer time). Spenser, Aunt Agatha's butler, was offering me the fried potatoes at the moment, and such was my emotion that I lofted six of them on to the sideboard with the spoon. Shaken to the core, if you know what I mean.

Mark you, I was in a pretty enfeebled condition already. I had been engaged to Honoria Glossop nearly two weeks, and during all that time not a day had passed without her putting in some heavy work in the direction of what Aunt Agatha had called "moulding" me. I had read solid literature till my eyes bubbled; we had legged it together through miles of picture-galleries; and I had been compelled to undergo classical concerts to an extent you would hardly believe. All in all, therefore, I was in no fit state to receive shocks, especially shocks like this. Honoria had lugged me round to lunch at Aunt Agatha's, and I had just been saying to myself, "Death, where is thy jolly old sting?" when she hove the bomb.

'Bertie,' she said, suddenly, as if she had just remembered it, 'what is the name of that man of yours – your valet?'

'Eh? Oh, Jeeves.'

'I think he's a bad influence for you,' said Honoria. 'When we are married, you must get rid of Jeeves.'

It was at this point that I jerked the spoon and sent six of the best and crispest sailing on to the sideboard, with Spenser gambolling after them like a dignified old retriever.

'Get rid of Jeeves!' I gasped.

'Yes. I don't like him.'

'*I* don't like him,' said Aunt Agatha.

'But I can't. I mean – why, I couldn't carry on for a day without Jeeves.'

'You will have to,' said Honoria. 'I don't like him at all.'

'*I* don't like him at all,' said Aunt Agatha. 'I never did.'

Ghastly, what? I'd always had an idea that marriage was a bit of a wash-out, but I'd never dreamed that it demanded such frightful sacrifices from a fellow. I passed the rest of the meal in a sort of stupor.

The scheme had been, if I remember, that after lunch I should go off and caddy for Honoria on a shopping tour down Regent Street; but when she got up and started collecting me and the rest of things, Aunt Agatha stopped her.

'You run along dear,' she said. 'I want to say a few words to Bertie.'

So Honoria legged it, and Aunt Agatha drew up her chair and started in.

'Bertie,' she said, 'dear Honoria does not know it, but a little difficulty has arisen about your marriage.'

'By Jove! not really?' I said, hope starting to dawn.

'Oh, it's nothing at all, of course. It is only a little exasperating. The fact is, Sir Roderick is being rather troublesome.'

'Thinks I'm not a good bet? Wants to scratch the fixture? Well, perhaps he's right.'

'Pray do not be so absurd, Bertie. It is nothing so

serious as that. But the nature of Sir Roderick's profession unfortunately makes him – over-cautious.'

I didn't get it.

'Over-cautious?'

'Yes. I suppose it is inevitable. A nerve specialist with his extensive practice can hardly help taking a rather warped view of humanity.'

I got what she was driving at now. Sir Roderick Glossop, Honoria's father, is always called a nerve specialist, because it sounds better, but everybody knows that he's really a sort of janitor to the looney-bin. I mean to say, when your uncle the Duke begins to feel the strain a bit and you find him in the blue drawing-room sticking straws in his hair, old Glossop is the first person you send for. He toddles round, gives the patient the once-over, talks about over-excited nervous systems, and recommends complete rest and seclusion and all that sort of thing. Practically every posh family in the country has called him in at one time or another, and I suppose that, being in that position – I mean constantly having to sit on people's heads while their nearest and dearest phone to the asylum to send round the wagon – does tend to make a chappie take what you might call a warped view of humanity.

'You mean he thinks I may be a looney, and he doesn't want a looney son-in-law?' I said.

Aunt Agatha seemed rather peeved than otherwise at my deadly intelligence.

'Of course, he does not think anything so ridiculous. I told you he was simply exceedingly cautious. He wants to satisfy himself that you are perfectly normal.' Here she paused, for Spenser had come in with the coffee. When he had gone, she went on: 'He appears to have got hold of some extraordinary story about your having pushed his son Oswald into the lake at Ditteredge Hall.

Incredible, of course. Even you would hardly do a thing like that.'

'Well, I did sort of lean against him, you know, and he shot off the bridge.'

'Oswald definitely accuses you of having pushed him into the water. That has disturbed Sir Roderick, and unfortunately it has caused him to make inquiries, and he has heard about your poor Uncle Henry.'

She eyed me with a good deal of solemnity, and I took a grave sip of coffee. We were peeping into the family cupboard and having a look at the good old skeleton. My late Uncle Henry, you see, was by way of being the blot on the Wooster escutcheon. An extremely decent chappie personally, and one who had always endeared himself to me by tipping me with considerable lavishness when I was at school; but there's no doubt he did at times do rather rummy things, notably keeping eleven pet rabbits in his bedroom; and I suppose a purist might have considered him more or less off his onion. In fact, to be perfectly frank, he wound up his career, happy to the last and completely surrounded by rabbits, in some sort of a home.

'It is very absurd, of course,' continued Aunt Agatha. 'If any of the family had inherited poor Henry's eccentricity – and it was nothing more – it would have been Claude and Eustace, and there could not be two brighter boys.'

Claude and Eustace were twins, and had been kids at school with me in my last summer term. Casting my mind back, it seemed to me that "bright" just about described them. The whole of that term, as I remembered it, had been spent in getting them out of a series of frightful rows.

'Look how well they are doing at Oxford. Your Aunt Emily had a letter from Claude only the other day saying that they hoped to be elected shortly to a very important college club, called The Seekers.'

'Seekers?' I couldn't recall any club of the name in my time at Oxford. 'What do they seek?'

'Claude did not say. Truth or knowledge, I should imagine. It is evidently a very desirable club to belong to, for Claude added that Lord Rainsby, the Earl of Datchet's son, was one of his fellow-candidates. However, we are wandering from the point, which is that Sir Roderick wants to have a quiet talk with you quite alone. Now I rely on you, Bertie, to be – I won't say intelligent, but at least sensible. Don't giggle nervously; try to keep that horrible glassy expression out of your eyes: don't yawn or fidget; and remember that Sir Roderick is the president of the West London branch of the anti-gambling league, so please do not talk about horse-racing. He will lunch with you at your flat tomorrow at one-thirty. Please remember that he drinks no wine, strongly disapproves of smoking, and can only eat the simplest food, owing to an impaired digestion. Do not offer him coffee, for he considers it the root of half the nerve-trouble in the world.'

'I should think a dog-biscuit and a glass of water would about meet the case, what?'

'Bertie!'

'Oh, all right. Merely persiflage.'

'Now it is precisely that sort of idiotic remark that would be calculated to arouse Sir Roderick's worst suspicions. Do please try to refrain from any misguided flippancy when you are with him. He is a very serious-minded man . . . Are you going? Well, please remember all I have said. I rely on you, and, if anything goes wrong, I shall never forgive you.'

'Right-o!' I said.

And so home, with a jolly day to look forward to.

I breakfasted pretty late next morning and went for a stroll afterwards. It seemed to me that anything I could do to clear the old lemon ought to be done, and a bit of fresh air generally relieves that rather foggy feeling that comes over a fellow early in the day. I had taken a stroll in the park, and got back as far as Hyde Park Corner, when some blighter sloshed me between the shoulder-blades. It was young Eustace, my cousin. He was arm-in-arm with two other fellows, the one on the outside being my cousin Claude and the one in the middle a pink-faced chappie with light hair and an apologetic sort of look.

'Bertie, old egg!' said Eustace affably.

'Hallo!' I said, not frightfully chirpily.

'Fancy running into you, the one man in London who can support us in the style we are accustomed to! By the way, you've never met old Dog-Face, have you? Dog-Face, this is my cousin Bertie. Lord Rainsby – Mr Wooster. We've just been round to your flat, Bertie. Bitterly disappointed that you were out, but were hospitably entertained by old Jeeves. That man's a corker, Bertie. Stick to him.'

'What are you doing in London?' I asked.

'Oh, buzzing round. We're just up for the day. Flying visit, strictly unofficial. We oil back on the three-ten. And now, touching that lunch you very decently volunteered to stand us, which shall it be? Ritz? Savoy? Carlton? Or, if you're a member of Ciro's or the Embassy, that would do just as well.'

'I can't give you lunch. I've got an engagement myself. And, by Jove,' I said, taking a look at my watch, 'I'm late.' I hailed a taxi. 'Sorry.'

'As man to man, then,' said Eustace, 'lend us a fiver.'

I hadn't time to stop and argue. I unbelted the fiver and hopped into the cab. It was twenty to two when I got to the flat. I bounded into the sitting-room, but it was empty.

Jeeves shimmied in.

'Sir Roderick has not yet arrived, sir.'

'Good egg!' I said. 'I thought I should find him smashing up the furniture.' My experience is that the less you want a fellow, the more punctual he's bound to be, and I had had a vision of the old lad pacing the rug in my sitting-room, saying "He cometh not!" and generally hotting up. 'Is everything in order?'

'I fancy you will find the arrangements quite satisfactory, sir.'

'What are you giving us?'

'Cold consommé, a cutlet, and a savoury, sir. With lemon-squash, iced.'

'Well, I don't see how that can hurt him. Don't go getting carried away by the excitement of the thing and start bringing in coffee.'

'No, sir.'

'And don't let your eyes get glassy, because, if you do, you're apt to find yourself in a padded cell before you know where you are.'

'Very good, sir.'

There was a ring at the bell.

'Stand by, Jeeves,' I said. 'We're off!'

=5=

SIR RODERICK COMES TO LUNCH

I had met Sir Roderick Glossop before, of course, but only when I was with Honoria; and there is something about Honoria which makes almost anybody you meet in the same room seem sort of under-sized and trivial by comparison. I had never realized till this moment what an extraordinarily formidable old bird he was. He had a pair of shaggy eyebrows which gave his eyes a piercing look which was not at all the sort of thing a fellow wanted to encounter on an empty stomach. He was fairly tall and fairly broad, and he had the most enormous head, with practically no hair on it, which made it seem bigger and much more like the dome of St Paul's. I suppose he must have taken about a nine or something in hats. Shows what a rotten thing it is to let your brain develop too much.

'What ho! What ho! What ho!' I said, trying to strike the genial note, and then had a sudden feeling that that was just the sort of thing I had been warned not to say. Dashed difficult it is to start things going properly on an occasion like this. A fellow living in a London flat is so handicapped. I mean to say, if I had been the young squire greeting the visitor in the country, I could have said, "Welcome to Meadowsweet Hall!" or something zippy like that. It sounds silly to say "Welcome to Number 6A, Crichton Mansions, Berkeley Street, W."

'I am afraid I am a little late,' he said as we sat down. 'I was detained at my club by Lord Alastair Hungerford, the Duke of Ramfurline's son. His Grace, he informed me, had exhibited a renewal of the symptoms which have been causing the family so much concern. I could not leave him immediately. Hence my unpunctuality, which I trust has not discommoded you.'

'Oh, not at all. So the Duke is off his rocker, what?'

'The expression which you use is not precisely the one I should have employed myself with reference to the head of perhaps the noblest family in England, but there is no doubt that cerebral excitement does, as you suggest, exist in no small degree.' He sighed as well as he could with his mouth full of cutlet. 'A profession like mine is a great strain, a great strain.'

'Must be.'

'Sometimes I am appalled at what I see around me.' He stopped suddenly and sort of stiffened. 'Do you keep a cat, Mr Wooster?'

'Eh? What? Cat? No, no cat.'

'I was conscious of a distinct impression that I had heard a cat mewing either in the room or very near to where we are sitting.'

'Probably a taxi or something in the street.'

'I fear I do not follow you.'

'I mean to say, taxis squawk, you know. Rather like cats in a sort of way.'

'I had not observed the resemblance,' he said, rather coldly.

'Have some lemon-squash,' I said. The conversation seemed to be getting rather difficult.

'Thank you. Half a glassful, if I may.' The hell-brew appeared to buck him up, for he resumed in a slightly more pally manner. 'I have a particular dislike for cats. But I was saying – Oh, yes. Sometimes I am positively appalled at what I see around me. It is not only the cases which come under my professional notice, painful as many of those are. It is what I see as I go about London. Sometimes it seems to me that the whole world is mentally unbalanced. This very morning, for example, a most singular and distressing occurrence took place as I was driving from my house to the club. The day being clement, I had instructed my chauffeur to open my landaulette, and I was leaning back, deriving no little pleasure from the sunshine, when our progress was arrested in the middle of the thoroughfare by one of those blocks in the traffic which are inevitable in so congested a system as that of London.'

I suppose I had been letting my mind wander a bit, for when he stopped and took a sip of lemon-squash I had a feeling that I was listening to a lecture and was expected to say something.

'Hear, hear!' I said.

'I beg your pardon?'

'Nothing, nothing. You were saying – '

'The vehicles proceeding in the opposite direction had also been temporarily arrested, but after a moment they were permitted to proceed. I had fallen into a meditation, when suddenly the most extraordinary thing took place. My hat was snatched abruptly from my head! And as I looked back I perceived it being waved in a kind of feverish triumph from the interior of a taxicab, which, even as I looked, disappeared through a gap in the traffic and was lost to sight.'

I didn't laugh, but I distinctly heard a couple of my floating ribs part from their moorings under the strain.

'Must have been meant for a practical joke,' I said. 'What?'

This suggestion didn't seem to please the old boy.

'I trust,' he said, 'I am not deficient in an appreciation

of the humorous, but I confess that I am at a loss to detect anything akin to pleasantry in the outrage. The action was beyond all question that of a mentally unbalanced subject. These mental lesions may express themselves in almost any form. The Duke of Ramfurline, to whom I had occasion to allude just now, is under the impression – this is in the strictest confidence – that he is a canary: and his seizure today, which so perturbed Lord Alastair, was due to the fact that a careless footman had neglected to bring him his morning lump of sugar. Cases are common, again, of men waylaying women and cutting off portions of their hair. It is from a branch of this latter form of mania that I should be disposed to imagine that my assailant was suffering. I can only trust that he will be placed under proper control before he – Mr Wooster, there *is* a cat closer at hand! It is *not* in the street! The mewing appears to come from the adjoining room.'

This time I had to admit there was no doubt about it. There was a distinct sound of mewing coming from the next room. I punched the bell for Jeeves, who drifted in and stood waiting with an air of respectful devotion.

'Sir?'

'Oh, Jeeves,' I said. 'Cats! What about it? Are there any cats in the flat?'

'Only the three in your bedroom, sir.'

'What!'

'Cats in his bedroom!' I heard Sir Roderick whisper in a kind of stricken way, and his eyes hit me amidships like a couple of bullets.

'What do you mean,' I said, 'only the three in my bedroom?'

'The black one, the tabby and the small lemon-coloured animal, sir.'

'What on earth – ?'

I charged round the table in the direction of the door. Unfortunately, Sir Roderick had just decided to edge in that direction himself, with the result that we collided in the doorway with a good deal of force, and staggered out into the hall together. He came smartly out of the clinch and grabbed an umbrella from the rack.

'Stand back!' he shouted, waving it overhead. 'Stand back, sir! I am armed!'

It seemed to me that the moment had come to be soothing.

'Awfully sorry I barged into you,' I said. 'Wouldn't have had it happen for worlds. I was just dashing out to have a look into things.'

He appeared a trifle reassured, and lowered the umbrella. But just then the most frightful shindy started in the bedroom. It sounded as though all the cats in London, assisted by delegates from outlying suburbs, had got together to settle their differences once for all. A sort of augmented orchestra of cats.

'This noise is unendurable,' yelled Sir Roderick. 'I cannot hear myself speak.'

'I fancy, sir,' said Jeeves respectfully, 'that the animals may have become somewhat exhilarated as the result of having discovered the fish under Mr Wooster's bed.'

The old boy tottered.

'Fish! Did I hear you rightly?'

'Sir?'

'Did you say that there was a fish under Mr Wooster's bed?'

'Yes, sir.'

Sir Roderick gave a low moan, and reached for his hat and stick.

'You aren't going?' I said.

'Mr Wooster, I *am* going! I prefer to spend my leisure time in less eccentric society.'

'But I say. Here, I must come with you. I'm sure the whole business can be explained. Jeeves, my hat.'

Jeeves rallied round. I took the hat from him and shoved it on my head.

'Good heavens!'

Beastly shock it was! The bally thing had absolutely engulfed me, if you know what I mean. Even as I was putting it on I got a sort of impression that it was a trifle roomy; and no sooner had I let it go than it settled down over my ears like a kind of extinguisher.

'I say! This isn't my hat!'

'It is *my* hat!' said Sir Roderick in about the coldest, nastiest voice I'd ever heard. 'The hat which was stolen from me this morning as I drove in my car.'

'But – '

I suppose Napoleon or somebody like that would have been equal to the situation, but I'm bound to say it was too much for me. I just stood there goggling in a sort of coma, while the old boy lifted the hat off me and turned to Jeeves.

'I should be glad, my man,' he said, 'if you would accompany me a few yards down the street. I wish to ask you some questions.'

'Very good, sir.'

'Here, but, I say – !' I began, but he left me standing. He stalked out, followed by Jeeves. And at that moment the row in the bedroom started again, louder than ever.

I was about fed up with the whole thing. I mean, cats in your bedroom – a bit thick, what? I didn't know how the dickens they had got in, but I was jolly well resolved that they weren't going to stay picnicking there any longer. I flung open the door. I got a momentary flash of about a hundred and fifteen cats of all sizes and colours scrapping in the middle of the room, and then they all shot past me with a rush and out of the front door; and all that was left of the mob-scene was the head of a whacking big fish, lying on the carpet and staring up at me in a rather austere sort of way, as if it wanted a written explanation and apology.

There was something about the thing's expression that absolutely chilled me, and I withdrew on tiptoe and shut the door. And, as I did so, I bumped into someone.

'Oh, sorry!' he said.

I spun round. It was the pink-faced chappie, Lord Something or other, the fellow I had met with Claude and Eustace.

'I say,' he said apologetically, 'awfully sorry to bother you, but those weren't my cats I met just now legging it downstairs, were they? They looked like my cats.'

'They came out of my bedroom.'

'Then they *were* my cats!' he said sadly. 'Oh, dash it!'

'Did you put cats in my bedroom?'

'Your man, what's his-name, did. He rather decently said I could keep them there till my train went. I'd just come to fetch them. And now they've gone! Oh, well, it can't be helped, I suppose. I'll take the hat and the fish, anyway.'

I was beginning to dislike this chappie.

'Did you put that bally fish there, too?'

'No, that was Eustace's. The hat was Claude's.'

I sank limply into a chair.

'I say, you couldn't explain this, could you?' I said. The chappie gazed at me in mild surprise.

'Why, don't you know all about it? I say!' He blushed profusely. 'Why, if you don't know about it, I shouldn't wonder if the whole thing didn't seem rummy to you.'

'Rummy is the word.'

'It was for The Seekers, you know?'

'The Seekers?'

'Rather a blood club, you know, up at Oxford, which your cousins and I are rather keen on getting into. You have to pinch something, you know, to get elected. Some sort of a souvenir, you know. A policeman's helmet, you know, or a door-knocker or something, you know. The room's decorated with the things at the annual dinner, and everybody makes speeches and all that sort of thing. Rather jolly! Well, we wanted rather to make a sort of special effort and do the thing in style, if you understand, so we came up to London to see if we couldn't pick up something here that would be a bit out of the ordinary. And we had the most amazing luck right from the start. Your cousin Claude managed to collect a quite decent top-hat out of a passing car and your cousin Eustace got away with a really goodish salmon or something from Harrods, and I snaffled three excellent cats all in the first hour. We were fearfully braced, I can tell you. And then the difficulty was to know where to park the things till our train went. You look so beastly conspicuous, you know, tooling about London with a fish and a lot of cats. And then Eustace remembered you, and we all came on here in a cab. You were out, but your man said it would be all right. When we met you, you were in such a hurry that we hadn't time to explain. Well, I think I'll be taking the hat, if you don't mind.'

'It's gone.'

'Gone?'

'The fellow you pinched it from happened to be the man who was lunching here. He took it away with him.'

'Oh, I say! Poor old Claude will be upset. Well, how about the goodish salmon or something?'

'Would you care to view the remains?' He seemed all broken up when he saw the wreckage.

'I doubt if the committee would accept that,' he said sadly. 'There isn't a frightful lot of it left, what?'

'The cats ate the rest.'

He sighed deeply.

'No cats, no fish, no hat. We've had all our trouble for nothing. I do call that hard! And on top of that – I say, I hate to ask you, but you couldn't lend me a tenner, could you?'

'A tenner? What for?'

'Well, the fact is, I've got to pop round and bail Claude and Eustace out. They've been arrested.'

'Arrested!'

'Yes. You see, what with the excitement of collaring the hat and the salmon or something, added to the fact that we had rather a festive lunch, they got a bit above themselves, poor chaps, and tried to pinch a motor-lorry. Silly, of course, because I don't see how they could have got the thing to Oxford and shown it to the committee. Still, there wasn't any reasoning with them, and when the driver started making a fuss, there was a bit of a mix-up, and Claude and Eustace are more or less languishing in Vine Street police-station till I pop round and bail them out. So if you could manage a tenner – Oh, thanks, that's fearfully good of you. It would have been too bad to leave them there, what? I mean, they're both such frightfully good chaps, you know. Everybody likes them up at the Varsity. They're fearfully popular.'

'I bet they are!' I said.

When Jeeves came back, I was waiting for him on the mat. I wanted speech with the blighter.

'Well?' I said.

'Sir Roderick asked me a number of questions, sir, respecting your habits and mode of life, to which I replied guardedly.'

'I don't care about that. What I want to know is why you didn't explain the whole thing to him right at the start? A word from you would have put everything clear.'

'Yes, sir.'

'Now he's gone off thinking me a looney.'

'I should not be surprised, from his conversation with me, sir, if some such idea had not entered his head.'

I was just starting in to speak, when the telephone bell rang. Jeeves answered it.

'No, madam, Mr Wooster is not in. No, madam, I do not know when he will return. No, madam, he left no message. Yes, madam, I will inform him.' He put back the receiver. 'Mrs Gregson, sir.'

Aunt Agatha! I had been expecting it. Ever since the luncheon-party had blown out a fuse, her shadow had been hanging over me, so to speak.

'Does she know? Already?'

'I gather that Sir Roderick has been speaking to her on the telephone, sir, and – '

'No wedding bells for me, what?'

Jeeves coughed.

'Mrs Gregson did not actually confide in me, sir, but I fancy that some such thing may have occurred. She seemed decidedly agitated, sir.'

It's a rummy thing, but I'd been so snootered by the old boy and the cats and the fish and the hat and the pink-faced chappie and all the rest of it that the bright side simply hadn't occurred to me till now. By Jove, it was like a bally weight rolling off my chest! I gave a yelp of pure relief.

'Jeeves!' I said, 'I believe you worked the whole thing!'

'Sir?'

'I believe you had the jolly old situation in hand right from the start.'

'Well, sir, Spenser, Mrs Gregson's butler, who inadvertently chanced to overhear something of your conversation when you were lunching at the house, did mention certain of the details to me; and I confess that, though it may be a liberty to say so, I entertained hopes that something might occur to prevent the match. I doubt if the young lady was entirely suitable to you, sir.'

'And she would have shot you out on your ear five minutes after the ceremony.'

'Yes, sir. Spenser informed me that she had expressed some such intention. Mrs Gregson wishes you to call upon her immediately, sir.'

'She does, eh? What do you advise, Jeeves?'

'I think a trip abroad might prove enjoyable, sir.'

I shook my head. 'She'd come after me.'

'Not if you went far enough afield sir. There are excellent boats leaving every Wednesday and Saturday for New York.'

'Jeeves,' I said, 'you are right, as always. Book the tickets.'

6

JEEVES AND THE YULE-TIDE SPIRIT

The letter arrived on the morning of the sixteenth. I was pushing a bit of breakfast into the Wooster face at the moment and, feeling fairly well-fortified with coffee and kippers, I decided to break the news to Jeeves without delay. As Shakespeare says, if you're going to do a thing you might just as well pop right at it and get it over. The man would be disappointed, of course, and possibly even chagrined: but, dash it all, a splash of disappointment here and there does a fellow good. Makes him realize that life is stern and life is earnest.

'Oh, Jeeves,' I said.

'Sir?'

'We have here a communication from Lady Wickham. She has written inviting me to Skeldings for the festives. So you will see about bunging the necessaries together. We repair thither on the twenty-third. Plenty of white ties, Jeeves, also a few hearty country suits for use in the daytime. We shall be there some little time, I expect.'

There was a pause. I could feel he was directing a frosty gaze at me, but I dug into the marmalade and refused to meet it.

'I thought I understood you to say, sir, that you proposed to visit Monte Carlo immediately after Christmas.'

'I know. But that's all off. Plans changed.'

'Very good, sir.'

At this point the telephone bell rang, tiding over very nicely what had threatened to be an awkward moment. Jeeves unhooked the receiver.

'Yes? . . . Yes, madam . . . Very good, madam. Here is Mr Wooster.' He handed me the instrument. 'Mrs Spenser Gregson, sir.'

You know, every now and then I can't help feeling that Jeeves is losing his grip. In his prime it would have been with him the work of a moment to have told Aunt Agatha that I was not at home. I gave him one of those reproachful glances, and took the machine.

'Hullo?' I said. 'Yes? Hullo? Hullo? Bertie speaking. Hullo? Hullo? Hullo?'

'Don't keep on saying Hullo,' yipped the old relative in her customary curt manner. 'You're not a parrot. Sometimes I wish you were, because then you might have a little sense.'

Quite the wrong sort of tone to adopt towards a fellow in the early morning, of course, but what can one do?

'Bertie, Lady Wickham tells me she has invited you to Skeldings for Christmas. Are you going?'

'Rather!'

'Well, mind you behave yourself. Lady Wickham is an old friend of mine.'

I was in no mood for this sort of thing over the telephone. Face to face, I'm not saying, but at the end of a wire, no.

'I shall naturally endeavour, Aunt Agatha,' I replied stiffly, 'to conduct myself in a manner befitting an English gentleman paying a visit – '

'What did you say? Speak up. I can't hear.'

'I said Right-ho.'

'Oh? Well, mind you do. And there's another reason why I particularly wish you to be as little of an imbecile as you can manage while at Skeldings. Sir Roderick Glossop will be there.'

'What!'

'Don't bellow like that. You nearly deafened me.'

'Did you say Sir Roderick Glossop?'

'I did.'

'You don't mean Tuppy Glossop?'

'I mean Sir Roderick Glossop. Which was my reason for saying Sir Roderick Glossop. Now, Bertie, I want you to listen to me attentively. Are you there?'

'Yes, still here.'

'Well, then, listen. I have at last succeeded, after incredible difficulty, and in face of all the evidence, in almost persuading Sir Roderick that you are not actually insane. He is prepared to suspend judgment until he has seen you once more. On your behaviour at Skeldings, therefore – '

But I had hung up the receiver. Shaken. That's what I was. S. to the core.

Stop me if I've told you this before: but, in case you don't know, let me just mention the facts in the matter of this Glossop. He was a formidable old bird with a bald head and out-size eyebrows, by profession a looney-doctor. How it happened, I couldn't tell you to this day, but I once got engaged to his daughter, Honoria, a ghastly dynamic exhibit who read Nietzsche and had a laugh like waves breaking on a stern and rock-bound coast. The fixture was scratched owing to events occurring which convinced the old boy that I was off my napper; and since then he has always had my name at the top of his list of "Loonies I have Lunched With".

It seemed to me that even at Christmas time, with all the peace on earth and goodwill towards men that there is knocking about at that season, a reunion with this bloke was likely to be tough going. If I hadn't had more than one particularly good reason for wanting to go to Skeldings, I'd have called the thing off.

'Jeeves,' I said, all of a twitter. 'Do you know what? Sir Roderick Glossop is going to be at Lady Wickham's.'

'Very good, sir. If you have finished breakfast, I will clear away.'

Cold and haughty. No symp. None of the rallying-round spirit which one likes to see. As I had anticipated, the information that we were not going to Monte Carlo had got in amongst him. There is a keen sporting streak in Jeeves, and I knew he had been looking forward to a little flutter at the tables.

We Woosters can wear the mask. I ignored his lack of decent feeling.

'Do so Jeeves,' I said proudly, 'and with all convenient speed.'

Relations continued pretty fairly strained all through the rest of the week. There was a frigid detachment in the way the man brought me my dollop of tea in the mornings. Going down to Skeldings in the car on the afternoon of the twenty-third, he was aloof and reserved. And before dinner on the first night of my visit he put the studs in my dress-shirt in what I can only call a marked manner. The whole thing was extremely painful, and it seemed to me, as I lay in bed on the morning of the twenty-fourth, that the only step to take was to put the whole facts of the case before him and trust to his native good sense to effect an understanding.

I was feeling considerably in the pink that morning. Everything had gone like a breeze. My hostess, Lady Wickham, was a beaky female built far too closely on the lines of my Aunt Agatha for comfort, but she had seemed matey enough on my arrival. Her daughter, Roberta, had welcomed me with a warmth which, I'm bound to say, had set the old heart-strings fluttering a bit. And Sir Roderick, in the brief moment we had had together, appeared to have let the Yule-Tide Spirit soak into him to the most amazing extent. When he saw me, his mouth sort of flickered at one corner, which I took to be his idea of smiling, and he said, 'Ha, young man!' Not particularly chummily, but he said it: and my view was that it practically amounted to the lion lying down with the lamb.

So, all in all, life at this juncture seemed pretty well all to the mustard, and I decided to tell Jeeves exactly how matters stood.

'Jeeves,' I said, as he appeared with the steaming.

'Sir?'

'Touching on this business of our being here, I would like to say a few words of explanation. I consider that you have a right to the facts.'

'Sir?'

'I'm afraid scratching that Monte Carlo trip has been a bit of a jar for you, Jeeves.'

'Not at all, sir.'

'Oh, yes, it has. The heart was set on wintering in the world's good old Plague Spot. I know, I saw your eye light up when I said we were due for a visit there. You snorted a bit and your fingers twitched. I know, I know. And now that there has been a change of programme the iron has entered into your soul.'

'Not at all, sir.'

'Oh, yes, it has. I've seen it. Very well, then, what I wish to impress upon you, Jeeves, is that I have not been actuated in this matter by any mere idle whim. It was through no light and airy caprice that I accepted this invitation to Lady Wickham's. I have been angling for it for weeks, prompted by many considerations. In the first place, does one get the Yule-tide spirit at a spot like Monte Carlo?'

'Does one desire the Yule-tide spirit, sir?'

'Certainly one does. I am all for it. Well, that's one thing. Now here's another. It was imperative that I should come to Skeldings for Christmas, Jeeves, because I knew that young Tuppy Glossop was going to be here.'

'Sir Roderick Glossop, sir?'

'His nephew. You may have observed hanging about the place a fellow with light hair and a Cheshire-cat grin. That is Tuppy, and I have been anxious for some time to get to grips with him, I have it in for that man of wrath. Listen to the facts, Jeeves, and tell me if I am not justified in planning a hideous vengeance.' I took a sip of tea, for the mere memory of my wrongs had shaken me. 'In spite of the fact that young Tuppy is the nephew of Sir Roderick Glossop, at whose hands, Jeeves, as you are aware. I have suffered much, I fraternized with him freely, both at the Drones Club and elsewhere. I said to myself that a man is not to be blamed for his relations, and that I would hate to have my pals hold my Aunt Agatha, for instance, against me. Broad-minded, Jeeves, I think?'

'Extremely, sir.'

'Well, then, as I say, I sought this Tuppy out, Jeeves, and hobnobbed, and what do you think he did?'

'I could not say, sir.'

'I will tell you. One night after dinner at the Drones he betted me I wouldn't swing myself across the swimming-bath by the ropes and rings. I took him on and was buzzing along in great style until I came to the last ring. And then I found that this fiend in human shape had looped it back against the rail, thus leaving me hanging in the void with no means of getting ashore to my home and loved ones. There was nothing for it but to drop into the water. He told me that he had often caught fellows that way: and what I maintain, Jeeves, is that, if I can't get back at him somehow at Skeldings – with all the vast resources which a country-house affords at my disposal – I am not the man I was.'

'I see, sir.'

There was still something in his manner which told me that even now he lacked complete sympathy and understanding, so, delicate though the subject was, I decided to put all my cards on the table.

'And now, Jeeves, we came to the most important reason why I had to spend Christmas at Skeldings. Jeeves,' I said, diving into the old cup once more for a moment and bringing myself out wreathed in blushes, 'the fact of the matter is, I'm in love.'

'Indeed, sir?'

'You've seen Miss Roberta Wickham?'

'Yes, sir.'

'Very well, then.'

There was a pause, while I let it sink in.

'During your stay here, Jeeves,' I said, 'you will, no doubt, be thrown a good deal together with Miss Wickham's maid. On such occasions, pitch it strong.'

'Sir?'

'You know what I mean. Tell her that I'm rather a good chap. Mention my hidden depths. These things get round. Dwell on the fact that I have a kind heart and was runner-up in the Squash Handicap at the Drones this year. A boost is never wasted, Jeeves.'

'Very good, sir. But – '

'But what?'

'Well, sir – '

'I wish you wouldn't say "Well, sir" in that soupy

tone of voice. I have had to speak of this before. The habit is one that is growing upon you. Check it. What's on your mind?'

'I hardly like to take the liberty – '

'Carry on, Jeeves. We are always glad to hear from you, always.'

'What I was about to remark, if you will excuse me, sir, was that, I would scarcely have thought Miss Wickham a suitable – '

'Jeeves,' I said coldly, 'if you have anything to say against that lady, it had better not be said in my presence.'

'Very good, sir.'

'Or anywhere else, for that matter. What is your kick against Miss Wickham?'

'Oh, really, sir!'

'Jeeves, I insist. This is a time for plain speaking. You have beefed about Miss Wickham. I wish to know why.'

'It merely crossed my mind, sir, that for a gentlemen of your description Miss Wickham is not a suitable mate.'

'What do you mean by a gentleman of my description?'

'Well, sir – '

'Jeeves!'

'I beg your pardon, sir. The expression escaped me inadvertently. I was about to observe that I can only asseverate – '

'Only what?'

'I can only say that, as you have invited my opinion – '

'But I didn't.'

'I was under the impression that your desired to canvass my views on the matter, sir.'

'Oh? Well, let's have them anyway.'

'Very good, sir. Then briefly, if I may say so, sir, though Miss Wickham is a charming young lady – '

'There, Jeeves, you spoke an imperial quart. What eyes!'

'Yes, sir.'

'What hair!'

'Very true, sir.'

'And what *espièglerie*, if that's the word I want.'

'The exact word, sir.'

'All right, then. Carry on.'

'I grant Miss Wickham the possession of all these desirable qualities, sir. Nevertheless, considered as a matrimonial prospect for a gentleman of your description, I cannot look upon her as suitable. In my opinion Miss Wickham lacks seriousness, sir. She is too volatile and frivolous. To qualify as Miss Wickham's husband, a gentleman would need to possess a commanding personality and considerable strength of character.'

'Exactly!'

'I would always hesitate to recommend as a life's companion a young lady with quite such a vivid shade of red hair. Red hair, sir, in my opinion, is dangerous.'

I eyed the blighter squarely.

'Jeeves,' I said, 'you're talking rot.'

'Very good, sir.'

'Absolute drivel.'

'Very good, sir.'

'Pure mashed potatoes.'

'Very good, sir.'

'Very good, sir – I mean very good, Jeeves, that will be all,' I said.

And I drank a modicum of tea, with a good deal of hauteur.

It isn't often that I find myself able to prove Jeeves in

the wrong, but by dinner-time that night I was in a position to do so, and I did it without delay.

'Touching on that matter we were touching on, Jeeves,' I said, coming in from the bath and tackling him as he studied the shirt, 'I should be glad if you would give me your careful attention for a moment. I warn you that what I am about to say is going to make you look pretty silly.'

'Indeed, sir?'

'Yes, Jeeves. Pretty dashed silly it's going to make you look. It may lead you to be rather more careful in future about broadcasting these estimates of yours of people's characters. This morning, if I remember rightly, you stated that Miss Wickham was volatile, frivolous and lacking in seriousness. Am I correct?'

'Quite correct, sir.'

'Then what I have to tell you may cause you to alter that opinion. I went for a walk with Miss Wickham this afternoon: and, as we walked, I told her about what young Tuppy Glossop did to me in the swimming-bath at the Drones. She hung upon my words, Jeeves, and was full of sympathy.'

'Indeed, sir?'

'Dripping with it. And that's not all. Almost before I had finished, she was suggesting the ripest, fruitiest, brainiest scheme for bringing young Tuppy's grey hairs in sorrow to the grave that anyone could possibly imagine.'

'That is very gratifying, sir.'

'Gratifying is the word. It appears that at the girls' school where Miss Wickham was educated, Jeeves, it used to become necessary from time to time for the right-thinking element of the community to slip it across certain of the baser sort. Do you know what they did, Jeeves?'

'No, sir.'

'They took a long stick, Jeeves, and – follow me closely here – they tied a darning-needle to the end of it. Then at dead of night, it appears, they sneaked privily into the party of the second part's cubicle and shoved the needle through the bed-clothes and punctured her hot-water bottle. Girls are much subtler in these matters than boys, Jeeves. At my old school one would occasionally heave a jug of water over another bloke during the night-watches, but we never thought of effecting the same result in this particularly neat and scientific manner. Well, Jeeves, that was the scheme which Miss Wickham suggested I should work on young Tuppy, and this is the girl you call frivolous and lacking in seriousness. Any girl who can think up a wheeze like that is my idea of a helpmeet. I shall be glad, Jeeves, if by the time I came to bed to-night you have for me in this room a stout stick with a good sharp darning-needle attached.'

'Well, sir – '

I raised my hand.

'Jeeves,' I said. 'Not another word. Stick, one, and needle, darning, good, sharp, one, without fail in this room at eleven-thirty to-night.'

'Very good, sir.'

'Have you any idea where young Tuppy sleeps?'

'I could ascertain, sir.'

'Do so, Jeeves.'

In a few minutes he was back with the necessary informash.

'Mr Glossop is established in the Moat Room, sir.'

'Where's that?'

'The second door on the floor below this, sir.'

'Right ho, Jeeves. Are the studs in my shirt?'

'Yes, sir.'

'And the links also?'

'Yes, sir.'

'Then push me into it.'

The more I thought about this enterprise which a sense of duty and good citizenship had thrust upon me, the better it seemed to me. I am not a vindictive man, but I felt, as anybody would have felt in my place, that if fellows like young Tuppy are allowed to get away with it the whole fabric of Society and Civilization must inevitably crumble. The task to which I had set myself was one that involved hardship and discomfort, for it meant sitting up till well into the small hours and then padding down a cold corridor, but I did not shrink from it. After all, there is a lot to be said for family tradition. We Woosters did our bit in the Crusades.

It being Christmas Eve, there was, as I had foreseen, a good deal of revelry and what not. First, the village choir surged round and sang carols outside the front door, and then somebody suggested a dance, and after that we hung around chatting of this and that, so that it wasn't till past one that I got to my room. Allowing for everything, it didn't seem that it was going to be safe to start my little expedition till half-past two at the earliest: and I'm bound to say that it was only the utmost resolution that kept me from snuggling into the sheets and calling it a day. I'm not much of a lad now for late hours.

However, by half-past two everything appeared to be quiet. I shook off the mists of sleep, grabbed the good old stick-and-needle and off along the corridor. And presently, pausing outside the Moat Room, I turned the handle, found the door wasn't locked, and went in.

I suppose a burglar – I mean a real professional who works at the job six nights a week all the year round –

gets so that finding himself standing in the dark in somebody else's bedroom means absolutely nothing to him. But for a bird like me, who has had no previous experience, there's a lot to be said in favour of washing the whole thing out and closing the door gently and popping back to bed again. It was only by summoning up all the old bulldog courage of the Woosters, and reminding myself that, if I let this opportunity slip another might never occur, that I managed to stick out what you might call the initial minute of the binge. Then the weakness passed, and Bertram was himself again.

At first when I beetled in, the room had seemed as black as a coal-cellar: but after a bit things began to lighten. The curtains weren't quite drawn over the window and I could see a trifle of the scenery here and there. The bed was opposite the window, with the head against the wall and the end where the feet were jutting out towards where I stood, thus rendering it possible after one had sown the seed, so to speak, to make a quick getaway. There only remained now the rather tricky problem of locating the old hot-water bottle. I mean to say, the one thing you can't do if you want to carry a job like this through with secrecy and dispatch is to stand at the end of a fellow's bed, jabbing the blankets at random with a darning-needle. Before proceeding to anything in the nature of definite steps, it is imperative that you locate the bot.

I was a good deal cheered at this juncture to hear a fruity snore from the direction of the pillows. Reason told me that a bloke who could snore like that wasn't going to be awakened by a trifle. I edged forward and ran a hand in a gingerly sort of way over the coverlet. A moment later I had found the bulge. I steered the good old darning-needle on to it, gripped the stick, and shoved. Then, pulling out the weapon, I sidled towards the door, and in another moment would have been outside, buzzing for home and the good night's rest, when suddenly there was a crash that sent my spine shooting up through the top of my head and the contents of the bed sat up like a jack-in-the-box and said:

'Who's that?'

It just shows how your most careful strategic moves can be the very ones that dish your campaign. In order to facilitate the orderly retreat according to plan I had left the door open, and the beastly thing had slammed like a bomb.

But I wasn't giving much thought to the causes of the explosion, having other things to occupy my mind. What was disturbing me was the discovery that, whoever else the bloke in the bed might be, he was not young Tuppy. Tuppy has one of those high, squeaky voices that sound like the tenor of the village choir failing to hit a high note. This one was something in between the last Trump and a tiger calling for breakfast after being on a diet for a day or two. It was the sort of nasty, rasping voice you hear shouting "Fore!" when you're one of a slow foursome on the links and are holding up a couple of retired colonels. Among the qualities it lacked were kindliness, suavity and that sort of dove-like cooing note which makes a fellow feel he has found a friend.

I did not linger. Getting swiftly off the mark, I dived for the door-handle and was off and away, banging the door behind me. I may be a chump in many ways, as my Aunt Agatha will freely attest, but I know when and when not to be among those present.

And I was just about to do the stretch of corridor leading to the stairs in a split second under the record time for the course, when something brought me up with a sudden jerk. One moment, I was all dash and fire and speed; the next, an irresistible force had checked me in my stride and was holding me straining at the leash, as it were.

You know, sometimes it seems to me as if Fate were going out of its way to such an extent to snooter you that you wonder if it's worth while continuing to struggle. The night being a trifle chillier than the dickens, I had donned for this expedition a dressing-gown. It was the tail of this infernal garment that had caught in the door and pipped me at the eleventh hour.

The next moment the door had opened, light was streaming through it, and the bloke with the voice had grabbed me by the arm.

It was Sir Roderick Glossop.

The next thing that happened was a bit of a lull in the proceedings. For about three and a quarter seconds or possibly more we just stood there, drinking each other in, so to speak, the old boy still attached with a limpet-like grip to my elbow. If I hadn't been in a dressing-gown and he in pink pyjamas with a blue stripe, and if he hadn't been glaring quite so much as if he were shortly going to commit a murder, the tableau would have looked rather like one of those advertisements you see in the magazines, where the experienced elder is patting the young man's arm, and saying to him, "My boy, if you subscribe to the Mutt-Jeff Correspondence School of Oswego, Kan., as I did, you may some day, like me, become Third Assistant Vice-President of the Schenectady Consolidated Nail-File and Eyebrow Tweezer Corporation".

'You!' said Sir Roderick finally. And in this connection I want to state that it's all rot to say you can't hiss a word that hasn't an "s" in it. The way he pushed out that "You!" sounded like an angry cobra, and I am betraying no secrets when I mention that it did me no good whatsoever.

By rights, I suppose, at this point I ought to have said something. The best I could manage, however, was a faint, soft bleating sound. Even on ordinary social occasions, when meeting this bloke as man to man and with a clear conscience, I could never be completely at my ease: and now those eyebrows seemed to pierce me like a knife.

'Come in here,' he said, lugging me into the room. 'We don't want to wake the whole house. Now', he said, depositing me on the carpet and closing the door and doing a bit of eyebrow work, 'kindly inform me what is this latest manifestation of insanity?'

It seemed to me that a light and cheery laugh might help the thing along. So I had a pop at one.

'Don't gibber!' said my genial host. And I'm bound to admit that the light and cheery hadn't come out quite as I'd intended.

I pulled myself together with a strong effort.

'Awfully sorry about all this,' I said in a hearty sort of voice. 'The fact is, I thought you were Tuppy.'

'Kindly refrain from inflicting your idiotic slang on me. What do you mean by the adjective "tuppy"?'

'It isn't so much an adjective, don't you know. More of a noun, I should think, if you examine it squarely. What I mean to say is, I thought you were your nephew.'

'You thought I was my nephew? Why should I be my nephew?'

'What I'm driving at is, I thought this was his room.'

'My nephew and I changed rooms. I have a great dislike for sleeping on an upper floor. I am nervous about fire.'

For the first time since this interview had started, I braced up a trifle. The injustice of the whole thing stirred me to such an extent that for a moment I lost that sense of being a toad under the harrow which had been cramping my style up till now. I even went so far as to eye this pink-pyjamed poltroon with a good deal of contempt and loathing. Just because he had this craven fear of fire and this selfish preference for letting Tuppy be cooked instead of himself should the emergency occur, my nicely-reasoned plans had gone up the spout. I gave him a look, and I think I may even have snorted a bit.

'I should have thought that your man-servant would have informed you,' said Sir Roderick, 'that we contemplated making this change. I met him shortly before luncheon and told him to tell you.'

I reeled. Yes, it is not too much to say that I reeled. This extraordinary statement had taken me amidships without any preparation, and it staggered me. That Jeeves had been aware all along that this old crumb would be the occupant of the bed which I was proposing to prod with darning-needles and had let me rush upon my doom without a word of warning was almost beyond belief. You might say I was aghast. Yes, practically aghast.

'You told Jeeves that you were going to sleep in this room?' I gasped.

'I did. I was aware that you and my nephew were on terms of intimacy, and I wished to spare myself the possibility of a visit from you. I confess that it never occurred to me that such a visit was to be anticipated at three o'clock in the morning. What the devil do you mean,' he barked, suddenly hotting up, 'by prowling about the house at this hour? And what is that thing in your hand?'

I looked down, and found that I was still grasping the stick. I give you my honest word that, what with the maelstrom of emotions into which his revelation about Jeeves had cast me, the discovery came as an absolute surprise.

'This?' I said. 'Oh, yes.'

'What do you mean, Oh yes? What is it?'

'Well, it's a long story – '

'We have the night before us.'

'It's this way. I will ask you to picture me some weeks ago, perfectly peaceful and inoffensive, after dinner at the Drones, smoking a thoughtful cigarette and – '

I broke off. The man wasn't listening. He was goggling in a rapt sort of way at the end of the bed, from which there had now begun to drip on to the carpet a series of drops.

'Good heavens!'

'– thoughtful cigarette and chatting pleasantly of this and that – '

I broke off again. He had lifted the sheets and was gazing at the corpse of the hot-water bottle.

'Did you do this?' he said in a low, strangled sort of voice.

'Er – yes. As a matter of fact, yes. I was just going to tell you – '

'And your aunt tried to persuade me that you were not insane!'

'I'm not. Absolutely not. If you'll just let me explain.'

'I will do nothing of the kind.'

'It all began – '

'Silence!'

'Right-ho.'

He did some deep-breathing exercises through the nose.

'My bed is drenched!'

'The way it all began – '

'Be quiet!' He heaved somewhat for awhile. 'You wretched, miserable idiot,' he said, 'kindly inform me which bedroom you are supposed to be occupying?'

'It's on the floor above. The Clock Room.'

'Thank you. I will find it.'

'Eh?'

He gave me the eyebrow.

'I propose' he said, 'to pass the remainder of the night in your room, where, I presume, there is a bed in a condition to be slept in. You may bestow yourself as comfortably as you can here. I will wish you good-night.'

He buzzed off, leaving me flat.

Well, we Woosters are old campaigners. We can take the rough with the smooth. But to say that I liked the prospect now before me would be paltering with the truth. One glance at the bed told me that any idea of sleeping there was out. A goldfish could have done it, but not Bertram. After a bit of a look round, I decided that the best chance of getting a sort of night's rest was to doss as well as I could in the arm-chair. I pinched a couple of pillows off the bed, shoved the hearth-rug over my knees, and sat down and started counting sheep.

But it wasn't any good. The old lemon was sizzling much too much to admit of anything in the nature of slumber. This hideous revelation of the blackness of Jeeves's treachery kept coming back to me every time I nearly succeeded in dropping off: and, what's more, it seemed to get colder and colder as the long night wore on. I was just wondering if I would ever get to sleep again in this world when a voice at my elbow said 'Good-morning, sir' and I sat up with a jerk.

I could have sworn I hadn't so much as dozed off for even a minute, but apparently I had. For the curtains were drawn back and daylight was coming in through the window and there was Jeeves standing beside me with a cup of tea on a tray.

'Merry Christmas, sir!'

I reached out a feeble hand for the restoring brew. I swallowed a mouthful or two, and felt a little better. I was aching in every limb and the dome felt like lead, but I was now able to think with a certain amount of clearness, and I fixed the man with a stony eye and prepared to let him have it.

'You think so, do you?' I said. 'Much, let me tell you, depends on what you mean by the adjective "merry". If, moreover, you suppose that it is going to be merry for you, correct that impression, Jeeves,' I said, taking another half-oz., of tea and speaking in a cold, measured voice, 'I wish to ask you one question. Did you or did you not know that Sir Roderick Glossop was sleeping in this room last night?'

'Yes, sir.'

'You admit it!'

'Yes, sir.'

'And you didn't tell me!'

'No, sir. I thought it would be more judicious not to do so.'

'Jeeves – '

'If you will allow me to explain, sir.'

'Explain!'

'I was aware that my silence might lead to something in the nature of an embarrassing contretemps, sir – '

'You thought that, did you?'

'Yes, sir.'

'You were a good guesser,' I said, sucking down further Bohea.

'But it seemed to me, sir, that whatever might occur was all for the best.'

I would have put in a crisp word or two here, but he carried on without giving me the opp.

'I thought that possibly, on reflection, sir, your views being what they are, you would prefer your relations with Sir Roderick Glossop and his family to be distant rather than cordial.'

'My views? What do you mean, my views?'

'As regards a matrimonial alliance with Miss Honoria Glossop, sir.'

Something like an electric shock seemed to zip through me. The man had opened up a new line of thought. I suddenly saw what he was driving at, and realized all in a flash that I had been wronging this faithful fellow. All the while I supposed he had been landing me in the soup, he had really been steering me away from it. It was like those stories one used to read as a kid about the traveller going along on a dark night and his dog grabs him by the leg of his trousers and he says "Down, sir! What are you doing, Rover?" and the dog hangs on and he gets rather hot under the collar and curses a bit but the dog won't let him go and then suddenly the moon shines through the clouds and he finds he's been standing on the edge of a precipice and one more step would have – well, anyway, you get the idea: and what I'm driving at is that much the same sort of thing seemed to have been happening now.

It's perfectly amazing how a fellow will let himself get off his guard and ignore the perils which surround him. I give you my honest word, it had never struck me till this morning that my Aunt Agatha had been scheming to get me in right with Sir Roderick so that I should eventually be received back into the fold, if you see what I mean, and subsequently pushed off on Honoria.

'My God, Jeeves!' I said, paling.

'Precisely, sir.'

'You think there was a risk?'

'I do, sir. A very grave risk.'

A disturbing thought struck me.

'But, Jeeves, on calm reflection won't Sir Roderick have gathered by now that my objective was young Tuppy and that puncturing his hot-water bottle was just one of those things that occur when the Yule-tide spirit is abroad – one of those things that have to be overlooked and taken with the indulgent smile and the fatherly shake of the head? I mean to say, Young Blood and all that sort of thing? What I mean is he'll realize that I wasn't trying to snooter him, and then all the good work will have been wasted.'

'No, sir. I fancy not. That might possibly have been Sir Roderick's mental reaction, had it not been for the second incident.'

'The second incident?'

'During the night, sir, while Sir Roderick was occupying your bed, somebody entered the room, pierced his hot-water bottle with some sharp instrument, and vanished in the darkness.'

I could make nothing of this.

'What! Do you think I walked in my sleep?'

'No, sir. It was young Mr Glossop who did it. I encountered him this morning, sir, shortly before I came here. He was in cheerful spirits and enquired of me how you were feeling about the incident. Not being aware that his victim had been Sir Roderick.'

'But, Jeeves, what an amazing coincidence!'

'Sir?'

'Why, young Tuppy getting exactly the same idea as I did. Or, rather, as Miss Wickham did. You can't say that's not rummy. A miracle, I call it.'

'Not altogether, sir. It appears that he received the suggestion from the young lady.'

'From Miss Wickham?'

'Yes, sir.'

'You mean to say that, after she had put me up to the scheme of puncturing Tuppy's hot-water bottle, she went away and tipped Tuppy off to puncturing mine?'

'Precisely, sir. She is a young lady with a keen sense of humour, sir.'

I sat there, you might say stunned. When I thought how near I had come to offering the heart and hand to a girl capable of double-crossing a strong man's honest love like that, I shivered.

'Are you cold, sir?'

'No, Jeeves. Just shuddering.'

'The occurrence, if I may take the liberty of saying so, sir, will perhaps lend colour to the view which I put forward yesterday that Miss Wickham, though in many respects a charming young lady – '

I raised a hand.

'Say no more, Jeeves,' I replied. 'Love is dead.'

'Very good, sir.'

I brooded for a while.

'You've seen Sir Roderick this morning, then?'

'Yes, sir.'

'How did he seem?'

'A trifle feverish, sir.'

'Feverish?'

'A little emotional, sir. He expressed a strong desire to meet you, sir.'

'What would you advise?'

'If you were to slip out by the back entrance as soon as you are dressed, sir, it would be possible for you to make your way across the field without being observed and reach the village, where you could hire an automobile to take you to London. I could bring on your effects later in your own car.'

'But London, Jeeves? Is any man safe? My Aunt Agatha is in London.'

'Yes, sir.'

'Well, then?'

He regarded me for a moment with a fathomless eye. 'I think the best plan, sir, would be for you to leave England, which is not pleasant at this time of the year, for some little while. I would not take the liberty of dictating your movements, sir, but as you already have accommodation engaged on the Blue Train for Monte Carlo for the day after to-morrow – '

'But you cancelled the booking?'

'No, sir.'

'I thought you had.'

'No, sir.'

'I told you to.'

'Yes, sir. It was remiss of me, but the matter slipped my mind.'

'Oh?'

'Yes, sir.'

'All right, Jeeves. Monte Carlo ho, then.'

'Very good, sir.'

'It's lucky, as things have turned out, that you forgot to cancel that booking.'

'Very fortunate indeed, sir. If you will wait here, sir, I will return to your room and procure a suit of clothes.'

7

JEEVES AND THE SONG OF SONGS

Another day had dawned all hot and fresh and, in pursuance of my unswerving policy at that time, I was singing "Sonny Boy" in my bath, when there was a soft step without and Jeeves's voice came filtering through the woodwork.

'I beg your pardon, sir.'

I had just got to that bit about the Angels being lonely, where you need every ounce of concentration in order to make the spectacular finish, but I signed off courteously.

'Yes, Jeeves? Say on.'

'Mr Glossop, sir.'

'What about him?'

'He is in the sitting-room, sir.'

'Young Tuppy Glossop?'

'Yes, sir.'

'In the sitting-room?'

'Yes, sir.'

'Desiring speech with me?'

'Yes, sir.'

'H'm!'

'Sir?'

'I only said H'm.'

And I'll tell you why I said H'm. It was because the man's story had interested me strangely. The news that

Tuppy was visiting me at my flat, at an hour when he must have known that I would be in my bath and consequently in a strong strategic position to heave a wet sponge at him, surprised me considerably.

I hopped out with some briskness and, slipping a couple of towels about the limbs and torso, made for the sitting-room. I found young Tuppy at the piano, playing "Sonny Boy" with one finger.

'What ho!' I said, not without a certain hauteur.

'Oh, hullo, Bertie,' said young Tuppy. 'I say, Bertie, I want to see you about something important.'

It seemed to me that the bloke was embarrassed. He had moved to the mantelpiece, and now he broke a vase in rather a constrained way.

'The fact is, Bertie, I'm engaged.'

'Engaged?'

'Engaged,' said young Tuppy, coyly dropping a photograph frame into the fender. 'Practically, that is.'

'Practically?'

'Yes. You'll like her, Bertie. Her name is Cora Bellinger. She's studying for Opera. Wonderful voice she has. Also dark, flashing eyes and a great soul.'

'How do you mean, practically?'

'Well, it's this way. Before ordering the trousseau, there is one little point she wants cleared up. You see, what with her great soul and all that, she has a rather serious outlook on life: and the one thing she absolutely bars is anything in the shape of hearty humour. You know, practical joking and so forth. She said if she thought I was a practical joker she would never speak to me again. And unfortunately she appears to have heard about that little affair at the Drones – I expect you have forgotten all about that, Bertie?'

'I have not!'

'No, no, not forgotten exactly. What I mean is,

nobody laughs more heartily at the recollection than you. And what I want you to do, old man, is to seize an early opportunity of taking Cora aside and categorically denying that there is any truth in the story. My happiness, Bertie, is in your hands, if you know what I mean.'

Well, of course, if he put it like that, what could I do? We Woosters have our code.

'Oh, all right,' I said, but far from brightly.

'Splendid fellow!'

'When do I meet this blighted female?'

'Don't call her "this blighted female", Bertie, old man. I have planned all that out. I will bring her round here to-day for a spot of lunch.'

'What!'

'At one-thirty. Right. Good. Fine. Thanks. I knew I could rely on you.'

He pushed off, and I turned to Jeeves, who had shimmered in with the morning meal.

'Lunch for three to-day, Jeeves,' I said.

'Very good, sir.'

'You know, Jeeves, it's a bit thick. You remember my telling you about what Mr Glossop did to me that night at the Drones?'

'Yes, sir.'

'For months I have been cherishing dreams of getting a bit of my own back. And now, so far from crushing him into the dust, I've got to fill him and fiancée with rich food and generally rally round and be the good angel.'

'Life is like that, sir.'

'True, Jeeves. What have we here?' I asked, inspecting the tray.

'Kippered herrings, sir.'

'And I shouldn't wonder,' I said, for I was in thoughtful mood, 'if even herrings haven't troubles of their own.'

'Quite possibly, sir.'

'I mean, apart from getting kippered.'

'Yes, sir.'

'And so it goes on, Jeeves, so it goes on.'

I can't say I exactly saw eye to eye with young Tuppy in his admiration for the Bellinger female. Delivered on the mat at one-twenty-five, she proved to be an upstanding light-heavyweight of some thirty summers, with a commanding eye and a square chin which I, personally, would have steered clear of. She seemed to me a good deal like what Cleopatra would have been after going in too freely for the starches and cereals. I don't know why it is, but women who have anything to do with Opera, even if they're only studying for it, always appear to run to surplus poundage.

Tuppy, however, was obviously all for her. His whole demeanour, both before and during lunch, was that of one striving to be worthy of a noble soul. When Jeeves offered him a cocktail, he practically recoiled as from a serpent. It was terrible to see the change which love had effected in the man. The spectacle put me off my food.

At half-past two, the Bellinger left to go to a singing lesson. Tuppy trotted after her to the door, bleating and frisking a goodish bit, and then came back and looked at me in a goofy sort of way.

'Well, Bertie?'

'Well, what?'

'I mean, isn't she?'

'Oh, rather,' I said, humouring the poor fish.

'Wonderful eyes?'

'Oh, rather.'

'Wonderful figure?'

'Oh, quite.'

'Wonderful voice?'

Here I was able to intone the response with a little more heartiness. The Bellinger, at Tuppy's request, had sung us a few songs before digging in at the trough, and nobody could have denied that her pipes were in great shape. Plaster was still falling from the ceiling.

'Terrific,' I said.

Tuppy sighed, and, having helped himself to about four inches of whisky and one of soda, took a deep, refreshing draught.

'Ah!' he said. 'I needed that.'

'Why didn't you have it at lunch?'

'Well, it's this way,' said Tuppy. 'I have not actually ascertained what Cora's opinions are on the subject of taking of slight snorts from time to time, but I thought it more prudent to lay off. The view I took was that laying off would seem to indicate the serious mind. It is touch-and-go, as you might say, at the moment, and the smallest thing may turn the scale.'

'What beats me is how on earth you expect to make her think you've got a mind at all – let alone a serious one.'

'I have my methods.'

'I bet they're rotten.'

'You do, do you?' said Tuppy warmly. 'Well, let me tell you, my lad, that that's exactly what they're anything but. I am handling this affair with consummate generalship. Do you remember Beefy Bingham who was at Oxford with us?'

'I ran into him only the other day. He's a parson now.'

'Yes. Down in the East End. Well, he runs a Lads' Club for the local toughs – you know the sort of thing

– cocoa and backgammon in the reading-room and occasional clean, bright entertainments in the Oddfellows' Hall: and I've been helping him. I don't suppose I've passed an evening away from the backgammon board for weeks. Cora is extremely pleased. I've got her to promise to sing on Tuesday at Beefy's next clean, bright entertainment.'

'You have?'

'I absolutely have. And now mark my devilish ingenuity, Bertie. I'm going to sing, too.'

'Why do you suppose that's going to get you anywhere?'

'Because the way I intend to sing the song I intend to sing will prove to her that there are great deeps in my nature, whose existence she has not suspected. She will see that rough, unlettered audience wiping the tears out of its bally eyes and she will say to herself "What ho! The old egg really has a soul!" For it is not one of your mouldy comic songs, Bertie. No low buffoonery of that sort for me. It is all about Angela being lonely and what not – '

I uttered a sharp cry.

'You don't mean you're going to sing "Sonny Boy"?'

'I jolly well do.'

I was shocked. Yes, dash it, I was shocked. You see, I held strong views on "Sonny Boy". I considered it a song only to be attempted by a few of the elect in the privacy of the bathroom. And the thought of it being murdered in open Oddfellows' Hall by a man who could treat a pal as young Tuppy had treated me that night at the Drones sickened me. Yes, sickened me.

I hadn't time, however, to express my horror and disgust, for at this juncture Jeeves came in.

'Mrs Travers has just rung up on the telephone, sir.

She desired me to say that she will be calling to see you in a few minutes.'

'Contents noted, Jeeves,' I said. 'Now listen, Tuppy – '

I stopped. The fellow wasn't there.

'What have you done with him, Jeeves?' I asked.

'Mr Glossop has left, sir.'

'Left? How can he have left? He was sitting there – '

'That is the front door closing now, sir.'

'But what made him shoot off like that?'

'Possibly Mr Glossop did not wish to meet Mrs Travers, sir.'

'Why not?'

'I could not say, sir. But undoubtedly at the mention of Mrs Travers' name he rose very swiftly.'

'Strange, Jeeves.'

'Yes, sir.'

I turned to a subject of more moment.

'Jeeves,' I said. 'Mr Glossop proposes to sing "Sonny Boy" at an entertainment down in the East End next Tuesday.'

'Indeed, sir?'

'Before an audience consisting mainly of costermongers, with a sprinkling of whelk-stall owners, purveyors of blood-oranges, and minor pugilists.'

'Indeed, sir?'

'Make a note to remind me to be there. He will infallibly get the bird, and I want to witness his downfall.'

'Very good, sir.'

'And when Mrs Travers arrives, I shall be in the sitting-room.'

Those who know Bertram Wooster best are aware that in his journey through life he is impeded and generally snootered by about as scaly a platoon of aunts as was ever assembled. But there is one exception to the general ghastliness – viz., my Aunt Dahlia. She married old Tom Travers the year Blue-bottle won the Cambridgeshire, and is one of the best. It is always a pleasure to me to chat with her, and it was with a courtly geniality that I rose to receive her as she sailed over the threshold at about two fifty-five.

She seemed somewhat perturbed, and snapped into the agenda without delay. Aunt Dahlia is one of those big, hearty women. She used to go in a lot for hunting, and she generally speaks as if she had just sighted a fox on a hillside half a mile away.

'Bertie,' she cried, in a manner of one encouraging a bevy of hounds to renewed efforts. 'I want your help.'

'And you shall have it, Aunt Dahlia,' I replied suavely. 'I can honestly say that there is no one to whom I would more readily do a good turn than yourself; no one to whom I am more delighted to be – '

'Less of it,' she begged, 'less of it. You know that friend of yours, young Glossop?'

'He's just been lunching here.'

'He has, has he? Well, I wish you'd poisoned his soup.'

'We didn't have soup. And, when you describe him as a friend of mine, I wouldn't quite say the term absolutely squared with the facts. Some time ago, one night when we had been dining together at the Drones – '

At this point Aunt Dahlia – a little brusquely, it seemed to me – said that she would rather wait for the story of my life till she could get it in book-form. I could see now that she was definitely not her usual sunny self, so I shelved my personal grievances and asked what was biting her.

'It's that young hound Glossop,' she said.

'What's he been doing?'

'Breaking Angela's heart.' (Angela. Daughter of above. My cousin. Quite a good egg.)

'Breaking Angela's heart?'

'Yes . . . Breaking . . . Angela's HEART!'

'You say he's breaking Angela's heart?'

She begged me in rather a feverish way to suspend the vaudeville cross-talk stuff.

'How's he doing that?' I asked.

'With his neglect. With his low, callous, double-crossing duplicity.'

'Duplicity is the word, Aunt Dahlia,' I said. 'In treating of young Tuppy Glossop, it springs naturally to the lips. Let me just tell you what he did to me one night at the Drones. We had finished dinner – '

'Ever since the beginning of the season, up till about three weeks ago, he was all over Angela. The sort of thing which, when I was a girl, we should have described as courting – '

'Or wooing?'

'Wooing or courting, whichever you like.'

'Whichever *you* like, Aunt Dahlia,' I said courteously.

'Well, anyway, he haunted the house, lapped up daily lunches, danced with her half the night, and so on, till naturally the poor kid, who's quite off her oats about him, took it for granted that it was only a question of time before he suggested that they should feed for life out of the same crib. And now he's gone and dropped her like a hot brick, and I hear he's infatuated with some girl he met at a Chelsea tea-party – a girl named – now, what was it?'

'Cora Bellinger.'

'How do you know?'

'She was lunching here to-day.'

'He brought her?'

'Yes.'

'What's she like?'

'Pretty massive. In shape, a bit on the lines of the Albert Hall.'

'Did he seem very fond of her?'

'Couldn't take his eyes off the chassis.'

'The modern young man,' said Aunt Dahlia, 'is a congenital idiot and wants a nurse to lead him by the hand and some strong attendant to kick him regularly at intervals of a quarter of an hour.'

I tried to point out the silver lining.

'If you ask me, Aunt Dahlia,' I said, 'I think Angela is well out of it. This Glossop is a tough baby. One of London's toughest. I was trying to tell you just now what he did to me one night at the Drones. First having got me in a sporting mood with a bottle of the ripest, he betted I wouldn't swing myself across the swimming-bath by the ropes and rings. I knew I could do it on my head, so I took him on, exulting in the fun, so to speak. And when I'd done half the trip and was going as strong as dammit, I found he had looped the last rope back against the rail, leaving me no alternative but to drop into the depths and swim ashore in correct evening costume.'

'He did?'

'He certainly did. It was months ago, and I haven't got really dry yet. You wouldn't want your daughter to marry a man capable of a thing like that?'

'On the contrary, you restore my faith in the young hound. I see that there must be lots of good in him, after all. And I want this Bellinger business broken up, Bertie.'

'How?'

'I don't care how. Any way you please.'

'But what can I do?'

'Do? Why, put the whole thing before your man Jeeves. Jeeves will find a way. One of the most capable fellers I ever met. Put the thing squarely up to Jeeves and tell him to let his mind play round the topic.'

'There may be something in what you say, Aunt Dahlia,' I said thoughtfully.

'Of course there is,' said Aunt Dahlia. 'A little thing like this will be child's play to Jeeves. Get him working on it, and I'll look in to-morrow to hear the result.'

With which, she biffed off, and I summoned Jeeves to the presence.

'Jeeves,' I said, 'you have heard all?'

'Yes, sir.'

'I thought you would. My Aunt Dahlia has what you might call a carrying voice. Has it ever occurred to you that, if all other sources of income failed, she could make a good living calling the cattle home across the Sands of Dee?'

'I had not considered the point, sir, but no doubt you are right.'

'Well, how do we go? What is your reaction? I think we should do our best to help and assist.'

'Yes, sir.'

'I am fond of my Aunt Dahlia and I am fond of my cousin Angela. Fond of them both, if you get my drift. What the misguided girl finds to attract her in young Tuppy, I cannot say, Jeeves, and you cannot say. But apparently she loves the man – which shows it can be done, a thing I wouldn't have believed myself – and is pining away like – '

'Patience on a monument, sir.'

'Like Patience, as you very shrewdly remark, on a monument. So we must cluster round. Bend your brain to the problem, Jeeves. It is one that will tax you to the uttermost.'

Aunt Dahlia blew in on the morrow, and I rang the bell for Jeeves. He appeared looking brainier than one could have believed possible – sheer intellect shining from every feature – and I could see at once that the engine had been turning over.

'Speak, Jeeves,' I said.

'Very good, sir.'

'You have brooded?'

'Yes, sir.'

'With what success?'

'I have a plan, sir, which I fancy may produce satisfactory results.'

'Let's have it,' said Aunt Dahlia.

'In affairs of this description, madam, the first essential is to study the psychology of the individual.'

'The what of the individual?'

'The psychology, madam.'

'He means the psychology,' I said. 'And by psychology, Jeeves, you imply – ?'

'The natures and dispositions of the principals in the matter, sir.'

'You mean, what they're like?'

'Precisely, sir.'

'Does he talk like this to you when you're alone, Bertie?' asked Aunt Dahlia.

'Sometimes. Occasionally. And, on the other hand, sometimes not. Proceed, Jeeves.'

'Well, sir, if I may say so, the thing that struck me most forcibly about Miss Bellinger when she was under my observation was that hers was a somewhat hard and intolerant nature. I could envisage Miss Bellinger applauding success. I could not so easily see her pitying and sympathizing with failure. Possibly you will recall, sir, her attitude when Mr Glossop endeavoured to light her cigarette with his automatic lighter? I thought I detected a certain impatience at his inability to produce the necessary flame.'

'True, Jeeves. She ticked him off.'

'Precisely, sir.'

'Let me get this straight,' said Aunt Dahlia, looking a bit fogged. 'You think that, if he goes on trying to light her cigarettes with his automatic lighter long enough, she will eventually get fed up and hand him the mitten? Is that the idea?'

'I merely mentioned the episode, madam, as an indication of Miss Bellinger's somewhat ruthless nature.'

'Ruthless,' I said, 'is right. The Bellinger is hard-boiled. Those eyes. That chin. I could read them. A woman of blood and iron, if ever there was one.'

'Precisely, sir. I think, therefore, that, should Miss Bellinger be a witness of Mr Glossop appearing to disadvantage in public, she would cease to entertain affection for him. In the event, for instance, of his failing to please the audience on Tuesday with his singing – '

I saw daylight.

'By Jove, Jeeves! You mean if he gets the bird, all will be off?'

'I shall be greatly surprised if such is not the case, sir.'

I shook my head.

'We cannot leave this thing to chance, Jeeves. Young Tuppy, singing "Sonny Boy," is the likeliest prospect for the bird that I can think of – but, no – you must see for yourself that we can't simply trust to luck.'

'We need not trust to luck, sir. I would suggest that you approach your friend, Mr Bingham, and volunteer your services as a performer at his forthcoming entertainment. It could readily be arranged that you sang immediately before Mr Glossop. I fancy, sir, that, if Mr Glossop were to sing "Sonny Boy" directly after you, too, had sung "Sonny Boy", the audience would respond satisfactorily. By the time, Mr Glossop began to sing, they would have lost their taste for that particular song and would express their feelings warmly.'

'Jeeves,' said Aunt Dahlia, 'you're a marvel!'

'Thank you, madam.'

'Jeeves,' I said, 'you're an ass!'

'What do you mean, he's an ass?' said Aunt Dahlia hotly. 'I think it's the greatest scheme I ever heard.'

'Me sing "Sonny Boy" at Beefy Bingham's clean, bright entertainment? I can see myself!'

'You sing it daily in your bath, sir. Mr Wooster,' said Jeeves, turning to Aunt Dahlia, 'has a pleasant, light baritone – '

'I bet he has,' said Aunt Dahlia.

I froze the man with a look.

'Between singing "Sonny Boy" in one's bath, Jeeves, and singing it before a hall full of assorted blood-orange merchants and their young, there is a substantial difference.'

'Bertie,' said Aunt Dahlia, 'you'll sing, and like it!'

'I will not.'

'Bertie!'

'Nothing will induce – '

'Bertie,' said Aunt Dahlia firmly, 'you will sing "Sonny Boy" on Tuesday, the third *prox.*, and sing it like a lark at sunrise or may an aunt's curse – '

'I won't'

'Think of Angela!'

'Dash Angela!'

'Bertie!'

'No, I mean, hang it all!'

'You won't?'

'No, I won't.'

'That is your last word, is it?'

'It is. Once and for all, Aunt Dahlia, nothing will induce me to let out so much as a single note.'

And so that afternoon I sent a pre-paid wire to Beefy Bingham, offering my services in the cause, and by nightfall the thing was fixed up. I was billed to perform next but one after the intermission. Following me, came Tuppy. And, immediately after him, Miss Cora Bellinger, the well-known operatic soprano.

'Jeeves,' I said that evening – and I said it coldly – 'I shall be obliged if you will pop round to the nearest music-shop and procure me a copy of "Sonny Boy". It will now be necessary for me to learn both verse and refrain. Of the trouble and nervous strain which this will involve, I say nothing.'

'Very good, sir.'

'But this I do say – '

'I had better be starting immediately, sir, or the shop will be closed.'

'Ha!' I said.

And I meant it to sting.

Although I had steeled myself to the ordeal before me and had set out full of the calm, quiet courage which makes men do desperate deeds with careless smiles, I must admit that there was a moment, just after I had entered the Oddfellows' Hall at Bermondsey East and run an eye over the assembled pleasure-seekers, when it needed all the bull-dog pluck of the Woosters to keep me from calling it a day and taking a cab back to civilization. The clean, bright entertainment was in full swing when I arrived, and somebody who looked as if he might be the local undertaker was reciting "Gunga Din". And the audience, though not actually chi-yiking in the full technical sense of the term, had a grim look which I didn't like at all. The mere sight of them gave me the sort of feeling Shadrach, Meshach and Abednego must have had when preparing to enter the burning, fiery furnace.

Scanning the multitude, it seemed to me that they were for the nonce suspending judgment. Did you ever tap on the door of one of those New York speakeasy places and see the grille snap back and a Face appear? There is one long, silent moment when its eyes are fixed on yours and all your past life seems to rise up before you. Then you say that you are a friend of Mr Zinzinheimer and he told you they would treat you right if you mentioned his name, and the strain relaxes. Well, these costermongers and whelkstallers appeared to me to be looking just like that Face. Start something, they seemed to say, and they would know what to do about it. And I couldn't help feeling that my singing "Sonny Boy" would come, in their opinion, under the head of starting something.

'A nice, full house, sir,' said a voice at my elbow. It was Jeeves, watching the proceedings with an indulgent eye.

'You here, Jeeves?' I said, coldly.

'Yes, sir. I have been present since the commencement.'

'Oh?' I said. 'Any casualties yet?'

'Sir?'

'You know what I mean, Jeeves,' I said sternly, 'and don't pretend you don't. Anybody got the bird yet?'

'Oh, no, sir.'

'I shall be the first, you think?'

'No, sir. I see no reason to expect such a misfortune. I anticipate that you will be well received.'

A sudden thought struck me.

'And you think everything will go according to plan?'

'Yes, sir.'

'Well, I don't,' I said. 'And I'll tell you why I don't. I've spotted a flaw in your beastly scheme.'

'A flaw, sir?'

'Yes. Do you suppose for a moment that, if when Mr Glossop hears me singing that dashed song, he'll come calmly on a minute after me and sing it too? Use your intelligence, Jeeves. He will perceive the chasm in his path and pause in time. He will back out and refuse to go on at all.'

'Mr Glossop will not hear you sing, sir. At my advice, he has stepped across the road to the Jug and Bottle, an establishment immediately opposite the hall, and he intends to remain there until it is time for him to appear on the platform.'

'Oh?' I said.

'If I might suggest it, sir, there is another house named the Goat and Grapes only a short distance down the street. I think it might be a judicious move – '

'If I were to put a bit of custom in their way?'

'It would ease the nervous strain of waiting, sir.'

I had not been feeling any too pleased with the man for having let me in for this ghastly binge, but at these words, I'm bound to say, my austerity softened a trifle. He was undoubtedly right. He had studied the psychology of the individual, and it had not led him astray. A quiet ten minutes at the Goat and Grapes was exactly what my system required. To buzz off there and inhale a couple of swift whisky-and-sodas was with Bertram Wooster the work of a moment.

The treatment worked like magic. What they had put into the stuff, besides vitriol, I could not have said; but it completely altered my outlook on life. That curious, gulpy feeling passed. I was no longer conscious of the sagging sensation at the knees. The limbs ceased to quiver gently, the tongue became loosened in its socket, and the backbone stiffened. Pausing merely to order and swallow another of the same, I bade the barmaid a cheery good night, nodded affably to one or two fellows in the bar whose faces I liked, and came prancing back to the hall, ready for anything.

And shortly afterwards I was on the platform with about a million bulging eyes goggling up at me. There was a rummy sort of buzzing in my ears, and then through the buzzing I heard the sound of a piano starting to tinkle: and, commending my soul to God, I took a good, long breath and charged in.

Well, it was a close thing. The whole incident is a bit blurred, but I seem to recollect a kind of murmur as I hit the refrain. I thought at the time it was an attempt on the part of the many-headed to join in the chorus, and at the moment it rather encouraged me. I passed the thing over the larynx with all the vim at my disposal, hit the high note, and off gracefully into the wings. I didn't come on again to take a bow. I just receded and oiled round to where Jeeves awaited me among the standees at the back.

'Well, Jeeves,' I said, anchoring myself at his side and brushing the honest sweat from the brow, 'they didn't rush the platform.'

'No, sir.'

'But you can spread it about that that's the last time I perform outside my bath. My swan-song, Jeeves. Anybody who wants to hear me in future must present himself at the bathroom door and shove his ear against the keyhole. I may be wrong, but it seemed to me that towards the end they were hotting up a trifle. The bird was hovering in the air. I could hear the beating of its wings.'

'I did detect a certain restlessness, sir, in the audience.

I fancy they had lost their taste for that particular melody.'

'Eh?'

'I should have informed you earlier, sir, that the song had already been sung twice before you arrived.'

'What!'

'Yes, sir. Once by a lady and once by a gentleman. It is a very popular song, sir.'

I gaped at the man. That, with this knowledge, he could calmly have allowed the young master to step straight into the jaws of death, so to speak, paralysed me. It seemed to show that the old feudal spirit had passed away altogether. I was about to give him my views on the matter in no uncertain fashion, when I was stopped by the spectacle of young Tuppy lurching on to the platform.

Young Tuppy had the unmistakable air of a man who has recently been round to the Jug and Bottle. A few cheery cries of welcome, presumably from some of his backgammon-playing pals who felt that blood was thicker than water, had the effect of causing the genial smile on his face to widen till it nearly met at the back. He was plainly feeling about as good as a man can feel and still remain on his feet. He waved a kindly hand to his supporters, and bowed in a regal sort of manner, rather like an Eastern monarch acknowledging the plaudits of the mob.

Then the female at the piano struck up the opening bars of "Sonny Boy", and Tuppy swelled like a balloon, clasped his hands together, rolled his eyes up at the ceiling in a manner denoting Soul, and began.

I think the populace was too stunned for the moment to take immediate steps. It may seem incredible, but I give you my word that young Tuppy got right through the verse without so much as a murmur. Then they all seemed to pull themselves together.

A costermonger, roused, is a terrible thing. I had never seen the proletariat really stirred before, and I'm bound to say it rather awed me. I mean, it gave you some idea of what it must have been like during the French Revolution. From every corner of the hall there proceeded simultaneously the sort of noise which you hear, they tell me, at one of those East End boxing places when the referee disqualifies the popular favourite and makes the quick dash for life. And then they passed beyond mere words and began to introduce the vegetable motive.

I don't know why, but somehow I had got it into my head that the first thing thrown at Tuppy would be a potato. One gets these fancies. It was, however, as a matter of fact, a banana, and I saw in an instant that the choice had been made by wiser heads than mine. These blokes who have grown up from childhood in the knowledge of how to treat a dramatic entertainment that doesn't please them are aware by a sort of instinct just what to do for the best, and the moment I saw the banana splash on Tuppy's shirt-front I realized how infinitely more effective and artistic it was than any potato could have been.

Not that the potato school of thought had not also its supporters. As the proceedings warmed up, I noticed several intelligent-looking fellows who threw nothing else.

The effect on young Tuppy was rather remarkable. His eyes bulged and his hair seemed to stand up, and yet his mouth went on opening and shutting, and you could see that in a dazed, automatic way he was still singing "Sonny Boy". Then, coming out of his trance, he began to pull for the shore with some rapidity. The last seen of him, he was beating a tomato to the exit by a short head.

Presently the tumult and the shouting died. I turned to Jeeves.

'Painful, Jeeves,' I said. 'But what would you?'

'Yes, sir.'

'The surgeon's knife, what?'

'Precisely, sir.'

'Well, with this happening beneath her eyes, I think we may definitely consider the Glossop-Bellinger romance off.'

'Yes, sir.'

At this point old Beefy Bingham came out on to the platform.

'Ladies and gentlemen,' said old Beefy.

I supposed that he was about to rebuke his flock for the recent expression of feeling. But such was not the case. No doubt he was accustomed by now to the wholesome give-and-take of these clean, bright entertainments and had ceased to think it worth while to make any comment when there was a certain liveliness.

'Ladies and gentlemen,' said old Beefy, 'the next item on the programme was to have been Songs by Miss Cora Bellinger, the well-known operatic soprano. I have just received a telephone-message from Miss Bellinger, saying that her car has broken down. She is, however, on her way here in a cab and will arrive shortly. Meanwhile, our friend Mr Enoch Simpson will recite "Dangerous Dan McGrew".'

I clutched at Jeeves.

'Jeeves! You heard?'

'Yes, sir.'

'She wasn't there!'

'No, sir.'

'She saw nothing of Tuppy's Waterloo.'

'No, sir.'

'The whole bally scheme has blown a fuse.'

'Yes, sir.'

'Come, Jeeves,' I said, and those standing by wondered, no doubt, what had caused that clean-cut face to grow so pale and set. 'I have been subjected to a nervous strain unparalleled since the days of the early Martyrs. I have lost pounds in weight and permanently injured my entire system. I have gone through an ordeal, the recollection of which will make me wake up screaming in the night for months to come. And all for nothing. Let us go.'

'If you have no objection, sir, I would like to witness the remainder of the entertainment.'

'Suit yourself, Jeeves,' I said moodily. 'Personally, my heart is dead and I am going to look in at the Goat and Grapes for another of their cyanide specials and then home.'

It must have been about half-past ten, and I was in the old sitting-room sombrely sucking down a more or less final restorative, when the front door bell rang, and there on the mat was young Tuppy. He looked like a man who has passed through some great experience and stood face to face with his soul. He had the beginnings of a black eye.

'Oh, hullo, Bertie,' said young Tuppy.

He came in, and hovered about the mantelpiece as if he were looking for things to fiddle with and break.

'I've just been singing at Beefy Bingham's entertainment,' he said after a pause.

'Oh?' I said. 'How did you go?'

'Like a breeze,' said young Tuppy. 'Held them spellbound.'

'Knocked 'em, eh?'

'Cold,' said young Tuppy. 'Not a dry eye.'

And this, mark you, a man who had had a good upbringing and had, no doubt, spent years at his mother's knee being taught to tell the truth.

'I suppose Miss Bellinger is pleased?'

'Oh, yes. Delighted.'

'So now everything's all right?'

'Oh, quite.'

Tuppy paused.

'On the other hand, Bertie – '

'Yes?'

'Well, I've been thinking things over. Somehow I don't believe Miss Bellinger is the mate for me after all.'

'You don't?'

'No, I don't.'

'Why don't you?'

'Oh, I don't know. These things sort of flash on you. I respect Miss Bellinger, Bertie. I admire her. But – er – well, I can't help feeling now that a sweet, gentle girl – er – like your cousin Angela, for instance, Bertie, – would – er – in fact – well, what I came round for was to ask if you would 'phone Angela and find out how she reacts to the idea of coming out with me tonight to the Berkeley for a segment of supper and a spot of dancing.'

'Go ahead. There's the 'phone.'

'No, I'd rather you asked her, Bertie. What with one thing and another, if you paved the way – You see, there's just a chance that she may be – I mean, you know how misunderstandings occur – and – well, what I'm driving at, Bertie, old man, is that I'd rather you surged round and did a bit of paving, if you don't mind.'

I went to the 'phone and called up Aunt Dahlia's.

'She says come right along,' I said.

'Tell her,' said Tuppy in a devout sort of voice, 'that I will be with her in something under a couple of ticks.'

He had barely biffed, when I heard a click in the keyhole and a soft padding in the passage without.

'Jeeves,' I called.

'Sir?' said Jeeves, manifesting himself.

'Jeeves, a remarkably rummy thing has happened. Mr Glossop has just been here. He tells me that it is all off between him and Miss Bellinger.'

'Yes, sir.'

'You don't seem surprised.'

'No, sir. I confess I had anticipated some such eventuality.'

'Eh? What gave you that idea?'

'It came to me, sir, when I observed Miss Bellinger strike Mr Glossop in the eye.'

'Strike him!'

'Yes, sir.'

'In the eye?'

'The right eye, sir.'

I clutched the brow.

'What on earth made her do that?'

'I fancy she was a little upset, sir, at the reception accorded to her singing.'

'Great Scott! Don't tell me she got the bird, too?'

'Yes, sir.'

'But why? She's got a red-hot voice.'

'Yes, sir. But I think the audience resented her choice of a song.'

'Jeeves!' Reason was beginning to do a bit of tottering on its throne. 'You aren't going to stand there and tell me that Miss Bellinger sang "Sonny Boy", too!'

'Yes, sir. And – rashly, in my opinion – brought a large doll on to the platform to sing it to. The audience affected to mistake it for a ventriloquist's dummy, and there was some little disturbance.'

'But, Jeeves, what a coincidence!'

'Not altogether, sir. I ventured to take the liberty of accosting Miss Bellinger on her arrival at the hall and recalling myself to her recollection. I then said that Mr Glossop had asked me to request her that as a particular favour to him – the song being a favourite of his – she would sing "Sonny Boy". And when she found that you and Mr Glossop had also sung the song immediately before her, I rather fancy that she supposed that she had been made the victim of a practical pleasantry by Mr Glossop. Will there be anything further, sir?'

'No, thanks.'

'Good night, sir.'

'Good night, Jeeves,' I said reverently.

8

EPISODE OF THE DOG MCINTOSH

I was jerked from the dreamless by a sound like the rolling of distant thunder; and, in the mists of sleep clearing away, was enabled to diagnose this and trace it to its source. It was my Aunt Agatha's dog, McIntosh, scratching at the door. The above, an Aberdeen terrier of weak intellect, had been left in my charge by the old relative while she went off to Aix-les-Bains to take the cure, and I had never been able to make it see eye to eye with me on the subject of early rising. Although a glance at my watch informed me that it was barely ten, here was the animal absolutely up and about.

I pressed the bell, and presently in shimmered Jeeves, complete with tea-tray and preceded by dog, which leaped upon the bed, licked me smartly in the right eye, and immediately curled up and fell into a deep slumber. And where the sense is in getting up at some ungodly hour of the morning and coming scratching at people's doors, when you intend at the first opportunity to go to sleep again, beats me. Nevertheless, every day for the last five weeks this looney hound had pursued the same policy, and I confess I was getting a bid fed.

There were one or two letters on the tray; and, having slipped a refreshing half-cupful into the abyss, I felt equal to dealing with them. The one on top was from my Aunt Agatha.

'Ha!' I said.

'Sir?'

'I said "Ha!" Jeeves. And I meant "Ha!" I was registering relief. My Aunt Agatha returns this evening. She will be at her town residence between the hours of six and seven, and she expects to find McIntosh waiting for her on the mat.'

'Indeed, sir? I shall miss the little fellow.'

'I, too, Jeeves. Despite his habit of rising with the milk and being hearty before breakfast, there is sterling stuff in McIntosh. Nevertheless, I cannot but feel relieved at the prospect of shooting him back to the old home. It has been a guardianship fraught with anxiety. You know what my Aunt Agatha is. She lavishes on that dog a love which might better be bestowed on a nephew: and if the slightest thing had gone wrong with him while I was *in loco parentis*; if, while in my charge, he had developed rabies or staggers or the botts, I should have been blamed.'

'Very true, sir.'

'And, as you are aware, London is not big enough to hold Aunt Agatha and anybody she happens to be blaming.'

I had opened the second letter, and was giving it the eye.

'Ha!' I said.

'Sir?'

'Once again "Ha!" Jeeves, but this time signifying mild surprise. This letter is from Miss Wickham.'

'Indeed, sir?'

I sensed – if that is the word I want – the note of concern in the man's voice, and I knew he was saying to himself "Is the young master about to slip?" You see, there was a time when the Wooster heart was to some extent what you might call ensnared by this

Roberta Wickham, and Jeeves had never approved of her. He considered her volatile and frivolous and more or less of a menace to man and beast. And events, I'm bound to say, had rather borne out his view.

'She wants me to give her lunch to-day.'

'Indeed, sir?'

'And two friends of hers.'

'Indeed, sir?'

'Here. At one-thirty.'

'Indeed, sir?'

I was piqued.

'Correct this parrot-complex, Jeeves,' I said, waving a slice of bread-and-butter rather sternly at the man. 'There is no need for you to stand there saying "Indeed, sir?" I know what you're thinking, and you're wrong. As far as Miss Wickham is concerned, Bertram Wooster is chilled steel. I see no earthly reason why I should not comply with this request. A Wooster may have ceased to love, but he can still be civil.'

'Very good, sir.'

'Employ the rest of the morning, then, in buzzing to and fro and collecting provender. The old King Wenceslas touch, Jeeves. You remember? Bring me fish and bring me fowl – '

'Bring me flesh and bring me wine, sir.'

'Just as you say. You know best. Oh, and roly-poly pudding, Jeeves.'

'Sir?'

'Roly-poly pudding with lots of jam in it. Miss Wickham specifically mentions this. Mysterious, what?'

'Extremely, sir.'

'Also oysters, ice-cream, and plenty of chocolates with that gooey, slithery stuff in the middle. Makes you sick to think of it, eh?'

'Yes, sir.'

'Me, too. But that's what she says. I think she must be on some kind of diet. Well, be that as it may, see to it, Jeeves, will you?'

'Yes, sir.'

'At one-thirty of the clock.'

'Very good, sir.'

'Very good, Jeeves.'

At half past twelve I took the dog McIntosh for his morning saunter in the Park; and, returning at about one-ten, found young Bobbie Wickham in the sitting-room, smoking a cigarette and chatting to Jeeves, who seemed a bit distant, I thought.

I have an idea I've told you about this Bobbie Wickham. She was the red-haired girl who let me down so disgracefully in the sinister affair of Tuppy Glossop and the hot-water bottle, that Christmas when I went to stay at Skeldings Hall, her mother's place in Hertfordshire. Her mother is Lady Wickham, who writes novels which, I believe, command a ready sale among those who like their literature pretty sloppy. A formidable old bird, rather like my Aunt Agatha in appearance. Bobbie does not resemble her, being constructed more on the lines of Clara Bow. She greeted me cordially as I entered – in fact, so cordially that I saw Jeeves pause at the door before biffing off to mix the cocktails and shoot me the sort of grave, warning look a wise old father might pass out to the effervescent son on seeing him going fairly strong with the local vamp. I nodded back, as much as to say "Chilled steel!" and he oozed out, leaving me to play the sparkling host.

'It was awfully sporting of you to give us this lunch, Bertie,' said Bobbie.

'Don't mention it, my dear old thing,' I said. 'Always a pleasure.'

'You got all the stuff I told you about?'

'The garbage, as specified, is in the kitchen. But since when have you become a roly-poly pudding addict?'

'That isn't for me. There's a small boy coming.'

'What!'

'I'm awfully sorry,' she said, noting my agitation. 'I know just how you feel, and I'm not going to pretend that this child isn't pretty near the edge. In fact, he has to be seen to be believed. But it's simply vital that he be cosseted and sucked up to and generally treated as the guest of honour, because everything depends on him.'

'How do you mean?'

'I'll tell you. You know mother?'

'Whose mother?'

'My mother.'

'Oh, yes. I thought you meant the kid's mother.'

'He hasn't got a mother. Only a father, who is a big theatrical manager in America. I met him at a party the other night.'

'The father?'

'Yes, the father.'

'Not the kid?'

'No, not the kid.'

'Right. All clear so far. Proceed.'

'Well, mother – my mother – has dramatized one of her novels and when I met this father, this theatrical manager father, and, between ourselves, made rather a hit with him, I said to myself, "Why not?" '

'Why not what?'

'Why not plant mother's play on him.'

'Your mother's play?'

'Yes, not his mother's play. He is like his son, he hasn't got a mother, either.'

'These things run in families, don't they?'

'You see, Bertie, what with one thing and another,

my stock isn't very high with mother just now. There was that matter of my smashing up the car – oh, and several things. So I thought, here is where I get a chance to put myself right. I cooed to old Blumenfeld – '

'Name sounds familiar.'

'Oh, yes, he's a big man over in America. He has come to London to see if there's anything in the play line worth buying. So I cooed to him a goodish bit and then asked him if he would listen to mother's play. He said he would, so I asked him to come to lunch and I'd read it to him.'

'You're going to read your mother's play – here?' I said, paling.

'Yes.'

'My God!'

'I know what you mean,' she said. 'I admit it's pretty sticky stuff. But I have an idea that I shall put it over. It all depends on how the kid likes it. You see, old Blumenfeld, for some reason always banks on his verdict. I suppose he thinks the child's intelligence is exactly the same as an average audience's and – '

I uttered a slight yelp, causing Jeeves, who had entered with cocktails, to look at me in a pained sort of way. I had remembered.

'Jeeves!'

'Sir?'

'Do you recollect, when we were in New York, a dish-faced kid of the name of Blumenfeld who on a memorable occasion snootered Cyril Bassington-Bassington when the latter tried to go on the stage?'

'Very vividly, sir.'

'Well, prepare yourself for a shock. He's coming to lunch.'

'Indeed, sir?'

'I'm glad you can speak in that light, careless way. I

only met the young stoup of arsenic for a few brief minutes, but I don't mind telling you the prospect of hob-nobbing with him again makes me tremble like a leaf.'

'Indeed, sir?'

'Don't keep saying "Indeed, sir?" You have seen this kid in action and you know what he's like. He told Cyril Bassington-Bassington, a fellow to whom he had never been formally introduced, that he had a face like a fish. And this not thirty seconds after their initial meeting. I give you fair warning that, if he tells me I have a face like a fish, I shall clump his head.'

'Bertie!' cried the Wickham, contorted with anguish and apprehension and what not.

'Yes, I shall.'

'Then you'll simply ruin the whole thing.'

'I don't care. We Woosters have our pride.'

'Perhaps the young gentleman will not notice that you have a face like a fish, sir,' suggested Jeeves.

'Ah! There's that, of course.'

'But we can't just trust to luck,' said Bobbie. 'It's probably the first thing he will notice.'

'In that case, miss,' said Jeeves, 'it might be the best plan if Mr Wooster did not attend the luncheon.'

I beamed on the man. As always, he had found the way.

'But Mr Blumenfeld will think it so odd.'

'Well, tell him I'm eccentric. Tell him I have these moods, which come upon me quite suddenly, when I can't stand the sight of people. Tell him what you like.'

'He'll be offended.'

'Not half so offended as if I socked his son on the upper maxillary bone.'

'I really think it would be the best plan, miss.'

'Oh, all right,' said Bobbie. 'Push off, then. But I

wanted you to be here to listen to the play and laugh in the proper places.'

'I don't suppose there are any proper places,' I said. And with these words I reached the hall in two bounds, grabbed a hat, and made for the street. A cab was just pulling up at the door as I reached it, and inside it were Pop Blumenfeld and his foul son. With a slight sinking of the old heart, I saw that the kid had recognized me.

'Hullo!' he said.

'Hullo!' I said.

'Where are you off to?' said the kid.

'Ha, ha!' I said, and legged it for the great open spaces.

I lunched at the Drones, doing myself fairly well and lingering pretty considerably over coffee and cigarettes. At four o'clock I thought it would be safe to think about getting back; but, not wishing to take any chances, I went to the 'phone and rang up the flat.

'All clear, Jeeves?'

'Yes, sir.'

'Blumenfeld junior nowhere about?'

'No, sir.'

'Not hiding in any nook or cranny, what?'

'No, sir.'

'How did everything go off?'

'Quite satisfactory, I fancy, sir.'

'Was I missed?'

'I think Mr Blumenfeld and young Master Blumenfeld were somewhat surprised at your absence, sir. Apparently they encountered you as you were leaving the building.'

'They did. An awkward moment, Jeeves. The kid appeared to desire speech with me, but I laughed hollowly and passed on. Did they comment on this at all?'

'Yes, sir. Indeed, young Master Blumenfeld was somewhat outspoken.'

'What did he say?'

'I cannot recall his exact words, sir, but he drew a comparison between your mentality and that of a cuckoo.'

'A cuckoo, eh?'

'Yes, sir. To the bird's advantage.'

'He did, did he? Now you see how right I was to come away. Just one crack like that out of him face to face, and I should infallibly have done his upper maxillary a bit of no good. It was wise of you to suggest that I should lunch out.'

'Thank you, sir.'

'Well, the coast being clear, I will now return home.'

'Before you start, sir, perhaps you would ring Miss Wickham up. She instructed me to desire you to do so.'

'You mean she asked you to ask me?'

'Precisely, sir.'

'Right ho. And the number?'

'Sloane 8090. I fancy it is the residence of Miss Wickham's aunt, in Eaton Square.'

I got the number. And presently young Bobbie's voice came floating over the wire. From the *timbre* I gathered that she was extremely bucked.

'Hullo? Is that you, Bertie?'

'In person. What's the news?'

'Wonderful. Everything went off splendidly. The lunch was just right. The child stuffed himself to the eyebrows and got more and more amiable, till by the time he had had his third go of ice-cream he was ready to say that any play – even one of mother's – was the goods. I fired it at him before he could come out from under the influence, and he sat there absorbing it in a sort of gorged way, and at the end old Blumenfeld said

"Well, sonny, how about it?" and the child gave a sort of faint smile, as if he was thinking about roly-poly pudding, and said "O.K., pop," and that's all there was to it. Old Blumenfeld has taken him off to the movies, and I'm to look in at the Savoy at five-thirty to sign the contract. I've just been talking to mother on the 'phone, and she's quite consumedly braced.'

'Terrific!'

'I knew you'd be pleased. Oh, Bertie, there's just one other thing. You remember saying to me once that there wasn't anything in the world you wouldn't do for me?'

I paused a trifle warily. It is true that I had expressed myself in some such terms as she had indicated, but that was before the affair of Tuppy and the hot-water bottle, and in the calmer frame of mind induced by that episode I wasn't feeling quite so spacious. You know how it is. Love's flame flickers and dies, Reason returns to her throne, and you aren't nearly as ready to hop about and jump through hoops as in the first pristine glow of the divine passion.

'What do you want me to do?'

'Well, it's nothing I actually want you to do. It's something I've done that I hope you won't be sticky about. Just before I began reading the play, that dog of yours, the Aberdeen terrier, came into the room. The child Blumenfeld was very much taken with it and said he wished he had a dog like that, looking at me in a meaning sort of way. So naturally, I had to say "Oh, I'll give you this one!" '

I swayed somewhat.

'You. . . . you. . . . What was that?'

'I gave him the dog. I knew you wouldn't mind. You see, it was vital to keep cosseting him. If I'd refused, he would have cut up rough and all that roly-poly pudding and stuff would have been thrown away. You see – '

I hung up. The jaw had fallen, the eyes were protruding. I tottered from the booth and, reeling out of the club, hailed a taxi. I got to the flat and yelled for Jeeves.

'Jeeves!'

'Sir?'

'Do you know what?'

'No, sir.'

'The dog . . . my Aunt Agatha's dog . . . McIntosh . . .'

'I have not seen him for some little while, sir. He left me after the conclusion of luncheon. Possibly he's in your bedroom.'

'Yes, and possibly he jolly dashed well isn't. If you want to know where he is, he's in a suite at the Savoy.'

'Sir?'

'Miss Wickham has just told me she gave him to Blumenfeld junior.'

'Sir?'

'Gave him to Jumenfeld blunior, I tell you. As a present. As a gift. With warm personal regards.'

'What was her motive in doing that, sir?'

'I explained the circs. Jeeves did a bit of respectful tongue-clicking.

'I have always maintained, if you will remember, sir,' he said, when I had finished, 'that Miss Wickham, though a charming young lady – '

'Yes, Yes, never mind about that. What are we going to do? That's the point. Aunt Agatha is due back between the hours of six and seven. She will find herself short one Aberdeen terrier. And, as she will probably have been considerably sea-sick all the way over, you will readily perceive, Jeeves, that, when I break the news that her dog has been given away to a total stranger, I shall find her in no mood of gentle charity.'

'I see, sir, most disturbing.'

'What did you say it was?'

'Most disturbing, sir.'

I snorted a trifle.

'Oh?' I said. 'And I suppose, if you had been in San Francisco when the earthquake started, you would just have lifted up your finger and said "Tweet, tweet! Shush, shush! Now, now! Come, come!" The English language, they used to tell me at school, is the richest in the world, crammed full from end to end with about a million red-hot adjectives. Yet the only one you can find to describe this ghastly business is the adjective "disturbing". It is not disturbing, Jeeves. It is . . . what's the word I want?'

'Cataclysmal, sir.'

'I shouldn't wonder. Well, what's to be done?'

'I will bring you a whisky-and-soda, sir.'

'What's the good of that?'

'It will refresh you, sir. And in the meantime, if it is your wish, I will give the matter consideration.'

'Carry on.'

'Very good, sir. I assume that it is not your desire to do anything that may in any way jeopardize the cordial relations which now exist between Miss Wickham and Mr and Master Blumenfeld?'

'Eh?'

'You would not, for example, contemplate proceeding to the Savoy Hotel and demanding the return of the dog?'

It was a tempting thought, but I shook the old onion firmly. There are things which a Wooster can do and things which, if you follow me, a Wooster cannot do. The procedure which he had indicated would undoubtedly have brought home the bacon, but the thwarted kid would have been bound to turn nasty and change his mind about the play. And, while I didn't think that any drama written by Bobbie's mother was likely to do the theatre-going public much good, I couldn't dash the cup of happiness, so to speak, from the blighted girl's lips, as it were. *Noblesse oblige* about sums the thing up.

'No, Jeeves,' I said. 'But if you can think of some way by which I can oil privily into the suite and sneak the animal out of it without causing any hard feelings, spill it.'

'I will endeavour to do so, sir.'

'Snap into it, then, without delay. They say fish are good for the brain. Have a go at the sardines and come back and report.'

'Very good, sir.'

It was about ten minutes later that he entered the presence once more.

'I fancy, sir – '

'Yes, Jeeves?'

'I rather fancy, sir, that I have discovered a plan of action.'

'Or scheme.'

'Or scheme, sir. A plan of action or scheme which will meet the situation. If I understood you rightly, sir, Mr and Master Blumenfeld have attended a motion-picture performance?'

'Correct.'

'In which case, they should not return to the hotel before five-fifteen?'

'Correct once more. Miss Wickham is scheduled to blow in at five-thirty to sign the contract.'

'The suite, therefore, is presently unoccupied.'

'Except for McIntosh.'

'Except for McIntosh, sir. Everything, accordingly, must depend on whether Mr Blumenfeld left instructions that, in the event of her arriving before he did,

Miss Wickham was to be shown straight up to the suite, to await his return.'

'Why does everything depend on that?'

'Should he have done so, the matter becomes quite simple. All that is necessary is that Miss Wickham shall present herself at the hotel at five o'clock. She will go up to the suite. You will also have arrived at the hotel at five, sir, and will have made your way to the corridor outside the suite. If Mr and Master Blumenfeld have not returned, Miss Wickham will open the door and come out and you will go in, secure the dog, and take your departure.'

I stared at the man.

'How many tins of sardines did you eat, Jeeves?'

'None, sir. I am not fond of sardines.'

'You man, you thought of this great, this ripe, this amazing scheme entirely without the impetus given to the brain by fish?'

'Yes, sir.'

'You stand alone, Jeeves.'

'Thank you sir.'

'But I say!'

'Sir?'

'Suppose the dog won't come away with me? You know how meagre his intelligence is. By this time, especially when he's got used to a new place, he may have forgotten me completely and will look on me as a perfect stranger.'

'I had thought of that, sir. The most judicious move will be for you to sprinkle your trousers with aniseed.'

'Aniseed?'

'Yes, sir. It is extensively used in the dog-stealing industry.'

'But Jeeves . . . dash it . . . aniseed?'

'I consider it essential, sir.'

'But where do you get the stuff?'

'At any chemist's, sir. If you will go out now and procure a small bottle, I will be telephoning to Miss Wickham to apprise her of the contemplated arrangements and ascertain whether she is to be admitted to the suite.'

I don't know what the record is for popping out and buying aniseed, but I should think I hold it. The thought of Aunt Agatha getting nearer and nearer to the Metropolis every minute induced a rare burst of spped. I was back at the flat so quick that I nearly met myself coming out.

Jeeves had good news.

'Everything is perfectly satisfactory, sir. Mr Blumenfeld did leave instructions that Miss Wickham was to be admitted to his suite. The young lady is now on her way to the hotel. By the time you reach it, you will find her there.'

You know, whatever you may say about old Jeeves – and I, for one, have never wavered in my opinion that his views on shirts for evening wear are hidebound and reactionary to a degree – you've got to admit that the man can plan a campaign. Napoleon could have taken his correspondence course. When he sketches out a scheme, all you have to do is to follow it in every detail, and there you are.

On the present occasion everything went absolutely according to plan, I had never realized before that dog-stealing could be so simple, having always regarded it rather as something that called for the ice-cool brain and the nerve of steel. I see now that a child can do it, if directed by Jeeves. I got to the hotel, sneaked up the stairs, hung about in the corridor trying to look like a potted palm in case anybody came along, and presently the door of the suite opened and Bobbie appeared, and suddenly, as I approached, out shot McIntosh, sniffing passionately, and the next moment his nose was up against my Spring trouserings, and he was drinking me in with every evidence of enjoyment. If I had been a bird that had been dead about five days, he could not have nuzzled me more heartily. Aniseed isn't a scent that I care for particularly myself, but it seemed to speak straight to the deeps of McIntosh's soul.

The connection, as it were, having been established in this manner, the rest was simple. I merely withdrew, followed by the animal in the order named. We passed down the stairs in good shape, self reeking to heaven and animal inhaling the bouquet, and after a few anxious moments were safe in a cab, homeward bound. As smooth a bit of work as London had seen that day.

Arrived at the flat, I handed McIntosh to Jeeves and instructed him to shut him up in the bathroom or somewhere where the spell cast by my trousers would cease to operate. This done, I again paid the man a marked tribute.

'Jeeves,' I said, 'I have had occasion to express the view before, and I now express it again fearlessly – you stand in a class of your own.'

'Thank you very much, sir. I am glad that everything proceeded satisfactorily.'

'The festivities went like a breeze from start to finish. Tell me, were you always like this, or did it come on suddenly?'

'Sir?'

'The brain. The grey matter. Were you an outstanding brilliant boy?'

'My mother thought me intelligent, sir.'

'You can't go by that. My mother thought *me* intelligent. Anyway, setting that aside for the moment, would a fiver be any use to you?'

'Thank you very much, sir.'

'Not that a fiver begins to cover it. Figure to yourself, Jeeves – try to envisage, if you follow what I mean, the probable behaviour of my Aunt Agatha if I had gone to her between the hours of six and seven and told her that McIntosh had passed out of the picture. I should have had to leave London and grow a beard.'

'I can readily imagine, sir, that she would have been somewhat perturbed.'

'She would. And on the occasions when my Aunt Agatha is perturbed heroes dive down drain-pipes to get out of her way. However, as it is, all has ended happily. . . . Oh, great Scott!'

'Sir?'

I hesitated. It seemed a shame to cast a damper on the man just when he had extended himself so notably in the cause, but it had to be done.

'You've overlooked something, Jeeves.'

'Surely not, sir?'

'Yes, Jeeves, I regret to say that the late scheme or plan of action, while gilt-edged as far as I am concerned, has rather landed Miss Wickham in the cart.'

'In what way, sir?'

'Why, don't you see that, if they know that she was in the suite at the time of the outrage, the Blumenfelds, father and son, will instantly assume that she was mixed up in McIntosh's disappearance, with the result that in their pique and chagrin they will call off the deal about the play? I'm surprised at you not spotting that, Jeeves. You'd have done much better to eat those sardines, as I advised.'

I waggled my head rather sadly, and at this moment there was a ring at the front-door bell. And not an ordinary ring, mind you, but one of those resounding peals that suggest that somebody with a high blood-pressure and a grievance stands without. I leaped in my tracks. My busy afternoon had left the old nervous system not quite in mid-season form.

'Good Lord, Jeeves!'

'Somebody at the door, sir.'

'Yes.'

'Probably Mr Blumenfield, senior, sir.'

'What!'

'He rang up on the telephone, sir, shortly before you returned, to say that he was about to pay you a call.'

'You don't mean that?'

'Yes, sir.'

'Advise me, Jeeves.'

'I fancy the most judicious procedure would be for you to conceal yourself behind the settee, sir.'

I saw that his advice was good. I had never met this Blumenfeld socially, but I had seen him from afar on the occasion when he and Cyril Bassington-Bassington had had their falling out, and he hadn't struck me then as a bloke with whom, if in one of his emotional moods, it would be at all agreeable to be shut up in a small room. A large, round, flat, overflowing bird, who might quite easily, if stirred, fall on a fellow and flatten him to the carpet.

So I nestled behind the settee, and in about five seconds there was a sound like a mighty, rushing wind and something extraordinarily substantial bounded into the sitting-room.

'This guy, Wooster,' bellowed a voice that had been strengthened by a lifetime of ticking actors off at dress-rehearsals from the back of the theatre.

'Where is he?'

Jeeves continued suave.

'I could not say, sir.'

'He's sneaked my son's dog.'

'Indeed, sir?'

'Walked into my suite as cool as dammit and took the animal away.'

'Most disturbing, sir.'

'And you don't know where he is?'

'Mr Wooster may be anywhere, sir. He is uncertain in his movements.'

The bloke Blumenfeld gave a loud sniff.

'Odd smell here!'

'Yes, sir?'

'What is it?'

'Aniseed, sir.'

'Aniseed?'

'Yes, sir. Mr Wooster sprinkles it on his trousers.'

'Sprinkles it on his trousers?'

'Yes, sir.'

'What on earth does he do that for?'

'I could not say, sir. Mr Wooster's motives are always somewhat hard to follow. He is eccentric.'

'Eccentric? He must be a loony.'

'Yes, sir.'

'You mean he is?'

'Yes, sir!'

There was a pause. A long one.

'Oh?' said old Blumenfeld, and it seemed to me that a good deal of what you might call the vim had gone out of his voice.

He paused again.

'Not *dangerous*?'

'Yes, sir, when roused.'

'Er – what rouses him chiefly?'

'One of Mr Wooster's peculiarities is that he does

not like the sight of gentlemen of full habit, sir. They seem to infuriate him.'

'You mean, fat men?'

'Yes, sir.'

'Why?'

'One cannot say, sir.'

There was another pause.

'*I'm* fat!' said old Blumenfeld in a rather pensive sort of voice.

'I would not venture to suggest it myself, sir, but as you say so. . . . You may recollect that, on being informed that you were to be a member of the luncheon party, Mr Wooster, doubting his power of self-control, refused to be present.'

'That's right. He went rushing out just as I arrived. I thought it odd at the time. My son thought it odd. We both thought it odd.'

'Yes, sir. Mr Wooster, I imagine, wished to avoid any possible unpleasantness, such as has occurred before. . . . With regard to the smell of aniseed, sir, I fancy I have now located it. Unless I am mistaken it proceeds from behind the settee. No doubt Mr Wooster is sleeping there.'

'Doing what?'

'Sleeping, sir.'

'Does he often sleep on the floor?'

'Most afternoons, sir. Would you desire me to wake him?'

'No!'

'I thought you had something that you wished to say to Mr Wooster, sir.'

Old Blumenfeld drew a deep breath. 'So did I,' he said. 'But I find I haven't. Just get me alive out of here, that's all I ask.'

I heard the door close, and a little while later the

front door banged. I crawled out. It hadn't been any too cosy behind the settee, and I was glad to be elsewhere. Jeeves came trickling back.

'Gone, Jeeves?'

'Yes, sir.'

I bestowed an approving look on him.

'One of your best efforts, Jeeves.'

'Thank you, sir.'

'But what beats me is why he ever came here. What made him think that I had sneaked McIntosh away?'

'I took the liberty of recommending Miss Wickham to tell Mr Blumenfeld that she had observed you removing the animal from his suite, sir. The point which you raised regarding the possibility of her being suspected of complicity in the affair had not escaped me. It seemed to me that this would establish her solidly in Mr Blumenfeld's good opinion.'

'I see. Risky, of course, but possibly justified. Yes, on the whole, justified. What's that you've got there?'

'A five pound note, sir.'

'Ah, the one I gave you?'

'No, sir. The one Mr Blumenfeld gave me.'

'Eh? Why did he give you a fiver?'

'He very kindly presented it to me on my handing him the dog, sir.'

I gaped at the man.

'You don't mean to say – ?'

'Not McIntosh, sir. McIntosh is at present in my bedroom. This was another animal of the same species which I purchased at the shop in Bond Street during your absence. Except to the eye of love, one Aberdeen terrier looks very much like another Aberdeen terrier, sir. Mr Blumenfeld, I am happy to say, did not detect the innocent subterfuge.'

'Jeeves,' I said – and I am not ashamed to confess

that there was a spot of chokiness in the voice – 'there is none like you, none.'

'Thank you very much, sir.'

'Owing solely to the fact that your head bulges in unexpected spots, thus enabling you to do about twice as much bright thinking in any given time as any other two men in existence, happiness, you might say, reigns supreme. Aunt Agatha is on velvet, I am on velvet, the Wickhams, mother and daughter, are on velvet, the Blumenfelds, father and son, are on velvet. As far as the eye can reach, a solid mass of humanity, owing to you, all on velvet. A fiver is not sufficient, Jeeves. If I thought the world thought that Bertram Wooster thought a measly five pounds an adequate reward for such services as yours, I should never hold my head up again. Have another?'

'Thank you, sir.'

'And one more?'

'Thank you very much, sir.'

'And a third for luck?'

'Really, sir, I am exceedingly obliged. Excuse me, sir, I fancy I heard the telephone.'

He pushed out into the hall, and I heard him doing a good deal of the "Yes, madam", "Certainly, madam!" stuff. Then he came back.

'Mrs Spencer Gregson on the telephone, sir.'

'Aunt Agatha?'

'Yes, sir. Speaking from Victoria Station. She desires to communicate with you with reference to the dog McIntosh. I gather that she wishes to hear from your own lips that all is well with the little fellow, sir.'

I straightened the tie. I pulled down the waistcoat. I shot the cuffs. I felt absolutely all-righto.

'Lead me to her,' I said.

— 9 —

INDIAN SUMMER OF AN UNCLE

Ask anyone at the Drones, and they will tell you that Bertram Wooster is a fellow whom it is dashed difficult to deceive. Old Lynx-Eye is about what it amounts to. I observe and deduce. I weigh the evidence and draw my conclusions. And that is why Uncle George had not been in my midst more than about two minutes before I, so to speak, saw all. To my trained eye the thing stuck out a mile.

And yet it seemed so dashed absurd. Consider the facts, if you know what I mean.

I mean to say, for years, right back to the time when I first went to school, this bulging relative had been one of the recognized eyesores of London. He was fat then, and day by day in every way has been getting fatter ever since, till now tailors measure him just for the sake of the exercise. He is what they call a prominent London clubman – one of those birds in tight morning-coats and grey toppers whom you see toddling along St James's Street on fine afternoons, puffing a bit as they make the grade. Slip a ferret into any good club between Piccadilly and Pall Mall, and you would start half a dozen Uncle Georges.

He spends his time lunching and dining at the Buffers and, between meals, sucking down spots in the smoking-room and talking to anyone who will listen about the lining of his stomach. About twice a year his liver lodges a formal protest and he goes off to Harrogate or Carlsbad to get planed down. Then back again and on with the programme. The last bloke in the world, in short, who you would think would ever fall a victim to the divine pash. And yet, if you will believe me, that was absolutely the strength of it.

This old pestilence blew in on me one morning at about the hour of the after-breakfast cigarette.

'Oh, Bertie,' he said.

'Hullo?'

'You know those ties you've been wearing. Where did you get them?'

'Blucher's, in the Burlington Arcade.'

'Thanks.'

He walked across to the mirror and stood in front of it, gazing at himself in an earnest manner.

'Smut on your nose?' I asked courteously.

Then I suddenly perceived that he was wearing a sort of horrible simper, and I confess it chilled the blood to no little extent. Uncle George, with face in repose, is hard enough on the eye. Simpering, he goes right above the odds.

'Ha!' he said.

He heaved a long sigh, and turned away. Not too soon, for the mirror was on the point of cracking.

'I'm not so old,' he said, in a musing sort of voice.

'So old as what?'

'Properly considered, I'm in my prime. Besides, what a young and inexperienced girl needs is a man of weight and years to lean on. The sturdy oak, not the sapling.'

It was at this point that, as I said above, I saw all.

'Great Scott, Uncle George!' I said. 'You aren't thinking of getting married?'

'Who isn't?' he said.

'You aren't,' I said.

'Yes, I am. Why not?'

'Oh, well – '

'Marriage is an honourable state.'

'Oh, absolutely.'

'It might make you a better man, Bertie.'

'Who says so?'

'I say so. Marriage might turn you from a frivolous young scallywag into – er – a non-scallywag. Yes, confound you, I *am* thinking of getting married, and if Agatha comes sticking her oar in I'll – I'll – well, I shall know what to do about it.'

He exited on the big line, and I rang the bell for Jeeves. The situation seemed to me one that called for a cosy talk.

'Jeeves,' I said.

'Sir?'

'You know my Uncle George?'

'Yes, sir. His lordship has been familiar to me for some years.'

'I don't mean do you know my Uncle George. I mean do you know what my Uncle George is thinking of doing?'

'Contracting a matrimonial alliance, sir.'

'Good Lord! Did he tell you?'

'No, sir. Oddly enough, I chance to be acquainted with the other party in the matter.'

'The girl?'

'The young person, yes, sir. It was from her aunt, with whom she resides, that I received the information that his lordship was contemplating matrimony.'

'Who is she?'

'A Miss Platt, sir. Miss Rhoda Platt. Of Wistaria Lodge, Kitchener Road, East Dulwich.'

'Young?'

'Yes, sir.'

'The old fathead!'

'Yes, sir. The expression is one which I would, of course, not have ventured to employ myself, but I confess to thinking his lordship somewhat ill-advised. One must remember, however, that it is not unusual to find gentlemen of a certain age yielding to what might be described as a sentimental urge. They appear to experience what I may term a sort of Indian summer, a kind of temporarily renewed youth. The phenomenon is particularly noticeable, I am given to understand, in the United States of America among the wealthier inhabitants of the city of Pittsburgh. It is notorious, I am told, that sooner or later, unless restrained, they always endeavour to marry chorus-girls. Why this should be so, I am at a loss to say, but – '

I saw that this was going to take some time. I tuned out.

'From something in Uncle George's manner, Jeeves, as he referred to my Aunt Agatha's probable reception of the news, I gather that this Miss Platt is not of the *noblesse*.'

'No, sir. She is a waitress at his lordship's club.'

'My God! The proletariat!'

'The lower middle classes, sir.'

'Well, yes, by stretching it a bit, perhaps. Still, you know what I mean.'

'Yes, sir.'

'Rummy thing, Jeeves,' I said thoughtfully, 'this modern tendency to marry waitresses. If you remember, before he settled down, young Bingo Little was repeatedly trying to do it.'

'Yes, sir.'

'Odd!'

'Yes, sir.'

'Still, there it is, of course. The point to be considered now is, what will Aunt Agatha do about this? You know her, Jeeves. She is not like me. I'm broad-minded. If Uncle George wants to marry waitresses, let him, say I. I hold that the rank is but the penny stamp – '

'Guinea stamp, sir.'

'All right, guinea stamp. Though I don't believe there is such a thing. I shouldn't have thought they came higher than five bob. Well, as I was saying, I maintain that the rank is but the guinea stamp and a girl's a girl for all that.'

' "For *a*' that," sir. The poet Burns wrote in the North British dialect.'

'Well, "a' that," then, if you prefer it.'

'I have no preference in the matter, sir. It is simply that the poet Burns – '

'Never mind about the poet Burns.'

'No, sir.'

'Forget the poet Burns.'

'Very good, sir.'

'Expunge the poet Burns from your mind.'

'I will do so immediately, sir.'

'What we have to consider is not the poet Burns but the Aunt Agatha. She will kick, Jeeves.'

'Very probably, sir.'

'And, what's worse, she will lug me into the mess. There is only one thing to be done. Pack the toothbrush and let us escape while we may, leaving no address.'

'Very good, sir.'

At this moment the bell rang.

'Ha!' I said. 'Someone at the door.'

'Yes, sir.'

'Probably Uncle George back again. I'll answer it. You go and get ahead with the packing.'

'Very good, sir.'

I sauntered along the passage, whistling carelessly, and there on the mat was Aunt Agatha. Herself. Not a picture.

A nasty jar.

'Oh, hullo!' I said, it seeming but little good to tell her I was out of town and not expected back for some weeks.

'I wish to speak to you, Bertie,' said the Family Curse. 'I am greatly upset.'

She legged it into the sitting-room and volplaned into a chair. I followed, thinking wistfully of Jeeves packing in the bedroom. That suitcase would not be needed now. I knew what she must have come about.

'I've just seen Uncle George,' I said, giving her a lead.

'So have I,' said Aunt Agatha, shivering in a marked manner. 'He called on me while I was still in bed to inform me of his intention of marrying some impossible girl from South Norwood.'

'East Dulwich, the *cognoscente* informed me.'

'Well, East Dulwich, then. It is the same thing. But who told you?'

'Jeeves.'

'And how, pray, does Jeeves come to know all about it?'

'There are very few things in this world, Aunt Agatha,' I said gravely, 'that Jeeves doesn't know all about. He's met the girl.'

'Who is she?'

'One of the waitresses at the Buffers.'

I had expected this to register and it did. The relative let out a screech rather like the Cornish Express going through a junction.

'I take it from your manner, Aunt Agatha,' I said, 'that you want this thing stopped.'

'Of course it must be stopped.'

'Then there is but one policy to pursue. Let me ring for Jeeves and ask his advice.'

Aunt Agatha stiffened visibly. Very much the *grande dame* of the old *régime*.

'Are you seriously suggesting that we should discuss this intimate family matter with your man-servant?'

'Absolutely. Jeeves will find the way.'

'I have always known that you were an imbecile, Bertie,' said the flesh-and-blood, now down at about three degrees Fahrenheit, 'but I did suppose that you had some proper feeling, some pride, some respect for your position.'

'Well, you know what the poet Burns says.'

She squelched me with a glance.

'Obviously the only thing to do,' she said, 'is to offer this girl money.'

'Money?'

'Certainly. It will not be the first time your uncle has made such a course necessary.'

We sat for a bit, brooding. The family always sits brooding when the subject of Uncle George's early romance comes up. I was too young to be actually in on it at the time, but I've had the details frequently from many sources, including Uncle George. Let him get even the slightest bit pickled, and he will tell you the whole story, sometimes twice in an evening. It was a barmaid at the Criterion, just before he came into the title. Her name was Maudie and he loved her dearly, but the family would have none of it. They dug down into the sock and paid her off. Just one of those human-interest stories, if you know what I mean.

I wasn't so sold on this money-offering scheme.

'Well, just as you like, of course,' I said, 'but you're taking an awful chance. I mean, whenever people do it in novels and plays, they always get the dickens of a welt. The girl gets the sympathy of the audience every time. She just draws herself up and looks at them with clear, steady eyes, causing them to feel not a little cheesy. If I were you, I would sit tight and let Nature take its course.'

'I don't understand you.'

'Well, consider for a moment what Uncle George looks like. No Greta Garbo, believe me. I should simply let the girl go on looking at him. Take it from me, Aunt Agatha, I've studied human nature and I don't believe there's a female in the world who could see Uncle George fairly often in those waistcoats he wears without feeling that it was due to her better self to give him the gate. Besides, this girl sees him at meal-times, and Uncle George with his head down among the food-stuffs is a spectacle which – '

'If it is not troubling you too much, Bertie, I should be greatly obliged if you would stop drivelling.'

'Just as you say. All the same, I think you're going to find it dashed embarrassing, offering this girl money.'

'I am not proposing to do so. *You* will undertake the negotiations.'

'Me?'

'Certainly. I should think a hundred pounds would be ample. But I will give you a blank cheque, and you are at liberty to fill it in for a higher sum if it becomes necessary. The essential point is that, cost what it may, your uncle must be released from this entanglement.'

'So you're going to shove this off on me?'

'It is quite time you did something for the family.'

'And when she draws herself up and looks at me with clear, steady eyes, what do I do for an encore?'

'There is no need to discuss the matter any further. You can get down to East Dulwich in half an hour.

There is a frequent service of trains, I will remain here to await your report.'

'But, listen!'

'Bertie, you will go and see this woman immediately.'

'Yes, but dash it!'

'Bertie!'

I threw in the towel.

'Oh, right ho, if you say so.'

'I do say so.'

'Oh, well, in that case, right ho.'

I don't know if you have ever tooled off to East Dulwich to offer a strange female a hundred smackers to release your Uncle George. In case you haven't, I may tell you that there are plenty of things that are lots better fun. I didn't feel any too good driving to the station. I didn't feel any too good in the train. And I didn't feel any too good as I walked to Kitchener Road. But the moment when I felt least good was when I had actually pressed the front-door bell and a rather grubby-looking maid had let me in and shown me down a passage and into a room with pink paper on the walls, a piano in the corner and a lot of photographs on the mantelpiece.

Barring a dentist's waiting-room, which it rather resembles, there isn't anything that quells the spirit much more than one of these suburban parlours. They are extremely apt to have stuffed birds in glass cases standing about on small tables, and if there is one thing which gives the man of sensibility that sinking feeling it is the cold, accusing eye of a ptarmigan or whatever it may be that has had its interior organs removed and sawdust substituted.

There were three of these cases in the parlour of Wistaria Lodge, so that, wherever you looked, you were sure to connect. Two were singletons, the third a family group, consisting of a father bullfinch, a mother bullfinch, and little Master Bullfinch, the last-named of whom wore an expression that was definitely that of a thug, and did more to damp my *joie de vivre* than all the rest of them put together.

I had moved to the window and was examining the aspidistra in order to avoid this creature's gaze, when I heard the door open and, turning, found myself confronted by something which, since it could hardly be the girl, I took to be the aunt.

'Oh, what ho,' I said. 'Good morning.'

The words came out rather roopily, for I was feeling a bit on the stunned side. I meant to say, the room being so small and this exhibit so large, I had got that sensation of wanting air. There are some people who don't seem to be intended to be seen close to, and this aunt was one of them. Billowy curves, if you know what I mean. I should think that in her day she must have been a very handsome girl, though even then on the substantial side. By the time she came into my life, she had taken on a good deal of excess weight. She looked like a photograph of an opera singer of the 'eighties. Also the orange hair and the magenta dress.

However, she was a friendly soul. She seemed glad to see Bertram. She smiled broadly.

'So here you are at last!' she said.

I couldn't make anything of this.

'Eh?'

'But I don't think you had better see my niece just yet. She's just having a nap.'

'Oh, in that case – '

'Seems a pity to wake her, doesn't it?'

'Oh, absolutely,' I said, relieved.

'When you get the influenza, you don't sleep at night,

and then if you doze off in the morning – well, it seems a pity to wake someone, doesn't it?'

'Miss Platt has influenza?'

'That's what we think it is. But, of course, you'll be able to say. But we needn't waste time. Since you're here, you can be taking a look at my knee.'

'Your knee?'

I am all for knees at their proper time and, as you might say, in their proper place, but somehow this didn't seem the moment. However, she carried on according to plan.

'What do you think of that knee?' she asked, lifting the seven veils.

Well, of course, one has to be polite.

'Terrific!' I said.

'You wouldn't believe how it hurts me sometimes.'

'Really?'

'A sort of shooting pain. It just comes and goes. And I'll tell you a funny thing.'

'What's that?' I said, feeling I could do with a good laugh.

'Lately I've been having the same pain just here, at the end of the spine.'

'You don't mean it!'

'I do. Like red-hot needles. I wish you'd have a look at it.'

'At your spine?'

'Yes.'

I shook my head. Nobody is fonder of a bit of fun than myself, and I am all for Bohemian camaraderie and making a party go, and all that. But there is a line, and we Woosters know when to draw it.

'It can't be done,' I said austerely. 'Not spines. Knees, yes. Spines, no,' I said.

She seemed surprised.

'Well,' she said, 'you're a funny sort of doctor, I must say.'

I'm pretty quick, as I said before, and I began to see that something in the nature of a misunderstanding must have arisen.

'Doctor?'

'Well, you call yourself a doctor, don't you?'

'Did you think I was a doctor?'

'Aren't you a doctor?'

'No. Not a doctor.'

We had got it straightened out. The scales had fallen from our eyes. We knew where we were.

I had suspected that she was a genial soul. She now endorsed this view. I don't think I have ever heard a woman laugh so heartily.

'Well, that's the best thing!' she said, borrowing my handkerchief to wipe her eyes. 'Did you ever! But, if you aren't the doctor, who are you?'

'Wooster's the name. I came to see Miss Platt.'

'What about?'

This was the moment, of course, when I should have come out with the cheque and sprung the big effort. But somehow I couldn't make it. You know how it is. Offering people money to release your uncle is a scaly enough job at best, and when the atmosphere's not right the shot simply isn't on the board.

'Oh, just came to see her, you know.' I had rather a bright idea. 'My uncle heard she was seedy, don't you know, and asked me to look in and make enquiries,' I said.

'Your uncle?'

'Lord Yaxley.'

'Oh! So you are Lord Yaxley's nephew?'

'That's right. I suppose he's always popping in and out here what?'

'No. I've never met him.'

'You haven't?'

'No. Rhoda talks a lot about him, of course, but for some reason she's never so much as asked him to look in for a cup of tea.'

I began to see that this Rhoda knew her business. If I'd been a girl with someone wanting to marry me and knew that there was an exhibit like this aunt hanging around the home, I, too, should have thought twice about inviting him to call until the ceremony was over and he had actually signed on the dotted line. I mean to say, a thoroughly good soul – heart of gold beyond a doubt – but not the sort of thing you wanted to spring on Romeo before the time was ripe.

'I suppose you were all very surprised when you heard about it?' she said.

'Surprised is right.'

'Of course, nothing is definitely settled yet.'

'You don't mean that? I thought – '

'Oh, no. She's thinking it over.'

'I see.'

'Of course, she feels it's a great compliment. But then sometimes she wonders if he isn't too old.'

'My Aunt Agatha has rather the same idea.'

'Of course, a title *is* a title.'

'Yes, there's that. What do you think about it yourself?'

'Oh, it doesn't matter what I think. There's no doing anything with girls these days, is there?'

'Not much.'

'What I often say is, I wonder what girls are coming to. Still, there it is.'

'Absolutely.'

There didn't seem much reason why the conversation shouldn't go on for ever. She had the air of a woman who had settled down for the day. But at this point the maid came in and said the doctor had arrived.

I got up.

'I'll be tooling off, then.'

'If you must.'

'I think I'd better.'

'Well, pip pip.'

'Toodle-oo,' I said, and out into the fresh air.

Knowing what was waiting for me at home, I would have preferred to have gone to the club and spent the rest of the day there. But the thing had to be faced.

'Well?' said Aunt Agatha, as I trickled into the sitting-room.

'Well, yes and no,' I replied.

'What do you mean? Did she refuse the money?'

'Not exactly.'

'She accepted it?'

'Well, there again, not precisely.'

I explained what had happened. I wasn't expecting her to be any too frightfully pleased, and it's as well that I wasn't, because she wasn't. In fact, as the story unfolded, her comments became fruitier and fruitier, and when I had finished she uttered an exclamation that nearly broke a window. It sounded something like "Gor!" as if she had started to say "Gorblimey!" and had remembered her ancient lineage just in time.

'I'm sorry,' I said. 'And can a man say more? I lost my nerve. The old *morale* suddenly turned blue on me. It's the sort of thing that might have happened to anyone.'

'I never heard of anything so spineless in my life.'

I shivered, like a warrior whose old wound hurts him.

'I'd be most awfully obliged, Aunt Agatha,' I said, 'if

you would not use that word spine. It awakens memories.'

The door opened. Jeeves appeared.

'Sir?'

'Yes, Jeeves?'

'I thought you called, sir.'

'No, Jeeves.'

'Very good, sir.'

There are moments when, even under the eye of Aunt Agatha, I can take the firm line. And now, seeing Jeeves standing there with the light of intelligence simply fizzing in every feature, I suddenly felt how perfectly footling it was to give this pre-eminent source of balm and comfort the go-by simply because Aunt Agatha had prejudices against discussing family affairs with the staff. It might make her say "Gor!" again, but I decided to do as we ought to have done right from the start – put the case in his hands.

'Jeeves,' I said, 'this matter of Uncle George.'

'Yes, sir.'

'You know the circs?'

'Yes, sir.'

'You know what we want.'

'Yes, sir.'

'Then advise us. And make it snappy. Think on your feet.'

I heard Aunt Agatha rumble like a volcano just before it starts to set about the neighbours, but I did not wilt. I had seen the sparkle in Jeeves's eye which indicated that an idea was on the way.

'I understand that you have been visiting the young person's home, sir?'

'Just got back.'

'Then you no doubt encountered the young person's aunt?'

'Jeeves, I encountered nothing else but.'

'Then the suggestion which I am about to make will, I feel sure, appeal to you, sir. I would recommend that you confront his lordship with this woman. It has always been her intention to continue residing with her niece after the latter's marriage. Should he meet her, this reflection might give his lordship pause. As you are aware, sir, she is a kind-hearted woman, but definitely of the people.'

'Jeeves, you are right! Apart from anything else, that orange hair!'

'Exactly, sir.'

'Not to mention the magenta dress.'

'Precisely, sir.'

'I'll ask her to lunch to-morrow, to meet him. You see,' I said to Aunt Agatha, who was still fermenting in the background, 'a ripe suggestion first crack out of the box. Did I or did I not tell you – '

'That will do, Jeeves,' said Aunt Agatha.

'Very good, madam.'

For some minutes after he had gone, Aunt Agatha strayed from the point a bit, confining her remarks to what she thought of a Wooster who could lower the prestige of the clan by allowing menials to get above themselves. Then she returned to what you might call the main issue.

'Bertie,' she said, 'you will go and see this girl again to-morrow and this time you will do as I told you.'

'But, dash it! With this excellent alternative scheme, based firmly on the psychology of the individual – '

'That is quite enough, Bertie. You heard what I said. I am going. Good-bye.'

She buzzed off, little knowing of what stuff Bertram Wooster was made. The door had hardly closed before I was shouting for Jeeves.

'Jeeves,' I said, 'the recent aunt will have none of your excellent alternative schemes, but none the less I propose to go through with it unswervingly. I consider it a ball of fire. Can you get hold of this female and bring her here for lunch to-morrow?'

'Yes, sir.'

'Good. Meanwhile, I will be 'phoning Uncle George. We will do Aunt Agatha good despite herself. What is it the poet says, Jeeves?'

'The poet Burns, sir?'

'Not the poet Burns. Some other poet. About doing good by stealth.'

' "These little acts of unremembered kindness," sir?'

'That's it in a nutshell, Jeeves.'

I suppose doing good by stealth ought to give one a glow, but I can't say I found myself exactly looking forward to the binge in prospect. Uncle George by himself is a mouldy enough luncheon companion, being extremely apt to collar the conversation and confine it to a description of his symptoms, he being one of those birds who can never be brought to believe that the general public isn't agog to hear all about the lining of his stomach. Add the aunt, and you have a little gathering which might well dismay the stoutest. The moment I woke, I felt conscious of some impending doom, and the cloud, if you know what I mean, grew darker all the morning. By the time Jeeves came in with the cocktails, I was feeling pretty low.

'For two pins, Jeeves,' I said, 'I would turn the whole thing up and leg it to the Drones.'

'I can readily imagine that this will prove something of an ordeal, sir.'

'How did you get to know these people, Jeeves?'

'It was through a young fellow of my acquaintance,

sir, Colonel Mainwaring-Smith's personal gentleman's gentleman. He and the young person had an understanding at the time, and he desired me to accompany him to Wistaria Lodge and meet her.'

'They were engaged?'

'Not precisely engaged, sir. An understanding.'

'What did they quarrel about?'

'They did not quarrel, sir. When his lordship began to pay his addresses, the young person, naturally flattered, began to waver between love and ambition. But even now she has not formally rescinded the understanding.'

'Then, if your scheme works and Uncle George edges out, it will do your pal a bit of good?'

'Yes, sir. Smethurst – his name is Smethurst – would consider it a consummation devoutly to be wished.'

'Rather well put, that Jeeves. Your own?'

'No, sir. The Swan of Avon, sir.'

An unseen hand without tootled on the bell, and I braced myself to play the host. The binge was on.

'Mrs Wilberforce, sir,' announced Jeeves.

'And how I'm to keep a straight face with you standing behind and saying "Madam, can I tempt you with a potato?" is more than I know,' said the aunt, sailing in, looking larger and pinker and matier than ever. 'I know him, you know,' she said, jerking a thumb after Jeeves. 'He's been round and taken tea with us.'

'So he told me.'

She gave the sitting-room the once-over.

'You've got a nice place here,' she said. 'Though I like more pink about. It's so cheerful. What's that you've got there? Cocktails?'

'Martini with a spot of absinthe,' I said, beginning to pour.

She gave a girlish squeal.

'Don't you try to make me drink that stuff! Do you

know what would happen if I touched one of those things? I'd be racked with pain. What they do to the lining of your stomach!'

'Oh, I don't know.'

'I do. If you had been a barmaid as long as I was, you'd know, too.'

'Oh – er – were you a barmaid?'

'For years, when I was younger than I am. At the Criterion.'

I dropped the shaker.

'There!' she said, pointing the moral. 'That's through drinking that stuff. Makes your hand wobble. What I always used to say to the boys was, "Port, if you like. Port's wholesome. I appreciate a drop of port myself. But these new-fangled messes from America, no." But they would never listen to me.'

I was eyeing her warily. Of course, there must have been thousands of barmaids at the Criterion in its time, but still it gave one a bit of a start. It was years ago that Uncle George's dash at a *mésalliance* had occurred – long before he came into the title – but the Wooster clan still quivered at the name of the Criterion.

'Er – when you were at the Cri.,' I said, 'did you ever happen to run into a fellow of my name?'

'I've forgotten what it is. I'm always silly about names.'

'Wooster.'

'Wooster! When you were there yesterday I thought you said Foster. Wooster! Did I run into a fellow named Wooster? Well! Why, George Wooster and me – Piggy, I used to call him – were going off to the registrar's, only his family heard of it and interfered. They offered me a lot of money to give him up, and, like a silly girl, I let them persuade me. If I've wondered once what became of him, I've wondered a thousand times. Is he a relation of yours?'

'Excuse me,' I said. 'I just want a word with Jeeves.'

I legged it for the pantry.

'Jeeves!'

'Sir?'

'Do you know what's happened?'

'No, sir.'

'This female – '

'Sir?'

'She's Uncle George's barmaid!'

'Sir?'

'Oh, dash it, you must have heard of Uncle George's barmaid. You know all the family history. The barmaid he wanted to marry years ago.'

'Ah, yes, sir.'

'She's the only woman he ever loved. He's told me so a million times. Every time he gets to the fourth whisky-and-potash, he always becomes maudlin about this female. What a dashed bit of bad luck! The first thing we know, the call of the past will be echoing in his heart. I can feel it, Jeeves. She's just his sort. The first thing she did when she came in was to start talking about the lining of her stomach. You see the hideous significance of that, Jeeves? The lining of his stomach is Uncle George's favourite topic of conversation. It means that he and she are kindred souls. This woman and he will be like – '

'Deep calling to deep, sir?'

'Exactly.'

'Most disturbing, sir.'

'What's to be done?'

'I could not say, sir.'

'I'll tell you what I'm going to do – 'phone him and say the lunch is off.'

'Scarcely feasible, sir. I fancy that is his lordship at the door now.'

And so it was. Jeeves let him in, and I followed him as he navigated down the passage to the sitting-room. There was a stunned silence as he went in, and then a couple of the startled yelps you hear when old buddies get together after long separation.

'Piggy!'

'Maudie!'

'Well, I never!'

'Well, I'm dashed!'

'Did you ever!'

'Well, bless my soul!'

'Fancy you being Lord Yaxley!'

'Came into the title soon after we parted.'

'Just to think!'

'You could have knocked me down with a feather!'

I hung about in the offing, now on this leg, now on that. For all the notice they took of me, I might just have well been the late Bertram Wooster, disembodied.

'Maudie, you don't look a day older, dash it!'

'Nor do you, Piggy.'

'How have you been all these years?'

'Pretty well. The lining of my stomach isn't all it should be.'

'Good Gad! You don't say so? I have trouble with the lining of *my* stomach.'

'It's a sort of heavy feeling after meals.'

'*I* get a sort of heavy feeling after meals. What are you trying for it?'

'I've been taking Perkins' Digestine.'

'My dear girl, no use! No use at all. Tried it myself for years and got no relief. Now, if you really want something that is some good – '

I slid away. The last I saw of them, Uncle George was down beside her on the Chesterfield, buzzing hard.

'Jeeves,' I said, tottering into the pantry.

'Sir?'

'There will only be two for lunch. Count me out. If they notice I'm not there, tell them I was called away by an urgent 'phone message. The situation has got beyond Bertram, Jeeves. You will find me at the Drones.'

'Very good, sir.'

It was latish in the evening when one of the waiters came to me as I played a distrait game of snooker pool and informed me that Aunt Agatha was on the 'phone.

'Bertie!'

'Hullo?'

I was amazed to note that her voice was that of an aunt who feels that things are breaking right. It had the birdlike trill.

'Bertie, have you that cheque I gave you?'

'Yes.'

'Then tear it up. It will not be needed.'

'Eh?'

'I say it will not be needed. Your uncle has been speaking to me on the telephone. He is not going to marry that girl.'

'Not?'

'No. Apparently he has been thinking it over and sees how unsuitable it would have been. But what is astonishing is that he *is* going to be married!'

'He is?'

'Yes, to an old friend of his, a Mrs Wilberforce. A woman of a sensible age, he gave me to understand. I wonder which Wilberforces that would be. There are two main branches of the family – the Essex Wilberforces and the Cumberland Wilberforces. I believe there is also a cadet branch somewhere in Shropshire.'

'And one in East Dulwich.'

'What did you say?'

'Nothing,' I said. 'Nothing.'

I hung up. Then back to the old flat, feeling a trifle sandbagged.

'Well, Jeeves,' I said, and there was censure in the eyes. 'So I gather everything is nicely settled?'

'Yes, sir. His lordship formally announced the engagement between the sweet and cheese courses, sir.'

'He did, did he?'

'Yes, sir.'

I eyed the man sternly.

'You do not appear to be aware of it, Jeeves,' I said, in a cold, level voice, 'but this binge has depreciated your stock very considerably. I have always been accustomed to look upon you as a counsellor without equal. I have, so to speak, hung upon your lips. And now see what you have done. All this is the direct consequence of your scheme, based on the psychology of the individual. I should have thought, Jeeves, that, knowing the woman – meeting her socially, as you might say, over the afternoon cup of tea – you might have ascertained that she was Uncle George's barmaid.'

'I did, sir.'

'What!'

'I was aware of the fact, sir.'

'Then you must have known what would happen if she came to lunch and met him.'

'Yes, sir.'

'Well, I'm dashed!'

'If I might explain, sir. The young man Smethurst, who is greatly attached to the young person, is an intimate friend of mine. He applied to me some little while back in the hope that I might be able to do something to ensure that the young person followed the dictates of her heart and refrained from permitting herself to be lured by gold and the glamour of his lordship's position. There will now be no obstacle to their union.'

'I see. "Little acts of unremembered kindness," what?'

'Precisely, sir.'

'And how about Uncle George? You've landed him pretty nicely in the cart.'

'No, sir, if I may take the liberty of opposing your view. I fancy that Mrs Wilberforce should make an ideal mate for his lordship. If there was a defect in his lordship's mode of life, it was that he was a little unduly attached to the pleasures of the table – '

'Ate like a pig, you mean?'

'I would not have ventured to put it in quite that way, sir, but the expression does meet the facts of the case. He was also inclined to drink rather more than his medical adviser would have approved of. Elderly bachelors who are wealthy and without occupation tend somewhat frequently to fall into this error, sir. The future Lady Yaxley will check this. Indeed, I overheard her ladyship saying as much as I brought in the fish. She was commenting on a certain puffiness of the face which had been absent in his lordship's appearance in the earlier days of their acquaintanceship, and she observed that his lordship needed looking after. I fancy, sir, that you will find the union will turn out an extremely satisfactory one.'

It was – what's the word I want? – it was plausible, of course, but still I shook the onion.

'But, Jeeves!'

'Sir?'

'She *is*, as you remarked not long ago, definitely of the people.'

He looked at me in a reproachful sort of way.

'Sturdy lower-middle-class stock, sir.'

'H'm!'

'Sir?'

'I said "H'm!" Jeeves.'

'Besides, sir, remembering what the poet Tennyson said: "Kind hearts are more than coronets".'

'And which of us is going to tell Aunt Agatha that?'

'If I might make the suggestion, sir, I would advise that we omitted to communicate with Mrs Spenser Gregson in any way. I have your suitcase practically packed. It would be a matter of but a few minutes to bring the car round from the garage – '

'And off over the horizon to where men are men?'

'Precisely, sir.'

'Jeeves,' I said. 'I'm not sure that even now I can altogether see eye to eye with you regarding your recent activities. You think you have scattered light and sweetness on every side. I am not so sure. However, with this latest suggestion you have rung the bell. I examine it narrowly and I find no flaw in it. It is the goods. I'll get the car at once.'

'Very good, sir.'

'Remember what the poet Shakespeare said, Jeeves.'

'What was that, sir?'

' "Exit hurriedly, pursued by a bear." You'll find it in one of his plays. I remember drawing a picture of it on the side of the page, when I was at school.'